MARY L...

was born in East Walpole, Massachusetts, ... brought home to Ireland by her parents when she was nine and has lived there ever since.

In 1938 she wrote her first short story, "Miss Holland", which was published by the *Dublin Magazine* where it was read by Lord Dunsany who gave her great encouragement and subsequently wrote an enthusiastic preface to her first collection, *Tales From Bective Bridge* (1942), which was awarded the James Tait Black Memorial Prize. Apart from two early novels, Mary Lavin has concentrated on the short story and the novella and has been held by many critics to be one of the greatest living writers of the short story. Her work, which has been widely translated, includes: *The Long Ago* (1944), *The Becker Wives* (1946), *At Sallygap* (1947), *A Single Lady* (1951), *The Patriot Son* (1956), *A Likely Story . . .* (1957), *The Great Wave* (1961), *In the Middle of the Fields* (1967), *Happiness* (1969), *A Memory* (1972), *The Shrine* (1977) and *A Family Likeness* (1985). Stories from the above have also been collected into three volumes under the title *Stories of Mary Lavin*, and a volume of *Selected Stories* was published in 1984. She has also published one children's book, *The Second Best Children in the World* (1972), illustrated by Edward Ardizzone. Mary Lavin's novels are: *The House in Clewe Street* (to be published by Virago in 1987) which was published in 1945 after serialisation in the *Atlantic Monthly* under the title "Gabriel Galloway", and *Mary O'Grady* (1950).

Mary Lavin has been awarded two Guggenheim Fellowships, the Katherine Mansfield Prize, the Eire Society Gold Medal (USA), the Literary Award of the American Irish Foundation and the Gregory Medal, founded by Yeats to be "the supreme award of the Irish Nation". In 1968 Mary Lavin was made a D. Litt by her *alma mater*, the National University of Ireland. In 1964-5 she was the President of Irish PEN and in 1971-3 was President of the Irish Academy of Letters.

Mary Lavin was married in 1942 to William Walsh, by whom she had three daughters. After his death in 1954 she was a widow for fifteen years, until she married Michael MacDonald Scott in 1969. Her home is in Bective, County Meath but she also has a small studio in Dublin where she does most of her work.

VIRAGO
MODERN
CLASSIC

NUMBER
209

MARY O'GRADY

MARY LAVIN

With a New Afterword by
AUGUSTINE MARTIN

Virago

Published by VIRAGO PRESS Limited 1986
41 William IV Street, London WC2N 4DB

First published in Great Britain by Michael Joseph 1950

British Library Cataloguing in Publication Data

Lavin, Mary
  Mary O'Grady (Virago modern classics)
  I. Title
  823'.912[F]   PS3523.A914

  ISBN 0-86068-679-5

Printed in Finland by Werner Söderström Oy

Contents

★

PART I

Mary

ABOUT the beginning of this century, in the city of Dublin, there was upon the bank of the Grand Canal a small stretch of vacant ground. Vacant lots were more common then than now, but even in those days it was odd to come upon one within the city borough. But here for a few years this plot of green grass was to remain, encircled by the stately Georgian buildings of Pembroke and Fitzwilliam. And here, when she first came to Dublin as a young bride, was the place Mary O'Grady loved best to be in all the city.

Day after day when she brought Tom's dinner pail to him at the tram barn, Mary was always eager to get away in order to spend a little while walking up and down outside the railings of this grassy place.

'Are you all right, Tom?'

'I ought to be!'

Tom was so proud of the way she brought him that dinner pail, in all seasons, and in all weathers. 'None of the other men have a hot meal like me,' he said. 'All they have at midday is a few cuts of bread and a hunk of cheese they bring with them in the morning. You can see for yourself!' he said, and he nodded towards the end of the big shed, where the other tram men sat on the steps of a disused tram, their caps pushed back on their foreheads, munching their bread, their eyes upon her all the time.

'Why don't you let me do that?' he said one day. 'I could take something with me and have something hot when I come home in the evening. It would save you coming all this way . . . !'

'Do you not want me to come?'

'Ah, Mary . . .'

'Well then! What are you talking about?' To hide the glow of

9

colour in her face, she turned aside. 'No one wants to start getting a hot meal at the end of the day! I'm glad enough to sit down when evening comes, without having to turn around to cook a dinner for you!'

But she didn't deceive him, and blushing deeper, it seemed to her that the other men at the end of the shed must surely see the love light in his eyes.

'I must go home now,' she cried, embarrassed, and anxious anyway to get to the Lots, and take a few breaths of the air that seemed so much purer there than anywhere else in the city.

And when, after a few years, she was accompanied in her daily trip to the barns by her children, running by her side, she always paused for a few moments when she came to the Lots. Winter and summer she loved to fill her lungs with the air that blew across the high coarse grass.

Inadequately railed by a rickety wooden paling, in winter this wild grass washed over the pavements in places, and in other places its yellow tufts knotted by the wind, and lashed by the rain, rose up in points like the waves of an angry sea.

How Mary loved to stand and look over that paling, but there was danger for the children in the piercing winds and she never delayed there long at that time of year.

Ah, but in summer! Then she could stand as long as she liked. Then the air was mild and balmy, and the children could have no better place to play and get the sun. Then the bleached old sward was lanced with a million shafts of young green grass, and lo! in the middle of the city there was the full splendour of a country meadow, of rich as any in the Midlands; a meadow tossing with myriad grasses, rye and timothy, cocksfoot, fescue, and the delicate tremble-grass; a meadow glowing bronze upon its surface, but lit in flashes everywhere by big white daisies. And when the wind swayed, it revealed an underworld of baby-faced blossoms hiding their heads in the cooler depths, out of reach of the burning, golden sun that, in those days, seemed ever to sail the high blue heavens.

Here, if she stood but for a moment, and leaned over the rickety paling, she could get the close, secretive scent of the clover, and her ear would catch the drone of insects, whilst against her cheek a pale butterfly, white, or whitish blue, might flutter by. And were she but silent for a moment, closing her eyes, the sounds of the city would begin to fall away, and the soft drone of a passing bee would become louder and louder, until the whole tumult of summer sounded in her ears, the tumult not of one short summer only, but of all the summers that were gone; the long, golden summers of childhood—and of Tullamore!

It was just like being in Tullamore.

'Look, children!' Mary O'Grady cried, drawing her small family around her. 'Look, Patrick! Look, Ellie! You're always asking me to tell you about Tullamore, and what it was like there. Well, there you are! There's Tullamore for you!' she cried, and her eyes shone love alike upon the daisied mead and the starry faces of the children.

Summer after summer, it was always the same. Summer after summer, with a flush on her cheeks, brushing her soft hair back from her brow with a firm, strong hand, the young mother uttered the same exclamations, and summer after summer, to the small brood fidgeting about her on the hot pavement, her words were new, and sweet, and stirring.

Mary was only a few months married when she first came upon the vacant Lots. It was one day in early summer before Patrick, her first child, was born, and nowhere else in the strange city all that summer did she feel so happy as walking heavily up and down outside the railings of this rich and teeming place.

Once, on her way back with the empty dinner pail, she bent down awkwardly, and got under the paling to get the feel of the grasses against her ankles, but it made her too homesick, and, as well as that, she didn't want to make herself remarkable; not at that particular time.

When Patrick was born, it was a different matter. Then she had an excuse for loitering. And, as she told Tom, it was very noticeable the way the little fellow always fell asleep when they reached the Lots. Perhaps the sound of the insects made him drowsy? Sometimes she pushed the pram on to the grass, through a gap in the railing, and sat down beside it, until the baby woke again. It was so lovely sitting on the grass, and—say what you liked—a pram was great company.

~   ~   ~   ~

Her neighbours never seemed to realize how much she loved setting out with the pram. They thought the baby was a burden upon her; and they were always proffering to mind him for her. Everyone in the terrace wanted to mind him and let her go away for a day with Tom.

'Go out with your man while you're still young enough to enjoy each other's company.'

The pale, jaded women in the little suburban terrace meant no harm. They did not mean to cast a shadow on the young couple's happiness. It was just that a shadow fell on their own hearts at the sight of Mary's comely figure; so slim, and yet so softly moulded into curves by motherhood.

'You're so kind.' Mary blushed till the pink glow in her face spread right down to her bosom. 'You're so kind,' she murmured, 'but I couldn't leave him for another little while.'

'Come now! Do you think I couldn't mind him? My dear girl, he wouldn't be the first baby I dandled on my knees! I suppose, like all mothers, you think nobody else would know how to hold him? I suppose you think I'd let him fall out of my arms on the top of his head!'

It was all Mary could do not to let it be seen how words like that made her shudder. More than anything in the world, even when she held him tightly in her own arms, she was afraid of his falling. She had heard stories—Oh! she couldn't bear to think of them now that she had a baby of her own, soft and pulsing in her arms.

'Oh, not at all!' she said, and she tried to laugh, or even to smile, but it was easy to see what she thought and felt.

'Well, what do you make of that!' cried the woman who had made the offer, and she laughed, but later she took Mary's arm. 'Take my advice, child,' she said, 'enjoy your youth while you can. Leave the little fellow here with me, and go out with your husband.'

But Mary only blushed deeper.

'Perhaps later in the year,' she murmured. How was it the woman did not understand? 'I can't leave him just yet a while,' she said.

'Later in the year! What nonsense is that? Isn't now the time to go; now in this glorious weather? Thanks be to God for sending it to us! Nonsense, girl, you do as I say, and bring the boy around here next Sunday after Mass. Is that settled?'

Mary felt helpless.

'You're very kind,' she said again, 'but——'

'No excuses!' said the woman.

'I'm not making excuses,' said poor Mary, 'it's only that——' But at this point Tom came on the scene.

'What's that?' said Tom, for he seemed to take a pride in what, to Mary, was and for ever would be, if not a shameful, at least a secretive necessity of her maternity. 'What's that?' he said again.

Mary told him of their neighbour's kind offer to them.

'Oh! That's very kind of you indeed, ma'am,' he said, 'but this isn't a city girl, you know. This is a country lass. She isn't up to your city tricks yet; your feeding bottles and soothers. But thank you kindly, all the same. It was very nice of you, indeed, and we're both very thankful to you. And I can tell you one thing, as soon as the little fellow is weaned, and doesn't need to have his mother within call all the time, I'll hand him over the wall to you some Sunday and take her away with me for the whole day. I promise you that!'

Still blushing, and conscious now of a sudden swell in her breasts inside the straining silk of her bodice, Mary looked with distressed eyes at the other woman, as if Tom in his unconscious pride had dealt the kind creature a wound.

'There's no one we'd rather leave him with than you,' she said, but she felt insincere and false, because never would she contemplate for an instant leaving him with anyone.

If they were near Tullamore, of course, it would be a different matter, because she could have left him with her own mother. It might even be different if he were able to walk, or to use his limbs.

'It's only while they haven't the use of their limbs,' she said seriously, explaining things to Tom, as with the baby in her arms they made their way to their own front door. 'It's only while they are powerless to put out their little hands, and protect themselves, that a fall would be so bad. It will be different when he is able to walk.'

But Tom wasn't listening to her now. They had reached their own house, and then, no sooner were they inside their dark and narrow little hall than, baby and all, he had caught her against him, and held her tight in his arms.

'There may be another little fellow in the cradle by then,' he said, and once again, although they were alone, she felt the blush rising in her face like a flood, and now the pain of her breasts was excruciating, pressed like that against him.

But not for worlds would she say he was hurting her.

'Oh Tom, it's time for the baby's feed,' she cried instead. 'Let me go,' because she knew that the needs of the baby were laws under which he humbly bowed his big curly head.

It seemed then that it would be an eternity until the little thing in her arms would be able to stir, but after all it was no time until the little fellow was able to sit up, to stand, and indeed, before she realized how the months were passing, he was able to take a few steps when she held out her arms to him. After that, when she reached the Lots, she used to take him out of his pram, and let him toddle about in the grass. But soon his little legs got sturdy, and if Tom had not bought her a set of reins with jingle bells, she would have had to give up the pleasure of going there, because she would never have been able to keep him by her side, particularly as it would not have been easy for her to run after him just then: she was expecting another child.

When Ellie, her second child, was born, however, she was as sprightly and lightfooted as ever, and off they went, every day, the three of them, with the dinner pail dangling from the handle of the pram that had now passed into the possession of Ellie, and on the way back they came to a stop as soon as they reached the waste ground. Patrick was big enough now to have sense, and to do what he was told. How big he was growing! And little Ellie too was getting big and fat. Her little fingers reached out for the daisies they threw into the pram to her, and her little face was always wreathed with smiles. She loved the daisies. And Mary looked forward to the next summer when the child would be able to run and pick them with her own little hands.

And so summer stole on summer, and time went past so gently that neither she nor Tom once heard its footfall. When Patrick had to go to school at last, and soon after him, Ellie, and these two were no longer with her when she went to the Lots, there was Angie then to take the place of Ellie, and to look up at her with serious eyes to hear the long, summer story about Tullamore.

'Aren't you tired, Mary?' Tom asked more and more anxiously as time passed, and she still insisted on bringing him a hot meal at midday. He used to wait for her at the door of the big tram shed, and when he saw her coming he went to meet her and took the dinner pail from her. 'Are you sure you're able for this long walk every day?' he asked one day, cautiously, because he knew her too well to make any stronger protests against her coming.

But Mary only laughed.

'I'll go back by the Lots as usual,' she said, 'and maybe I'll sit and rest for a bit if the grass is dry. The baby will probably fall asleep.'

There was always a baby to fill the big, ramshackle pram that was beginning at last to have a dilapidated air, in spite of the care that Tom gave it, cleaning the metal and patching the hood, and greasing and oiling the big high wheels. Indeed it was not so much that it was dilapidated as that it had the outmoded look of all vehicles that have seen too many seasons.

'It will do fine for another while,' said Mary, one day when Tom drew her attention to how shabby it had become.

He looked at her with tenderness.

'I hope it will soon be put away for good.'

'Oh, don't say that, Tom,' she cried. For how could she bear to think of a time when there wouldn't be one of the children with her when she made the daily trip to the tram barn and came home by the Lots. For although Angie, too, would soon be going to school, her youngest son, Larry, was big enough to run along by her side.

'You must be a familiar figure leaning over that paling,' said Tom one day.

For it was summer once again, and as sure as in the midmost meadows of the land the bees were suckling the clover nipples on the broad white breast of June, Mary O'Grady was to be seen with her children round her, leaning over the palings as she told them about Tullamore.

'Come here, Angie. Come here, Larry. You're always asking me to tell you something about Tullamore; well, that's Tullamore for you! That's what it was like, big meadows, just like that, only bigger and higher, so big and so high they washed up to the doors of the house, and washed back from it to the mearing at the road. There were times when you couldn't see that mearing hedge with the height of the growth around it. Yes; that's true. The growth was something wonderful in our parts. My father used to say that the grass would come out over the ditches if the people weren't careful. He was always the first man in Tullamore to cut his meadow. He used to say that it would flood over the house, and drown us all, if he didn't take a scythe to it in the first week of June.'

The children looked up at her eager, glowing face, and listened to those faraway tales of long dead Junes in that dreamy place Tullamore, where it seemed to them that it must always have been midsummer—always the heart of June.

June! Like the word 'Tullamore,' the word 'June' used to take an effect upon Mary's heart. June was the month in which she herself was born, and in the simplicity of her heart, she used to tell the children, as she used to tell their father too, in the days when there were still things about her undiscoverable to him, that this was the reason she loved roses.

It was true that she had a passionate love for the rose. In the back yard of the small, ugly house in Ranelagh, where she had gone as a bride, and would no doubt one day be made straight for her burial, she had stuck into the earth scores and scores of slips and cuttings, shamelessly taken from the rose bushes that decorated the front gardens of the fashionable residences of Pembroke and Fitzwilliam. For unless you stole a root, or damaged the growth of a plant, it was no harm surely to take a little cutting? And some of these slips took root, and to a certain extent throve, but it must be said that what flourished most was stalk and foliage, which furthermore showed strong inclinations to revert to their briary origins. Yet, in spite of this, there was a pleasant bowery look about the O'Grady back yard, and from it there wafted over the more orderly gardens to either side of it a faint old-fashioned fragrance. There was no back yard like it in the whole of Ranelagh.

Yes, Mary loved roses, and although she soberly chose the names of her first two daughters from the sanctified source of family tradition, names that could be ultimately traced to the Calendar of the Saints, when her third daughter was born in the middle of a sweet June day, Mary O'Grady looked out from her bed by the window into the briary tangle of the yard, and seeing one pale pink rose that had opened its petals flat, she decided to call the little girl Rose.

'Rosie's a lovely name for a young girl,' she said. 'I don't believe there's a girl in all Ranelagh called Rosie. It isn't a Dublin name. It's a real Tullamore name!'

Tom laughed. He went over to the cradle where the little girl lay.

'So you're to be the Rose of Ranelagh, are you?' he said. 'I can well believe it.' He looked back at Mary. 'She's going to be a beauty,' he said. 'Like her mother.'

But Mary frowned. One of the neighbours who had tended her at the birth of the child was outside on the landing sorting sheets. Dublin people didn't understand talk like that from married couples.

'Ssh!' she said softly, and she began to ask questions about the christening, to pretend she had not heard what he said; but she had heard all right. 'Anyway,' she said, after a minute, 'I hope we'll be gone out of Ranelagh before this little creature is grown up!'

Perhaps it was only a natural feeling of depression after the strain she had undergone, but never before had Mary felt so dissatisfied with Ranelagh, and their small box of a house. Perhaps a vague idea for their betterment lay at the back of her mind, or perhaps her discontent was due to nothing more than having been shut up in the house for so long. Even when she was on her feet again, it was a long time before she was able to go for a nice long walk, because the new baby made a lot of work. And so although the little thing had not quite cut her teeth, two little peaks of ivory stuck up in the pink ridge of her lower gum before the O'Grady cavalcade was once more on its way to the Lots.

It was a day in May, and the baby was nearly a year old. They had made their journey to the tram barn a bit earlier perhaps than usual, because it was an exceptionally mild day, and there seemed to be wings on Mary's heels. And as for the pram, it sped forward like a chariot.

Oh, such a day! The sky was so blue, the clouds were so white, and in the parks the hawthorn trees were beaded with tight pink buds. So when they had waved their last at Tom, with Angie and Larry at each side of her, and Rosie in her chariot, Mary, with her firm figure and her quick, easy step, began to walk down Fitzwilliam Street.

From the time she crossed the tram lines at Merrion Square, it was a straight walk right down Fitzwilliam Street to their resting place on the Canal side, but a slight rise in the level of the street for a time hid the grassy plot from sight, and so, until the moment when it came into view, Mary's eye followed the blue line of the Dublin Hills, which rose up in front of her, and in particular she dwelt upon the blue peak that was supposed to be the ruin of the Hell Fire Club.

'I wonder why it was called the Hell Fire Club,' she pondered as she tried to discern upon the misty blue slope the deeper and bluer mass of that famous ruin. 'I must ask Tom; he will know,' she thought, because Tom was a Dublin man from his head to his toes; his big black curly head and his big strong toes that were hard to pinch into even the biggest boots to be had in the city.

Tom knew all about Dublin. He used to go up the Hills when he was a boy, and after they were married, he was always saying he'd take Mary up there some Sunday afternoon. It was a pity for his sake that she could not go with him. Indeed there were times when she saw him standing at the hall door in his shirt sleeves, looking out at the hot street, that she knew that if he was single he'd take a tram and go out to Rathfarnham. It would be very nice out there. She knew that; but still, it was only for him that she fretted. She didn't mind for herself at all. If only, she thought, he was on the Rathfarnham tram route he would get a bit of country air while the tram was waiting at the terminus. Or if he was even on the Terenure tram, he'd get a view of the Dublin Mountains going up Rathmines Road. But he always seemed to be changed from one short run to another. First he was on the link line that only went from Rathmines to Ballsbridge. And after that he was on the Parkgate line that only went back and forth from Nelson's Pillar to the terminus. It was too bad. Poor Tom!

One summer he had been on the Kingstown tram for a while, but it was in the busy season, and his heart was scourged with the crowds, and with all the pushing and shoving at every stop along the line. There were times when he didn't so much as glance at the sea, he was so bothered with children yelling, and babies squalling. He used to be afraid of his life some child would fall over the top of the tram, and come down on the rails in front of him.

'It could happen in a minute,' he said.

'God preserve us from all harm!' Silently, secretly, Mary murmured her talisman against all evil, because, since her babies were born, the slightest word of hurt or harm to any creature was almost more than she could bear, such a shaft of pain went through her heart.

'When they get bigger, we can take them with us,' she said, 'we'll take them out into the country, won't we?' she said, for she was still fearful at the thought of that toppling tram load of children, bound for Kingstown Pier, teetering and rocking on the rails, and the noisy gulls wheeling inland at Merrion Gates, screeching, and dropping their dirt.

It would be much nicer to go out into the country. It would be like home. Or else to go up the mountains, because as time passed they seemed to smoulder more and more mysteriously in the blue haze of distance. But they never went out to the country; and they never went up the mountains. And when, after a while, there were almost as many blue eyes in the family as there were beads upon the blue necklace that Mary wore on her wedding day, Tom gave up hope of their ever going.

But as Tom's desires for wandering afield grew fainter, their son Patrick, who was a big boy now, was beginning to wonder about the world beyond his own back yard.

The mountains, above all, seemed to fascinate him.

'What's on the other side of them?' he asked one day. 'Do people live up there?'

'Run away and play like a good child, and don't bother me with your silly questions,' his mother said sharply, because she was beginning to be afraid of the fascination they had for him.

That settled him for a while. But one day shortly afterwards she heard him talking to Tom. She happened to catch what he said as she raised up her head from over the tub of suds where she was washing a pair of blue pants for him.

'What tram would you take if you wanted to get to the mountains, Dad?'

That was all he said, but something in his voice made her turn around, and something in his eyes made her take up her hands from the suds and wipe them at her sides, while Tom in his shirt sleeves at the window sat placidly smoking his pipe, as if there were nothing strange in the question at all.

'Come here, Patrick!' she cried. 'Show me what you have in your hand?' and prizing open a dirty little fist, she found what she expected: the three copper pennies she had given him that morning for turning the handle of the mangle for her.

'Patrick O'Grady!' she cried then, in a voice that was thunder to the little boy. 'Patrick O'Grady! Don't you dare think of such a thing!' And she stared at him with a look so stern that the three big pennies that were to have charioted him to the blue hills fell to the floor and rolled away into the darkness under the kitchen table.

Such prescience was too much for any little boy, and even Tom was amazed at it.

'How did you know what he had in his head?' he asked later.

'Oh, I just knew!' said Mary, making light of her vision, but she was trembling. It was the first time she had looked straight into the little boy's heart.

There was no more said about the mountains after that until Patrick was in bed, but before she went to bed herself that night, Mary had persuaded Tom to take the little boy up the mountains the following Sunday.

It was a fine Sunday, too. Mary stood at the door and watched them go down the street.

'Don't be too late,' she called.

All the same, she was not a bit surprised to find it was long past teatime when she saw a tired pair appear at the end of the street.

'Oh, Tom, are you tired? Did you have to carry him much of the way?' she cried, as she went to the gate to meet them and held out her arms for the child.

'It's all right,' said Tom. 'Leave him to me. I'll carry him up to his bed. He's dead to the world.'

'Did he have a good time?' whispered Mary. 'What did he think of the mountains?' She peered over Tom's shoulder at the sleeping child. 'Are you sure he is asleep?' she asked. 'Are you sure he does not want his supper? It's a long fast till morning.'

It was a bitter disappointment to her that she was not going to hear what Patrick thought of the mountains, and when, after Tom had laid him on his bed, and she had covered him, the little boy smiled in his dreams, she felt a strange sadness as if, already, her son had penetrated to the heart of a mystery that might be for ever hidden from her, his mother.

'Come on. Mary,' said Tom. 'Is my supper ready?'

Although he didn't say a word, she knew how Tom's arms must ache after the heavy weight of the child, but she had to know if the trip was a success.

'He'll tell you himself in the morning,' said Tom. 'I'm too tired to open my mouth except to swallow a drink of tea.'

'I'll have it ready in five minutes,' said Mary, going down the stairs, but at the foot of the stairs she paused. 'I think morning will never come,' she said.

Next morning, the moment Patrick opened his eyes, she was smiling down at him. 'Well, Patrick, did you see the mountains?'

'Oh yes, we saw them,' said Patrick. Beside her eager face his little face looked stolid and unmoved.

'What did you think of them, son?' she cried. 'Aren't you going to tell Mother about them?'

'They're not a bit the same when you get near them.'

That was what she would have thought. They must be indeed very strange and beautiful when you were nearer to them.

'What were they like?' she said, stirred by faint imaginings of their strangeness and their beauty.

But Patrick pulled away from her.

'Put on my shoes,' he said. He always wanted to get out of the house in time to see the morning trains pass over the bridge.

'Well!' Mary could only stare at him in amazement. 'Oh, Patrick! Is that all you're going to tell me about your trip after the way I made your father take you?' She still held him by the strap of his belt.

'But there's nothing to tell,' said Patrick, shaking himself free. 'When you're up near them they're not the same at all; they're not like mountains any more, they're just ordinary fields.'

'Ordinary fields!'

'Fields—and hedges—and sheep.' Patrick cocked his head to one side. He thought he heard the whistle of an engine far away. Probably it was only leaving Harcourt Street Station now, but in a few seconds it would be going over the bridge at the side of the house. He hadn't much time. Still, he didn't want his mother to look at him with that sad look in her face.

'Yes,' he said impatiently, and he sought around in his mind for something that might bring home to her quickly how unlike it had all been from what he expected.

'Yes, sheep—and houses; little white houses—and meadows.'

There! Unmistakably it was the whistle of the train.

'I'll tell you, Mother,' he said, with a flash of inspiration. 'When we got near them they weren't like mountains at all! It was just like Tullamore!'

Then he was out in the hallway; but at the door he stopped for an instant.

'Why are you laughing, Mother?' he asked, but he didn't wait for an answer.

'Tullamore! Oh, son!' How could she help but laugh! Did she talk about Tullamore so much that her children, who had never been there in their lives, could talk about it as familiarly as that?

Still laughing, she stooped down and picked up the discarded nightshirt, that was warm with the heat of her son's small body, and slightly smelling of his small, fat person. But Patrick's words had stirred her more deeply than she knew, and a gentle wave of longing lapped lightly against her heart.

One of these days, when the baby is big enough to do without the pram, I'll take them all, and we'll go home for a few days to Tullamore!

It would be so mild and milky there just now, with the cows going out to pasture, their udders yellow with pollen.

Ah dear! What was that?

No matter how many times a day the shrill whistle of a train shattered the air, it seemed to startle her.

And Patrick? Was he all right? Uneasily she moved over to the window, and looked out at him where he stood on the pathway a few paces from the house, looking upwards at the railway line which bridged the street at that point. He was all right, she saw, and as usual he had timed things well, for as she stood looking out, the train rattled over the bridge above them, filling the air with smoke and steam. That steam! How she detested it! And how she detested the damp archway where the steam dissolved into moisture that streamed down the walls, and here and there dripped into the street in heavy oily drops.

The O'Grady house was the last house in the terrace, and nearest to the railway.

'I think it's an advantage to be at the end of the terrace,' Tom said, when they were trying to make up their minds about the house. 'It's better than being stuck up against other houses on both sides. And the garden is bigger than any of the other gardens in the terrace.'

The garden had been a great attraction for Tom. And all the way home to her aunt's house that day he kept telling her how quickly he would get it under control, when he rolled up his sleeves and tackled it.

When they eventually made up their minds and took the house, Tom was as good as his word about the manner in which he rolled up his sleeves. Every evening that spring, as soon as he had eaten his supper, and taken off his big boots for a while to cool his feet, he put them on again and went out in the garden.

But it was a losing game from the start. It wasn't that things didn't grow in it. On the contrary, never in her life had Mary seen grass as brilliant as the long, shiny, green blades that seemed to sprout overnight in the moist clay. It was impossible to keep it down. It wasn't like real grass at all, though; it was queer and unnatural like the weeds.

Perhaps it was the steam from the trains that made the weeds grow so strong, and so persistently. Except in wayside ditches, Mary had never known weeds to flourish as they flourished in that garden, and not only the common weeds with which she was familiar, nettles and thistles, dock, ragwort and wild parsley, but other weeds, so huge and so ugly she had never before seen anything like them. One of these, in particular, which she had grown to dread was a foul-smelling thing with a stem that seemed to thicken while you were looking at it. At first this foul thing had only grown upon the railway bank, but at last it invaded their own garden, and it was impossible to keep it from spreading, no matter how Tom hacked at it. He used to attack it as if it were some living thing at first, but after a while he began to have such a loathing for it that he hated to go near it. And Mary didn't blame him. For hours after it was cut, like the windpipe of a living thing, the great hairy stem would be wet about the edges, and slowly excreting a slimy white fluid.

Oh, how had she stood it all those years?

If only they lived in a nicer locality, not so near the railway, or in some place where it would be a little more like the country!

Once she had said that to Tom, and it made him feel bad.

'You're fretting for home,' he said. 'You'll never content yourself in Dublin.'

Well, that was before the children were born, and perhaps now and then she used to dream that something would happen so that Tom could give up his job, and she could go back to Tullamore, and bring him with her. How he'd love the country if he was in it for a while.

But now they had the children to consider. And that made a big difference. They couldn't take children down to the country and deprive them of all the advantages they had in Dublin. And so, fret as she might, for their sake she put out of her head all thought of going back to Tullamore. Didn't the whole world know that the city was the place for opportunity and advancement?

~ ~ ~ ~

In the early years of their marriage, their children came to Mary and Tom as seasonally as the flowers came up in the fields, or as the stock in the pasture at home had their young to run at foot with them.

There was less than a year between Patrick and Ellie, and not much more than a year between Ellie and Angie.

But after the birth of Angie, nature seemed to take things more indolently, and Angie was nearly four years old before their second son, Larry, was born, while Larry was a full four years and more, in the June that Rosie was born.

Yet, in spite of having nursed them all, and minded them without any help from anyone, Mary seemed to be only now in the full bloom of her womanhood.

'I'm so proud of you, Mary,' said Tom impulsively one evening when, after putting the other children, big and small, to bed for the night, she had brought down the baby to the kitchen fire to be fed and made ready for the long hours of darkness.

'Are you fooling?' she said, looking up at him, because on her way down the stairs she had caught a glimpse of herself in the hall mirror, and seen the way her hair was all loosened from its coils, and the bodice of her dress all rumpled from carrying the child in her arms.

But as their eyes met, she knew that it was not only in her looks that he took pride. He was proud of her in ways she could hardly understand.

He was proud of the number of children she had borne him. He was proud of her good health and good spirits when she was with child on each occasion. And he was proud of the way her confinements had been accomplished so easily and safely in her own home, with only the help of the district nurse. But above all, he was proud of the fact that, unlike the pale, papery wives of other men, out of the fullness and plentitude of her body she had nourished her children. And when, after the birth of Rosie, he walked by her side on the Sunday she went to be churched, he looked as proud as he did upon the first Sunday of all that they went abroad together as man and wife, and he had seen out of the corner of his eye how other men had glanced at her, at her pink cheeks, and her soft hair, and at her twinkling ankles.

Not that those days were altogether gone. For in its proper time her figure regained its trimness, and, in spite of dark forebodings to the contrary, after each child had taken its toll, her lovely almond teeth still shone upon him softly when she smiled.

'You're just the same as the first day I met you, Mary,' he said, as she sat down at the kitchen fire with the baby.

'Are you joking?' she said again, looking at him with a pleased surprise.

But there was no mistaking the look in his eyes. It was indeed the same look she had seen in them the first day they met. Across the sleeping child they smiled at each other. And Mary's mind was filled with a mild surprise that they were sitting there together, man and wife, with so many years behind them, so many children born to them, and—who could tell—so many more, perhaps, yet to come. For although after each child was weaned, and, once more, she took her place as the most important member of her family, deep in her heart she always felt that it was not upon her alone that all the attention was centred, but upon the nameless, unborn child that would begin before long to form within her body.

And yet it seemed such a short time since she and Tom had stood outside this very house, then vacant, and made up their minds to pay a deposit upon it and secure it for their home.

How had they ever brought their minds to a decision about that, or indeed about anything? How had they, two strangers as it were, and so young, so terribly young, alone and secretly, without telling their parents or anyone else, made up their minds to marry and live out their lives together, for ever and ever? And having made the decision, how had they dared to tell their parents what they meant to do? How had they dared to ask for the few pounds they needed to buy their wedding clothes and to get together the few bits of things that would set them up in a house? How had they done it? How had they dared?

It all seemed so much more difficult now, looking back on it, than it had seemed at the time, or else she had forgotten a lot about that time, as well as all the other things that people forget, good things and bad, as life goes onward.

Mary looked across at her husband.

How was it that out of all the young fellows in the city, Tom should have been the conductor on the first tram she boarded outside her aunt's house, on that one and only visit that she had ever made to the city? How was it that among all the people getting on and getting off that tram every minute of the day, he should have noticed her? And how had he dared to speak to her when he was giving her a ticket, and how had he dared to come and sit on the seat beside her when they got to the end of the line and the other passengers got out? And how had she dared to answer him, she who had always been warned against talking to a stranger? To think that she actually consented to meet him that evening, she, a country girl, she who was always considered shy! She must have been very country-looking too! What made him take such a fancy to her, he who must have been used to such smart girls? And yet, he made up his mind about her in a few days, and asked her to pledge him her word. And she did. She pledged him her word at the end of the week, and when she went home and her parents met her at the train she didn't wait till they were out of the station before she told them that she would be going up to Dublin again in the middle of the month; to get married!

A feeling of admiration came over Mary for the Mary of long ago, who had had this strength in her desire, and who had the courage to pack up her belongings and leave her father and mother, and her dear kind brother John, and all the places she knew so well, to go to a strange city, to live with a strange man.

How had she done it? How had she made that wrench with her old home; she who had never slept out of her own old feather bed except on that one fateful visit to her aunt? And above all, how she had let the parting become so final and complete? She had meant to go back home so soon, and to bring Tom with her; the two of them walking up the aisle of the chapel to the very front seat, with everyone looking at them, even the altar boys giving sly glances back over their shoulders, and the priest himself darting a look at them as he came out through the little sacristy door. But she did not go back. And why? She couldn't say. When she let the first summer pass without going it was less easy to arrange to go in the summers that followed. Somehow it always seemed easier for her father and mother to come up and stay with them, than for them to go down to Tullamore. The old couple liked the city. They liked the lights, and they liked seeing so many people on the streets. Not that she and Tom would not have liked a change too, but it was so hard to go anywhere when you had to bring children. Patrick's love for trains did not stop him from being sick after the first few miles. And some of the others couldn't be got on to a station platform at all, but began to scream and cry as soon as they heard the whistle of the train, and smelled the steam and the smoke. Indeed, whatever change came over her, Mary herself didn't care too much for stations and trains. She got a reel in her head when she heard the whistle of the engine, and she flew into an absolute panic if the children were not within reach of her. She used to shout at Tom to take hold of them, and she used to grab at them, although they were always well back against the wall of the waiting room, and although Tom told her that she was making them all look silly. That was the last thing she wanted, to look silly. Would she ever forget the day they were all made to look so foolish! It was one day they were taking an excursion train to Bray, and just as they went into the station a gust of wind came around the corner and what did it do but blow Angie's white straw hat right off the child's head and right down on to the rails in front of the engine. Oh, how she screamed! Not that she cared tuppence about the hat, although it was a new one, but because she was terrified out of her life that the child might break away from her and run to the edge of the platform. Oh, the terror she felt that day, and the terrible feeling that came over her as she saw the familiar little straw hat lying on the line in front of that engine that was advancing so relentlessly upon it. It would have been just the same if it had been the child herself that lay upon the line in front of it.

Even now, years afterwards, she could not bear to think long about that incident. Yes; train journeys might be all right if you didn't have a crowd of youngsters to keep your eyes upon all the time. After that excursion to Bray, she put out of her head all thought of going to Tullamore until the children were old enough to mind themselves. And that, in spite of the many times the old people had begged her to go down to them, when they became too feeble to venture journeying to her.

Ah! But how cruel it was that when the supreme call came to go back, when first her father, and then her mother, lay dying, that she should on both occasions be helpless in childbed!

Her father! Her mother! And to think that she had not even gone to see their graves.

Oh, how had she been so careless? How had she treated so lightly the ties that, when it came to binding her own children to her, seemed so sacred and so secure?

~   ~   ~   ~

'I thought you were asleep!'

One evening when Tom came home from work Mary was sitting in the dark kitchen. She was all alone. Rosie was in bed, and Larry was up in his bedroom where he would not be interrupted, doing his homework. Patrick and the girls had finished their supper and were gone out somewhere for the evening. They were no longer children. Patrick was almost nineteen now, and he was going to the Technical School. The girls also had left day school, and both of them were going to a commercial college in Harcourt Street.

'When did you ever see me asleep in a chair?' said Mary, and she got up at once and began to set Tom's supper before him. She had hardly put his food in front of him, however, when she sat down again in the same attitude as before, not moving, not speaking, just looking listlessly into the fire.

Tom was hungry, so he pulled up his chair to the table and began to eat what had been set before him. Once in a while, however, he looked over his shoulder at Mary, but he knew better than to question her, and so when he had finished his food he stood up and went over to the press in the corner of the room and took out a wooden box filled with tins of polish and old dusters. Still without talking, he began to polish the brass buttons on the blue jacket that was supplied to him by the Tramway Company. But before he had done more than the two top buttons Mary looked up.

'Here, Tom,' she said, 'give me that jacket and sit down. I'll do those buttons for you to-night. You must be tired after standing on your feet all day.'

Tom drew a deep breath. So it wasn't because of anything he had done that she was depressed. He handed over the jacket, but he was upset by the dejected look on her face.

'Sit down, can't you?' she said at last.

Tom sat down. He would eventually hear what was troubling her but not until she was ready.

Meanwhile, one after the other, the buttons that had been so dull and foggy had begun to shine like pure gold.

'Tom?'

The last button was done. Mary laid the jacket across the back of a chair. 'Did it ever occur to you, Tom,' she said, 'that Patrick is very restless?'

Oh, was that all that was troubling her? Tom relaxed. For a long time now she had worried about Patrick, imagining that he was getting too full of his own importance and that he was too fond of being out of the house.

'He's hardly ever at home except to swallow his food, and then he's gone, only coming home in time to tramp upstairs to bed!'

That was an allegation that she frequently made. To please her, Tom had to make some reply.

'Do you want me to speak to him?' he said.

That was what he had said upon other occasions, and for the time being at least it had satisfied her anxieties.

To-night, however, she seemed to be more deeply disturbed.

'Oh, don't say anything to him,' she cried. 'It might only——' But there she paused.

'——Only what?'

For a minute or two she said nothing, and then when she spoke her voice was troubled.

'It might only make him more anxious to get away from us,' she said.

This was something new. So the boy wanted to get away from them, did he? Tom had not been prepared for anything as definite as that.

'When did he tell you this?' he asked.

But she threw a scornful glance at him.

'You don't think he'd tell me such a thing to my face, do you?' she said.

'Well then——' Tom looked at her. Her hand was resting on her heart.

'It's just that I know,' she said.

And looking at her, Tom suddenly felt a strange sadness steal into his own heart.

'Are you sure he didn't say something to upset you?' he asked, his face darkening.

But Mary only sighed.

'No,' she said dully. 'He said nothing; nothing definite anyway.'

Nor had Patrick said anything.

That evening she had set his meal before him as usual, and as usual she sat down at the other end of the table to give herself the pleasure of seeing him satisfy his big appetite with the food she had prepared with such care for him. But to her disappointment he was bolting it down too fast.

'Are you going out again, son?' she asked.

His mouth was full but he nodded his head.

'Do you want a message?' he asked after a minute.

She had shaken her head.

'You'd never think of staying at home for an evening, would you, son?' she said bitterly.

How could his food do him any good when he attacked it like that, his elbows stuck out to either side—as if he was riding a bicycle, she thought irritably.

But the bitterness was lost on him. He only laughed and it gave her some solace to see his strong white teeth; not one decayed tooth in his whole head. Then he stood up.

She had stayed sitting at the table.

'I often think you hate this house, Patrick,' she said then, slowly and gravely.

'Oh, there's nothing wrong with the house,' he said, and as a matter of fact he glanced around him as if he had a warm regard for the little kitchen.

But she had not been able to let things rest at that.

'You'd never know,' she said, 'one of these days we might take it into our heads to move.'

'To a new house?'

He was putting on his coat, but he stopped with his arm halfway out in his sleeve.

'Would you like that?' she cried, her heart beating faster with eagerness for his answer.

But his coat was on, and he was at the door, and he laughed again, lightly, carelessly, not knowing what he was doing to her.

'Where will I be then?' he said, and something in his own words put him into good humour.

Where will I be then? Just a few simple words, but they had filled her heart with anguish.

'He has something in the back of his mind, Tom,' she said, and again her heart was pierced by pain; pain that was like the first arrowy pangs of sundering that she had felt within her the day before he was born.

'My poor Mary.' Tom stood up and coming behind her he laid a hand upon her shoulder. 'We can't keep him with us forever,' he said, and his voice was so gentle it seemed to feel its way through her thoughts.

'I know that,' she said, but Tom's words had only made her feel worse.

Helpless, he looked at her. Could he do nothing to make her feel better? He stumbled on.

'As a matter of fact,' he said, 'I have been thinking lately that Patrick may not be the first to leave us, in spite of his being the eldest. I see the girls, Ellie and Angie, whispering and giggling a lot between themselves lately. They're not such children as we think!'

Mary looked up.

'Yes,' said Tom, 'I didn't tell you, but the other day when I was doing a temporary run on the Clonskea tram I caught sight of the pair of them standing at the corner of Earlsfort Terrace, and you wouldn't believe what they were doing? Well, I'll tell you! They were talking to a couple of students out of the University. Now! There's something to think about for a change, instead of always worrying about your precious Patrick! I tell you, Mary, you thought you had trouble bearing them and rearing them, but your troubles are only beginning. Well, if they want to go, let them go, I say. We were all right before they came to us, weren't we? We were happy together then, the two of us, weren't we? Well, we'll be happy again. Let them spread their wings if they like. We can't stop them. But when they're gone, we'll still have each other.'

Poor Tom! He meant well, but the tears rushed into her eyes and fell down her face. The next instant his arms were around her.

'Why, Mary,' he cried, 'what's the matter! What did I say?'

'I'm sorry, Tom.' Lifting the corner of her apron Mary wiped her wet eyes. 'I'd better save my tears,' she said. 'A day may come when I'll need them worse than to-day.'

But they smiled at each other. That day seemed well below the rim of the horizon.

PART II

Tom

ONE Saturday afternoon about a year later Tom O'Grady was seated at the kitchen table buttering his bread. Patrick was at the sink, washing his hands, and the girls would be home at any minute, Mary said. She did not want to wet the tea until they were all at the table.

With a little worried frown, Mary glanced at the chairs that were crowded around the table.

'Will there be room for all of us?' she murmured, partly to herself and partly aloud to Patrick.

'Won't we manage the same as we do every day?' said Patrick casually, as he dried his hands on the towel behind the door. But suddenly he lowered the towel. 'Is Alice Maguire going to be here for tea?' he asked.

Something in his voice annoyed Mary.

'Well!' she said shortly. 'When the girl was so kind as to take Rosie out for the afternoon, and walk about the Park with her for two or three hours, I think the least we might do is to offer her a cup of tea. The poor child, when does she see any company at all only when she comes in here on an evening?'

'Oh, I'm not saying anything against her coming,' said Patrick hastily. 'I'll be going out anyway as soon as I get a cup of tea. What's the cause of the delay anyway, Mother? God knows when the girls will be back. And Alice Maguire——'

But just at that moment there were voices in the hall, and the next minute three young girls came into the kitchen in a bunch. Two were linked; these were Ellie and Angie, the first a gay vivacious girl, with bright hair and light brown eyes freckled with dancing lights, the latter slimmer and paler and more serious looking, with

33

black hair and blue eyes. The third was Alice, and clinging to her was Rosie, a pretty child with flossy, curling hair that lolloped about her pink cheeks. Alice also had fair flossy hair, and pink cheeks, but her face was not as animated as the face of the little girl clinging to her.

'Well, Alice, did you have a nice afternoon?' said Mary.

'We had a lovely time, Mrs. O'Grady,' said Alice, but almost at once she turned her attention to Rosie, undoing her hair and tying it up again.

Mary cast a look at Ellie and Angie.

'It's a wonder one of you girls wouldn't attend to your little sister,' she said, 'and not leave it all to poor Alice.'

'Oh, Alice likes doing it, don't you, Alice?' said Angie.

'That's because she was an only child herself,' said Ellie over her shoulder, as she elbowed Patrick for room in front of the mirror over the sink. 'Anyway the child is old enough to look after herself,' she said.

Mary's lips parted. She would like to have said something more but she did not say it. Larry was still absent.

'I'm not going to wait any longer for anyone,' said Mary. 'Will you please sit down at the table and I'll wet the tea!'

The next minute the room was filled with the scraping of chairs and under cover of the noise made by his elders, Larry slipped in through the back door and took his place among them.

'Who's going to pour out the tea? For goodness' sake, Mother, will you sit down and give us a cup of tea! What are you standing up again for?'

'Ellie! The sugar.'

'Patrick, give me the loan of your spoon?'

'Ellie! Did you hear me talking to you, are you asleep? Will you pass the sugar?'

'I'll pass it to Alice; that's what I'll do. I have manners if you have none.'

'Children! Children!'

The meal had begun.

It was seven o'clock at least before anyone at the table gave signs of being satisfied, and even then the fury of the talk and laughter was unabated, although one member of the party had departed to bed. This was Rosie, who midway through the meal had begun to loll about in her chair and yawn, and who after a few protests had consented to go to bed so long as Alice went upstairs with her.

'Please, please, Mrs. O'Grady?' Holding Rosie close, and entreating

Mary with shining eyes, Alice had pleaded to be allowed to go up with the little girl.

'Please, Mrs. O'Grady?'

'Very well, child,' said Mary, still mildly reluctant, but unable to resist the plea in Alice's mild eyes.

Rosie was delighted. She ran out of the room.

'Hold the banisters, Rosie,' cried Mary, following them out into the hall.

For a moment she stood looking after them, as Alice went up the stairs behind the child.

'Make her wash her hands, Alice,' she said anxiously, but it was habit that made her speak, because there was no need to tell Alice. She was such a sensible child.

Child? As she and Rosie reached the small dark landing at the top of the narrow stairs, Mary smiled with surprised amusement, for under the vanishing flash of Alice's blue dress, she caught sight of a pair of slim ankles clad in shining silk. Gracious me! So Alice had begun to wear silk stockings. Oh well, she was growing up like the rest of them. And as well as that, she was tall for her age. But there was one thing certain, she might begin to wear more grown-up clothes, but she was never likely to discard any of her girlish modesty.

I like that girl, she thought, as she went back into the noisy room.

It was only chance that made Mary's eyes fall first upon Patrick in the crowd that still sat around the table, but as her eye fell on him the thought came into her mind that it would be a nice thing if Alice came to see them oftener. But she resolved that the next time the girl came, she would see that Rosie was put to bed at an earlier hour, and not by Alice either, but by Ellie or Angie.

How well neither of them made a move to put the little girl to bed, she thought, looking impatiently at the two elder girls. Who did they take after at all, she wondered, standing at the door and watching their complacent smiles, as, with their elbows on the table, they listened indolently to some story that Tom was recounting over the empty cups. They never showed any warmth to Alice, she thought. For that matter they never seemed to want anyone but themselves. They never asked to bring any friends to the house, and they went everywhere together. What kind of girls are they, she wondered. I should think they would like to have Alice with them for company now and then when they went out for a walk in the evenings. But they didn't. On the few occasions the girl had ventured to suggest going with them, they had managed to shake her off by making some flimsy excuse.

Selfish!

The word rose involuntarily to Mary's lips. Selfish! It would be so nice for Patrick, and indeed for them all, she amended hastily, if there were more young people dropping in occasionally; like Alice. Yes: it would be nice for all of them, but particularly for Patrick. If there were a few young people like Alice dropping in and out of the house, they might hear less of those unsettled remarks they had had from him of late. They might hear less criticisms of Dublin, and fewer hints that he was getting tired of it. Not much of a city indeed! That was something she had overheard him say recently. The idea of it! There was gratitude for you!

Not much of a city indeed! Supposing she had married and settled down in Tullamore, what would he have had to say about that? For her children were so much a part of her now that it seemed to Mary that, irrespective of what course her life had taken, or of whom she had married, she would still at that moment have been surrounded by the same laughing faces that circled her as she took her chair among them again.

But Mary was no sooner sitting down again than her attention was drawn to the end of the table where some altercation had broken out between Larry and Ellie; an argument that was rapidly developing into a wrangle.

'Careful there, Larry!' said Tom, but it was too late, for in dragging his arm free from an admonitory clutch that Ellie had laid upon it, Larry's elbow had brushed against his cup, and the next minute it was smashed to fragments on the floor.

Although in the chatter and uproar of the others, the sound of falling crockery was almost unheard, Mary felt compelled to stand up again.

'Pick up the pieces, Ellie,' she said. 'It was partly your fault. And as for you, young man,' she said, looking at Larry, whose frightened eyes were fastened upon her, 'as for you, young man, it's time you started your homework. Get up at once and get your books.' Then as Alice at that minute came back into the room, Mary stayed on her feet. 'Here, Alice,' she cried. 'Take my chair. There's something spilled on your own chair. Come, Larry!'

At that moment, however, there was a sudden knock at the front door. At once the din died. And one and all, those in the kitchen stared into the hallway through the door that Alice had left open.

'Who can that be?' Mary asked the question that was in all eyes.

'There's a way to find out, isn't there?' said Patrick impatiently, and he pushed his chair back with a grating noise.

But Tom O'Grady was on his feet as well.

'I'll attend to it,' he said, and he squeezed his bulk out between the back of Ellie's chair and the wall.

Who could it be? If it was a neighbour, wouldn't he know enough to put his hand through the letter box and pull the piece of string that was connected to the latch? For, in common with the occupants of every other house in the terrace, and every other terrace all over the whole city of Dublin, by this simple device, the O'Gradys believed themselves to be combining convenience with caution, and defeating the wit of burglars who would assuredly find a key if it were hidden under a mat or a stone.

When Tom went into the hall, he was careful to close the door of the kitchen behind him, for although it was their custom to eat their meals in the kitchen, it would not do for a stranger to discover them doing so. It was not as if they did not have a parlour; they had a very nice parlour. But how could it be kept clean and tidy if they did not take their meals elsewhere on ordinary days of the week, and when they had no visitors. It was all very well for Ellie and Angie to protest that it was common to eat your food in the same room where it was cooked. As Mary was obliged to say to them, on more than one occasion, it wasn't they who had to run the house, and when the parlour was used it was not they who had to put it to rights again. And there was another point to consider. If they were having their meal in the parlour, and, as on this occasion, a knock came on the door while they were taking it, what would happen? What would be done with the caller? Would he be ushered in upon them, as they were, with the table in disarray and the room all in disorder?

'Now!' As she fumbled to untie the strings of her apron, Mary could not forbear a triumphant look at Ellie, as, listening in dead silence, those he had left behind him in the kitchen heard Tom, first, opening the hall door, then exclaiming, and finally, after an exchange of excited talk in which another voice mingled, they heard him opening the door of the parlour and inviting the caller to step inside. Then he was back in the kitchen.

'Guess who I have in the parlour!' he cried, his face flushed with excitement, and his forehead glistening with sweat. 'Your brother John, all the way up from Tullamore!'

~   ~   ~   ~

'Look here, Mother, I don't have to stay at home to-night, do I?'

It was the night after Uncle John's surprise visit, and to-night he was coming to spend the whole evening with Mary and her family.

'It's the least he might do,' said Mary. For after the first excitement of seeing him, she had been greatly disturbed to find that her brother had made arrangements to stay in a hotel on the other side of the city.

'He wanted to be near the Cattle Market,' said Tom, taking his part later that evening after he had gone back to the hotel. 'He was telling me he came up all the way for the purpose of buying a pedigree bull, and I suppose he wanted to be at the sales in good time.'

'I hope that's the real reason,' said Mary, and she looked around the house with a critical glance. 'I always feel that he doesn't like this house: he said something once about it being like a little box!'

'Oh nonsense!' said Tom, and she tried to be reassured.

At any rate Uncle John was coming to spend his last evening with them and she was determined that everything would be at its best. It was in the middle of her preparations that she became aware that Patrick was getting ready to go out.

'But, son! Don't you want to be here to meet your Uncle John?'

'I met him last night, didn't I?' said Patrick.

The look of disappointment on his mother's face cut him to the heart, but some perversity prevented him from taking back his words. Instead he turned aside and began to fiddle with the bunch of keys he had found upon the table, but out of the corner of his eye he watched her, and after a minute, although she said nothing more, he threw down the keys.

'All right, all right, Mother!' he said hastily. 'I'll be back before he goes. Will that do?'

The sun flashed back into Mary's face.

'You'll be back early, so?' she said.

That wasn't exactly what Patrick meant. He put out his hand and patted Mary condescendingly on the shoulder.

'No one is ever able to tear themselves away from this house before the last tram, Mother, you know that?'

It was true. They did not have many visitors, but those they had were well used to walking home, because whatever charm there was in the little house, the last tram was usually gone by the time they thought of making a move towards the door.

Everyone said there was a charm about the little house. Many and many a time, particularly if Ellie started playing the piano, and they all began to sing, one of the young people had to run out to try to hold the last tram at the corner of the street, while their visitors sprinted after them, half in and half out of their coats.

Yes, the little house seemed to have a charm, and, as Patrick said, all their friends found it hard to tear themselves away from it.

'All except you!' thought Mary suddenly, as she heard the hall door slam after her elder son.

Fortunately, however, this evening there was so much to do, there was no time for brooding. It was a quarter past seven and Uncle John had been asked for eight o'clock.

The meal was already laid; that was one good thing, but there were several small preparations yet to be made, if the evening was to run smoothly, and occasions for going back and forth between the parlour and the kitchen were to be reduced to the lowest possible number.

It would have been so much more homely to have had supper as usual in the kitchen, and John would have liked it better too, Mary knew, but Ellie had put her foot down firmly on such a proposal, and she had been strongly supported by Angie.

The girls had taken a surprising interest in the party, for as such they insisted on calling the evening ahead.

It was of no avail for Mary to protest that it would only be a cup of tea taken in the hand, with a bit of cake and a few sandwiches, although indeed after the girls had ransacked the pilgrim basket under Mary's bed, where she kept her store of linen and her few pieces of silver, the parlour had taken on quite a festive air. The big lace cloth, with the tatting work on it, that had been given to Mary by her aunt—the same aunt with whom she had stayed that time long ago when she first met Tom—that had come out of its camphor and borax. And the six silver spoons that had been brought to Mary from America by a servant girl who had worked for her mother long ago in Tullamore: they came out of their little chamois bag. And, last but not least, the great pontifical tea cosy, all cutwork and hand-done lace, that Mary cherished above everything else because it had been made by Tom's mother, that too came out, and was sitting on the tea table waiting to come down snug and close over the big brown teapot that made such a good brew of tea.

'It makes nicer tea than I ever got anywhere else,' said Mary with asperity, when, earlier in the evening, some criticisms had been levelled against this homely article.

The girls, it seemed, had put their eye on a handsome teapot in a shop window in Ranelagh.

'It has a border of roses round the middle, Mother,' said Ellie, knowing Mary's weakness for the queen of flowers, 'and the knob on top of the lid is in the shape of a little rose! You should see it, Mother. It's a dream!'

'No doubt,' said Mary drily, 'and a dream is all it would be in this house before long, it it were to get the abuse that is given to Old

Faithful.' This was Mary's name for the old crock teapot. 'I wonder how long your fancy teapots would last if they were put standing on the stove, waiting until everyone in this house was pleased to sit down to the table. No thank you! This teapot is good enough for me,' she said, and she filled it with boiling water, and set it on the stove, to ensure that it would be piping hot when the time came to make the tea in it.

'Why don't you buy it yourself?' she said suddenly. 'Why don't you buy it and put it in your bottom drawer?' For something had capriciously brought to her mind Tom's words about seeing Angie and Ellie in Earlsfort Terrace talking to two young men.

For a moment Ellie stared at her in surprise.

'No thank you,' she said then, and catching up a tray with a cup and saucer on it, she flounced into the parlour. 'When I get married I'll expect to have my pots and pans bought for me!'

There was an air of strain in the house.

'I hope you won't be disappointed,' said Mary.

Latterly there was always some sharpness in the atmosphere when she and the girls were alone. But it had never taken quite this form before. It seemed to Mary that there was a more serious note than hitherto in their bickering. And she regretted the nature of her own remarks. As a matter of fact for some time past she had noticed that even in front of her, the girls had indulged in flippant talk that she did not like: talk about boys and that kind of thing. Mary pursed her lips. Boys indeed!

And watching Ellie flouncing out of the room she made a firm resolve.

I won't have any more of it, she resolved. I'll soon put a stop to it the next time it starts. They're too young for talk of that kind. They were too precocious, both of them, from the time they learned how to talk.

A small feeling of disappointment in them stole into her heart. Once or twice before she had had the same feeling. Perhaps she had thought they would have been more like she had been in her own girlhood. Perhaps she had hoped to find again in them her own youth that had now vanished. But they were altogether different from what she had been. They had grown up in the city, of course. That made a difference.

Thank goodness I have Rosie, she thought, but her thoughts were interrupted as her eyes fell on Ellie, who had come back into the kitchen again, and who had begun to help Angie to cut bread and butter it.

'What are you doing?' she asked, because if she wasn't making a mistake, they were cutting the crusts off the bread. 'Surely you're not——'

'Now, Mother, please leave this to us,' said Ellie, who seemed to know what her mother was going to say. 'Please don't interfere. If you went about more, Mother, you'd realize how common it is to leave the crust on the bread.'

'I see I may as well say nothing,' said Mary, because they had already finished the job and were arranging the bread on the bread plates.

All at once, Mary got the feeling that the evening was not hers, but theirs. They had certainly put their hearts into the preparation of the supper.

Then, just a few minutes before their uncle was due to arrive, one of them made the most extraordinary statement. Perhaps Mary hadn't been intended to hear it, but they were speaking quite openly, as, having finished the table to their satisfaction, they were washing themselves at the sink and doing their hair.

'I wonder will it be a success?' said Ellie.

'Of course it will,' said Angie.

'It's a pity about Uncle John, isn't it?' said Ellie.

A pity about him? What did they mean?

'Oh, he may go early,' said Angie.

Go early? John? But wasn't the party for him?

Mary didn't understand.

But seeing her looking perplexedly at them, then, at the last minute, when it would have been impossible to have done anything about it, Ellie threw light upon all their activity.

'By the way, Mother,' she said, and daughter or no daughter, Mary thought there was a sly look in her eyes, 'I hope you won't mind if a friend of mine should happen to call during the evening?'

Mind? What use would it be to mind now at this hour? How could this friend—or did she say friends—be stopped at the last minute?

'Well, Ellie,' she said coldly—it was impossible to be warm—'I think it's late in the day to ask if I mind.'

'Oh, they'll only call for a few minutes, Mother.' Once she had broached the matter at all, Ellie was full of assurance.

'Did you say one or did you say two friends?'

'Two!' said Ellie, and she looked at Angie and gave a silly titter.

'I see,' said Mary. Well, she would say nothing. It was unfortunate that they would not be alone, but it was too late now to mend matters. It would spoil the evening for her brother John; there could be no intimate talk. But they would just have to put up with it. Her mind turned to more practical questions. Would there be enough cups? Would there be enough chairs? Those were the things that concerned her first, but suddenly she thought of something more pressing.

'Have I met them before?' she asked, because she hated above all things to have to meet people for the first time.

Reluctantly Angie answered her.

'I don't think so,' she said.

So much the worse! There would be a strain in the atmosphere all evening. It was certainly very disappointing. She had counted so much on the evening being a success. She had counted so much on a homely chat with John.

'Well, there's just one thing,' she said, 'if there are strange girls being asked to the house, I hope you took care to ask Alice Maguire as well. I don't want Alice to feel slighted.'

'Oh, Alice!' Ellie and Angie looked at each other. Mary knew what was in their minds. How was it that none of them felt the same as she did about Alice?

'Oh, Alice will probably come in if she hears the piano,' said Ellie at last.

'Ellie O'Grady!' Mary was downright angry. 'You know that's the last thing Alice Maguire would do—to come without being asked, particularly if she knew there was other company. It is easily seen you know very little about the girl if you think she is that kind of person. Now listen to me! You can just get your coat this minute and go down the street and ask her.'

For a moment it seemed as if Ellie were going to refuse. There was a defiant gleam in her eyes, but just then Angie broke into the conversation. She had kicked off the broken-down shoes in which she had plodded about the house, and in her stocking feet, she was about to go upstairs for her best pumps.

'I think Mother doesn't understand, Ellie,' she said, and she looked nervously at her sister. Ellie looked back at her and it could be seen that she calculated something in her mind. Then she looked straight at Mary.

'I think you didn't understand, Mother,' she said, 'about our friends, I mean. You thought they were girls too. Well—they're not!'

There! She had said it. Now she must make light of it, rush on to another topic, in short, by some means or other, she must distract her mother.

'And so you see, Mother,' she cried hastily, remembering the argument about Alice, 'and so you see there might be too many girls if I went down for Alice Maguire!'

'Oh dear! This must be John!'

The exclamation came from Mary. There was a knock at the door.

'And I haven't changed my blouse yet,' cried Ellie. 'Will you answer it. Mother?'

What a good thing the knock came at that moment! Angie drew a deep breath, but, as her mother hastily pulled at her apron strings and wiped her hands, she made a sly sally.

'What about Alice, Mother?' she queried in a whisper. 'Will I go for her?'

'Oh, don't bother me now,' said Mary. 'Do as you please, but I'll tell you one thing, let you and your sister make sure that you're here to open the door when your own visitors come!'

~ ~ ~ ~

As Mary hurried into the hall, prepared to open the door to her brother, she was surprised to hear voices outside, not one but several voices. Could it be that the girls' friends had arrived also? She stood. Yes indeed, there were several people on the doorstep. She could hear them laughing and talking. She had half a mind to go back and call one of the girls, but just as this ignominious thought occurred to her, her ear caught a familiar voice mingled among the others, and a moment later the letter box was opened by a violent poke from without, and to her relief a stubby and familiar finger squeezed its way into the opening and began to fumble for the string that opened the latch.

At the sight of this familiar finger, Mary's confidence surged back.

'Just a minute, Tom. It's all right,' she cried. 'I'm coming!'

Without her aid, however, the door had already been opened, and there upon the threshold, smiling at her, stood not only Tom and her brother John, but two strange young men.

Such tall young men! And so broad-shouldered. Mary stared. She wasn't prepared for their being altogether such a good-looking couple. How on earth would they find room in her little parlour to stretch their long legs! And one of them, the older it seemed of the two, was not standing to his full height at all, but was leaning backwards, supported by his hands upon the little iron rail that separated the path from the small front garden.

They were so fair! Mary's eyes flew from one young man to the other. And so freckled. Not since she was a girl, long ago, had Mary seen grown men with such fair hair or such freckled faces. Tullamore faces! The thought came into her mind. Country faces, anyway, she conceded, that was certain.

'Well, Mary? Are you going to let us into your house, or are you going to keep us all evening on the doorstep?'

Tom was smiling, and as he spoke he glanced jovially at his brother-in-law and then at the young men. He was trying, Mary could see, to appear as if at his ease, and yet she knew by the slight glisten on his face that he was at heart uncomfortable. What did he make of the two young men, she wondered, and her eyes went back to them as she stood aside to let all of them file into the little hallway. The two young men, at any rate, were not in the least uncomfortable.

'Good evening, Mrs. O'Grady ma'am,' they said, both together, and both together they smiled at her with such big, country smiles that her heart as well as her hand went out to them at once. She almost forgot to greet John.

'Good evening, John,' she said, 'won't you step inside?'

But as John made no move she turned and saw that Tom, who had stepped into the hallway first of any, still stood there, uncertainly, and that, like a boulder fallen into the mouth of a cave, he had completely blocked the way into the parlour.

'Make way there, please, Tom,' she said, and a little rasp had come into her voice, for it had occurred to her suddenly that there was need for some introduction. 'Some friends of the girls, Tom,' she murmured, and she turned to the visitors. 'I'm afraid I don't know your names, young men,' she said. That was the best she could do at the moment. To get them all into the parlour was the thing that mattered.

But what was wrong with Tom? Was he turned into stone, that he gave no help in the matter?

Suddenly, however, Mary felt a hand at her elbow and looking up she saw a smiling face looking down into hers, and gently but firmly, she was herself being urged into the parlour.

'Come on, Mrs. O'Grady. Let you and I lead the way.'

It was the taller of the two young men, and almost at once the other young man followed his example, giving Uncle John a helping push from behind.

'Don't bother your head about making us acquainted, ma'am,' said the first young man. 'We did that ourselves on the doorstep, didn't we, sir?' he said, as taking the hat that Uncle John was vaguely holding in his hand, he slung it carelessly down on the little hall table. 'Yes, indeed,' he went on, 'and if we didn't do a good job of it, the evening is long for doing a better one. Don't trouble your head about us. Wait till you see, ma'am; in a few minutes we'll all be one big happy family. As I say——' and, having caught sight of the tea table in the parlour the young man pushed the door wide open and before she knew what he was doing, he had planted her in an arm-chair—'as I always say,' he said, 'it's only your mean-minded city man that waits for an introduction before he opens his mouth. But that's not the way with us, is it?'

And here, having settled Mary in the most comfortable chair, Bart, for that seemed to be his name, pulled over another chair, and planted Uncle John in it.

'We don't stand on ceremony, do we? Thanks be to goodness but it's a change to meet an honest man from the land, because I can see——' and the young man smiled and looked at Mary—'I can see that however much of the world your brother has travelled, ma'am, he set out from the right place at the start!'

Now wasn't that quick of him, thought Mary, to have seen that John was her brother, and to know that he came from the country.

'You're from the country too, aren't you?' she asked timidly, be-cause even as she spoke she saw that both of the young men were dressed in smart suits of clothes, not in any way countrified. They might not like to think she had sized them up as easily as they had sized up John, because of course, on second thoughts, looking at John's flannel waistcoat and the gold watch and chain that stretched across it, she could see that it wasn't hard to guess whence he had come. But Bart seemed to be delighted.

'Of course I'm from the country, ma'am.' With a comical smile he bent down his big head of yellow hair until it was almost in her lap. 'Don't you see the hayseed is still in my hair?' he said.

Mary laughed.

'Where are you going to sit?' she asked. Then she turned to the other young man. He was still standing too, but he was talking to Tom. She was relieved to see that he wasn't awkward either, although as well as she could judge, he was a good deal more quiet than Bart. Indeed when, at that moment, he turned to her she saw that he was as shy as a girl.

'You're from Tullamore, Mrs. O'Grady?' he said, and his voice was soft and gentle like his eyes. 'Bart and I pass through Tullamore on our way to Dublin. It seems to be a nice place.'

'Oh, Tullamore is lovely,' said Mary, and her eyes dwelt more particularly upon him.

He's Angie's boy, she thought, and Bart belongs to Ellie.

'Are you Willie?' she asked, smiling at him, because she had caught that name in the cross talk that now filled the room.

He nodded.

'I'm Willie Haslip,' he said. 'Bart and I come from the same parish.'

He's a nice boy too, thought Mary, but Bart was her favourite. What did Tom think of them, she wondered, and she looked at him, but before she had time to make out the expression on his face, there was a sound of light feet tapping down the stairs and the next minute Ellie opened the door and put in her head.

'Oh!' she exclaimed on seeing the young men.

Mary was conscience-stricken. I should have told the girls the boys had come, she thought, and she looked anxiously at her daughter. It was quite clear from the almost indifferent way in which Ellie had stuck her head inside the door that she did not know the young men had come. But to Mary's relief, and indeed to her secret admiration, Ellie did not appear in the least daunted.

'Good evening, Uncle John,' she said. 'Hello, Bart! Hello, Willie! So you got here!' Then, turning to her parents, she addressed them offhandedly. 'I didn't know the boys had come,' she said.

'My dear girl, we're all one happy family,' said Bart, and Mary nodded in approval of this sentiment.

It pleased her to see the way the young men jumped to their feet at sight of Ellie. Uncle John also struggled to get up from his chair, but he was motioned back at once by Tom, who had made no effort to rise. A flash of impatience came over Mary. What harm would it have done Tom to get to his feet for a moment? How would his manners look in the eyes of their visitors? A little frown gathered on her brow. Perhaps Bart saw it, because the next moment he said something that smoothed it away.

'Stay where you are, Mr. O'Grady,' he said. 'Chivalry is chivalry, but home is home! Isn't that right?' And he and Tom began to laugh.

'Hello, Uncle John. Hello, Willie! Hello, Bart!'

Angie had come downstairs.

First Willie; then Bart.

Mary noted the order. With Ellie it had been the other way round, Bart and then Willie. They were well matched. Yes; they were well matched. That was the thought that came into Mary's mind again, when Ellie and Bart seated themselves together on the settee, side by side. Not but that Willie and Angie seemed to be well suited too, she thought, as they seated themselves one on each arm of the settee, separated by Ellie and Bart, but undivided, it seemed, in the attention they gave each other across the heads of their companions.

'Are you all right there, Angie?'

Mary was not heeding everything that was said, and she was startled a little by the burst of laughter that greeted Bart's simple question. For that matter, however, it was soon clear that with young people laughter was like a galloping fever. Almost every word from one brought laughter from the others.

The room was filled with laughter. And Tom and John laughed loudest of all, throwing back their heads. What they were laughing at she could not say, but she knew that Bart would make anyone laugh, he was such a character. He was the heart and soul of the evening.

To think that she had been nervous in case these young men would interfere with the success of the evening! Why, it was they who had made it a success. Without them, it seemed to her now, the evening might very well have been dull. They were such good company.

And as the room became more and more noisy with talk and laughter, she leaned back in her chair and gave herself up to watching the others. She watched the young men in particular, and she watched their behaviour and attitude to the girls, and she had to admit that it was a long time since she had met two such nice young men.

The odd thing was that they should have taken such a liking to Ellie and Angie! There must be something about them to have caught the fancy of two young men such as these. Mary looked at the girls more closely than she had looked at them for some time. They were, she supposed, pretty enough in their own way, but it wasn't exactly the kind of looks that were admired long ago, in her own girlhood, that was to say in Tullamore. Although Ellie indeed was looking quite different from what she had looked earlier in the evening: different indeed, thought Mary, from what she had ever looked before; at least in her own home. Her face was always animated, but this evening she had more colour in her cheeks than ever before, and altogether there was something bolder and more open about her, you might almost say something more beautiful. Mary stared at her with surprise and pleasure. Then she looked at Angie, and as she did she remembered something she used to say to Tom about them long ago, when they were little girls, dressed the same in white dresses with blue sashes and white Panama hats.

'Isn't it funny, Tom,' she used to say, 'in spite of being dressed exactly alike, they look so different. They're not a bit alike really. They're not like sisters at all.'

Angie used to be so quiet-faced and so shy. And her hair always seemed so silky and docile compared with Ellie's wild, wavy masses. Angie barely looked at you when she spoke to you and then her lids dropped over her big blue eyes again. And when a stranger spoke to her she seemed to tremble, at least her little pointed face, so pale and so pure an oval, trembled and quivered as if beseeching one to look away from her. Ellie was so different. Her eyes invited you, teased you, drew you onwards and then, shining suddenly with a colder light, tossed you aside. As children, that was. When they grew up they seemed to be more alike, or else the similarity of the habits and ways they learned at school, and afterwards at the commercial college, made them seem not only like each other, but like hundreds of girls all over the city that Mary saw in the streets and in the trams, and behind the counters of the big shops.

But now suddenly in the parlour, she saw again that long forgotten disparity.

There was such glowing warmth in Ellie's eyes. And she had a mischievous air about her that Mary had almost forgotten. Indeed, as every instant passed, Ellie seemed to glow the more, to become more alive. It was as if with every laugh she gave, every look she cast, and every stir she made, some flame within her was fanned and leaped higher and higher.

It's no wonder he's looking at her like that, thought Mary, as Bart leaned over, and all for Ellie alone whispered something softly.

'Oh, Bart!'

Looking up into his eyes Ellie only laughed; but higher and higher, till Mary felt nervous, the flame leaped upwards.

Was she only nineteen? She looked so much older than that just now. Instead of being surprised that she had a young man, Mary realized it was a wonder she had not a dozen of them, and long before this!

But Angie! Looking at her after looking at the flushed and glowing face of Ellie, Mary felt as if she had suddenly entered into a tranquil and shaded place; not deeply shadowed, but letting in a scattered light: a shade such as might be made by leafy branches swaying this way and that and casting a patterned shade. Her little face was so serene; so pale; so quiet. She was like a child. Was it possible that she was seventeen at all? She looked hardly older than when she made her First Holy Communion. And on her face, indeed, there was the same look that it had worn that day: a look of ineffable peace. And as she used to do when she was a child, Angie had folded her hands in her lap and her lids were shaded downwards so that her lashes lay on her skin, like the painted lashes of a big china doll that had been sent to Rosie by her grand-aunt Ella in America.

Was Rosie all right, she wondered suddenly? It was time she tiptoed upstairs to see if the child had uncovered herself in her sleep. But still she lingered downstairs. In the haze of cigarette smoke that filled the room, and in which the bright dresses of the girls smouldered like the lights in an opal, she saw that John and Tom were talking more soberly now, disregarding the younger people, although from time to time Ellie and Bart interrupted them and they took the interruption in good part. Indeed Ellie and Bart too were talking more confidentially. Young as they were, and although this was the first time she had ever seen them together, Mary felt an absolute certainty that these two would want to get married. And soon.

But the others? Angie and Willie still sat, one on each arm of the old settee. For the most part they were silent, but now and then they exchanged a few words quietly over the heads of the other two. And almost all the time they exchanged their quiet glances. They were so very young; just a girl and a boy. They were like sister and brother! Indeed Willie Haslip was far more like Angie than either Patrick or Larry, with his thin face and his light eyes, and the serenity of his gaze. Yes, they were only children, and it would be hard to say what the future held for anyone, much less for two children like them, and yet there had been young people who knew their own minds even at their age. What were they saying to each other? And what were they thinking as, calm and serious, they listened quietly, now to each other, and now to what was being said around them. The most that could be said about them was that they appeared as if they were biding their time. That was it.

They're waiting for something, thought Mary. And in a flash she knew what it was.

They're waiting for the settee, she thought. They're waiting for Ellie and Bart to vacate it, to be gone upon their ways, until they take their place. And looking at them, she felt that they too, like the other couple, were in some way ringed around, drawn into one circle together.

Was she sad, or was she happy? Mary could not have told. From time to time she took part in one or other of the various conversations around her, but for the most part she leaned her head back against her chair, and letting her hands lie in her lap, she postponed the moment of going up to look at Rosie.

As for the supper, in spite of the fact that the table was there in the middle of the room, all showery with its lace cloth, all sparkling with its little china cups, the thought of food had gone completely out of her head.

It was only when, after having fancied it once or twice, she realized upon a third occasion that Ellie was looking queerly at her, and trying to make her understand something by vigorously frowning, that Mary suddenly sprang to her feet.

'Oh dear,' she exclaimed, 'I must make the tea! I nearly forgot all about it. What will you think of me!' she cried, and she addressed herself to her brother John, but it was not upon him alone, but upon Bart and Willie also, that her looks of apology fell. 'Young people are always hungry,' she said as she made her way past the settee to get to the door. 'Why didn't you say something sooner?' she whispered, as she went past Ellie. But Bart heard her too.

'Oh come now, Mrs. O'Grady,' he said, and he was on his feet at once. 'You know why they didn't say anything. They were afraid they would draw down trouble on themselves. If we were all to sit here till morning I don't suppose they would have made one stir! Oh, I know them! But they didn't fool me, ma'am. Oh no! Because the minute I came into the room I put my eye on the lovely table you had set for us!'

How Mary's heart warmed to that kind of talk. No foolish protests against putting her to trouble, but a good honest appetite that he wasn't trying to hide.

'I'm afraid, Mrs. O'Grady, that I know them better than you do, in spite of your being their mother, and I'm afraid I have to tell you that they are a lazy pair, or perhaps I should only speak for one of them? Perhaps Angie isn't quite as bad as this one!'

But as he spoke, Bart cast on Ellie a look that belied all his banter. Then he turned again to Mary and taking her by the arm he was about to go with her into the kitchen.

'Let them stay here,' he said. 'You and I can manage without them, can't we, Mrs. O'Grady! You don't know me properly yet. You don't know how useful I can be in the house. And what a good job I am like that, with young ladies such as they are nowadays. Come on, Mrs. O'Grady!'

But Mary knew better than to let him come any further than the door with her. Even without the warning glances that flashed at her from all corners of the room, she knew better than to let the young man follow her into the kitchen. It was in such a mess after the preparation of the meal. At another time she would be proud to let it be seen, for thanks to Tom it was always brightly painted and in a shade of yellow that would make you think the sun was always shining in it. But she didn't want anyone to see it as it was to-night.

'Now just sit right down again,' she said, disengaging Bart's hand from her arm with difficulty.

'Well!' said Bart. 'Well! I suppose I must do as I'm told on my first visit.' He shook his finger at Mary. 'But I warn you, I won't always be so easy to handle. Wait till you see! If you could hear what my landlady has to say about me. She says I'm as good as any woman in the kitchen.'

Landlady! So they were in lodgings. A warm, motherly feeling for them overcame Mary. They must be students, she thought, and at the same moment she remembered something Tom said a long time back about seeing the girls at the corner of Earlsfort Terrace talking to two University students.

University students! A mild astonishment passed over Mary. University students, no less. Well! She had always wanted something better for the girls than they had seemed, at times, to want for themselves.

But the poor boys! If she had known they were in lodgings! She would have had something substantial to offer them. Her eye fell critically on the supper table with its thin bread, and thin sandwiches, so bare looking, she thought, with the crusts cut from them, and the little fancy cakes in their frilly papers. They looked a poor fare for big strong young men; but it was too late to do anything about it now.

'What are you studying?' she asked, with her hand on the knob of the door.

'Oh, we're doing engineering.' It was Willie Haslip who answered her. 'This is our second year,' he said. 'As a matter of fact our second exam is in the morning.'

'In the morning! An examination!' Mary was aghast. First of all her eyes flew to the clock. They should have been in bed hours ago. And it seemed it was all her fault that this was not so, because she had forgotten about the supper. But her next thought was more practical. If they had an examination in the morning they would certainly have to get something substantial for their supper. 'Why didn't you tell me about their examinations?' she said, turning to the girls. She was taken off her balance and her voice was fussy, and vaguely she knew that if she got any more fussed, she was liable to say or do something that would displease the girls. 'Wouldn't they like something more than this?' she cried, contemptuously waving her hand in the direction of the daintily laid table. 'Wouldn't they like an egg or something?'

But the young men only laughed. And as she had foreseen, the girls were annoyed.

'Oh, Mother, for goodness' sake!' cried Ellie.

Even Angie was upset.

'As far as I can see,' she said, 'they're not even going to get a cup of tea, at this rate, because it will be time for them to be going soon. They'll have to get the last tram, you know!'

'But it wouldn't take a minute to boil a little egg,' said Mary. 'Are you sure, Bart? Are you sure, Willie?'

She felt so anxious about them. And then, as she might have known she would, she made the awful blunder.

'Indeed,' she cried, 'there is not much comfort trying to make a good meal at this little table, whereas out in the kitchen——'

But there she stopped. What had she said? The girls, she knew, were staring at her, and she felt a sudden silence come down on the whole room; but the next minute Bart gave a loud laugh.

'Oh, look at their faces, Mrs. O'Grady,' he said, and he seemed to take delight in the expression of annoyance that had come over Ellie's face in particular. 'Trying to pretend they never ate a meal anywhere but in the parlour!'

That settled the girls. They had to take what had passed with as good a grace as possible.

'Not when there are visitors!' said Ellie hotly. Bart looked around him in mock bewilderment.

'Visitors?' he said. 'Where are the visitors? I don't see any, unless of course you consider your Uncle John is one!'

In the laughter that met this remark, Bart flung out his arm and put it around Mary's waist.

'I'll tell you what we'll do, ma'am,' he said. 'We'll have supper here to-night, just to humour them, and because the table is laid, but from now onwards we'll let these two fine ladies take their cups and saucers into the parlour if they like, but you, ma'am, and Mr. O'Grady and Willie and I will have ours where we'll feel happiest, out in the kitchen, the place where everyone in the whole world enjoys a meal the best. Isn't that right?' Bart looked around him, and from Tom and her brother John at least he had full assent to his words.

'I could tell you a good yarn about an old fellow in Tullamore,' said John. 'There was no one with him in the house, and he had two rooms downstairs, a parlour and a kitchen——'

As he began his story, Mary realized with a pang how little attention she had given to him all evening and even now she could not stay to listen to him. No matter how rude it might seem she would have to slip out without delay and make the tea. What would she do if the fire had gone out? Opening the door she hurried into the hall, but as she did, she almost ran into someone who was coming up the hallway against her.

'Oh, Patrick!' she exclaimed with joy. To have him home now was almost all she needed in order to make the evening perfect. 'I'm so glad you came home early, son,' she said.

'Early? It's after ten,' said Patrick. 'Did you not start supper yet? Good!' His hand was on the handle of the parlour door, but he turned back on an afterthought. 'Can I do anything to help?' he asked. Then, when she said there was nothing he could do, he remembered something else he had not told her. 'By the way,' he said, 'I thought I heard Rosie talking in her sleep.'

Mary glanced at the clock. She would have to run upstairs before doing another thing. But they could wait. They were so late now another few minutes would hardly matter. And Patrick would want a little time to get to know them. It was so splendid that he was home before they departed.

At the head of the stairs, she glanced down at him, his stocky frame standing out in the light from the parlour as he opened the door and was greeted by the others.

Her heart swelled with pride. He was a good son. She tiptoed into Larry's bedroom where all was dark except for a small colza oil lamp, with a red globe, that burned before a holy picture on the top of a marble washstand that reflected the lamp's red glow.

Larry was fast asleep, his face smothered in the pillow, in exactly the same position in which he had fallen asleep. She went across the landing to the room where Rosie slept. Rosie was asleep too, but it was a more restless sleep, and one pink arm was outflung through the bars of the cot in a curiously defenceless attitude. As Mary stood looking at her she stirred and muttered in her sleep. Sweet-tempered by day, healthy and happy, this child seemed to suffer strange disturbances in her sleep, and often her voice shattered the whole house with its loud protests against some terror that seized her in her dreams.

'My baby!' murmured Mary as, at her touch, the little girl drew back her arm. Bending over the bed she pulled the covers over her and then stood watching her sleeping face.

'Mother! What's keeping you?' Ellie was calling to her from the stairs.

'I'm coming!' she cried, and she hurried out to forestall, if she could, the wrath that must be to come. 'I had to run up to see if they were all right,' she whispered, as they met upon the landing.

To her surprise, however, Ellie was not impatient at all.

'What do you think of him, Mother?' she asked, her face as eager as when she was a schoolgirl.

'I think they're both very nice young men,' Mary said, and as she said so, she wondered mildly what she would have felt if it had been Patrick who had brought home a friend; a young lady. Not that he had shown much interest in girls up to this, but on the one or two occasions that she had seen him standing for a minute in the street talking to a girl, even some quite nice girl whom she had formerly liked, from that moment for some odd reason she began to dislike the girl. Always, of course, excepting Alice!

'That reminds me, Ellie,' she said, as on tiptoe she and Ellie went down the stairs into the kitchen, 'we did nothing about Alice. I meant to send Angie down to the house for her but I forgot about it.'

'Oh, don't worry about Alice, Mother,' said Ellie. 'When I was upstairs changing my blouse, I remembered that she would not be able to come anyway. She had one of her headaches all day. I met Mrs. Maguire at dinner time and she told me, but it went out of my head with the fuss.'

'I'm so glad,' said Mary—'that she won't feel slighted, I mean, but I don't like to hear of these headaches; the child is getting them so often lately.'

A little frown of worry settled on her face. Only for the visitors she would have called to the house to inquire for Alice, but there was no use thinking of that now. There was not a minute to lose if their visitors were to have their supper in time to get the last tram back to the city. How the time had flown! And to think she had not had a private word with John. She looked at the clock again. They would surely miss the last tram at this rate. Then there would be no sense in their hurrying away. She might get a few words with him yet.

But long after the midnight tram was housed in the darkened tram barn, and she stood with her family in the doorway to watch their guests depart, she could only excuse herself as best she could to John.

'I didn't have a private word with you all evening,' she said, as she helped him with his overcoat.

'Well,' said John, 'you know where I am to be found if you want me.'

'Oh, you'll come up to see us again before long,' she said lightly, because he was looking at her intently and she felt that he was trying to put all that was unsaid between them into those few last words upon the doorstep. But she had forgotten his heavy, plain, outspoken ways.

'I'll come up if you want me,' he said, and he might have said something else if Bart and Willie had not come to the end of their good-byes to Tom and the girls, and going one to either side of him began to urge upon him the lateness of the hour.

'Come now, sir,' said Bart, 'the city is a bad place at this hour of the night, you know.' And giving a last wave to Tom and the laughing girls, the three men made their way to the gate and began to walk down the empty street, where long after they were out of sight, their footsteps echoed with a lonely sound.

Mary looked after them. Now that it was too late, she was filled with remorse for her neglect of her brother. She turned to Tom.

'I hardly spoke two words to John,' she said sadly.

Tom only laughed.

'Maybe we'll take a trip down to see him next summer,' he said, but it was clear that it was their other visitors that occupied his mind. He turned to the girls. 'As for those young men,' he said, 'I don't think we've seen the last of them.'

That was enough for the girls.

'Oh, did you like them, Father?' cried Angie, and then as she found her words were the same as those on the lips of her sister, she laughed.

'My only trouble,' said Tom, 'was to know which of them I liked best.'

And putting an arm around each of them, as Mary stayed back to put the chain on the door, he led them back into the parlour.

'And which one do you think you liked best?' cried Ellie, while Angie protested that the question was not fair.

Tom was able for them both.

'I expect I'll have plenty of time to make up my mind in the matter,' he said. And they all laughed again, except Mary. She had taken the young men to her heart in such a way that she did not want to hear comparisons made between them. Willie was a bit quiet, but wasn't he the younger of the two? Bart was inclined to tease, but wasn't it all only fun?

Suddenly she thought of something.

'I'll tell you what we'll do,' she said, as, each taking hold of one of the white deal chairs that lined the wall, they knelt down on the floor, supporting themselves by resting their elbows on the seat of the chairs, 'I'll tell you what we'll do. We'll offer up a decade of the

Rosary for them,' and she put her hand up to her forehead. 'In the name of the Father, and of the Son——' she murmured, and she began to feel in her pocket for her Rosary beads.

~   ~   ~   ~

The manner in which the O'Gradys had accepted Bart and Willie was best seen by the way in which proper names were considered unnecessary when, a week later, the girls came bursting into the kitchen.

'They passed! They passed their examinations!'

'Both of them?' cried Mary, anxiously, coming out of the kitchen, because it was Ellie's voice only she heard.

Angie was there too though, and her eyes were gleaming.

'Yes, Mother,' she said.

'Yes, both of them,' said Ellie. But all at once her excitement seemed to flag somewhat and going over to the mirror, that hung above the sink, she peered into it. 'As a matter of fact, Willie got honours,' she said. 'Didn't he, Angie?'

This time Angie only nodded, but the gleam in her eyes spoke louder than any words.

'Well now, isn't that splendid!' said Mary, and expecting to hear more she at once pulled out a chair and sat down. Tom sat down also.

'How far more have they got to go now before they're through?' he asked.

'Well, you see——' Angie hadn't even taken off her hat. She still stood in the middle of the floor, and her lips eagerly parted to answer her parents' questions but Ellie, having made whatever investigations she wanted to make in the little mirror, turned around.

'Oh, ages!' she said, abruptly. 'What about supper, Mother?'

Mary knew Ellie. She stood up with a sigh. That girl was like a flame, ready to flare up one minute and just as ready to flicker out. They wouldn't get any more satisfaction from Ellie.

Later, however, when she was passing her cup for the second time, Ellie seemed prepared to return to the matter.

'I suppose we should ask them over again some evening to celebrate?' she said, looking inquiringly at Mary. Tom also was looking at her.

'What did I tell you?' he said.

And indeed, his prophecy was more than fulfilled, for shortly after this there began a long series of evenings, all much alike, in many ways, to the first evening that the young men had called. But there was one important difference. After that first evening they were never entertained anywhere except in the kitchen.

And after a while it became clear to the girls that it was very nice to have the parlour empty if there should happen to be anything about which the young men might want to have a private word with one or other of them, always, of course, leaving the door slightly ajar, because upon this convention Mary insisted.

~ ~ ~ ~

It was a sunny morning and Mary and Rosie were walking down the street. Mary was on her way to do her shopping, when coming towards her, in her blue dress and her white straw hat, she saw Alice Maguire.

'Good morning, child! I'm glad to see you,' she cried, calling out to her as soon as she saw her. 'That's the dress I like best on you, Alice,' she said as they came nearer to each other. 'Say hello to Alice, Rosie,' she said, looking down at the child. 'I had to take her with me,' she exclaimed, 'she wouldn't stay at home with Larry.'

'But how will you manage to get your shopping done, Mrs. O'Grady?' Alice was all concern.

'Oh, I'll manage,' said Mary. 'I'm used to it.'

Now up to this point the meeting was quite ordinary, just such as might have occurred on any day since Alice left school. But this morning Alice said something very odd.

'Oh, it's well for you!' she said.

Mary looked at her in surprise.

'What did you say, Alice?' she asked.

'Oh nothing,' said Alice, and then, disengaging Rosie's hand from Mary's, she drew the little girl to her side, 'You go and do your shopping,' she said. 'I'll take Rosie down to Stephen's Green and I'll bring her back in time for her dinner.'

'Oh, Alice! You'll do nothing of the kind! Do you think I'd allow you? Why surely you didn't think——'

'I thought nothing,' said Alice, and to cut short all argument she turned to Rosie. 'You'd like to come with me, wouldn't you, Rosie?'

'I'd love it,' said Rosie at once.

'There!' said Alice triumphantly, and she began to move away backwards. 'Don't you know I love minding her?' she said.

She did. Mary knew that. It was strange to think that the girl loved children so much; she who was an only child. There were Ellie and Angie, both big girls when Rosie was born, and yet they never took any interest in her, never wanted to mind her, or do anything for her, in spite of all it would mean to their mother. There was no doubt about it that it would be a great help to have the little girl taken out of her hands for a short spell.

A feeling of release rose within her like a bubble, and in a sudden jocularity she called after Alice.

'Wait till you have a family of your own to mind one of those days, Alice,' she said. It was a remark unlike any she had ever made, and she had no sooner uttered it than it sounded coarse and unnecessary, but yet she knew that she could not have recalled her words, so spontaneously had they risen at the sight of the girl smiling so sweetly down on the little girl by her side.

It was then, however, that the second odd thing happened. To her absolute astonishment, Mary saw two big tears swim into Alice's eyes, and, almost at once, before the girl had time to turn aside, they coursed like two blue beads down her cheeks.

'Why, Alice!' Mary had time only to make this one exclamation, for the next minute Alice had turned, and grasping Rosie's hand tighter, she hurried down the street. Mary did not know what to do. She did not know what to think. For a minute she stared after them, but in that minute they had reached the corner of the street and were lost in the crowds of early morning shoppers.

Disturbed, Mary stood for another minute and then she too began to mingle with the crowds. But she could not keep Alice out of her thoughts, and it occurred to her that the girl was paler than usual. It was true that she had never been considered strong, but it wasn't always the strongest people who were the healthiest in the long run. And it was not as if Alice would ever have to put up with much hardship. She would never have to go out to work. Ever since she left school her parents had kept her at home. They liked having her around the house. And it was no wonder. Didn't Mary herself love to have her come in to see her, as she did now and again, and just sit down at the table in the kitchen, while she went about her work.

Just to see her sitting there, just to smile at her, and have her smile back, once in a while, gave her some curious satisfaction that was hard to understand, since it always aggravated her if Ellie or Angie sat down idly, even for a few minutes, although they worked hard all day.

Indeed, both her own girls had cause to be tired these days; Ellie perhaps even more than Angie, because she was now working in a solicitor's office in Dame Street. Angie had still to finish her course, but she was at present doing temporary work in the evenings as well. Nevertheless, Mary did not spare them in the house. Wasn't it odd, then, that she felt so lenient to Alice, who thought nothing of idling away two or three hours at a time sitting down with her elbows on the table, and only opening her mouth to say an odd word now and again?

She did not sit there without offering to help, of course, but feeling she was not strong Mary never allowed her to do very much for her. She was probably useless in the house anyway. But there was one thing Alice could do and that was mind children. Young as she was, she already had the heart of a little mother. And she was always the same. Mary could recall when Alice was only a child herself, playing in the street with her doll's pram. She was a picture, with her blue starched dresses and white starched pina-fores and her little white drawers with stiff white frills that stuck out like a hen's tail feathers when she bent down to tuck her dolls into the little doll's pram. Even when she was a big girl in long stockings she used to go around with a doll in her arms. Oh, there was no mistake about it, the man that got Alice would have a good mother for his children. She would probably spoil them, lifting them every time they cried, cuddling them, and spending the livelong day stooping to pick up what they flung on the floor from over the sides of their cots or their prams. She would be their slave. But was that such a fault? Mary recalled the way people had warned her against letting her own children play upon her.

'Don't give them bad habits,' they cried.

Every time she and Tom went outside the door long ago with the children they met someone or other to give them this advice; some poor unfortunate worn-out mother of a sickly brood that were hard to bear and harder to rear. She only laughed at their advice and tolerantly smiled at the children.

'They have bad habits already,' she said, and then, as some urge of love came over her, making her want to be within the sanctuary of their little house again, she would quicken her steps, and soon they would all be hurrying forward; their feet flying over the pave-ment to keep up with the rolling wheels of the perambulator, as if it were some vehicle entirely disassociated from them with which they must at all costs keep pace.

'The bad habits of love!' she said.

Thinking of those days now, however, she sighed. It was so easy then to satisfy the needs of her little family, whereas now—with another sigh she turned and began to make her purchases.

Mary had come home from her shopping and indeed dinner was

long over before she found time to think of Alice again. But then, when the house was quiet, she thought uneasily about her.

Why was she so unhappy this morning in the street? Those tears! Surely no girl ever had less cause for tears. There she was, living with an adoring mother and father, who gave her everything she wanted. She had only to make a wish for it to be granted at once. And as for the future. She had no cause to worry about that! If her father died, her mother would have a good pension; not indeed that there was much likelihood of anything happening to Fred Maguire, a fine strong man, in his prime, you might say. He'd live to draw his own pension, and it wouldn't be long till he would be drawing it. He'd still be well able to take another job if he wanted. But he wouldn't have to do that, Alice said. She said he was looking forward to his retirement, which went to prove, thought Mary, that the Maguires had a nice nest egg in the bank. And who would it go to in due course, but to Alice?

Then another thought occurred to her. Young men were blind, weren't they? There were Bart, and Willie Haslip, with no eyes for anyone except Ellie and Angie, who wouldn't have one penny to divide between them when it came to a dowry. The girls made no secret of it either, but were always joking and laughing about how penniless they were. Weren't men curious creatures after all? To think of all the nice girls these young men must have met at the University. And you might be sure the girls they met there had a few pence behind them or they wouldn't be idling away their time at a university.

Ah well, there was a lot to be said still for a pretty face, she thought, as Ellie's glowing countenance came before her eyes for a moment. Money wasn't everything. And Angie was pretty too. Tom used to say she was like an angel when she was small, and there was something angelic about her now too when she was sitting still not knowing anyone was looking at her.

Money or no money, they were two fine girls, and if Bart and Willie Haslip were to ask their hand in the morning Mary felt she could look them in the eyes and tell them they were getting a good bargain.

Not that she would hold it against a girl if she had a little money. Take Alice, for instance. Now if Patrick—

Ah, there was no denying it, in spite of his indifference towards her, and of her backwardness and shyness with him, secretly, deep in her heart, Mary cherished the hope that she would one day sit in St. Mary's Church, with her handkerchief tight as a ball in her hand, half crying and half smiling, as Patrick and Alice came down the aisle together, man and wife.

Alice would make such a nice little bride. She would look so lovely in white. And a wreath and veil would suit her very much, her face was so small and so fair. A lovely bride, she thought.

~ ~ ~ ~

It was evening time. Mary was going around the kitchen doing odd tasks of trifling importance. The young people were in the parlour, but the door was open, and someone, probably Ellie, had begun to tinkle a few notes on the piano. Tom was sitting in the kitchen, and although he was reading the paper, he looked up from time to time to say something to Mary. But he could see that she was not giving much attention to what he said. She was listening, politely, but he knew that her thoughts were elsewhere.

Then suddenly she raised her head and a brilliant smile flashed over her face.

'Is that someone at the door, Tom?' she asked, and at the same time Tom thought he heard a faint sound in the hall.

'I thought I heard a sound,' he said. 'Perhaps it was Patrick going out?'

'Oh, I never thought of that,' said Mary, her face clouding over. 'I thought it was someone coming in; I thought it was Alice. Hush!' she said, as she stood, listening intently, then her smile flashed out again. 'Listen!' she cried. 'Isn't that her voice in the parlour?'

'Alice?'

Tom put his head to one side, but it was impossible to distinguish one voice from amongst the rest in the noisy room, where, like the tinkle of a brook, through the noise and the talk there could be heard the sound of the piano. Indeed, at that moment the sound became more than a tinkle because whoever was at the piano was pressing too hard on the loud pedal.

All of a sudden Mary wanted to have the kitchen to herself.

'Isn't it a wonder you wouldn't go inside, Tom,' she said abruptly, 'you that's supposed to be so fond of music!'

Tom was taken by surprise. 'What about you?' he asked.

'I'll be listening out here,' she said, 'and I'll be in after a few minutes.'

Reluctantly Tom got to his feet.

'——and Tom!' He was just at the parlour door when she called him back. 'If Alice is inside would you ask her to come out here to me for a minute?'

'Oh, there you are, Alice!' Deliberately, Mary refrained from looking Alice in the eyes when she felt her come quietly into the kitchen a minute or two later. 'Close the parlour door, dear.' That was all the indication she gave that there was anything beyond the casual in her request for the girl's company.

When she had Alice safely inside the kitchen, however, and sitting down in her usual place at the end of the table, Mary came over and leaned her hand upon the other end of the board, looking across it.

'You look pale this evening, Alice,' she said, partly as a spontaneous observation, and partly as a covert reference to the episode of the morning.

Instantly, as if to deny Mary's words, a bright crimson flush came into the girl's face and rosied her cheeks all over. Mary had not expected her to take her words so seriously.

'Oh, you needn't mind me, Alice child,' she said hastily. 'You needn't pay any attention to what I say! The girls complain that I'm always saying they're pale. Don't mind me, child!'

'Oh, I don't mind, Mrs. O'Grady,' said Alice. 'Indeed I don't. I'd never mind anything you'd say to me—ever.' She hesitated. 'It's only that I thought of something Mother said to-day—that's all.'

For a moment it seemed as if she were going to say more, but she changed her mind. Then her lips parted once more. There was one thing, one thing only, she had to say.

'Mrs. O'Grady?'

'Yes, dear?'

'There is something I'd like to ask you.'

Mary stood still, waiting and listening.

'It's only that I'd be obliged if you should happen to meet Mother, that you wouldn't say anything to her about what you said just now; about my looking pale, I mean.'

'Why, Alice! What would make me say such a thing? Dear me! I see you're upset. What bad luck made me open my mouth at all, I wonder? Why, gracious child, I only fancied you didn't look as bonny as you usually look. But as for mentioning it to your mother! Such an idea! And anyway, when will I see your mother? Sometimes I don't see her from one end of the week to the other. And as for you, my love, why should I say anything about you? You may be a little bit pale to-night, but by to-morrow your cheeks will be as red as a peony rose. Indeed, they are that way now!'

Though her words were true, and there was a deep flush on the girl's face, it did not fully reassure Mary, but rather it distressed her the more. It was not a natural flush. It was too bright, too hectic.

'Why should it worry you even if I did say anything to your mother?' she asked on an impulse.

'Oh, you know Mother; she fusses so!' said Alice.

In spite of herself, Mary raised her eyebrows. Her impression of Mrs. Maguire was not that she fussed too much. On the contrary, it seemed at times to Mary that Alice's mother was in some respects too placid, too easygoing. But Alice evidently saw her mother in a different light.

'Oh yes, you have no idea how she fusses,' she cried, seeing that Mary's face wore an expression of doubt. 'The other day some busybody said something or other to her about me, about how I looked; and we've had a miserable time since, Father and I. Yes, you've no idea! She's been making all kinds of suggestions; the most absurd you ever heard!'

All at once, Mary's curiosity, no, more than that, her apprehensions, were aroused.

'For instance?' she said, deliberately speaking in a calm dispassionate voice, although she felt her heart pounding against her ribs.

'Oh, about my going away for a little while to rest, and that kind of thing.'

Mary's mind began to work furiously. Mrs. Maguire had a sister somewhere in the country with whom Alice used to spend a few days when she was a child.

'To your aunt's, I suppose?' she said.

But she could hardly catch what the girl said. Really Alice spoke so low sometimes one would be inclined to be impatient with her.

'Not to your aunt's? Is that what you said?' That was strange. 'To the sea then, I suppose?' she said, this being the only alternative she could imagine.

'Oh no, not to the sea,' said Alice, and to Mary's surprise she repudiated the suggestion with a peculiar vehemence. Indeed, to her utter astonishment, a shudder passed over the girl.

'Well, where then, in the name of goodness?' she cried.

'Oh, just for a few days' rest; a kind of a holiday,' said Alice.

'You said that,' said Mary impatiently. 'But where?'

That was what she wanted to know. But that was just what Alice seemed to find so difficult to tell her.

'To a place those people told her about,' she said slowly, and in so low a voice that Mary had to incline her head to hear her at all. 'Those people that were talking to her about me; about my looking pale, you know. They said they knew a place in the country where I could go; it would be a kind of a holiday, they said, and not very expensive, considering everything.'

Up to this point Mary had not been able to make head or tail of what Alice was saying. Now in an instant she understood, and a sudden rage swept over her.

'Considering what?' she said, and if Alice were not so confused and embarrassed, she would have been positively frightened at the look on Mrs. O'Grady's face.

'I don't know what,' she said miserably. 'The food, I suppose, and the air: the air in this place is supposed to be very good.'

'Well, Alice Maguire!'

All of a sudden, the anger and indignation, that had nearly swept Mary out the door and down the street to confront and confound the girl's mother, was pricked by this remark about the air. She began in spite of herself to laugh.

'The air?' she repeated. 'The air! Are you serious, Alice?' she said. 'Well, that's the best I ever heard. I heard some good things in my time, but I never heard better than that. And where, might I ask, is this wonderful place where they charge extra for the air you breathe? God's bountiful, free gift to all His creatures!'

But seeing that Alice was taking her seriously, and was about to give her the name of the place, she went quickly around the table and put her arm across the girl's shoulders.

'Don't tell me!' she said imperatively. 'I don't want to hear any more about it. And I can tell you this, Alice, that you will hear nothing more about it either. Whether you like it or not, I'm going to speak to your mother, Alice, and tell her that it ill becomes her to give ear to such notions. Tell me one thing—what on earth did your father say to all this? The poor man. He must be out of his mind with worry. Such an idea! Why I never heard the like! A little holiday indeed! I know what's wrong with your mother, Alice. She's trying to keep you too much under her wing; that's what is the matter with her. Holiday indeed—it would be fitter for her to be thinking of your honeymoon. Yes! I mean it. And I'm going to tell her so, too. I know what you need, my girl, to put roses in your cheeks. And so do you!'

The idea of it. Such a feeling of anger came over Mary that once again, there and then, she felt like going out the door and down the street to tell Mrs. Maguire what she thought about her and her little holidays. But again her anger subsided and instead she felt a curious weakness, almost a faintness, and quite suddenly she sat down.

Such an idea, she thought, but looking at Alice, she anxiously scanned her all over, face, throat, shoulders, down to her little flat virginal chest. The child was thin. There was no denying that. But was her mother out of her mind? Did she not know that in Ireland talk like that, about holidays and about going away, was only the beginning of terrible things? What about it, if one person felt a bit frailer than another! Let them ignore it. Let them reach out and take as good a grasp as they could get upon life and upon reality. Let there be no talk about delicacy. That word was like a curse. It ought never to be used without grave cause. If a boy or a girl had any little weakness the best thing to do was to fight against it. Hadn't she known several cases of young people that were well known to be a bit delicate, but they did not give in to the delicacy, they ignored it, and in time they got stronger and as likely as not they got married, and they were no sooner married than they began to put on flesh and in a few years they were so robust you'd pass them in the street and never know them for the same creatures. But there were others! Mary shuddered. There was a girl in Tullamore long ago, indeed she was not unlike Alice; the same golden hair and white skin, and the same pink, coming and going, in her pretty cheeks. Well, she had a mother like Alice's mother, and the next thing people heard was that she was going away for one of those little holidays. Just like Alice said. Mary shuddered again. Well! that was the beginning of it. But she wasn't going to think of the end of it!

There was one thing certain, however, and that was that no one was going to make any mistake about Alice.

She stood up again.

'I'm very glad you told me, Alice,' she said. 'I'm glad you took me into your confidence. But I want you to promise me something. I want you to promise me you'll forget all about those people and their nonsensical talk about going away. I'll put an end to that.'

'But, Mrs. O'Grady!' Alice looked frightened. 'Mother will be very annoyed with me for telling you about it. She was most particular about no one knowing our business.'

'Hmm! Is that so?' Mary bit her lip. Then she patted the girl on the back reassuringly. 'You leave your mother to me, child,' she said.

For one moment more Alice looked doubtful, and then she seemed to be reassured. Her mother would be no match for Mrs. O'Grady. She was overwhelmed by a feeling of pride in Patrick's mother.

'Oh, Mrs. O'Grady, you're so good,' she cried, 'You're so kind'— and standing up, she threw her arms around Mary. 'You're wonderful!' she cried.

'Oh nonsense!' said Mary, but she was pleased at the girl's words. 'But if I do this for you, Alice,' she said suddenly, disengaging herself from the thin childish arms that were hugging her close, 'if I do this for you, I want you to do something for me. I want you to take a little more trouble with your appearance. Oh no, your clothes are always very tasteful and neat,' she said hastily, as Alice drew back in surprise and looked down at her blue silk blouse, 'and you're as pretty as a picture,' she said with equal haste as Alice put up a hand to her face in vague distress. 'I mean you could do something more with your hair, for instance,' she said. 'You could crimp it up a bit, or make it soft looking. See. Did you ever do this?'

And to Alice's astonishment, and somewhat to her own surprise, Mary caught a strand of the girl's fine slippery hair and, holding it between her forefinger and thumb of one hand, with the same fingers of the other hand she began to push the loose hair lightly upwards until it began to have a soft fluffy appearance.

'There!' she said. 'If you did something like that, I mean.' And she stood back to observe the effect, trying to stifle the small voice that sought to remind her of the countless times that she had quarrelled with Ellie and Angie for doing this very thing with their hair.

And then, still refusing to listen to that small inner voice, she suddenly went over to the dresser, and standing on a chair, she put up her hand and took down an old battered chocolate box that rested on the top of it. It belonged to Ellie. And many and many were the times that Mary had vowed vengeance upon it, going so far as to threaten at one time to throw it into the fire. But now she stepped down from the chair with this box in her hand, and began to rummage in it. Then, finding what she sought, she suddenly held it forward to Alice.

'Did you ever try a dab of this on your cheeks, Alice?' she said. 'I don't approve of it all the time, and I don't like much of it either, but I can't see that it's any harm once in a while, to give a person a little confidence.'

Too surprised to say anything for a minute, Alice looked at the little gilt box in the shape of a heart, that Mary held guiltily towards her. It was Ellie's, and as far as she could see, it was a little box of rouge.

'Oh, Mrs. O'Grady,' she cried then, 'I couldn't! I couldn't really,' and she began to laugh hysterically.

'Well, maybe you're right,' said Mary, and she too began to laugh a little shamefacedly. 'You certainly don't want it now anyway,' she said. For the unnatural flush that had been upon Alice's face had ebbed away, and there was all over her countenance now the healthy glow and sparkle of animation.

I am so glad I spoke to her, thought Mary. The poor child must have been so worried, so frightened. Those tears! But now she was her happy self again. Everything was all right once more.

'And now you must go back to the others, Alice,' she said. 'They'll be wondering what is keeping you,' She listened. 'They seem to be having a great time judging by the noise and the laughing.' Then as there was a sound in the hall, Mary's face brightened still more. 'That must be Patrick. Hurry up, Alice. Here, wait a minute! Brush the hair out of your eyes! Straighten your collar. Now! Let me look at you.' For one minute she held the girl at arm's length. 'You're as pretty as a picture,' she said, but still she detained her. Thinking of all the girl must have suffered before she spoke to her, Mary longed to say something warmer and more affectionate still. Well, there was something she could say! And now was the time to say it. 'You know how I feel about you, my dear,' she said. 'You know what hopes I have about you and Patrick!'

There! She had said it. Yes: she had said it. She had said what she thought would have filled the girl with confidence and happiness. But what was the meaning of that look on her face, and the way she changed colour again?

For Alice had turned as white as a sheet.

'Oh, I know he's very careless, Alice,' said Mary, frightened, without knowing why, by the expression on her face. 'I know he's a very careless fellow now, but I can't believe that he won't come to his senses one of these days and realize what I realized long ago! I won't say any more: you know what I mean! But I shouldn't be saying things like this that might only upset you. Pay no heed to me. And in the meantime all you have to do is to be your own sweet self and time will do the rest.'

But Alice was either not listening, or else Mary had made some dreadful mistake. Without warning, the tears had gushed into the girl's eyes. And this time she didn't turn away, but let them stream down her face like a frightened child.

'Why, Alice, what is the matter? Come now! Come! You mustn't cry like this. You must tell me what is the matter. What's that?' For Alice was saying something in a voice too low for anyone to hear. 'What did you say?' Mary put her arm around her and drew her against her side.

'I said I used to think that it would be that way, too, myself, one time.'

Oh, so it was about Patrick that she was upset. Mary felt relieved.

'Of course you did! And that's the way it will be, too, you'll see,' she said. 'Come now, don't be a silly girl.'

But Alice looked up at her, her tears ceasing for a moment.

'How can it be that way now?' she cried. 'He'll forget me!'

'Forget you? When? What do you mean?' Mary didn't understand. 'What on earth do you mean?' she said, and then suddenly a thin arrow point of fear touched her heart for an instant.

For a moment she glanced away from Alice towards the fire. Had it gone low? For the room suddenly seemed to have grown chill; but the fire was all right. She turned back to Alice.

'What on earth do you mean, Alice?' she said, and her voice was suddenly colder.

But Alice noticed nothing.

'He'll see so many other girls,' she wailed, but then, becoming aware perhaps of a strange stillness in Mrs. O'Grady, she looked up in dismay.

What had she done? Her hands flew to her face.

'Oh, Mrs. O'Grady! Didn't you know? Oh, surely you knew?' she cried. But the look of pain on Mary's face was her answer. 'Oh, how can you ever forgive me?' she cried, and she flung herself upon Mary. 'I thought you'd be the first to know it,' she said, and she did not see how Mary winced at this, the sharpest stab of all, for pressing her head against Mary's shoulder, she sobbed; big sobs that shook her thin shoulders.

After a minute or two, however, realizing that Mrs. O'Grady still had said nothing, the girl raised her head. A vain, childish hope had flared up within her.

'Perhaps he hasn't made up his mind?' she cried. 'Perhaps that's why he said nothing to you?'

But Patrick's mother was looking down at her when she looked up, and their eyes met, but the eyes that looked into hers, and met their eager gaze, were so wise and so sad that a sadness and a wisdom seemed to grow inside in her own thin little breast.

'I suppose he must have meant it,' she said.

Gently, soothingly, Mary began to stroke the girl's hair.

'He meant it, child,' she said. 'His heart is set upon it! We cannot keep him.'

At these words, another sob broke from Alice, but after a few minutes her sobs ceased and she drew away abruptly from Mary.

'But I thought you didn't know?' she cried accusingly.

'I knew it always, Alice,' said Mary. 'Since he was a small child

I knew that he had a restless heart. I knew that he had a mind to wander. Some people are like that; they cannot rest or be easy in one place. We used to have a saying about such people long ago in Tullamore; we used to say they had an itching heel.'

Abruptly the hand that stroked the girl's hair was withdrawn, and Mary went over to the window and stood looking out.

'When he was a little boy, he used to stand all day long under the bridge just looking up at the locomotives passing overhead. I used to think it was only because he was a little boy that it was natural for him to be interested in trains and the like. But that wasn't it at all. It was more than that. Even then, small as he was, the sight of them was a torture to him, because they were going away, and he was always left behind, standing under the bridge looking after them, and listening to the sound of them dying away on the rails.'
As Mary's mind strayed back over those days gone past, a silence seemed to come down upon the whole house. The voices in the parlour had momentarily grown low, and were not heard, and except for her own voice, the kitchen was still and silent. But the silence was broken again by a great gulping sob from Alice.

'Oh, Mrs. O'Grady,' she cried, 'how terrible it is for you. What will you do at all? How can he do it to you?'

'Oh, hush, Alice,' said Mary. 'That's not it at all.'

'But surely if you asked him not to go, he would listen to you?'
Mary shook her head.

'I can't stand between him and what he thinks is best,' she said, and then she took Alice's hand. 'Why should I think that I know better than him? Perhaps it's right for him to go. No, child. If he wants to go, I cannot stop him. There's only one thing I can do.'

Alice knew. 'Pray for him?' she said softly.

Mary nodded.

Yes, she could do no more than that: pray for him. Pray that he would be guided and given good counsel; pray that whatever step he took would be to his advantage; pray that his affairs would prosper, and pray that he would be kept safe in body and soul wherever he might wander. Those would be the prayers that would rise daily from her lips, and only at the end of her litanies, only as she crossed herself, and began to rise from her knees, would the smallest and most urgent prayer of all be wrenched from her, with tightened hands and suppliant eyes, the prayer that in the end, whether he prospered, or whether he failed, he would come back to her, one day, sooner or later; that one day she would look upon his face again.

'We must both pray for him, Alice,' she said.

'I know,' said Alice, her eyes swimming once more, but beside the sorrow of Mary her own sadness seemed but a shadow, and when at that moment she heard Patrick's voice in the parlour, although she saw that, to Mary, it brought only a new kind of anguish, she was too young not to rise to the joy of the moment.

Mary saw her face.

'You'd better go in to the others, Alice,' she said. 'They'll wonder what is keeping you.'

Then as Alice hesitated, she put her hand on her shoulder and urged her forward.

'I'll go in, too, after a little while,' she said.

But just as Alice reached the parlour door, and put her hand upon the amber doorknob, she heard Mary call her back.

'Did you call me, Mrs. O'Grady?' she cried, going back to the kitchen reluctantly. Something that had weighted her down all day, all week, had been mysteriously lifted from her shoulders, and now she wanted only to get back to the others in the parlour, to stand at the piano that had struck up again since Patrick's return, but if Mrs. O'Grady wanted her—'Did you call?' she said, reaching the kitchen and putting her head inside the door.

Mary was sitting down in front of the fire, and there was a curiously stiff look about her as if she were bound to the chair; but she spoke gently and softly.

'No dear,' she said.

That was odd. Alice could have sworn that she had heard a call, but smiling as brightly as she was able, she ran back along the passage.

When Alice was gone, Mary relaxed. What good would it have been to have asked any questions? She would know all there was to know sooner or later. And though he was flesh of her flesh, she still had some pride, even where he was concerned. She could wait until he came to her himself and told her what he had to tell.

I must pretend I didn't hear a thing, she thought, sitting in her kitchen, giving herself counsel. Then, after a few minutes she stood up, and going over to a little mirror above the sink into which her daughters peered incessantly, but into which she seldom glanced from Sunday to Sunday, she now looked earnestly at her face, and stared deep into her own eyes.

This is my first sorrow, she thought, looking at the face, still so like the face that had stared back at her from another mirror on the morning of the day she was going out to be married. This is my first sorrow, she thought, but it will not be my last. And a violent shiver passed through her body. Like the first single drop of rain that falls some minutes before a storm, this single sorrow presaged more to come.

Behind her, still in a blaze of light, there lay the bright landscape of the past, radiant, rich and beautiful; but all, all behind her now.

~ ~ ~ ~

When Mary at last made up her mind to join the young people, in the parlour, they were singing so loudly that for a few minutes they did not notice that she had come into the room, nor see her standing in the doorway.

At the piano there sat a stout young man who was a stranger to her; but she knew all the others.

For all the world as if they were set in motion by some swinging pendulum, they swayed this way and that, in time to the music, while from their open mouths, as fragrance is spilled from a censer, there spilled out song to either side. And on the last note of the song every mouth in the room was as round as a ring, and through the smoke that filled the room the young people exchanged glad eyes. It was a happy scene. Mary stood at the door, and looked in upon them all, but especially her eyes sought and rested on her eldest son. All the others, she could see, were in one way or another touched by the sentiment of the old song, Tom was sad, and the young people stirred by secret longings. Patrick alone was unaffected. Sitting on the arm of a chair, he too was singing, and singing at the top of his voice, while, like them too, he swayed from side to side in time to the music, but if he felt anything at all, it was amusement, even perhaps a little contempt, for the simple taste of the others.

Alice is right, she thought, looking at him. He will not be content with us for much longer. Then, while she was looking at him, Patrick looked across the room and saw her.

'What's the matter, Mother? You look as if you'd buried your whole family.'

The song was at an end. The young man at the piano swung around on the piano stool, and everyone began to make room for Mary. Bart sprang to his feet at once, and wanted her to take his chair.

'Come over here, Mother,' he cried, but his last word was greeted by a peal of laughter.

'Well, what about it?' challenged Bart. 'Everyone else in the family calls her Mother, so I don't see why I shouldn't!'

At this, Ellie blushed furiously, and Angie had to make the retort that modesty demanded.

'Well, you're not one of the family, Bart!' she cried.

But she knew, and everyone else knew, the answer that fitted this like a glove.

Bart looked at Ellie.

'That's not my fault,' he said, and he addressed Mary again. 'Is it, Mother?' he asked.

But at this there was another peal of laughter, and as for Mary, she felt as if something warm had been thrown around her shoulders. How simple they were, all of them; how easily their fun and their happiness sprang up out of nothing.

How can he leave us? her heart cried, for amid the laughter and the teasing, she saw out of the corner of her eye that Patrick was yawning.

But the young man at the piano had dropped his hands upon the keys again.

'Do you know this?' he asked, and before anyone had time to give him an answer, a strong rich baritone, that somehow or other up to this had been smothered in the medley of voices, broke over the room with such strength and beauty that, although everyone present knew the old song word by word, and note for note, no one wanted to do anything but listen. It was the 'Irish Emigrant.'

> I'm sitting on the stile, Mary,
>   Where we sat side by side,
> On a bright May morning long ago,
>   When first you were my bride.

As if he had taken for granted that they would accompany him, the singer had at first been diffident, but then, finding himself soaring alone, after a line or two his voice took on a greater power and strength.

> The corn was springing fresh and green
>   And the larks sang loud and high,
> And the red was on your lips, Mary,
>   And the lovelight in your eyes.

All their lives, those who listened had been familiar with these words, but so potent was the voice of the singer that it was as if only now for the first time, they were touched by the feeling that underlay the sad and lovely plaint. Slowly, a change had come over the whole room, and whatever about the men, there was not one of the women but whose lips trembled and in whose eyes the tears had not begun to glisten.

I'm very lonely now, Mary,
   For the poor make no new friends,
But oh they love the better far
   The few Our Father sends!

I'm bidding you a long farewell.
   My Mary, kind and true!
But I'll not forget you, darling,
   In the land I'm going to!

They say there's bread and work for all,
   And the sun shines always there
But I'll not forget old Ireland,
   Were it fifty times as fair.

The glorious voice rose in a swell, and softly it sank again, and then where only a voice had been, there sat upon the piano stool the slightly rotund figure of the strange young man; but this time no one applauded him. A rich, deeply satisfying silence hung over all. And so silent were the young people in particular they seemed to have been put under a spell.

On the settee, Bart, with unaccustomed seriousness, was looking into Ellie's eyes, and across their heads Willie Haslip looked at Angie with his gentle gaze. Even Patrick's eyes rested with an odd reflective expression upon Alice. But Alice had bent her head.

She's crying, thought Mary, and she wondered if Patrick understood the reason for those tears. She would have liked to watch them, those two young people, but no one had complimented the singer. She turned to him.

'That was a beautiful song,' she said, 'and you have a beautiful voice.'

But her own voice sounded tired, and noticing this, and feeling a lowering of their own energy and vitality after the singing, the visitors became conscious of the lateness of the hour.

'Well, much as I hate to say it, I'm afraid we had better be thinking of the road, Willie,' said Bart, standing up.

Willie was instantly on his feet.

'I was just about to say the same,' he said, and remembering that he had brought no overcoat with him, he began to turn up the collar of his coat. 'I wonder what kind of a night it is?' he said, and he looked at Angie.

'I'll go as far as the door with you,' said Angie at once. 'It may be a nice fine night——' she hesitated a moment—'like last night,' she said.

'Where were you last night?' There was a sharp note in Willie's voice.

'Nowhere,' said Angie quickly, 'but I was looking out of my window when I went upstairs and I saw it was a bright starry night.'

Their eyes met. A look of shame came into the young man's eyes as if he had been guilty of some enormity, to obtain pardon for which, had they been alone, he would have thrown himself on his knees before her. But here, now, in front of the others, he could only look at her mutely. But perhaps his look was not so mute as it seemed. Perhaps it spoke with a thousand tongues, and received a thousand answers. Or perhaps it asked but one question:

'Will we, one night, look out together upon that starry sky?'

'Well?' It was Bart who broke in upon them. 'Did I hear you say you were coming to see us to the door, Angie? What about you, Ellie?'

Ellie was still sitting on the settee.

'I hate to stand up,' she said, yawning.

But it was so certain that she would do so, and more than that, that she and Angie would go out to the front gate, Mary went ahead of them all out into the hall and took down a coat from the rack.

'Here, Ellie,' she said, holding out the coat to her. 'Here, Angie,' she said, having found another one with some difficulty on the loaded rack. 'Put that on your shoulders. These evenings are getting very chilly. And don't stand many minutes in the cold. You know your father wouldn't like it.'

Tom, at that moment, however, was helping the strange young man into his coat and handing him his hat. Mary looked at them. She had not asked, and had not been told, the name of the visitor. Did Tom know him, she wondered. What does he think about it all, she wondered suddenly: about Bart and Ellie, and about Angie and her young man? And what will he think about Patrick when he hears about him? I suppose he'll just say I can't expect to keep them for ever.

If they all left us, he wouldn't mind a bit, she thought. He'd be just as content for us both to be sitting here in the house alone, one on either side of the fire, like we used to sit long ago before any of them were born.

As if things could ever be the same again! Men were so insensitive!

It was hard at times not to feel contempt for them. And indeed there was a slightly contemptuous look on Mary's face as, a few minutes later, having sent Patrick down the street with Alice, to see her safely to her door, and having warned the girls once more not to stay too long out at the gate in the cold, she and Tom turned back from the door and went together into the kitchen.

'Is the back door locked, Tom?' she asked impatiently. He took care of that for her on most nights of the week, but to-night he had made no effort to help her, but sat down by the dying fire looking into it. She went on with her chores, but more and more as the minutes went by she was aware of him. There was something on his mind.

'Mary?'

She was winding the clock, but she looked up. She knew there had been something troubling him.

As their eyes met, however, he stared at her in a curiously helpless way, a victim to the long habits of a lifetime of inarticulateness. In her heart Mary knew she could help him, as she had done on the few other occasions in their life when he had shown himself to be under stress of wanting to say something out of the ordinary. But to-night she was very tired, and beyond looking at him questioningly, she gave him no help.

For a moment some disturbance, caused by what was in his mind, showed itself upon his homely face, and in his honest, kind eyes, but when she made no effort to go to his assistance, he was unable to put it into words.

'It's after eleven,' he said at last, rising from his chair. 'I don't like the idea of the girls standing outside at the gate at this hour.'

'Is that what you wanted to say to me?' said Mary sarcastically.

'Isn't it something that ought to be said?' he replied, a shade of truculence in his voice, but she knew that he was not annoyed with her, nor indeed with the young people either, but with himself for not having been able to get out what was on his mind. She yawned.

I'll hear it in time, she thought, and giving a last look around the kitchen, she handed him the alarm clock.

'Are you coming up?' she asked, taking up a bundle of Rosie's clothes that had been airing all the evening at the side of the stove.

It was a long time since she had been so sleepy. At the foot of the stairs she yawned again. The young people were delaying a long time. Tom was right, though she would not want him to know that she agreed with him on the point. I won't be able to go to sleep until I hear them come back into the house, she thought; until I hear the door clap home, and the chain rattle into its socket. But as soon as these symbols of safety sounded in her ear, it would not be long until she lost her hold upon the day, and was fast asleep. Not until then, though, not until then; not until they are all safely back in the house, she thought, as she mounted the stairs wearily, and wearily folded back the covers of the bed and began to take off her clothes.

But she must have been more tired than she knew, for when Tom came up the stairs Mary was asleep.

She must have been very tired, he thought, as he stood still in the middle of removing his collar and tie, and listened to her steady breathing, and looked at her sleeping face. She never went to sleep before without waiting to hear the last one of the family come in and bang the door.

There!

Downstairs the hall door was closed with a thud, and one after the other, the different voices of the three young people could be heard as they made their way into the kitchen.

I suppose she wasn't worried when she knew they were only outside the door, he thought, as he put out the light and slipped quietly in by her side.

I'm tired too, he thought. But somehow he didn't go to sleep as quickly as usual. He didn't seem inclined to sleep at all.

It was hot. He felt inclined to toss and turn but he was restrained by the thought that he might disturb the peaceful sleeper by his side. Considerate always, to-night a new tenderness, a new anxiety such as he had never felt before in all their life together, took possession of him and as he listened to her breathing, his own breath was almost an agony to him, so desperately did he try to keep it even and gentle. In the darkness it seemed to him that it was stertorous and violent.

It would awaken her. For a time the dread of doing so made his heart beat faster, but as he lay there sleepless, a feeling of loneliness came over him, and there stole into his heart a wayward wish that she would waken.

If she were to waken now, in the darkness, where they were alone together, he would have no difficulty in pouring out all that had welled up within him downstairs when the young people were singing that song. That song: even now he could not get the words of it out of his head. And, as at the time it was sung in the parlour, and afterwards in the kitchen, he was almost overpowered by the flood of tenderness that swept over him. Only now, with no one to see, he did not try to stop the tears that flowed into his eyes. And he wasn't one for tears.

Not once, since he was a little boy, could he remember having shed a tear, although downstairs in the parlour he nearly made a fool of himself before them all. Because for him, Mary and the Mary in the song were one, and his heart had been rent in him while the song lasted. Then, looking up suddenly, he had seen her standing in the doorway.

She was in her prime. Fascinated, he had stared at her, his feelings of pride and joy only comparable to the way he felt the first evening she consented to meet him more than twenty years ago, when she was a young country girl with her hair down her back.

She was a woman now, but a woman in her prime, and there was still about her that curiously country air and manner that marked her out among all the women around about them in the locality. There she was, the mother of a grown-up family, and yet she was so strong and firm and straight, her skin so soft and clear, her cheeks so pink and her eyes so bright and eager. She was a mother five times over, and yet it was only by the softness of her breast and the wisdom in her eyes that this could be known to anyone.

She had borne him five children. Five times she had lain down in the pain of childbirth, here in this very house. How had she risen again so fair and so unbroken by what she had suffered? And more amazing still, how had he endured the torment of waiting, helpless, downstairs until her agony was spent?

What had he felt at those times? Had he not been frantic with fear as she hovered in those dark vales of pain? He tried hard to remember, but in the end he had to face the plain fact that he could not recall what he had felt, or even what he had done during those hours of her pain and anguish.

If he had again to face one of those long days of waiting for her confinement to come to an end, and her delivery to be accomplished, how would he endure it?

This thought had struck him in the parlour, but now in the dark room it came back to him, and with it there came another thought, swifter and more terrifying. What made him think of those days of her fecundity as days that were over and passed? She might even at this moment be carrying within her, unknown to them, another child for whose sake she would once again have to make that terrible journey through the vales of pain.

No: it could not be. He was once more fully awake, but all the same, fear gripped him like a vice, and it seemed to him that only by shouting could he free himself of it. To shout; to scream; to let one loud cry break from him: that only, it seemed, would give him ease. To let one single word tear its way from his strangled lungs: the word No. No! That one word alone would bring him ease if he could but shout it loud enough: loud; loud; loud.

If anything were to happen to her? A cold sweat broke over his face. For it was the first time in their lives together that the thought came to him that one day, sooner or later, they would have to part.

Right from that first day he had seen her sitting in the tram he had felt his heart leap, and ever after he had not been satisfied until he had settled things so that she was going to belong to him forever. But now for the first time he realized the limitations of that word; its earthly boundaries. One day, they must part, and, looking at her form, that he faintly discerned or fancied he could discern, beside him, the frailty and fragility of her sex made him feel uneasy about her. If he should ever lose her! How would he endure one day without her?

A terrible cold feeling had replaced the feverish heat of a moment before. He shuddered. They would one day be separated, and then, not until they lay together under the clay would they be stretched side by side again. He shuddered once more.

He would light the gas, he thought. That might dispel the dark fancies that tormented him.

But he didn't light it. Instead he made an effort to be practical. After all, he was always considered to be a man of good sense.

If only he could get some sleep. Perhaps if he turned over once, gently, he might not disturb her, and he might find it easier to sleep on his other side?

Before he turned, however, he reached out his hand, and gently, lightly, as if they were strolling outdoors in the daylight, he clasped her sleeping hand in his.

~   ~   ~   ~

It was sometime about the middle of the night that Mary began to stir uneasily in her sleep. Up to then her sleep had been disturbed, but about this time she passed from a state of dream to one of partial wakefulness, and she was not at once able to tell the difference between the dream and the reality.

For the most part her dreams had been about Patrick. She was looking at him across a short distance, such as that which stretched from the front gate to the hall door. He wore a new suit of clothes, and yet somehow she thought he had often looked better in one of his old suits, even the shabby and stained old suit he wore on Saturday mornings when he was cleaning and oiling his bicycle.

She did not like the suit, but this fact hardly accounted for the feeling of sadness and terror that was gathering around her heart.

I ought to be glad to see him, she thought, for he was not going away, but coming back it seemed from the manner in which he was facing towards her and looking up at the house.

If only she could call out to him, she thought, he might tell her what was wrong, but she was unable to part her lips or utter any sound, while he too, her son, seemed able only to stand and stare.

Confusion and perplexity added themselves to her feeling of heartbreak and sorrow.

It will be all right when he comes up the pathway, she told herself, and since her feet were rooted to the ground and she could not go towards him, she stretched out her hands to him.

Then, with the nightmare leap of a dream, his hand was in hers, holding it tightly in a hot convulsive grip.

Flesh of her flesh, son of her body, she yet recoiled from that hot convulsive palm, and desperately she tried to pull back her hand. But the more she pulled back her own hand, the tighter became the grip upon it of that other hand.

Was it Patrick's hand at all? Away at the end of the path, that had all at once become elongated, she saw Patrick again, far, far away, still staring at her silently, although she fancied that his lips were moving as if he were trying to say something, trying to make her hear. It was not his hand that was clasping hers.

Whose, then, was this sweated, burning hand from which she could not escape?

'Patrick!'

Ah! Now she could use her voice.

'Patrick!' Now she could make him come to her.

But he did not hear. The name that she cried was drowned by other voices, that suddenly sounded all about her, louder, louder, louder.

And then suddenly she was fully awake. The dream was ended. The long far vista was gone, and close by her side Tom tossed in some disturbance. And his hand was holding hers in a strangling grip.

So that was the dream, she thought, relieved for a moment, but the next moment she became conscious of something odd about Tom. He wasn't asleep.

'Tom?'

Roughly she pulled her hand from his, and leaning up on her elbow she caught his shoulder and shook him.

'Is there anything the matter, Tom?'

But before he answered her, he moaned again.

'Oh, Mary!'

It was more like a sigh than anything else: a sigh or a sob.

'Oh, Mary, I thought you'd never hear me—I'm weak from calling you.'

He sounded weak. His voice was choked, and after each word there was a kind of gasp that seemed to be involuntary to him.

'My God, Tom, what's the matter?' she cried, and turning, she scrambled out on the floor, at the other side of the bed, and fumbled her way around to him.

His forehead was on fire. He seemed to be in a kind of fever. Yet at the minute that she left her hand upon his head, he shuddered.

'It's so cold,' he said. 'My feet are like ice.'

Cold? She was incredulous. Oh dear God. What was the matter with him?

'Wait till I light the gas,' she said, but instead of the gas she lighted the small butt of candle she kept by their bed in case Rosie would waken in the night and need attention. The gaslight was too harsh for the eyes of a child, and by some instinct she did not use it now either.

'What happened you? When did you wake up?' Shielding the candle flame, she was able to gather her thoughts together and take command of the situation.

'I think the pain woke me,' said Tom.

In the light of the candle, he too felt better.

So it was only a pain! she thought. She had been so frightened. That hot hand and forehead; that moaning and gasping! It might have been anything! Like all people without much experience of illness, it seemed to her that these irregularities might mean anything. Fever! Pneumonia! Anything!

But a pain! That was a different matter. Pain was something with which she was familiar; something with which she was accustomed to deal. How many times had the children, from the first to the last of them, wakened up screaming with a pain? Not alone when they were infants, and only needed to be turned over on her knee, and rubbed hard till they put up wind, but right up till they were young men and young women.

Now if she had a sixpence for every pain she had had, she would be a rich woman to-day. Most of her pains had been natural, and had boded good not ill, yet if he knew what they were like he would have something to moan about, she thought, as she pulled on an old woollen robe and knotted the cord about her waist.

'Why didn't you say at the start that you had a pain?' she said again, fussy and motherly. 'I'll slip downstairs and light the gas under the kettle. A few sips of hot water are what you want; or else a drop of peppermint. But I'll put the kettle on to boil anyway first, just in case! Now! You'll be all right?'

She was going out of the door when he moaned again. She came back.

'I'm sorry—Mary.' His breath, that he had been afraid to let go, forced its way from him in a great sigh.

'Where is it, this pain?' she said, and all at once, even to go down the small hallway to the kitchen right below them seemed very far to go from him.

His voice was so weak she couldn't hear what he said, but she saw that he put his hand up to his arm; to his shoulder. Then he spoke again, and his voice was louder.

'All over me,' he said, and he looked up at her with a frightened look. 'It's coming on again,' he said, and reaching up he caught her hands with both of his in the same scorching convulsive grip that had seemed to be part of her nightmare.

'It's coming: it's coming!' he shouted.

'Hush, Tom!' she said, but her own confidence had been weakened a bit to think that the pain was not in his stomach. She was so familiar with disorders in that region. Still, there was no use getting into a panic.

'I'll get some hot water,' she said again; decidedly. But it would be impossible to get away from him if he insisted on holding on to her hands like that.

He was trying to say something.

'Don't try to talk if it's hard for you,' she said. 'Take your time.'

But he had to talk. '——Stay.'

It may have been more than one word that he gasped out, but one word was all she could hear.

'Very well.'

It seemed stupid, but what else could she do? She sat down on the side of the bed.

'Will I rub your chest?' she asked after a minute.

'——No.'

She made another effort to free her hands.

'If I rubbed your chest, it might ease you,' she said.

'——No—no.' He had strength enough to say that, to repeat it, it seemed any number of times.

'All right. All right!' It would be hard to keep her patience with him if he was going to take this attitude; going to behave like a child.

'There's nothing to be frightened about,' she said, using the old phrases so effective always with the children.

But he wasn't listening to her.

'The doctor!' he gasped. 'Do you think you could get a doctor?'

'A doctor?'

She looked at him in astonishment. Once, about nine or ten years ago, she had yielded to foolishness, and sent for a doctor when Ellie had a pain. She never forgot the way the doctor had looked at her.

'Oh, Tom, you don't mean to say it's that bad?' she said irritably. 'Let me get you a drop of whisky?' she coaxed.

This time it seemed that he was going to be sensible.

'Where is it?' he asked, after a little difficulty.

'Downstairs, of course,' she said.

'You haven't any up here?'

'Why would I have it up here?' Such a question! How could you keep your patience with that kind of thing? She stood up. 'You'll feel better after a sip of whisky,' she said.

But he wouldn't let her go.

'Don't mind it,' he said, and this time, if only for a moment, his voice was stronger, and his tone imperative. 'I don't want you to leave me.'

'But——'

'Mary!' As his voice failed again his eyes implored her to obey him, and with his finger he beckoned her nearer. 'Mary!' he said again, speaking with great difficulty. 'I'm very bad, I think.'

Saying it, like that, himself, in some way annoyed her.

'Nonsense, Tom,' she said. 'There's nothing wrong with you, it's only some kind of indigestion or flatulence. And you'd be all right if you'd let me get you something, and if you really think you'd like the doctor I'll go and fetch him. But it's a queer time of night to get a man out of his bed. Don't you think you could wait until morning? You don't look too bad,' she said, and now that the sweat had stopped pouring from his face, he didn't look so bad at all, except that his forehead where his hair started looked kind of white.

'Well! What do you think?' she asked, because he was evidently thinking hard. Seemingly, however, they had not been thinking about the same thing at all.

'If you knocked on the wall,' he said, 'Patrick would hear you and come out; he could go for the doctor. I don't want you to leave me,'

'There's no need to knock on the wall,' she said, 'I think the whole house is up.' For she had heard Patrick's sleepy tones calling out to the girls to know if there was anything wrong. And she thought too that she heard Ellie's voice, and even her steps outside their door. But she did not stir, because all at once he seemed quiet and peaceful again and he had closed his eyes.

'Well?' she said gently, after a few minutes.

But when he opened his eyes she did not like the way he looked at her, as if it were hard for him to see her; as if he were far away from her.

'Mary?'

His voice, too, sounded as if he were far away.

'Yes, Tom?'

'Don't be frightened.'

Why should she be frightened? What did he mean?

But suddenly she was frightened, terribly, terribly frightened. In an instant it had all flared up again, the terror, the panic that she had felt when she woke up in the dark and heard a moan.

'Tom!'

He didn't answer, but he was looking at her, and his look was so strange she didn't at once understand it, and then she saw that it was a look of pity.

'Mary?' It was an urgent whisper, and he raised himself slightly in the bed.

She bent towards him.

'Yes?'

But quite suddenly he sank back, and a short uneven sigh came from his lips. That was all. There was no more moaning; no other sound or movement.

But she sprang back with a scream, and running to the foot of the bed, she began with her two hands to beat against the wall of the room that separated her from the room where Patrick slept.

She didn't fully realize it, but she, who had never been a day sick in her life, who had never had to deal with a more serious illness than measles or chicken pox, was suddenly, at that moment, confronted with nothing other than death.

~　　　~　　　~　　　~

They had come back from Glasnevin Cemetery, and they were alone at last, the three grown children and the widow.

All day, and all the previous night and day, Mary had been waiting for this moment when they would be alone, and yet now that it had come, what was there for them to say?

'You ought to turn up the back of your dress before you sit down, Mother.' Ellie was the first to speak as they went into the kitchen, and Mary was about to sit down. 'Black is so hard to keep clean,' she said explaining, 'it shows up every speck.'

That was true. The truth of the remark weighed upon Mary, and before she sat down, she carefully turned up the back of her mourning gown.

'Wasn't it good of Alice,' she said, 'to take Larry and Rosie out?'

'I wonder where they've gone?' said Angie.

'Oh, to the Park, I suppose.'

Ellie and Angie smiled at each other. They had spoken together.

'That's a wish,' said Angie, and leaning towards each other, and crossing their fingers, with a little laugh the two sisters made their wishes.

Mary stared at them. She could hardly believe that she heard them correctly, with their small talk and their giggling. Was it to hear this that ever since they had stepped into the cab outside the cemetery gates, she had longed for the moment of being alone with them? Was it? Had they nothing after all to say to each other, now that they were alone, with no further need to keep up appearances?

As if they felt some compunction under her gaze, however, at that moment they sprang to her side.

'Poor Mother!' cried Angie.

'You'll have to take something,' cried Ellie.

'How about a cup of tea?' they said, but once more the sisters had spoken together, and a little nervous laugh broke from them.

Behind her back, a little guiltily, Mary knew they were crossing their little fingers again and making another wish.

'I don't want anything,' she said, dully.

'Oh, Mother!'

The sisters looked at each other as if this were what they expected. Then Ellie came and stood in front of her.

'Now, Mother, you mustn't act like that.'

'Like what?' she said.

'Like the way you're acting,' said Ellie, and suddenly she became more animated. 'When Bart's father died, he told me that——'

But Mary turned her head aside.

'If you don't mind,' she said, 'I can wait till another time to hear what Bart said.'

'Mother!' Two red spots lit in Ellie's cheeks. 'I think that's most unkind of you, Mother. Bart feels almost as bad as any of us. He said that Father was one of the nicest men he ever met. Didn't he? Angie!' For an instant Ellie turned to Angie, and then back to Mary. 'As a matter of fact he was wondering if he oughtn't to wear a little black diamond on his sleeve, like Patrick.'

'Well!' Mary couldn't prevent herself from sneering. 'That's what he ought to do indeed!' she said. 'Maybe!'

But no sooner had she said the bitter words than a frightened feeling came over her. Was this what it was going to be like without him: a house of bickering and petty quarrelling, with no man at the head of it to keep order and quiet? Not that she had ever heard him raise his voice beyond the normal, but somehow, now that he was gone there was, all over the house, a feeling that some discipline was broken.

Slowly and deliberately she looked from one face to another, as they sat aimlessly in a circle around the fire. They were a set of individuals, she thought with panic, herself included. The thread that had bound them into a family was broken.

And at the thought of this sundering, all that she had suffered in the past three days seemed nothing, and putting up her hands to her face, she burst into tears.

'Mother!'

Instantly they were all around, pressing close to her and jealously elbowing each other aside to get nearer to her. Ellie flung herself down on her knees.

'Poor Mother!' she cried, and her own face was wet with tears that ran freely down her cheeks and spotted her black silk mourning dress.

Angie too was crying, without trying to hide her tears or even to wipe her eyes. And Patrick, although there were no tears wet upon his face, as upon the faces of the girls, even he had the convulsed countenance of one who is trying to smother his feelings, and who by facial contortions keeps from brimming over the tears that have welled up within him.

This was the first time they had given way, and Mary, understanding suddenly that it was more for her than for their father that they wept, began to wipe her own face and dry her own tears. Something of the shock it must have given them to see her cry still showed in their eyes; but yet she felt that they were grateful to her also for showing her feelings thus openly before them. It brought her nearer to them.

'Poor Mother! Don't fret. Father wouldn't want you to fret, you know.'

Still on her knees, Ellie put out her warm young arms and embraced her, leaning her head down on Mary's lap.

'Yes, Mother, what Ellie says is true!'

More helplessly, Angie stood by her chair. She is like Ellie's shadow, thought Mary, seeing again for an instant an erratic fleeting likeness in the faces that stared so earnestly up into hers.

'Look here, you two——' Patrick stood up—'if you want to do something for Mother, why don't you get her that cup of tea you have been talking about ever since we came home!'

Oh dear! The poor boy was probably hungry. Mary had forgotten all about meals and mealtimes. What hour was it?

But the clock had stopped.

That was one of Tom's jobs: to wind it.

No matter: they must all be hungry anyway, whatever time it was. They had not eaten much going out to the funeral. She must set about preparing something for them. She tried to rise. But Ellie was answering Patrick.

'I suppose you want a cup of tea yourself!' she said, and partly to her regret and partly to her relief, Mary heard in Ellie's words, and saw in her eyes, the indestructible gaiety of youth. And she knew that the bickering of a moment or two earlier was just a passing thing, and that it had changed already into bantering and teasing.

'Well, what if I do want something? It's five hours since we broke our fast,' said Patrick, but as Mary put her hands on the arms of her chair to rise, he put her down again firmly. 'I could do with something to eat,' he said, 'but this is one day in your lifetime, Mother, that your daughters ought to be better able to prepare a meal than you.'

'But, Patrick——' She would have protested further, only that accidentally raising her head she intercepted a meaningful look pass between her children. And almost at once she knew that Patrick had something to say to her.

Go on, Patrick seemed to say to them, can't you see that now is my chance? Or so Mary read the expression upon his face.

She could have been mistaken, of course, but she did not think this was so, and as Ellie almost at once sprang to her feet and beckoned Angie with her, she felt certain that she was not mistaken. In another minute, although the girls went in and out between the pantry and the kitchen, and the kitchen and the scullery, she and her son were virtually alone, for the others were at once caught up in a conversation of their own that soon circled them round with as great a privacy as the highest, thickest wall. Moreover, not being experienced or expert about the house, they made a great clatter with the delft.

Reluctantly, resignedly, Mary sat back in her chair. Patrick, on the other hand, stood up, and placing himself with his back to the stove, he stood for a minute, his hands in his pockets jingling a few coins in them. Yes. He had something to say to her. She knew this restless habit well. Tom had been like that too. Patrick had something to say, but he didn't know how to begin.

Well, whether it was good or bad, what he had to say, she would have to help him. And by her old unerring instinct, although she spoke at random, her words were exactly the right ones to give him the opening he wanted.

'You're head of the house now, son.' That was what she said, and had he not at once eagerly taken up her words, she would have been overcome with the anguish they caused to surge up within her own heart. He gave her no time, however.

'I know that,' he said solemnly. 'That's what I wanted to talk to you about, Mother. Of course this means a great change for all of us'—as he said the word 'this' he pointed to where on the mantelpiece a long line of black-rimmed envelopes from sympathetic relatives and friends spared him the necessity of being more explicit about their loss.

For all of them? It had seemed to Mary that it was she alone who would be affected. Vaguely she supposed that there would have to be financial adjustments made, and it was partly with relief, and yet with a certain amount of humiliation also, that she realized that, in spite of her age, and her years of authority over him, some weakness in her sex was making her ready to defer to him in such matters, as the only man in the house.

'There will be your father's pension, if that's what you mean,' she said.

'Oh, I know all about that,' said Patrick. 'As a matter of fact I was speaking to one of the office staff about it at the funeral. There will be a few formalities to comply with, but you don't need to worry about that, Mother, I'll attend to them.'

Surprise, admiration, and gratitude were not strong enough to stifle the small feeling of humiliation that again passed through her. Was this her son, who, only the other day it seemed, was a helpless little bundle of pink flesh lying in the laundry basket looking up at her, but not seeing her, with his big blue eyes?

'It's about other matters I want to talk, about myself in fact. I'll have to give up the vocational classes, and look out for a job.'

'Oh, Patrick! Is that necessary?' she cried, startled and frightened. For the first time a possibility of privations came to her mind. But surely if there were any to be borne she could bear them, and not the children; not Patrick. 'Oh, son, that won't be necessary, I'm sure,' she cried. 'You'd hate to give up your classes, wouldn't you?'

But apparently she had not followed his meaning. He laughed, shortly and bitterly.

'Is that all you know about me?' he said. 'Why, even if this——' indicating the mourning cards again—'had never happened, I don't believe I could have faced another month of that place; but it was my only chance of——'

Without ending his sentence, however, he stopped, not with any idea of concealment, but as if he had been about to say something in the wrong way and thought it would be better to stop and try again.

'For goodness' sake, don't worry about the classes,' he said. 'All I'd ever learn at them wouldn't be much use to me in this country. In this country you've got to be either at the top or at the bottom.'

What did he mean?

'I mean you've got to have a university degree to get anywhere in this country,' he said, 'and if you haven't that, you may as well give up any idea of trying to rise above your boots.'

She was confused.

'But why did you go to the classes, Patrick? It was your own idea to go to them, I remember it well. Father and I thought it was a waste of time.'

'If I was staying in this country, yes,' said Patrick, 'but I knew that outside this country if you had a bit of education, and the right kind of guts, you could get to the top of the wheel.'

Outside this country?

She stared at him, bewildered, for Alice's conversation that had cast such a shadow over her, a few days previously, had been swept away by the events that followed, but now that shadow was over her again, darkening everything, filling her heart with dread. She looked up with fright. Patrick too looked frightened. Perhaps he had not meant to say what he had said, or at least not in just that way. Perhaps once again he had begun badly, but by this time his efforts to find the right way had unstrung his nerves and made him irritable. And, anyway, hadn't his plans been changed? What need was there then to be so careful?

'Now, Mother, there's no need to look at me like that,' he said crossly. 'You didn't think that I was going to spend my life in this one-horse town, did you? You must have known what I had in my mind?'

But when she put her hand to her breast, he saw that he still had not said what he wanted to say.

'Not that it matters now,' he said, urgently, because at last he began to see the damage that his clumsiness was doing to her. 'I told you that everything was changed, didn't I? I told you that, at the start. My plans are all changed now.'

But as she looked at him, saying nothing still, he thought she must not have understood.

'I'm not going now, Mother, don't you understand?'

But all that Mary understood was that he had been going. It was true; all Alice had said. For the first time since he had begun to talk to her, she became aware of the girls again. They were no longer making noise with the crockery, and they didn't seem to be talking: they were standing listening to herself and Patrick.

'You didn't tell me anything about your plans,' she said at last, and her voice sounded stiff in the silence, although she felt anything but stiff, sitting at his mercy in the chair that seemed all at once to be too big, and to enclose her like a cave. Then she saw Ellie give a peculiar look at Patrick.

So the girls had known his intentions! Did everyone in the family know them, except herself?

'Why wasn't I told something about this?' she cried.

'There was nothing definitely settled,' said Patrick. 'I didn't know until a few days ago that I'd get a passage at all. It's not as easy to get over there now as it was at one time,' he said aggressively.

'To get where?' she said, keeping her voice calm and low because of all the eyes upon her.

But Patrick's impatience with his own bad management of the whole conversation turned suddenly to irritation. Surely his mother hadn't been as much in the dark as all that? He flashed a look of suspicion at the girls. Surely they hadn't kept their mouths shut as tightly as all that? If so, it must have been for the first time in their lives!

'To America!' he snapped. 'Where else did you think?'

America!

It was beyond all that she had imagined—or dreaded.

Long ago, at home in Tullamore, in their rich and plenteous inland pastures, they had heard tales of the Irish emigrants from the barren sea coasts of the west and the south. It was to America these emigrants went, and an atmosphere of poverty and sorrow attended their departure.

'America?' she repeated incredulously, but her voice was only a faint whisper.

But suddenly the girls, who had stood silently behind her, seemed to swoop down around her, as if their arms were wings of shelter and protection, which they would unfold to enwrap her.

'But, Mother, he's not going at all now!' cried Ellie. 'That's what he wanted to tell you; that he's changed his plans!'

And as her warm and eager eyes flew over Mary's face, assessing the ravage of her grief, she looked up with a flash of scorn at Patrick.

'Aren't you a nice one!' she cried. 'Can you never be trusted to do anything right? You said you were going to cheer her up with what you had to tell her. A fine job you made of it! Look at her!'

For Mary was once more crying, softly, silently, and like the soft and silent rain of the Midlands, it was more frightening to the children about her than the wildest outburst, because it seemed as if the sad grey veil that came down over everything would never lift, or not until every blossom and petal, every trace of promised happiness, had been washed utterly away.

'Come, Mother. There now! You ought to know him better. Aren't men all alike; clumsy fools. He only meant to tell you he isn't going now, that he has changed his mind, and that he is going to look out for a good job here at home.'

But as Mary still wept without being able to cease, Ellie stopped trying to explain. She stood up and beckoned to Patrick.

'Tell her you're not going. Tell her!' she cried, and she motioned to him to bend down.

Poor Ellie. Mary raised her wet eyes and looked into the eyes of her eldest daughter.

She's a real woman, she thought. She's capable of all a woman's virtues, and all a woman's faults. She arranged all this, but her plans went wrong. She arranged for Patrick to tell his tidings to-day, in the hope that the house would be brightened a little by his words. But she had counted without the difference between herself and the man. He had handled his part of the plan in his own way, and he had spoiled everything. Mary saw with surprise the flashing of a fiery light in her daughter's eyes, almost as if a glint from the firelight were reflected there for an instant. It was more of the woman in her; it was the core of enmity in her heart against all men, be they brother or husband, the core of enmity that would keep her always, till the last minute of her life, a person with whom to contend. She would never allow herself to rest at ease in the slack chains of familiarity or intimacy. She would be always at heart a stranger to the man she married, and for that reason always, to the last minute, in command of his love. Not like me, thought Mary. I stopped being a woman. I became a mother. But she will always be a woman first, and a wife and mother afterwards.

Mary put out her hand suddenly and touched Ellie's warm, flushed cheek.

'I understand, Ellie,' she said. 'I understand quite well, but it came as a little shock all the same.'

'Of course it did!' Ellie's voice now was soothing, softening, expressing the gentler side of her, but in an instant she changed again and cast an inimical glance at Patrick.

How could you be so stupid!

The words to Patrick were not spoken, but they were there to be read by all in the fiery glow of her eyes.

'Oh Ellie! Don't speak to your brother like that,' said Mary.

'But I said nothing!'

'Well then, don't look at him like that,' said Mary. 'He meant well.'

He did. No matter what the girls thought, she knew Patrick. A smile came over her face.

'What are you smiling at, Mother?' said Angie. But Mary had turned to Patrick.

'I was just thinking,' she said, 'of when you were a little boy, Patrick.' Since her outburst of crying it was the first time she had looked at him. 'You never liked to see me tired or sad'—but as she spoke, a thought involuntarily flashed through her mind—was I ever sad then? 'I used to think you never liked to see me sit down; I had to be always busy about the kitchen, singing or humming to please you! But if I ever did sit down for a minute, or if you thought I was not as happy as you wanted me to be, you used to steal away for a while and when you came back, you crept up to me, a little bit like you did just now, not wanting the others to see or to overhear you, and I knew you had gone to get some of your little treasures to give to me, to cheer me up and put me in good humour. But'—here the tears came into Mary's eyes again for a moment, but this time they were tears of laughter—'but it was likely to be something queer that you pressed into my hand with your hot little fist; a beetle perhaps,' she shuddered, 'or a frog.'

'Oh, Mother!' the girls screamed.

'Yes!' said Mary, looking at them, now, and laughing still, 'so you see you must not say anything to him; I know him well.'

A slightly resigned look came on Ellie's face.

'All the same,' she said, hotly, 'I think men are the limit.'

Mary looked at her again with a frank curiosity, as if she did not know her. How alive this daughter of hers was, always, to the difference between men and women. She, herself, after the first few days of strangeness, had never thought of Tom as much different from herself in any way. That was why they were so easy with each other, so placid always, she supposed. Ellie would never be that way with any man. A further, deeper curiosity stirred in her, as to what Ellie's life would be like, when she and Bart married, and a vista seemed to break in the darkness of the years ahead. It would be strange and interesting to see what Ellie would make of those problems which, somehow, in her own life had been passed over by her almost unknowingly, without fully understanding them until they were behind her.

For the second time she put out her hand, and touched Ellie's cheek.

'And do you think Bart is the limit too?'

Although she took constant teasing from the rest of the family, at her mother's odd, unexpected words, Ellie blushed, but immediately she concealed her blushes by a toss of her rich chestnut curls.

'Oh, Bart is about the worst of them all,' she said, and then, almost exactly as Patrick had done a little while before, Ellie too glanced hesitatingly at the table where, after calling their attention to the fact that the tea was a long time made, and getting cold, Angie and Patrick had started to take their own meal. But seeing the sadness of Mary's face, she turned her back on the table.

'I have something to tell you too, Mother,' she said, speaking in a way that, for her, was wonderfully soft and shy. 'I hope I won't be as bad as Patrick, and make it sound like bad news instead of good! But I suppose, in my case, you can guess what I have to tell you.'

Yes. Mary could guess. Ellie too would be leaving her.

'I suppose you and Bart have come to an understanding?' she said, trying to hide the pain that lay under these tidings also. But she might have known that there would have been something unexpected in anything Ellie did.

'Pphf!' she said. 'I should think I'd expect things to be on a firmer footing than that! What is an understanding anyway? It doesn't bind you! It may satisfy some girls, but not me! Look!'

And slipping her fingers in between the buttons of her black bodice, from somewhere within, between her camisole and her waistband, to Mary's astonishment she pulled out a small jeweller's box, covered in purple plush, and presumably to be opened by means of the little pearl stud that gleamed against the rich pile.

Mary stared. Her surprise was absolute and undoubted. For an instant Ellie held out the little casket on the flat of her palm, and savoured her mother's astonished gaze. Then she pushed her hand forward almost into Mary's face.

'Open it, Mother,' she cried, quickly and urgently. 'I wanted you to see it before anyone else,' and she glanced over her shoulder at the others, busy with their meal.

With a curious timidity Mary advanced a hand towards the little bejewelled box, but Ellie could not wait.

'I'll do it,' she cried, and still holding the little casket flat on her hand, with the other hand, lightly, expertly, even sacrilegiously, so thought Mary, she pressed the pearl stud and the little casket opened with a spring. But there was nothing sacrilegious about the way that, once opened, daughter as well as mother stared at the little ring that looped upwards out of the silken lining. For Ellie, as well as for Mary, it might almost have been the first time that the little hoop of diamonds was revealed, so breathlessly did she behold it, and so reverently did she hush her voice as she looked up to hear her mother's opinion.

'Do you like it, Mother?'

What words could Mary find to match that shining little hoop of gold, with its starry diamonds sparkling. And what words could she have found to express, not just her admiration of the little ring itself, but her pride that her Ellie, her own daughter, was the possessor of it.

'Why, Ellie!' she cried, looking with amazement from the ring to the sparkling face above it. 'Put it on!' she cried, and then, before Ellie had time to comply with the command, Mary had lifted it out of the casket and with the unaccountable and undying vanity of her sex had slipped it on to her own finger.

'Your father never as much as thought of giving me a ring,' she said, and it was clear that it had never before occurred to her to notice his omission. 'Not that he wouldn't have died for me,' she added quickly, 'but I expect Bart would do that, too,' she said, and they smiled at each other. 'Did the others not see it yet?' she whispered, leaning nearer. 'When are you going to let them see it?'

For answer, however, Ellie looked over her mother's head and laughed. Mary turned around.

Behind her, with his mouth full, Patrick was standing staring at the ring. And, beside him, waiting only for the word to rush forward and take the little casket into her own hands, stood Angie, her face shining. It was Angie who spoke.

'Ellie!' she cried. 'You mean thing! You never told me! How long have you got it?' And in a moment she had the ring on her finger, flashing it round and round, and making the facets flash with light. 'Not that we didn't guess,' she added quickly. 'Willie said the other night that there was something in the wind.'

But it was not at Angie that Ellie was looking, but at Patrick.

'Well?' she said.

'I must say it's a surprise to me,' said Patrick, slowly. 'I suppose this means you'll be taking your leave of us sooner than we thought?'

There was an odd note in his voice.

I know what's in his mind, thought Mary. He had turned to Angie, and there was a rough note, now, in his voice.

'I suppose you'll be flashing a ring too one of these days,' he said.

Yes: I am right, thought Mary. He's afraid that they will all get out of here and that he will be left—a prisoner.

I must have a talk with him, she thought; but not until I have had a cup of tea.

It was the first time in several hours that she had felt the need for some sustenance, and finding that she still had the little plush ring-box in her hands, she held it out to her daughter.

'Here, Ellie,' she said, 'here's the box. Put back the ring in it, and come and have a cup of tea. You took nothing all day either.' But as they went over to the table she paused. 'Did you put back your ring in its box?' she asked suddenly.

'I did,' said Ellie absently.

'That's what I thought,' said Mary, looking at Angie, who stood dreamily, twisting something round and round upon the third finger of her left hand. For a minute Mary thought it might have been Ellie's ring, but the ring that Angie twisted round and round upon her finger was fashioned of a metal more precious than gold, and the diamonds that sparkled in it were as the stars compared with Ellie's pitiable little hoop of diamond chippings, for the ring that Angie twisted upon her finger was a dream ring, and the lights that flashed from its silver facets were little ghostly lights that she alone could see.

A strange shiver passed through Mary, and after taking a few sips of tea, she stood up.

'Ellie, I want to have a few words with Patrick.'

It was abrupt, but Ellie understood.

'Here, Angie,' she said. 'Help me to clear this table. Bart will probably be around any minute.'

Without a tray, inexpertly, she piled together all the cups and saucers she could carry, and went into the scullery, followed vaguely by Angie with a cup in one hand and a saucer in the other.

Mary looked around. She and Patrick were alone now, he self-consciously sitting at the table, and rolling into pellets the crumbs of bread that littered it. For a moment she had an impulse to stand up and brush away the crumbs. The girls were so slovenly. They never seemed to be able to do things the way she did them. They would probably leave the table like that all evening if she didn't do something about it. How they could look at it and be content to leave it that way was more than she could understand. They have a lot to learn, she thought: she who a moment before had marvelled at the wise depths in Ellie's eyes.

With an effort she forced herself to remain in her chair. It was an impulse of weakness that had prompted her to deal with the table. What she had to do was harder. There was no use postponing it.

'Patrick!'

'Yes, Mother?'

'Come over here, son,' she said. 'I want to talk to you. You said that your plans were changed. Well, I hope you haven't caused anyone any inconvenience by the change?'

She looked fixedly at him, but his face was expressionless as he sat awkwardly on the edge of the chair, his hands on his knees.

'Well?' she said, and she waited a minute. Then, when he didn't say anything, she altered her voice.

'Ah well! I suppose your plans weren't as definite as all that? I suppose you hadn't got beyond making inquiries? I expect it's not as easy as it used to be to get to America!'

'Oh, it's not so difficult if you go the right way about it,' he said. 'There is a bit of difficulty about passports and the like, but there's a way out of everything.'

'You didn't have your passport, did you?' she said, surprise getting the better of the cautious movements by which she had intended to approach the matter.

He nodded.

'You did?' She felt a stab, and then an impulse to stab back at him. 'Hadn't you better give that back, then?' she said sharply.

At another time he might have laughed at her, but he didn't feel like laughing. Instead he looked morosely down between his knees at the floor.

'You don't have to give them back,' he said. 'You don't pay anything for them. They're given out free. Plenty of people have passports without going anywhere at all—just in case.'

'In case of what?' She didn't like the way he gave such a superior air to his voice as he explained things to her.

'Oh, just in case!' he said limply.

'And they're given out free?' She took up this idea and turned it over for a minute. 'If that's the case I bet there's not much more given free! I always heard it cost a small fortune to get to America, and you have to have money in your pocket when you land there. That's a law! You have to have a five-pound note in your pocket. Did you know that?'

Patrick shuffled restlessly.

'I have that!' he said defiantly.

'Oh!' She was taken aback.

'I saved it up,' he said.

'Oh, you did!'

Two contradictory emotions met together within her. So that was why he was always asking for money when he was going out all last winter. He used to say it was for lemonade, but she used to find it hard to think he had spent all she gave him on lemonade alone, unless he was a proper fool, paying for other people's refreshments as well as for his own. Ah, it had worried her, this question of giving him money, and vague, dark forebodings had visited her at times. But now they were all swept away. Now she knew why he wanted the money: he was saving it and putting it aside to further his plans. Were it not that she hated duplicity she would have been greatly relieved that her fears had been unfounded.

'Hmmn!' she said, and made no other comment for a minute. Then another idea occurred to her.

'But your passage!' she said. 'You didn't save that up in pennies and farthings! Where were you going to get the money for that?'

Patrick squirmed.

'Isn't that what I told you,' he said, not roughly, but restively, 'I told you there were ways of getting there if you went about it the right way.'

'Yes?' She waited.

'I know a fellow in the office of the White Star Line. As a matter of fact you met him: he was here at the house one evening—a stout little fellow who played the piano for us.'

'Yes?' She couldn't help being sarcastic. 'He gave you the money, I suppose?' she said. 'Either that or he was so fond of you he got you a free passage!'

She had goaded him at last into a full statement.

'It amounts to that, if you want to know!' he exclaimed. 'I was going to work my passage.'

'What?'

It was beyond all she had imagined. She stared at him.

'In the purser's office!' he said coldly, disdaining the look of alarm in her eyes.

'Oh!' she said. Then another aspect of the thing occurred to her.

'Then you must have had everything settled? Might I ask when you were going to tell me about all this?'

Here Patrick came to life. He sat forward, and his eyes were bright and shining.

'I was going to tell you this week, Mother,' he said. 'Honestly I was. Honestly! Even if this hadn't happened——' here again he indicated the mourning cards on the laden mantel-shelf—'I was going to tell you, without fail, this week.'

He was so earnest. He was so desperately anxious to convince her of his sincerity that she could not help feeling mollified. But an unfortunate question came to her lips.

'And when were you—sailing?'

Visibly his eyes dulled, and the eagerness went out of his attitude. In a moment he had taken up again the same slightly sullen posture as before.

'What's that?' she said, for he was muttering so that she could hardly hear him.

'Next week!' he said.

Oh, Patrick! What have I ever done that you should treat my love like this? Did you think that, whoever else might impede you in your ambitions, I, your mother, would have set obstacles before you? My son, I love you; but I love you less.

These were the words that she spoke to him, but not from her lips. Then, with a sudden gesture, putting her hands on her knees, in a curiously elderly fashion for one of her years and looks, she rose from her chair, and without further calculation she went over to a long chest covered with a rug that occupied a corner of the kitchen, and the contents of which were not often revealed to the children. But now, throwing off the rug, and opening the lid with a little key she took from somewhere on her person, Mary raised the lid and took out a small metal cashbox, which had once been painted black but from which the black paint was gone in places, giving it a pattern of silver scratches. It was a kind of cashbox as far as Patrick could make out, but he did not get much chance to see it because in a minute the box was locked away in the chest again, and the rug thrown over it once more, and, as he still sat sheepishly in his chair, his mother was standing in front of him again, a little bundle in her hand, a bundle of bright green and white bank notes.

'I haven't much to give you, Patrick,' she said, 'and now that Father is gone from me, I have to think more about the other children that is to say, Larry and Rosie, than about you others who are old enough to look after yourselves, but I, like yourself, saved up these few pounds from time to time in pennies here and there, and as long as I have them there's no need for an O'Grady to work his passage anywhere!' She unrolled the little wad of notes. 'How much will it cost to pay for a proper passage?'

PART III

Patrick

Two weeks had passed since the day that Tom O'Grady had been laid to rest in Glasnevin Cemetery. It was early evening. Rosie had been in bed for some time, and Larry, having finished his lessons, had gone upstairs too. They could hear him hotly turning from side to side, creaking the springs of the old iron bed on which he slept. The rest of the family, with Mary, sat in the kitchen.

'Is Bart coming to-night, Ellie!' Patrick asked, after a long silence had lain over them.

'Yes, I suppose so. Why?' asked Ellie.

'Oh, no why,' said Patrick, and picking up a magazine, without interest he began to turn over the tattered leaves.

'Willie ought to be back in town soon, oughtn't he?' he said after another few minutes, looking up at Angie, who, like Mary, was sewing, but less expertly, because more than once she pricked her finger and brought out a little bead of blood upon it which she promptly put to her lips and sucked until the bleeding stopped. At the moment her brother spoke she was in the act of breaking a piece of thread between her small even teeth that were as neat as little pearl buttons on a draper's card, and so she was only able to nod her head in answer to him.

Willie was in Sligo, during a temporary job which he had recently undertaken.

'You'd miss him, wouldn't you, quiet as he is?' said Patrick.

It was only when he said this that Mary suddenly awoke to some strain in the atmosphere of the room.

'Children,' she said, looking around at them sitting, all three of them, so lifelessly in front of the fire, while beyond them, through the window over the sink, and out beyond the wall of the backyard, a fragment of the sky could be seen, blue and serene and still. 'Children! Why are you all indoors on such a fine evening? Surely you're not staying at home on my account?'

But as she spoke, she recalled that for the past fortnight not one of them had set foot outside the house after the evening meal. They had stayed at home to keep her company; to prevent her from feeling lonely.

'Nonsense!' she said, as if it were they who had spoken, and not she who had read their minds. 'Out of the house at once, the whole lot of you! I never heard of such a thing! If it's me you're thinking about, let me assure you I have too much to do to feel lonely for long. And anyway——'

But what she was about to say was not the kind of thing that could be said to them; or indeed to anyone. It was part of the secret agony of her loneliness, that not to a living soul could she say she missed Tom most at night, when she lay down in the great, cold bed where, night after night, for so many years, he had never failed, even in sleep, to reach out an arm to enfold her when she finally turned down the sheet and got in beside him.

Ah, the loneliness of that room, with its great brass-bound bed, that never now seemed to soften or grow warm.

The daytime was not so bad at all, or even the hours of the early evening. For one thing Tom had been out all day, and had often done late shifts on the Dalkey line, which kept him out till after midnight. She was not accustomed to having him much in the house by day. And so, now, downstairs she was hardly ever lonely. But even if she was! She wouldn't let her loneliness keep the children from their pleasure.

'I never heard such a thing,' she said, 'to stay indoors on a fine evening. That isn't going to do your poor father any good, you know.'

It was Angie who answered her. Ellie and Patrick only exchanged a glance in that language of the eyes which these two practised so much, but which she had never quite mastered.

'We don't feel like going out, Mother,' said Angie gently.

Mary turned to her. How pale she looked in her heavy mourning clothes.

'Just the same, child,' she said, 'you need fresh air.'

She didn't like the way the girl was looking. Her black clothes made her seem so much smaller and more frail than ever. With distaste Mary looked at the black bodice and skirt, the black shoes and black stockings. The child was shrouded in mourning, all but the pale oval of her face, and her two small hands so white the blue veins showed in them like pencil marks. Ellie looked a bit better in black, although she too was pale. Their mourning suddenly depressed Mary, and their pale faces and their subdued mien made her nervous. What if it was disloyal to Tom; what if it did seem unnatural, she found herself suddenly counting the months until they would be out of black. In the middle of her calculations, however, she noticed Ellie was looking at Patrick.

'Are you sure?' said Ellie.

Patrick nodded his head.

'Yes, I'm staying in all evening,' he replied. And then he looked across at Mary. 'I want to talk to you, Mother.'

The girls had got to their feet but they still looked uncertainly at their brother.

'Go on,' said Patrick impatiently. 'Get your hats.'

'Very well,' said Ellie then. 'We'll go up and get ready.'

The next minute they could be heard tripping upstairs, and in another minute tripping down again. Then Ellie put her head in the kitchen door.

'We won't be long,' she said, and she was gone.

Mary and Patrick heard the front door closed with a smart slap.

Mary turned to her son.

'Well, son?'

'Well, Mother,' said Patrick, 'I met that fellow again.'

At first she did not understand, and she looked at him inquiringly. But he was only making an opening for himself and he didn't bother to explain, but went on with what he had to tell.

'He was saying it was a great pity I let that opportunity slip.'

Ah, now she understood. What day was it? Ah yes. This was the day on which he was to have sailed.

'Why, son?' she said, trying to keep her voice quiet.

'Oh, you know your own mind better than I do,' said Patrick, 'but this fellow in the shipping office agrees with me that it's a great pity to throw away twenty or thirty pounds on passage money when I could get over free. And here's another thing. There'd be no sense in the like of me going any other way but steerage, and from all I hear, things aren't very choice in steerage. You're down in the bottom of the ship, almost in the hold, and you have only a bit of the forward deck for a promenade. I wouldn't mind that so much, but I hear we'd be railed off from the other sections as if we were cattle. That's the way you're treated, too, as cattle. And as for the other passengers, they regard you as dirt.'

Mary sat still. Only vaguely did she follow these differences of deck and class to which he referred in such familiar manner. But that there were other differences she could well understand.

'How much would it cost to go the other way,' she asked, 'on the other side of the ship?'

'Oh, second class, you mean?' Patrick laughed at her manner of expression.

'Isn't there another section?'

'Cabin? Oh, that's out of the question. In the first place I wouldn't have proper clothes; it's only the swells that go that way. Oh, second class is good enough for anyone, and if it goes to that, steerage would be good enough for me. What do I care about other people? Plenty of better people than I went out that way, and as the fellow in the White Star office says, a great many of them come back that way too, although, in nine cases out of ten, they could buy the boat when they were returning. I wouldn't mind what people thought of me: it's just that it seems a waste of money to pay for something when as good, and better, can be got for nothing!'

Mary was a little bewildered. She thought that it was a question of money that was agitating his mind. Now she felt unsure.

'What do you mean by as good or better?' she said, carefully feeling her way. 'If you pay your way, what could be better than that?'

'Well, it stands to reason,' said Patrick, 'that there's greater freedom for a member of the ship's personnel. There's no such thing as barriers for a member of the purser's office, you know, Mother. And then there's the uniform; that's supplied, you know, gold braid and all that——' Patrick tipped his sleeve as if the gold braid were there—'officer's cap,' he put a finger to his head. 'A fellow would look fairly smart in that outfit, you know.'

He smiled at her, and the charm in his smile affected her as it always did, but immediately an air of superiority that she disliked came into his voice.

'Ah yes,' he said, 'it's a pity you feel the way you do, Mother. Of course, if you changed your mind this chap down in the office thinks he might manage to get me another chance on the next sailing of the *Celtic*.'

She saw now what was confronting her.

'When would that be?'

All at once he was humble again.

'The week after next, Mother,' he said, like a little boy confessing to something secret and shameful in his heart.

For a few minutes she sat still, and then she looked at him steadily.

'I'd prefer you to pay your passage,' she said, 'and so would your father. Find out the amount of the passage money, on whatever part of the ship you'd like to go on, and let me know how much it will be.' Then, as there was no response from him, she went on. 'I suppose you could get a passage on that same boat; the one you were talking about just now?'

In spite of all his efforts to be collected, Patrick's face lit up.

'The *Celtic*?' he said. 'But it's sailing the week after next; maybe sooner.'

Mary could not look into that face, eager with feelings she could not share. She turned her head aside.

'As long as you're set on going,' she said, 'there's no sense in my trying to hold you back.'

It was so unexpected that she should have taken this attitude that Patrick lost his head. He sprang to his feet and caught her hands.

'That's the spirit, Mother,' he said. 'That's the way to look at it. And wait till you see! I'll be back home to see you, before two years, with my pockets heavier than they are now. And there's such a thing as a letter too, you know, Mother, and although I'm not saying anything now, I'm not making any promises, I understand it doesn't take an extra stamp to enclose a little banknote now and again, does it?'

He was so excited he tried to pull her to her feet, but as she resisted him, saying nothing, he tried to curb his excitement.

'Of course there's no need for me to go on that particular vessel,' he said, 'although I believe she's a very steady little steamer. She carries livestock, you see, and any boat carrying a cargo of cattle is always steady; well ballasted, that's the reason. But, as I say, there's no need for me to make a point of going on that particular vessel. Except of course that it's getting late in the year now. We're getting a bit near the equinox and you get a bit of rough seas about that time, but no matter, I'm not afraid of that. It's only you I'd be thinking about, lying in bed listening to the wind and thinking of me in the middle of the ocean. But that's a small matter.'

A spasm faint as a shadow passed over Mary's face.

'I think it would be nice for you to go on the boat you mentioned,' she said. 'I've got kind of used to it now and the name of it is familiar too: what's this you said it was?'

'The *Celtic*, Mother. Well, I suppose you're right. That's settled, then, I suppose. Let me see: is there a calendar handy?'

It occurred to Patrick suddenly that his mother was a very simple person. She's like a child, he thought. And all the complications and all the subtleties of an adult personality, with which he had credited her, seemed to him suddenly to have been illusory, as when from the deck of a liner, already far out to sea, one looks back at a great city, and sees with astonishment that all its intricacies, its thousand streets and alleyways, its million roofs and towers, and all, all its steeples, domes, wharves, and bridges have dwindled into a single mass: a solitary crag, or a low mud flat marked only by one tower.

A stab of loneliness assailed him, and made his heart ache.

And yet, I'll go, he thought. Indeed the ache in his heart made it seem as if he were already gone some way upon his voyage and that it was beyond his power to return.

Vaguely it crossed his mind to wonder why he was going at all. He looked around the little kitchen, so quiet and happy. I may never again be as happy as I am now, never in all my life, he thought. He looked at Mary. She is the creature I love most in all the world: why then, am I leaving her? And going so far away that the chances are that I may never see her again. Why? he asked, but he found no answer except in restless uneasy feeling which ever since he was a child made it intolerable to him to be long in one place. Even now, so near to the time when he would be leaving it, perhaps for ever, it was hard for him to endure the thought of staying at home all evening.

'Did the girls say when they would be home, Mother?' he asked.

The silence that had settled in the kitchen appalled him.

~   ~   ~   ~

'Look, Bart,' cried Ellie one evening, as she paused in the street to read a placard pasted on the window of a vacant house in Rathmines.

During the winter months, having come to the understanding that they would one day marry, Bart and Ellie had begun vaguely to look at the houses to either side of them, as they went for their evening walks along the suburban roads.

'Look, Bart!' said Ellie this evening. 'It says the key is next door,' she said, pulling him gently back by the arm, as he began to move away. Impatiently Bart stood, and looked up at the house.

'I wouldn't take it as a present,' he said.

It was a tall, gaunt house, with narrow windows and a narrow door like the lid of a coffin.

'Do you think I would!' cried Ellie. 'I only thought it would be fun to go inside when it would be so handy to get the key.'

Bart looked at her. Perhaps it would be fun to go into the tall old house with her, and to wander about its empty rooms. It would be the first time he would ever have been alone with her except out of doors in the city streets, which seemed, even late at night, to be always populated.

'I'll get the key,' he cried suddenly, breaking away from her.

Surprised a little by his abrupt change of mind, Ellie stood and watched him, as he knocked upon the door of the other house. A minute later she saw the door being opened to him by a thin wispish woman in black, a landlady probably, with a landlady's curious mind and eye. Then the creature vanished into the narrow black hallway and when she reappeared she handed something to Bart.

It was the key.

'I have it,' he cried.

Why was he so excited? A minute earlier he hadn't wanted to see the house at all.

'Oh, I'm sorry we bothered,' said Ellie. 'It's getting late and it's getting dark. We won't be able to see it properly. And anyway what good will it do us?'

She seemed to have forgotten that it was she who had suggested getting the key: she who had said it would have been fun. Now instead she looked critical and bored. A little stupidly, Bart looked at the key in his hand. And Ellie followed his gaze.

'I suppose we should make some use of it,' she said then, 'since we gave that woman the trouble of getting it for us. She's probably squinting out at us behind those hideous curtains.'

Bart looked at the windows of the other house. He could see no one, but not for an instant did he doubt Ellie's superior vision. And as he looked, it crossed his mind, humbly and contritely, that in the matter of the curtains also, if he were not guided by her superior taste, he would have thought that they were not too bad. Humbly he acknowledged to himself that without her he would, at best, have blundered through life, never knowing by what a hairsbreadth good taste and true feeling differed from their counterfeits. Then he looked back to the vacant house.

'Well! Will we just take a quick look over it?' he said.

'We'd better, I suppose,' said Ellie.

But there was a note in her voice that stung Bart.

'It was your idea, Ellie!' he said.

'How quick you were to take it up!' she said, but as he failed to get the key to turn in the lock, she put out her hand. 'Here, let me try,' she said.

'Ugh!' The smell that came out of the dark, ugly hallway was combined of dampness and stale dust, and perhaps even of some noxious fungus at work upon the unseen timbers beneath the neglected outer surfaces. 'Ugh! What a hideous hallway!' said Ellie, and she shuddered.

But Bart's voice was vibrant with subdued excitement.

'Come on,' he said roughly, eagerly, stopping only to hold back the door for her to pass ahead of him. The darkness, the foul odours, and the curious, damp atmosphere he did not notice at all, so great was the sudden access of excitement which came over him at the thought of entering with her into this sanctuary of silence and privacy. It was as if they stood together at the mouth of some strange cavern where mystery and ecstasy awaited them, and into which they were about to rush headlong, hand in hand together. Almost it seemed to him that he should reach out and lay his hand over her eyes, so great was the transport with which he felt himself carried forward. But as he glanced at her, with a look of rapture, he saw that Ellie was as cold as ice, and the glance she flashed at him was as cold as the little blue lights that, at that moment, gleamed from the diamonds on her finger.

'I'll wait here,' she said. 'You can take a look around the house and come back and tell me about it.'

With a shock of amazement Bart was brought back to earth.

'What did you say?' he asked. 'Do you mean to say you're not going to come inside at all?'

'Well, if you're quick about it,' said Ellie briskly, 'I'll take a look into some of the rooms when you come out.'

Did he hear her aright? Did she not trust him? Was that it? Did she think—? He looked at her, anger rising like a storm inside him.

But at the sight of her his anger fell away. She had taken out her little powder box with the mirrored lid, and unconcerned with him, she was looking into its shining pool. 'You hear queer stories about empty houses,' she said. 'We'll go in one at a time. But don't be long! I don't fancy standing here all evening.'

'Perhaps I won't bother going in at all,' said Bart suddenly, as, peering into the hallway, he saw it for the first time as it actually was, evil smelling and dank.

But he went in a few paces nevertheless, and finding a door on the right he opened it and turned into the large bleak room within, lit dimly by a north window almost completely overgrown with some green creeping weed.

'There's a fine mantelpiece here,' he said, calling out to Ellie.

'Oh, Bart! Do hurry! It's getting chilly!'

'Just one look at the rooms overhead,' he said, and the next thing she saw was his long legs going up the stairs two steps at a time.

Why on earth had she suggested their coming near the wretched place! Ellie was not only impatient, but beginning as well to feel cold. As the minutes went by she grew more and more irritable, for he seemed to be going into every room, if she were to judge by the sounds of doors opening and shutting far up in the now almost pitch-dark regions beyond the stairhead. A house that could not possibly have any interest for them! So like a man, she thought. Oh, they were all the same, tiresome, and without thought for others.

'Bart! For heaven's sake!'

How well he had never suggested looking at one of the little-red-brick terraced houses with bay windows that were so numerous everywhere all over the city. Oh no, he ignored little houses like that! Oh, trust a man, even a man like Bart, she thought, to be cautious when it came to taking the final step.

Ellie shivered, and drew her collar closer around her neck. And she quite, quite forgot the little diamond ring that Bart, all on his own initiative, had produced one evening from its little purple casket with the white pearl stud, and whose lights were now quenched in the darkness of her black kid glove.

'Oh, Bart! How you startled me. I thought you were still upstairs!' she cried, for there he was beside her, pulling the door closed after him and taking the key from the lock.

'Well, what was it like upstairs?' she asked grudgingly, but curious too, at the same time.

'I'll tell you,' said Bart, 'but wait till I give back this key.'

It was almost dark now, and when he came back to her he put his arm around her waist.

'Please, Bart!' she protested, and she tried to step aside from his encircling arm, for although it was warm and comfortable to have it around her, there were other people in the street besides themselves. 'Be careful!' she said warningly. 'What will people think!'

But where now was the caution with which she had thought to rule him a few minutes previously.

'Let them think what they like!' he said, and tightening his arm about her, with the other arm he indicated vaguely the houses to either side of them. 'We needn't worry about what people might think of us in this locality,' he said, and then, just exactly as if he had read the thoughts that had passed through her mind while she waited for him on the step of the old house, he said something else;

something that brought a lump into her throat, and made her want suddenly to cry. 'It would be a different matter altogether if this were one of those roads off Appian Way, with little red-brick houses to either side. You know the little houses I mean, with bay windows in front and little gardens back and front. We wouldn't want to give people a bad opinion of us in a locality like that.'

She just managed to ask one question in a low little voice, more like Angie's than her own.

'Why?'

'Because that's the kind of locality in which we're going to live, isn't it?' he said, and his voice grew more eager and excited. 'How is it we so seldom see one of those little villas vacant?' he demanded. 'I'll tell you why! Because they're so much in demand. That's why! They are no sooner vacant than they're snapped up again. I'm going to tell you something, Ellie, whether you like it or not. We ought to keep our eyes open; we ought to be more alert! It's all very well to say we're not getting married for some time, but there are things to be taken into consideration. Take the housing situation, for instance. How do we know that there'll be a suitable house available when we finally make up our minds about a date? How do we know that?'

To express his enthusiasm, Bart was forced to stand still in the street and wheel Ellie around to face him.

'I tell you, Ellie, it's not a bit too soon for us to start looking at houses in earnest. Not a bit too soon! As a matter of fact we should have begun sooner. We have lost a lot of time already. But that can't be helped now. From here on I have my mind made up that if we come across a suitable house we're not going to let it slip between our fingers! Do you hear me?'

Yes. Ellie heard him!

But she didn't answer him. In the pale light from a distant lamp he could only see her face faintly, turned a little aside from him as she stood patiently listening.

'Did you hear me?' he asked again, frowning with the force of his earnestness. But after another instant he looked more sharply at her. 'You're laughing!' he said accusingly.

And Ellie was laughing. She was laughing soundlessly, but when he looked closely he saw that her whole body was trembling with subdued laughter, and tears of laughter lay on her lashes.

'I'd like to know what you're laughing at!' he exclaimed. He was never so perplexed in all his life.

But Ellie too was perplexed. She was hardly aware that she was laughing. It was just that things seemed to have come together so oddly, so accidentally, you might say. There was that ridiculous incident about the vacant house: it had seemed so purposeless, so pointless, such a waste of time. She stood shivering on those cold grey steps, thinking what a shame it was that the evening should have been such a failure. And yet, when Bart came out of the old house, in the very moment that he appeared beside her, so suddenly and so startlingly, before he said a word of all this to which she had listened just now, before he did more than look into her eyes, she knew that, insignificant as it had been, in the course of that incident some change had come over him; some incalculable influence had worked upon him, and their destiny together had been advanced a pace.

How strange it all was: how little part one seemed after all to take in determining the course of one's own life. What a matter of hazard and chance it was. And how different, in so many hundreds and thousands of ways, was a man from a woman!

'I'm not laughing, Bart,' she said, speaking at last, 'truly I'm not!' And truly she was not laughing now. 'But hadn't we better hurry home?' she said. 'It's getting late.'

So different! That was her constant thought, as she pressed closer against him, while they made their way homeward. So different, she thought, and for the first time in the strong armour of her pride and her vanity, a chink was made, and she felt herself abased by a passionate longing for the time when she would explore that difference to the full.

And so, what had been a casual pastime for the young couple became an earnest occupation, and every other evening they set out in search of a house; and yet of all the houses in and out of which they trudged, not one single house, it seemed, in all the city, was the house that was meant for them.

'Patience! You must have patience, children,' cried Mary, as night after night they came back to her, tired and dispirited. 'After all, there is no great hurry. The sooner you get a house the sooner you'll have to pay rent on it!'

But this little sally was too mild to draw more than a watery smile from the young people.

'Here! Take a sip of this, and you'll feel better.'

Mary never failed to have the kettle boiling, and however late it was when they came home, she wouldn't let Bart leave the house without a drink of hot tea.

'Will you have a cup, Ellie?'

Mary looked anxiously at her daughter. Sometimes Ellie was so tired that all she wanted was to fall into bed as soon as the door closed

on Bart. Tea would only keep her awake, she said, having begun to
learn for the first time that there was not necessarily any relation
between physical fatigue and genuine sleepiness.

'No thank you, Mother,' she said, throwing back her coat from her
shoulders and sinking into a chair.

She was beginning to look the worse for this trudging about the
streets. Mary didn't like it. And another thing she didn't like was the
effect it was having upon the relations between the young people.

'Ellie!' she exclaimed in disapproval, as Ellie, without thought,
kicked her shoes from her feet one night as soon as she got inside the
kitchen, and taking up her little foot in one hand began to feel it all
over with the other hand, wincing as if it were calloused and sore.

'Oh, Mother! Bart doesn't mind!' A shade of asperity seemed to be
creeping back into the relationship of mother and daughter.

Mary wanted to give her daughter a sharp answer.

More shame to him if he doesn't! That was what she was prompted
to say, but as she looked at the young man, leaning so wearily upon
his elbow at the table, she saw that she and Ellie were at cross pur-
poses, and that what Ellie meant was that Bart was too fatigued to
take heed of what was going on about him. After that Mary made no
comment, no matter how Ellie behaved when they came home after a
hard evening's work. Indeed before long she found herself counselling
her to pull off her shoes and to put her feet up in a chair to rest them.

One such evening, after caressing her little foot in her hands for a
few minutes, Ellie stood up and hobbling over to the dresser took
down the canister in which they kept the sugar.

'You haven't any sugar, Bart,' she said, as he stirred his tea vaguely
and put the cup to his lips.

'Thanks,' said Bart, and then he laughed. 'I never missed it,' he
said.

'In that case,' said Mary, smiling at him, 'you can spare yourselves
the expense of a sugar bowl in your new house when you get it.'

'When we get it!' The phrase was unfortunate. Ellie sank back into
her chair, but this time her attitude was one of dejection more than of
fatigue. 'If we ever get it,' she said. 'I'm beginning to think we never
will.'

'Oh, Ellie!'

Mary had not thought to draw down this gloom upon herself and
upon Bart. She looked appealingly at the latter. Couldn't he do something to raise Ellie's spirits? But Bart was not looking in her direction.
Instead he was looking at Ellie, and his eyes, though weary-looking,
were filled with a tender compassion for her.

'Never mind, Ellie,' he said, 'we'll find some place to lay our heads.'
As he spoke he leaned across the table to the window, and putting up
his hand he drew aside the light, lace curtains that alone screened
them from the starry sky without. 'We won't be defeated,' he said,
partly teasing and partly serious. 'If necessary,' he said, 'we'll sleep
under the stars.'

'Oh, Bart!'

Whatever way he talked when they were alone, Ellie wasn't going
to listen to this kind of thing in her mother's presence. Overcome
with embarrassment, she darted an angry glance at him, and began
to feel around under the chair for her shoes.

'If you're so fond of the stars,' she said nervously, embarrassedly,
'you'd better hurry and get out under them.' And she went into
the hall to hasten his departure by taking down his coat from the hall
stand. 'Here's your coat,' she said crossly.

'Now, Mrs. O'Grady!' said Bart complainingly. 'See how she treats
me! Amn't I the foolish man to wear myself to the bone trying to
find a house for her?'

'You are indeed!' said Mary, but her voice was forced. She was
conscious of a growing feeling of exasperation in Ellie.

'Oh please, Mother! Please, Bart! It's not a laughing matter. I
meant what I said—I don't believe we'll ever get the right house,
Here!' she cried then, as there was a sound of voices in the hall, and
she thrust Bart's coat towards him. 'Here are the others,' she said.
'and I don't want to see them. I only want to go to bed and throw
myself down.'

'That's the sensible thing to do,' said Mary. 'I'll see you to the
door, Bart,' she said, turning to the young man.

The others, Angie and Willie, had gone into the parlour.

'Will you say good night to them?' asked Mary, as she and Bart
went out into the hallway. The parlour door was closed.

Bart shook his head.

What a beautiful night it was! After he had gone Mary stood there
at the door looking up into the sky, so studded with stars, so silent,
and so serene.

Why are they so impatient, she thought—all of them. Only the
other day they were up there somewhere, in those starry regions,
and now they are grown men and women consuming themselves
with their little worries. I must do something to keep Ellie from
getting into such an exhausted condition, she thought, as finally she
closed the door and went back into the kitchen. But what exactly she
was going to do she did not know.

The next evening, however, when Bart called, Mary made a weak effort to keep them at home.

'You used to have such enjoyable evenings,' she said, 'playing the piano and singing.'

'Mother, I'm surprised at you,' said Ellie. 'To talk about the piano and Father only a few weeks dead.'

'Oh dear.' A spasm of genuine pain passed over Mary's face. 'I forgot,' she cried.

But it was not Tom that she forgot; it was the fact that he was dead. And if he were to look down on them he would understand what she meant; understand and forgive her. She knew that. A little bit humiliated, however, she made no further effort to prevent the young people from going forth on their expedition.

'Don't stay out too long!' That was all she ventured to call after them as they went out of the house. But she didn't expect that they would take any heed of her words.

And so, when, about an hour later, she heard their voices in the hall, she was so surprised she thought for a long, terrible moment that something had happened: that there had been some accident. But instantly their voices reassured her. It was true they were high-pitched and excited, but at the same time they were so gay and so triumphant!

The next minute they burst into the kitchen, and both of them flung their arms around her.

'Now, Mother!' cried Ellie. 'You wanted to keep us at home. You tried to prevent us from going out. And it would have been your fault if we hadn't found it!'

'Found what?' cried Mary.

'Do you hear that, Bart?' cried Ellie. 'A house, of course!' she cried, standing back from Mary, and looking at her with shining eyes.

'Where?' The word came impulsively to Mary's lips, but she was hardly heeding the answer. Never in her life had she seen Ellie look as she looked just then. It was as if all the happiness of her whole future life shone for that moment in her face.

But as Bart opened his mouth to reply to Mary, Ellie ran around and pressed her hand to his lips.

'Don't tell her!' she cried urgently. 'We'll make her come and see it.' She turned to Mary. 'Oh, Mother, you have no idea! You never saw such a dear little house. Two bay windows! And on a corner, too—semidetached, you know! Oh, when you see it, you'll feel just the same as we did, won't she, Bart? And, Mother! What do you suppose? There seem to be apple trees in the back garden, or perhaps they're pears—we couldn't tell, because we could only see the tops of them.'

In spite of her bewilderment at the suddenness of their return, and their excited words, Mary began to gather her thoughts together.

'But didn't you see the garden?' she asked. 'Didn't you go into it?'

'How could we?' cried Ellie.

'You see, Mother,' said Bart, 'we weren't inside the house at all.'

'What?'

After all the stations they had made upon their tireless pilgrimage, and after the minute scrutiny to which they had subjected so many closets and cupboards, mantelpieces, drainpipes, window sashes, chimney pieces and cornice stones, was it possible that they had been brought to this state of excitement by a house they had only seen from the outside?

'We're getting the key to-morrow, first thing,' said Bart, reading the surprise in Mary's eyes.

'But I wouldn't care if we never saw the inside of it,' said Ellie. 'I mean I'd be prepared to walk into it this minute, without ever going over it at all, because I know, I know in my heart, that it's just the kind of house I always dreamed I'd live in some day.'

'And anyway we were able to see a good part of the hall,' said Bart, 'by looking in through the letter box, and we could see something of the sitting-room, too, through a crack in the shutters.'

'We're absolutely certain it's the house for us.' Ellie glanced at the clock. 'What on earth is keeping Angie out till this hour?' she said, although it was still within an hour of the normal time at which any of them came home in the evenings. 'And Patrick! I should think he'd stay at home a little more now that he's going away so soon.'

She so obviously wished Angie and Patrick were home in order to tell them about the new house, Mary almost felt under an obligation to provide someone else for the purpose.

'It's too bad Alice isn't here,' she said. 'Alice is so interested in your house hunting.'

'Oh, I didn't tell you, Mother!' Ellie's face clouded momentarily. 'Poor Alice is laid up again: only a chill or something, but they had the doctor for her, and he said they had better keep her in her room till the weather is better.'

'Oh dear!' cried Mary. 'Who told you that? When did you hear it? I missed her these last few days, but I didn't think anything of it. The poor child! I must make something nice and take it in to her. How long ago is it since she had the doctor?'

But Ellie couldn't remember, or else she couldn't concentrate.

'The children are asleep, I suppose?' she said suddenly.

'Now look here, Ellie!' It was Bart, this time, who saw what she had in mind. 'Whether they're asleep or awake you had better stay downstairs, and not get them into such a state of excitement that they won't go to sleep till morning. Come and sit down here, and try to be calmer, and we'll tell your mother how we came upon the house in the first place.'

But the telling was unsatisfactory. Every other minute Ellie glanced at the clock, or threw back her head to listen to the distant rattle of a tramcar.

Her whole pleasure in the house seemed now to have become weighted into a single drop, full and heavy, which she longed to let fall into the hands of her brother and sister. They would be so interested. Her mother, of course, was interested, but how could she understand like the others? Poor Mother thought they should all be perfectly happy to stay at home with her for the whole of their days! Oh, what was keeping those others! She couldn't stand much more of this waiting for them.

And yet when, not very much later, Angie and Patrick came in together, having met at the gate, where Willie Haslip had said good-bye to Angie, there was something lacking after all in the telling of Ellie's news, and instead of the satisfaction that she had expected to feel, there was a new problem put forward by Patrick, as soon as their mother's back was turned.

It was Ellie who drew down the problem upon them.

'You don't seem as pleased as you might, Patrick!' she said pettishly, looking at him.

'What makes you think that?' said Patrick sulkily, yet making no effort to deny that her observation was true.

'Oh, it's easy to be seen,' said Ellie. 'Isn't it?' she cried, appealing to Angie.

It was Angie who put into words what Patrick seemed able only to express by a growing glumness and taciturnity.

'I suppose Patrick didn't think you'd be settling down so soon,' she said. 'Isn't that it, Patrick?'

Still glumly, Patrick nodded his head.

'I suppose,' said Angie, timidly going a step further, 'that he's thinking you wouldn't like him to go away if the wedding is going to take place sooner than we thought. Isn't that it, Patrick?'

'Well,' said Patrick gruffly, 'isn't it only natural I'd want to be here to give her away?' he said, addressing himself to Angie. 'Who else is there to do it?' he asked angrily.

So that was it. It made it a bit better to have things out in the open, thought Ellie, but she could not help feeling a shadow fall already over the brightness of her joy.

'Well, Patrick O'Grady,' she said, 'you needn't think for one minute that Bart and I are going to go between you and your plans. In the first place, what gave you the idea we were going to get married as soon as all that? Just because we found the house doesn't mean we're going to rush things!'

But this seemed to make Patrick more angry than ever.

'Talk sense,' he said. 'If you take the house you'll have to start paying rent for it, and if you're paying rent for it you'll have to live in it.'

At this, however, Ellie tossed her head, and her eye flashed dangerously bright.

'Not necessarily!' she said, sharply. 'We're not all so mad about money as you, Patrick!'

'Oh hush, Ellie!' Much, much less contention than this affected Angie and made her tremble all over.

'Well, it's true,' said Ellie, but already she repented her words somewhat. 'As a matter of fact, though,' she said, looking at Patrick with remorse, 'it would be just as well for you to go ahead with your plans before we start to carry out ours, I mean for Mother's sake!'

'Why for her sake?' said Patrick.

'Well, this is the way I look at it,' said Ellie. 'If you go before the wedding, Mother will have the fuss of the wedding to distract her, and she'll get over her loneliness quicker. I don't mean that she'll miss you less but she won't have much time to sit around and think about you. On the other hand if you wait for the wedding, she'll be tired after all the fuss, and she'll have nothing ahead of her to which she can look forward, only the awful thought that you will be leaving her next——' But at this point Mary's footsteps were heard coming back into the kitchen.

'We'll talk about it again!' said Ellie.

And indeed, not only was it true that they would talk about it again, but in the next few days it could hardly be said that they talked about anything else, except for the fact that their talk had always to take place when Mary's back was turned and that when she was present they had to make a show of interest in other matters. At last, however, it was decided upon that Patrick was to sail on the date he had arranged.

First of all there was a hitch in the negotiations about the house, and although the owner had given Bart every assurance that he would not give the house to anyone before them, some uncertainty had arisen as to whether or not he intended to let the house at all.

'So you see,' cried Ellie in a final effort to convince Patrick, 'you may be home again before we get it, yet. You may be home again in time to give me away after all!'

'Well, I don't know about that,' said Patrick, and from his voice it seemed as if a heavy burden had been lifted from him, 'I don't know about you people and your plans,' he said, 'but I know one thing—you won't see me home again until I've made a nice packet!' Suddenly he sprang to his feet, an excited flush on his face. Mary was not in the room, and there was no need to spare anyone else.

'My God, how I'm longing to get out of here!' he cried. 'Two weeks more! I suppose they'll come to an end some time!'

And in this supposition Patrick was not wrong, and in exactly fifteen days, no more and no less, the fortnight came to an end; his hat was on his head, his coat was on his arm, his baggage was in the hall, and, all except Mary, the family clustered around him.

~   ~   ~   ~

If only Mother would come downstairs, things might not be so bad, so different from what he had expected. Patrick stood at the foot of the stairs.

'Would there be anything the matter with her?' he asked at last, going up a few steps of the stairs, and looking at Mary's closed door.

The others were ready and waiting to accompany him to the train, but their mother had not yet come down.

'I'll be late,' said Patrick. 'Are you sure there's nothing wrong with her? Why is she keeping us waiting so long?'

'Oh, you ought to know Mother! She'll be down in a minute,' said Ellie reassuringly.

As a matter of fact, Ellie herself had been uneasy about her mother. Undoubtedly Mary had taken the whole affair of Patrick's going much better than any of her children had expected. But he wasn't gone yet! And the worst part of the ordeal had yet to be endured—seeing him off from the station. Perhaps it was a mistake to have suggested her going to the station with him? Perhaps they should have persuaded her to stay at home? But if she stayed at home, someone would have had to stay with her. And who would have stayed? Not one of the family but would have been bitterly disappointed at having to forgo the excitement. Even Larry was excited. Even Rosie! Rosie had everyone at heads and hares, running from room to room, asking questions and pestering everyone to know if they were going to go in a cab.

'Don't bother me, Rosie,' cried Ellie at last. 'And get down from that suitcase this minute: do you want to make it twice as shabby as it is?'

'Is it very shabby, Ellie!' said Patrick anxiously.

'Not at all,' said Ellie crisply. 'I was only trying to make that child stay quiet for a minute. I don't know what need there is for her to come to the station!' But as, at this, a dangerous gleam came into Rosie's eyes, her older sister patted her on the head. 'All right,' she said, 'all right, I'm not stopping you! But don't keep pestering me about the cab; we haven't decided about it yet.'

'As a matter of fact you had better decide about it soon,' said Bart, coming up behind them at that moment, 'because it's getting late.'

'I know that,' said Ellie sharply. What kind of a family are we? she thought. What does Bart think of us? We can never make up our minds about anything. She turned back to Patrick.

'Well?' she said crossly, just exactly as if there were no such thing as the Atlantic Ocean, across which, out of their sight, he was so soon to be borne away. 'What about the cab?'

Patrick too seemed to have forgotten those great dividing waves.

'Well,' he said crossly, 'we won't all fit in one cab, you know. Some of you will have to go by tram!'

'Unless we hired another cab,' said Angie timidly, because although Bart and Alice were already there, and presumably accepted as members of the farewell party for the station, she was not sure whether they were counting Willie, who would of course be arriving any minute. 'We'd all fit in two cabs,' she said. 'Rosie could sit on Willie's knee.'

'Oh, is Willie coming too?' Angie frowned. Ellie sounded so patronizing. Angie looked at Patrick.

'Patrick asked him to come, didn't you, Patrick?'

'Yes, I believe I did,' Patrick said absently, because he was thinking about the cab.

'Look here,' he said suddenly, 'I'm not going to have a line of cabs drawn up outside the door as if we were going to a funeral!'

For a minute there was an awkward silence, but Bart, who was sitting on the lid of a big suitcase, gave Alice a nudge.

'I think Alice here regards it as a funeral,' he said. 'Isn't that so, Alice?'

Alice blushed furiously.

'Oh, Bart!' she exclaimed, but no words could belie the blushes in her face.

Patrick looked first at Bart, and then turned with an expression of surprise to Alice.

'Why should Alice think that?' he asked, and almost immediately another thought passed through his mind. She can look pretty when she likes, he thought. It's nice of her to come to see me off when I hardly ever took any notice of her. 'I'll send you a postcard, Alice,' he said.

Her blushes deepened. Why didn't she say something?

'I suppose you'll forget me in a week,' he said. He'd like to make her open her lips. They were pretty lips, too, though he hadn't noticed them ever before.

But Alice didn't open her lips. She only nodded her head miserably from one side to another.

'Does that mean yes or no?' he asked. What was the matter with her? Was it possible that she was shy of him? He used to think her quietness came from a sort of stupidity, but now he wondered if there might not have been some other cause for it. Come to think of it, she had hardly ever spoken two words together in his company.

Suddenly he wanted to hear her voice. He even moved over nearer to her, so that if she answered he would hear her, because her voice was always faint.

'If I write to you, you might write to me,' he said, and then he stepped still nearer. 'Will you?' he whispered.

But before he caught the single word with which in a low voice Alice answered him, he heard, overhead, the door of Mary's room opening, and the next minute Mary came down the stairs.

'I'm ready,' she said. 'What are we waiting for now? If you're going at all, son, you may as well be in good time. And who is going in the cab? Have you decided that?'

It was Ellie who answered: sharply.

'You and Patrick are going in it, Mother,' she said. 'The rest of us can go by tram.'

'And what about us?' said Larry and Rosie in unison.

'Oh, you can come in the cab!' said Mary.

Ellie frowned.

'They'll do no such thing,' she said shortly. 'They can come on the tram with the rest of us. There is always a charge for extra passengers in a cab. And you'll be crowded enough as it is!'

Mary looked at the disappointed faces of her younger children. She wanted to suggest that they should go in the cab instead of her, and that she would go by tram, but she was afraid of hurting Patrick's feelings; he might have something to say to her in his last few minutes with her.

Then another solution occurred to her.

'If you took the luggage on the tram,' she said, addressing Ellie and the others, 'then the children could come in the cab.'

This time Ellie looked severe indeed.

'Really, Mother, I sometimes wonder how you cannot see the absurdity of the things you say. Carry the luggage indeed! If it weren't for the luggage, we could all go by tram. There would be no need for a cab at all. Isn't that right, Patrick?'

Patrick, however, was not listening.

'Would we be able to make room for Alice?' he asked. 'She hasn't been well lately, you know,' he added, as Ellie seemed about to bridle again at his suggestion.

'Oh, I'm all right,' said Alice, confused at this unusual attention. 'You and your mother will want to be together I expect,' she added.

Once again Mary wanted to give up her place. But what would be the use, she thought, of throwing them together now like this, at the last moment, when it could make no difference whatever?

Instead she looked fondly at Alice.

'We'd only love to take you, child,' she said, 'if there is room.'

But there wouldn't be room. Already, as Bart and Larry each gave a hand to take it out of the house, Patrick's baggage was piling up into a formidable mound on the path outside the house. It was not so much that he had a great amount of things to take with him as that they were packed in a miscellany of small suitcases, and that, after they were closed and locked, a number of articles that had not been included in them had to be made up in brown paper parcels. These parcels, as well as the parting gifts of his family and friends, would certainly fill most of the space in the cab that was not taken up by Patrick and Mary.

There wouldn't be room for her, not without making it uncomfortable for the others, thought Alice, but fearing that they might overrule such an excuse she made another instead.

'Oh no, thank you,' she cried. 'I'd rather go on the tram. Truly I would, Mrs. O'Grady. A cab always upsets me; truly it does! All that rocking, you know!'

And as she said it, she swayed slightly from side to side, her light hair lifting away from her face, first to one side and then to the other, while the colour in her cheeks seemed also to rock slightly, a volatile fluid in a frail translucent vessel.

She doesn't mean a word of it, thought Patrick. She is just talking from nervousness. She's afraid of crowding up the cab; afraid of intruding upon us.

Glancing quickly at the pile of baggage outside the door, and glancing around him at the straggling group of his party, his eyes came finally to rest again upon Alice.

'Just a minute,' he said. 'Why don't we all go by tram? There are so many of us we ought to be able to manage the luggage between us.'

In the general exclamation of satisfaction that greeted this suggestion, the disappointment of the youngsters was drowned.

'Now you're talking!' said Bart. 'Here, give me that!' he cried, and snatching up the largest and heaviest of the suitcases he began to move down the path to the gate.

'Hello, Willie,' he said, as Willie at this moment came up to them. 'Try to hurry them,' he said.

Ellie alone was aware of the way time was passing.

'I'm coming, Bart,' she cried. 'Wait for me. Come on, Patrick,' she urged. But Patrick was arguing with Alice.

'That's too heavy for you, Alice,' he said, as Alice tried awkwardly to get a better grip upon the large parcel put into her hand by Angie. 'Here, give it to me,' he said. 'There's no need for her to carry anything at all,' he said crossly to Angie as with a laugh she pushed another parcel into the girl's hands. 'I'm quite serious, Alice,' said Patrick frowning, and this parcel also he took from her.

He looked at her then, right into her face, that should have been so familiar to him, but which all at once was as strangely fair and provocative as if he had never before seen her in all his life, or perhaps it was that in that fair, sweet face was symbolized all he was leaving behind him, all the frail sweet sanity of his childhood and youth. Under his gaze Alice turned away. She was embarrassed. Very well! He'd give her something to embarrass her. And as, still protesting, she tried to persuade one person after another to let her carry something, he reached out his hand.

'Very well, if you insist on taking something, take my arm,' he said, and he caught her little arm in its fragile blue silk sleeve, and drew it under his own arm, imprisoning it there with a tight clasp, and laughing down at her confusion.

This was more like what he had expected the trip to the station would be, he thought, as, at last, the party began to move down the street, every one of them carrying something, as if, he thought, when for a moment he surveyed them, as if they were all, every one of them, including Alice on his arm, all, all going with him.

'Supposing you were all coming with me,' he said, looking around him, but his eyes came to rest on Alice, and he lowered his voice so that even Mary, who walked on the other side of him, could not catch what he said. 'Supposing you were coming, Alice?' That was what he said.

Now what had he done? Surely those weren't tears shining on her lashes? He had only spoken in fun. Now what was he to do? Afraid to look at her, he pressed her arm tighter and stepped out with a swing. If only the tram would hurry!

Ah, here was the tram coming towards them, rolling and swaying upon its rails, almost as if it were dangling by its trolley from the high wires overhead, and only in places touched the shining rails below it.

'Up on top!' Patrick cried out to Bart and Ellie who were in front and who, when the tram came to a stop, were boarding it ahead of the others.

'Yes, the top of the tram was the place for them in the mood that Patrick was in at that moment. It was a great idea to come on the tram. It was a great idea having the whole family coming to see him off at the train. He was filled with the spirit of adventure.

Everything is going the way I wanted, he thought, as they got down from the tram at the station and stepped out on to the platform, and he paused to ask on which side of the station he would get his train, and walked gaily after the others up the platform.

The platform was as wide as a street. They walked together, all spread out in a line. More than ever, it seemed to Patrick as if they were all bent on the one journey; all tending towards one destination.

Ah, there was the train. It was coming down the siding, and pulling in to the platform, a porter already running alongside and opening the compartment doors while the carriages were still moving.

'What about your luggage?' said Bart over his shoulder. 'Is it going in the van, or are you taking it into the carriage with you?'

'Just dump it down anywhere,' said Patrick, 'until I see if I can get an empty carriage.'

They had to shout to each other over the heads of other people, because in the rush that took place on all sides, the line of their party was broken. But as, one after the other, Ellie, Angie, Bart, Willie, Mary, and the children, deposited what they had been carrying upon the platform beside him, islanding him around with suitcases and parcels, and then instinctively falling back to stand at a little distance from him, suddenly the sensation that they were one party ebbed away from Patrick, and all the feeling of excitement, all the desire to shout and sing and be rowdy, fell away from him too. He was alone; alone, and setting out upon a journey from which who could say if he would ever return.

Mother?

He looked around for her. How had he brought himself to leave her? Dearer than anyone in the whole world, dearer than anyone had ever been to him, or ever would be, how was he yet able to go away like this, perhaps never to see her again? A stab of absolute agony went through him. But even now, when the light of his ambition was thinnest and most feeble, not for one moment did he think of trying to turn back from the way he had chosen.

Meanwhile the others were getting uneasy.

'We didn't have much time so spare at all,' Mary was saying. 'Hadn't you better find a nice compartment, Patrick, and make sure of a comfortable seat?'

'Here's an empty carriage,' cried Bart, pulling open one door.

'This is a corridor carriage,' cried Willie, opening another.

It almost seemed as if they were hurrying to dispatch him.

'There's no hurry,' he said.

But there was. In all too brief a space, the other passengers had begun to board the train; friends began to cluster around the carriages, doors were slammed, and then, most final of all, the guard suddenly came down the platform locking the carriage doors.

'You'd better take your seat, Patrick,' said Bart.

It was time indeed to do so. Patrick looked straight into Mary's eyes, for the first time since he had told her he was going. She seemed to have been waiting for this moment, and in her eyes was all the desire that she had stifled up to now: the desire to hold out her arms to him and fold him against her breast.

'Son,' she said, 'are you quite sure?'

'About what?' he said, looking back at her; but he knew what she meant.

'That you want to go?'

'But, Mother——'

'I know, I know,' she said hastily. 'But if you wanted to go back on it, the money wouldn't matter.'

For a moment no one said anything. Patrick looked deep into Mary's eyes. Then he turned and looked at Alice.

But at this moment the guard, further down the line, put a whistle to his lips and the whistle of the train gave a long answering blast. And just exactly as if by invisible wires, the sound controlled his limbs, Patrick moved towards the door of the carriage nearest to him, into which, while they were talking, a porter had lifted his bags.

'It's for the best, Mother,' he said when, a moment later, he was inside the train, and the door was closed and locked, and he could talk to them only by leaning out over the window ledge. Already divided from them, already entered into his new world, he was like a person imprisoned in a high tower.

'Well kids?' he said unsteadily to Larry and Rosie, who were on the front row of the little group, that, like a group of mourners now, stood on the platform under him. 'Well? Will you be good youngsters till I come back?'

'Will you send us the postcards you promised?' they countered, speaking both at the same time.

'Send me one of a skyscraper!' said Larry.

'Send me one of the house where you live!' said Rosie.

'He'll live in a skyscraper, silly,' said Larry, turning to Rosie. 'There's nothing but skyscrapers in America, isn't that right, Patrick?'

'I'll tell you that when I get there!' said Patrick. 'But keep back. This train is liable to start moving any minute. Here, wait a minute!' Before Larry lowered himself from the ledge of the carriage upon which he had climbed to raise himself to the height of the window, Patrick put his hand into his pocket, and drew out some small change. Once in a while, in the past, he had given the two youngest members of the family a few coppers; but to-day as he fingered the coins in his hand he hesitated, and then suddenly took a bright silver florin and put it into Larry's hand.

The money was hardly his to squander, and he glanced sheepishly at Mary, but the gesture was a symbol of his hopes, and the measure of the ambition that was sending him forth.

'It will be a sovereign when I'm going next time,' he said, and he beckoned to Rosie. 'I suppose I'll have to give you one too?'

Rosie laughed, and reached up her hand, her face radiant with smiles.

'What do you say? Where are your manners?' said Ellie, who had been engaged in a few words with some friend she encountered on the platform, but who had now come back to the group around Patrick.

'Haven't you anything to say to the rest of us?' she said, a little crossly. She looked at her mother and Angie. 'Why are you letting those youngsters pester him? Hasn't he things to say to us? There!' She made a drive with her handbag as if she would scatter them to one side.

But Patrick leaned outward.

'Leave them alone,' he said. 'They're not doing anyone any harm.' Remembering the way they wanted to ride in the cab, he put his hand in his pocket. 'If I give you another five bob,' he said, 'will you take a cab down as far as the Pillar?' But a look from Ellie soon froze his fingers around the coins.

'I should think you'd have something to say to us,' she said, and she linked Angie conspiratorially. 'I suppose we'll both have changed our names by the time we see you again.'

'I suppose you will,' said Patrick. He was looking at Rosie, but he looked back at Ellie. 'That's all that will be changed about you,' he said. He looked at her for a moment affectionately. They hadn't seen much of each other of late years, but when they were growing up they had been good friends. 'I can't imagine you ever looking any different from the way I see you this minute—or Angie either,' he said, including her in the affection of his glance. 'But it's different with these two,' he said, turning again towards Larry and Rosie. 'I suppose that no matter how soon I come back they'll have changed so much I won't know them.'

'And what about Alice?' It was Rosie who looked up at him, and asked the question with the full simplicity of childhood.

Patrick looked at the friend of his childhood, and he said something, but at that moment a deafening blast of the whistle made it impossible to catch his words.

The train gave a jerk, clanked backwards, reversed itself and moved forward with a shuttle motion. With a steady churning sound it began to steam out of the station.

'You're off!' cried Bart, and there were various exclamations from the others.

Mary stared silently at the moving train that carried so precious a passenger out of her sight. And out of all the incidents that led up to that moment, and which she had borne with such calmness and fortitude, this one, single incident alone seemed incomprehensible: that the train had begun to move. He was gone, and she had said nothing to him. All the fears that had filled her heart in the past two weeks, all the anxieties that had kept her tossing wakeful on her bed at night, returned now, and threw her into a panic. The dangers against which he should have been warned, the exhortations and admonitions that should have been contained in her last parental words with him! Why had she said none of them? In the very last few minutes she had been talking not to him at all, but to Alice. And what had she been saying to Alice? Something so unimportant that already she had forgotten it. Was it possible that, with her son, her first-born, standing beside her, within reach of her hand, but now being borne so rapidly from her, perhaps for ever, she had been talking to a little girl, the daughter of a neighbour in the same street with her, whom she had seen every day since she was born, and whom she was likely to see every day of all the years to come?

'Son!'

If, over the noise of the train, over the boisterous shouting of Rosie and Larry, and the calling of messages by Bart and Ellie and Willie and Angie, she could but penetrate to him with even that one cry, it might speak to him of all the fear and all the love that somehow, although it had occupied her since the day he was born, was yet to this day unexpressed.

'Son!'

It was a faint and forlorn cry, and not only the din and commotion of engine and man, but the very mist and steam of the station seemed to stifle and drown it. And although she could still see Patrick's face, it was only a white flash in the steam and smoke which enwrapped the train as it gathered speed, and sped under the blackened bridge at the end of the platform. Then the steam and smoke became so thick that the flash of that white face was no longer to be seen, and soon the train itself was blotted out of existence. And then, suddenly, the mist was blown away, the steam evaporated, the train no longer blocked the bridge; it was clear of it, speeding into the open spaces beyond, and now, for the last time, like the arm of a swimmer far out to sea, those on the platform saw an arm upthrust.

The O'Gradys waved, although indeed it was not certain that that upflung hand belonged at all to Patrick.

PART IV

Bart and Ellie

'DON'T think, Mother,' said Bart, as they came out of the station, drifting aimlessly in the direction of the city, 'don't think that we are going to let you go home without us to-night.' For as they sauntered out of the station, Mary had said that the young people did not need to come all the way back to the house on her account; there might be something they'd like to do. But taking her arm, Bart drew it under his, linking her to him with an affectionate gesture.

In the distance, they could still detect the pulse of the engine that pulled Patrick's train, sleeper by sleeper, out of the city, but every minute the sound grew fainter, and the noise of the traffic gradually smothered it. Then, a large horse-drawn dray rattled down the street, over the cobblestones, deafening them to all else, and after it had passed into the station yard, their ears might seek in vain for the throb of the vanished train. It was gone, now; gone out of the city, a minute black shape, crawling like a caterpillar through the country-side, now between high grassy banks, now measuring its length against a stretch of flat water, now running abreast a white road, and now seeming to burrow under the earth, as it met, and passed under, a bridge, and finally speeding through large flat pasture lands, where cattle with grotesque bucketing gait and ridiculous tails like stuffed stockings threw up their heels in fright and fled at its approach.

'There is no need for anyone to come with me,' said Mary again.

She had kept up well all evening, for the sake of the others, but all she wanted now was to get home, and then? Well, she didn't quite know what she would do after that, but whatever it might be, she would be safe and secure in her own home, with the doors closed, and the world shut out from her.

'You can leave me as far as the tram,' she conceded reluctantly to Bart. 'You people can take your time and come home slowly,' she added, appealing to Ellie. 'You might like to walk.' She looked about her again. 'It's a lovely evening for a walk.'

It was a beautiful evening. High over the city roofs the sky was dappled with pink and yellow clouds, small, and delicately moulded, until the sky seemed like a shell-strewn shore, and gazing upwards, one was filled with sensations of pleasure.

Looking around them, the O'Gradys were silent for a minute; but Ellie's face was troubled. She was the first to break the silence.

'Are you sure you'll be all right, Mother?' she said.

Ellie had been undecided about what they would do after they left the station. Setting out together had been all right; they were all strung up, then, and excited, but now, even here in this strange part of the city where no one knew them, she had begun to feel that they were making themselves conspicuous, there were so many of them. And that Alice Maguire! What need had there been for her to tack herself on to them?

But Alice, it appeared, did not intend to stay with them.

'I'll go home with Mrs. O'Grady,' she cried, eagerly linking Mary on the other side from Bart.

'Oh, Alice, that's awfully nice of you,' said Angie, who had lagged behind with Willie, but who at this point drew level with them again, so that to Ellie's annoyance there was now again one long line stringing out over the entire path, Larry having to walk unevenly, with one leg up and one leg down, between the pavement and the gutter.

'Are you sure you don't mind, Alice?' said Ellie, feeling constrained to say it, but turning almost immediately she pulled Bart's sleeve. 'That child will be run over,' she said. 'What is the need for us all to walk in one line?'

By this time they had reached a street crossing, and, in the distance, Mary caught sight of a tram teetering down a distant line of rails that glinted greenly in the evening light. For a moment she pressed Alice's hand, and then she slipped her own arm free.

'You'll do no such thing, Alice!' she said. 'You'll stay and enjoy yourself with the others. Where are the children? Come now!' With a beckon she motioned them to her side, and but for the grip Bart still had upon her other arm, she was ready to leave them. When she attempted to draw her arm from his, however, Bart only tightened his hold.

'Ellie,' he said, and he pointed to Mary's arm locked in his own. 'Now is our chance. You know we never can get your mother to come out with us, but now we have her, and surely we're not going to let her go home?'

'Oh! I don't know that Mother would like to stay out with us,' said Ellie, looking at her young man, and speaking about Mary as if either she were not there at all, or she spoke another language. 'I think she'd probably prefer to go home.' She turned to Mary. 'Wouldn't you, Mother?' she said.

But Bart wasn't going to be put aside.

'Look here,' he said, 'we'll put it this way. Either your mother comes with us, or none of us go. Either she comes with us, or we all go home with her. How's that?' And looking around him, he questioned the others.

'Hear, hear!' said Willie Haslip, and, having had her sweetheart's approbation for a plan that had filled her with joy, there and then, in the street Angie put her arm around her mother's waist.

'Oh, Mother!' she cried. 'Say you'll come with us.' Her face was aglow with happiness. 'Where will we go, Bart?' she cried, turning to him.

'Wait a minute; wait a minute; let me speak, please,' cried Bart, trying to answer Angie's excited question over the din caused by Larry and Rosie, who had only just apprehended the importance to them of Mary's decision.

'Oh, Mother! Stay, won't you!'

'Please, please!'

'You put me in a very awkward position,' said Mary at last, looking from one animated face to another, but catching sight of Ellie's face, less eager than the others, she grew firm again in her resolve to go home.

'It would be very silly for me to stay,' she said. 'I have a lot of things to do at home, whereas you young people——' She looked at Bart, but Bart, although he still held her fast by the arm, was not looking at her.

'Ellie!' said Bart. 'You talk to her!'

Had he seen the slight reluctance in Ellie's face? Had her mother seen it? A feeling of shame came over Ellie. If only there weren't so many of them! That Alice Maguire! And the children! They made such a crowd! she thought. But under Bart's glance she felt ill at ease, and she put out her hand, and linked Mary, and putting aside all her hesitations and scruples, she turned to Bart, and looked confidently at him.

'What is the need of talking to her?' she said. 'We have her here now between us, and we won't let her escape from us.'

Yes; she was right. There had been a curious look in Bart's eyes. because now, looking into them, Ellie saw that unfamiliar glint melt away again, to be replaced by the old familiar look of approbation and pride.

'Now what have you to say for yourself, Mother?' said the young man.

'Well, I seem to be in your hands,' said Mary weakly.

'That's settled so,' said Bart. 'The next thing to decide,' he said, looking over his shoulder at the others who had been forced to walk behind them, as they moved down nearer to the centre of the city and the streets became more crowded, 'the next thing to decide is where will we go? Has anyone any suggestions?'

'What's wrong with the Palais?'

It was just like Angie, thought Ellie, to suggest the wrong place. All her irritation returned. The Palais was where they usually went for supper, Angie and Willie, and she and Bart, but somehow it didn't seem the place for them to go now when there were so many of them; such a crowd.

As a matter of fact she had been reluctant to go there herself at first, because it was the haunt of the University students, and she felt that even she and Angie might be out of place there. That was a foolish idea, however, that had quickly been forgotten, but now she looked critically at her mother's black mourning clothes that gave her a heavy, matronly appearance that fitted neither her face nor her figure. And then the youngsters! She looked at Larry and Rosie. That young fellow is getting gawkier every day, she thought with vexation, as her eye fell on her young brother, and as for Rosie, she had to refrain from looking at the child because assuredly if she had got her dress stained, it would be all she could do not to slap her there in the street.

But Bart was looking at her again.

'Well,' he said, 'will we go to the Palais?'

Was there again a challenge in his eyes?

'I don't mind,' said Ellie. 'The Palais is all right.'

'Good!' said Bart, and he smiled at her again.

How different we are from each other, really, in spite of everything, she thought, looking at Bart as they began to move down towards the Parnell Monument, near which the little restaurant was situated. Some frigidity and fastidiousness in her made her shrink from this exposure of themselves in a public restaurant. She did not like Bart to be seen with her like this, among all her people. It seemed so familiar; so intimate. It seemed to strike so much of a family note.

When they were married, doubtless there would be times when she and Bart would have to be seen with the others, but that would be different; then it would not be so embarrassing. Not that Bart was embarrassed: he seemed only too eager to run ahead, only too eager to anticipate all that was to come. Even the children, who were getting boisterous and noisy, seemed to amuse him, and he encouraged rather than discouraged them. And unless her ears deceived her, Ellie fancied he was addressing her mother as intimately as if they were at home. He was calling her 'Mother.'

It was as if he could not wait, but was throwing himself recklessly forward, into the turmoil and stress of the future.

But it hasn't come yet! thought Ellie, with one of the strange spasms of antagonism towards Bart for which she could not account, since they seemed always to be accompanied by the most contradictory desires, such as those which, now that they were inside the restaurant, made her push Alice aside almost rudely in order to sit by his side. Because Alice was stupid enough for anything; she was quite capable of seating herself down beside Bart, or between Angie and Willie. There! She knew it. Angie and Willie were separated. Fortunately they didn't seem to mind. Still, that wasn't the point. Ellie stared at Alice. What on earth did her mother see in the creature. She had always been pushing her at Patrick. It was a good thing Patrick had his head screwed on too well to have anything to do with an insipid creature like that. He'd probably marry some girl in America; some girl with plenty of money.

When they were all seated at last, Ellie felt better. Once seated they were not so conspicuous. And she could not help feeling pleased at the sight of her mother, so simple, and so happy, sitting among them all, and presiding over the big pot of tea that was presently set in front of them. To think that I grudged her this treat, she thought with compunction. To think that if I had my way she would have gone home to the empty house!

Ellie's remorse smote her the more since the restaurant was almost deserted.

What can I do, she thought, to make her enjoy the evening? But apart from the negative act of refraining from saying anything to hurt or upset her, she could think of nothing.

Above all, we won't mention my wedding, she resolved, and anxious to find her way back into the conversation from which she had wandered away, she tried to catch something that Alice was saying, and to which the others did not seem to be listening.

'What did you say, Alice?' she asked.

'I said we wouldn't feel the time passing now until your wedding, Ellie.'

She might have known! With a look of exasperation too great for words, Ellie turned away from Alice to look anxiously at her mother. But to her surprise Mary did not seem to be in any way disturbed.

'We'll have to begin to think of getting your clothes ready, Ellie,' she said.

Poor Ellie! It wasn't her doing that the conversation had taken this direction. It was as if the whole family had waited only until Patrick was gone to break into excited talk about the next event. It was as if their interest in it, too long stifled and suppressed, rushed forth headlong now; everyone wanting to talk at the same time. And Mary's face, that Ellie feared to find saddened by thoughts of the wedding, seemed instead to have softened.

'Is it to be a white wedding?' Alice asked over the din of the other voices.

It was Mary who answered Alice.

'If I had my way it would be a white wedding, Alice,' she said. 'She'd look lovely in a wreath and veil.'

'She'll look lovely in whatever she wears,' said Bart. And at his words, Mary's face was wreathed in smiles.

'Blue is a nice colour for a wedding,' she conceded.

'And Ellie looks lovely in blue,' said Angie, looking at her sister. 'I love your blue silk dress, the one with the white polka dots all over it.'

'Do you?' said Ellie, and it seemed, as she looked around the table at them, that all her family, even Larry and Rosie, were gazing at her with love and pride. Angie's words seemed to speak from every eye.

We love you in your blue polka dot, said their eyes. We love you in everything you say and do. You are the proudest flower in our garden.

How generous they were. How could she ever have been ashamed of them, even for a moment? How could she have wished the evening to have been other than it was?

'Do you like it, Angie?' she said, meaning the polka dot dress. 'Because I'll leave it to you when I go away.' And then as Angie protested, she pressed it upon her the more urgently. 'I'll be getting so many new clothes,' she said. 'And you'll have my side of the wardrobe to fill now as well as your own.'

'Oh, Ellie, I'll miss you.'

The thought of that crowded wardrobe where they had battled for space for their dresses, on so many, many occasions, brought a lump to Angie's throat.

'I'll leave you lots more things too,' said Ellie recklessly. 'You can have my blue coat, and my white jacket with the silver buttons. I won't ever wear them again.'

Dear Angie; Ellie wanted to give, and give, and give to her. Then she turned and looked at her mother. There were none of her things she could give to her mother, but she knew what would please her, and so she put her hand under Rosie's chin.

'Rosie,' she said, 'I'll give you my pink silk blouse, and my pink petticoat, and Mother can make them over into something nice for you.'

To Rosie, Ellie's words were like a dream, particularly as she was drowsy with sleep.

'Oh, Ellie!' she murmured ecstatically.

There was only Alice now left ungarlanded.

'I'd leave you something, Alice, only your mother buys everything you want.'

'Oh, Ellie, I wouldn't dream of taking anything from you,' cried Alice, 'but if there was anything you were throwing away——' She paused, and then she went on breathlessly, 'Mother is so good,' she said, 'she buys me everything, as you say, but she always picks things for me herself, because she says I haven't developed a good taste for clothes yet.'

Poor Alice, this was a long speech. Ellie stated at her for a moment, and then she laughed.

'Oh, I see what you mean,' she said. 'You'd like a little of my vulgar finery for a change!'

'Oh, Ellie, I meant no such thing!' cried Alice, but they were all laughing now so gaily that she wasn't able to make herself heard at all.

'Can I get a word in edgeways, I wonder,' said Bart at last, through the laughter. 'It's all very well for you women to spend the evening talking about finery and furbelows, but there's another important matter to be discussed.'

'Not here; not at this hour, I hope,' said Ellie, for Rosie's head was nodding to one side. The child would fall asleep in another minute.

'I just want to mention it,' said Bart, and he turned to Mary. 'Did you know, Mother,' he said, 'that your daughter here,' and he nodded his head at Ellie, 'refuses to have a honeymoon? What do you think of that! You think it's bad enough that she refuses to wear a wreath and veil. Well, I don't mind that. But I think I've stood enough anarchy when she refuses to come on a honeymoon!'

'Why——' Mary turned in some surprise to Ellie, but her voice was drowned again in the chorus of surprise from the rest of the party.

'Well!' said Ellie, looking at them defiantly, and then looking crossly at Bart, as much as to say that he had no right to give away this secret. She would have explained things in her own way when she was ready to do so; her eyes flashed.

'It's a waste of money,' she said limply, at last.

'Do you hear that?' cried Bart, appealing to Mary. 'Surely that is my worry, and if I want to spend a little money at that time above all, I think I ought to be allowed to do it.'

'There are plenty of things on which you can spend your money,' said Ellie.

'That may be true,' said Bart. 'But here's another question. What about a holiday? I've been postponing my holidays all the year to give myself a good, long honeymoon!'

'Oh, there's nothing to prevent you from taking your holidays at that time,' said Ellie. 'As a matter of fact it would be a good idea to take them then; there'll be so much to do in the new house; the garden will be in a dreadful state, judging by the condition it's in now.'

'Do you see what I'm up against?' said Bart, throwing out his hands in mock appeal to Mary. 'The fact of the matter is, Mrs. O'Grady, that it's the house she's marrying, and not me at all.'

'It is a dear little house,' said Alice, with a sigh.

'I wish——' said Angie, but she didn't finish her sentence, and under the tablecloth, across the thin knees of Alice, she felt for Willie's hand and held it for an instant.

'I think it's only proper,' said Ellie, 'to start life together in our own home, instead of in some ugly, cheap hotel.'

'But you're not serious, Ellie?' said Mary. 'Every young couple goes away for a while after the wedding, even for a few days.'

'And why?' challenged Ellie. 'Because most people are sheep. What one does, they all must do. And what about yourself, Mother? You didn't have a honeymoon!'

'Oh, that was a different matter,' said Mary, her face suffused with colour. 'I came straight up from the country. Dublin was new to me. It was as good as a honeymoon.'

'And so it will be to us,' cried Ellie, her eyes shining across at Bart.

'I see her point in a way, you know,' said Bart meditatively. 'It would be a different matter to go away for a few days later in the year when——'

'When nobody could sneer at us and make fools of us,' said Ellie.

'But what on earth makes you imagine anyone would sneer at you?' cried Mary.

'Oh, that's all you know about it, Mother,' said Ellie. 'You're so innocent, Mother. I don't know how things were in your day, but if you only knew the things I've heard. There was a girl in my class at the commercial college, and she told me about her honeymoon. She said she was never so miserable in her life; she thought she'd never get home.'

'But I don't understand!' said Mary.

'Oh, vulgar jokes, and that sort of thing,' said Ellie, reddening.

'Oh, how I'd hate that!' exclaimed Angie, and looking across Alice, she exchanged glances with Willie Haslip.

They looked exceptionally young, Mary thought, Angie and Willie, sitting, as usual, more silent than the others, with the curious expression on their faces that she had seen before, as if they were waiting for something; but they were losing nothing of what was going on at the same time. It was almost as if, in Bart and Ellie, they had found their mentors in some wonderful art, that they dared not yet to practise by themselves.

It must be getting late, she thought suddenly, turning back to Bart, who ever since the moment that Patrick's train had left the platform seemed to have become the head of the household. Then, as she stared at him, she glanced involuntarily at Larry. Would her younger son ever be to her what Patrick had been? She looked at his thin white face, and his eyes that looked darker now, under the strain of the late hour. He was nearly fourteen. At that age Patrick had been as broad as his father; not as tall perhaps, but all the stronger, all the sturdier for that. Larry was going to be tall, but it wasn't a quality Mary particularly admired in a man unless, like Bart, he had the girth to carry his height. Why was Larry so thin? She couldn't understand it. He had been reared like the rest of them, but for some reason he had not developed in the same way. He is indoors too much, she thought. He's always woolgathering. She frowned.

'Hadn't we better make a start for home?' she said abruptly. 'This young man will have to be up for school in the morning.' She turned to Alice. 'Your mother will be worried about you, child,' she said.

'Oh, not when I'm with you, Mrs. O'Grady!' said Alice. 'And that reminds me,' she added, 'she told me to tell you how sorry she was for you; about Patrick, I mean!'

Patrick! It was the only mention of him that had been made all evening. As Bart helped her on with her coat, Ellie threw another glance of contempt at the luckless Alice, who fortunately had her back turned. What need was there to remind them of Patrick just now, when they had succeeded so well all evening in distracting their mother from thinking of him?

When, however, a moment later they left the warm atmosphere of the restaurant, and stepped out into the dark street, the chill night wind upon their faces was like the slap of a wave, and it is doubtful if the thought of Patrick could have been far from any of their minds, except perhaps Rosie's, who was so drowsy now that, although she was able to walk, she did so like a rag doll, propped under both arms, and her legs, every minute, going limp under her.

'It's a calm night, anyway,' said Angie, feeling that vague fears assailed her mother.

Patrick was hardly midway across the country as yet, but somehow, in all their minds, it was impossible not to think of him as already far out to sea, and since they had never seen the sea, save where it tamely washed the shallow shores of Sandymount, they imagined it as a dark and heaving mass of turbulent waves, threatening ever to engulf the frail vessels that set out upon it.

'It's calm here anyway,' said Mary, a shudder passing through her body, 'but I always heard that when it's calm on land it's often rough and stormy at sea. Did you ever hear that, Bart?'

Bart was emphatic. 'I did not,' he said. 'And furthermore, I don't believe it's true. There is a lot of nonsense talked about the sea, by people who know nothing about it.'

'I suppose you're right,' said Mary, but that she was not convinced was shown a few minutes later. 'What about icebergs?' she said.

'Oh, Mother!' Both together, Ellie and Bart came to a stop. 'If you're going to let yourself think of things like that!' cried Ellie.

But Bart was more practical.

'There's no such thing as an iceberg now,' he said, 'or at least there's no such thing as a floating iceberg. There are special ships now, to patrol the seas, and keep a lookout for them, and if they come across one, they send out radio messages that can be picked up by any vessels in the vicinity. In the meantime they set about blowing it up; blasting it out of existence. They're equipped for the purpose.' It was an engineer speaking; Mary listened respectfully.

'For that matter,' cried Bart, seeing that he had gained her attention, 'the liners themselves are equipped in nearly every case nowadays to deal with eventualities that would have been the end of a ship not so long ago.' He pressed Mary's arm closer. 'I'm surprised at you, Mrs. O'Grady,' he said, 'to be so old-fashioned, with your talk about icebergs and storms. Those are all things of the past. When do we ever hear now of a disaster at sea? Why, they're so safe nowadays the next thing will be that people will be bored with sea travel and look for something more exciting; something with a bit of a thrill to it! Yes! Wait till you see! The next thing we know they'll be going by aeroplane. It's been done already, you know. The whole world will be at it soon. Think of it! Three thousand miles in the air without any chance of landing or refuelling. Man! That would be an adventure!'

An excited glow came into his face. The topic enthralled him.

'Mother!' he cried. 'Wait till you have a letter from Patrick one of these days, telling you that he's coming home in an aeroplane!'

'God forbid!' cried Mary in fright, and then, overcome by the thought that a day would probably come when, by some means or other, he would come back to her, the first tears she had shed since she had heard of his going welled into her eyes, but she winked them aside, for there was a tram coming towards them and Bart was hailing it, and a minute later she was sitting bolt upright in the brightly lighted tram, and forced to concern herself with the problem of Rosie.

For the dark night streets through which they had sauntered had seemed like the streets of a dream to Rosie, and she had been led along, as if in her sleep, moving effortlessly. Now, being lifted suddenly into the brightly lighted tram was like being awakened violently and unpleasantly. Digging her fists into her eyes, and rubbing them until they were red and sore, she struggled in Bart's arms, and began to get crosser and crankier every minute, pulling away from anyone who touched her or tried to make a suggestion for her comfort.

'No. I don't want to sit there,' she cried, crossly and pettishly, when Angie tried to make room for her on the seat beside her. 'Leave me alone. Go away, you,' she cried to Alice, always her friend in daylight.

'No, no, let me alone,' she screamed, when Willie Haslip tried to take her on his knee.

'She's overtired,' said Mary desperately to Bart, to Ellie, to the conductor, to the whole tram.

'We'll have to take her off the tram,' cried Ellie, her cheeks aflame, and her embarrassment turning into anger, against everyone, Mary included. 'I don't know why she was let stay up till this hour!' she cried. What would Bart think!

Bart, however, was the one person who did not seem to mind at all.

'What sort of nonsense is that?' he said, turning towards Ellie with a frown. 'Get off the tram? Why should we do that? We paid our fare, didn't we? Well!' He glared around the tram. 'If there is anyone unnatural enough to object to a little child that's tired out and nearly asleep, well! then let them get off and wait for another tram. Too much excitement! That's the trouble. And——' Bart turned to Ellie—'I suppose you never opened your mouth when you were her age?' he said. As Rosie's outbursts were more fitful now, he engaged Mary's glance. 'I suppose you never had a moment's trouble with Ellie, ma'am?' he said. But Ellie was still cross. She sat screwed up in the corner, looking at Rosie as if at any minute she would reach across and give her a good slap. Suddenly Bart took her hand, and leaning towards her, he whispered something in her ear.

'Oh, Bart!' All at once the hard spots of anger in Ellie's cheeks were diffused into a soft mist of colour that flooded her face all over, and forgetting Rosie, she looked up at him with shining eyes. 'Oh, Bart!'

'Ssh!' said Mary. For with one more blink Rosie had fallen asleep.

Now we're worse than ever, thought Ellie. But her more immediate concern was with the dark landscape beyond the tram window.

'Where are we, I wonder?' she asked again, as she rubbed the misty glass with her little glove and peered out. 'Oh, my goodness, we get out at the next stop,' she cried, and she looked with dismay at the sleeping Rosie, who had now slumped down until she was almost lying on the seat opposite.

Mary began to gather up her things.

'Will I wake her, I wonder?' she said.

But Bart stood up.

'Leave her to me,' he said, and as the tram drew to a stop, motioning the others to alight, he gathered up the sleeping child in his arms and then stepped carefully down into the street. She did not waken. 'Tell the others to go ahead,' he said, whispering to Ellie. 'We'll take it easy. Poor little thing,' he said, looking down into the child's face with an inscrutable expression upon his own.

The child's head had settled softly into place on his shoulder, and from her softly parted lips there came only a sleepy and incomprehensible murmur.

'There's no sense in waking her now,' he said. 'I'll carry her as far as the house and we'll put her down in her little bed. She won't give another stir until morning!'

Then, keeping behind the others, the young couple began to walk along the street.

Only dimly could they see the others, ahead of them in the darkness except when they passed into the yellow circles of light that underlay the infrequent street lamps. Then for an instant they could see the light flash of Alice's blue dress.

Because of the sleeping child, they themselves were silent, but a

current seemed to pass through them, so that the least movement of
one caused some chord to throb and vibrate within the other, and as
they, in their turn, passed into the circle of light under each lamp post,
they sought each other's eyes.

At the last lamp-post of all, however, forgetting their caution, or
throwing it to the winds, Ellie put her hand on Bart's sleeve, and her
voice was sharp and urgent.

'Wouldn't it be terrible, Bart, if we didn't have any children?' she
cried.

Her voice was so plaintive the young man came to a standstill. He
looked anxiously at her.

'What makes you say a thing like that?' he said, and his own voice
was sharp and urgent.

Ellie was looking at him with strange unfathomable gaze.

'I don't know,' she said, in a low agonized voice. She looked
around her at the enclosing darkness that, except for the medallion
of yellow light in which they stood, seemed to menace them like a
malevolent force. 'It's only,' she said, speaking haltingly, and shivering in the middle of a word, 'it's only that this——' she made a vague
gesture that included all three of them—'seems so unreal.'

'Oh, is that all?' There was relief in Bart's voice as, abruptly
shifting the weight of Rosie, so that she gave a little cry of protest,
he stepped out of the circle of light again into the last stretch of
the darkness that lay between them and the O'Gradys' lighted door
that Mary had left open for them. 'What you need is a good sleep,
my girl,' he said, 'to put an end to your foolish fancies. No children,
indeed. Wait till you see, my dear. Wait till this time next year!'

But Ellie's fancies had fled. Facing him in the lighted doorway, her
eyes flashed with their more habitual fire and spirit.

'There's no need to be familiar, Bart,' she said, and putting out her
arms, she suddenly caught hold of the unfortunate Rosie, and
snatching her out of the arms of her betrothed, she bundled her up
in her own arms. 'I'll carry her upstairs,' she said. 'And you can take
yourself home as fast as you like!'

No good night; no handshake; not as much as the lightest touch
of her cheek against his, that she sometimes bestowed upon him, with
a swift rush. Nothing but a tilt to her chin and a flash of her eyes and
she was gone.

That was Ellie. Bart looked after her for a moment as she went into
the hall, making straight for the stairs with Rosie in her arms, her
ankles twinkling for a minute, before she vanished into the darkness
at the top of the stairs.

That was Ellie. Life with her would never be upon an even plane. They would scale the high pinnacles and gaze upon the shining upper reaches, but as suddenly they would be dashed to the earth again. But that was the way he wanted it to be; that was what had attracted him to her from the first moment he had seen her—had he not divined it in the changing aspects of her face?—her rich capacity for all that life had to offer; the sufferings as well as the pleasure. She was so unlike Angie, he thought, as he walked slowly away from the door because he knew that in a few minutes Willie Haslip, having ascertained that he was not going into the house, would have said good night to Angie and hurried out into the street to overtake him.

How strangely lives were shaped, he thought. There was Willie Haslip, and in all likelihood he and Angie would end by uniting their destinies. Yet, only for him, Willie would probably never have laid eyes on Angie.

Was he coming? He looked back. There was no sign of him. He strolled onward. As he reached the lamp-post under which Ellie had poured out her foolish fears about the future, he stood for a moment, but the circle of light, like a fairy ring in the blackness, gave him a curiously nervous feeling, foreign to his practical, rational nature.

I wish this fellow would hurry up, he thought, watching the vacant space of light of the O'Grady doorway in the hope of seeing Willie appear in it. A curious feeling of affection for his friend came over him. They had been together since they were little boys, sitting together on the same school bench. Although he was only a bare year older than the other, Bart had a feeling of responsibility towards him that, for some reason, was at that moment heightened, until, as he waited for him in the dark street, it became almost oppressive, and he felt that in some way he was indeed the very author of the other's destiny.

Angie is a sweet and gentle girl anyway, he thought, recalling again that he had been the cause of Willie's having met her. Then, seeing two figures outlined for a moment in the golden doorway, he put his fingers to his lips and gave a short clear whistle, that sounded in the darkness like the shrill note of a bird.

Instantly, the two figures fell apart, one to remain for a few moments transfixed in light, the other dropping into the darkness.

~   ~   ~   ~

'Do you remember the night that Patrick went away?' said Bart one Saturday afternoon, as he came into the house, unannounced, letting himself in by the string on the latch like one of the family.

Mary looked up. Why was he so excited? He had taken Ellie by the hand.

Mary laid down her work, and Larry looked up from his books. The whole family was listening. Bart looked around him.

'Do you remember we were talking about the way aeroplanes were making such headway? You do! Well, what did I see in the papers to-day but a notice saying that some English company has brought over a few planes to this country and they're going to give pleasure trips, by the day, back and forth across Ireland. The first one is this afternoon. Just think of it. You can step into the plane in the Pheonix Park and in a few minutes you'd be looking down on the Shannon, and in another few minutes you'd be over Galway or Cork. It's a kind of stunt, I suppose,' he said, 'to advertise the planes, but that doesn't mean they're giving free runs. In fact the charges are going to be pretty steep, I hear. But I thought——'

Almost giddy with excitement, he turned to Ellie: so excited was he indeed that he hardly saw the desperate way she was signalling to him with her eyes to change the subject.

Just in time, before he began to speak again, she moved over to him.

'Be careful,' she whispered. 'Mother wouldn't hear of such a thing!'

But he hadn't said anything. Amazed, he looked into Ellie's eyes.

'How did you know what was in my mind?' he asked softly.

Ellie didn't deign to answer him except with her eyes. Why wouldn't I know! said her eyes. Aren't we, who are alike in so many ways, alike most of all in this: our love of danger and excitement?

That was true.

Bart looked at her with love and pride.

But Mary was looking suspiciously at them.

'They'll get no one in Dublin to go up in the air!' she said, tartly.

'Oh, you'll find they will, Mother!' said Bart, but he tried not to be too emphatic because Ellie was still nudging him to be careful.

'You'd want to be out of your mind, if you ask me!' said Mary, 'before you'd take your life in your hands by going up in one of those things.'

'Oh, I don't know about that,' said Bart, and in spite of the way Ellie was pressing his arm, and trying to keep him calm, the glow of excitement with which he had entered the house had faded and he was getting irritated.

'I'm afraid I don't look on this matter in the same light as you do, Mrs. O'Grady,' he said, argumentatively. Surely this was one province in which he might be supposed to have some knowledge: some authority of opinion. 'It's just——' He hesitated.

'——just what?' said Mary.

'——just a difference of generation,' said Bart reluctantly, but firmly.

'I see.' In spite of herself, Mary admired the firm stand he took in the matter, but she was not prepared to give in to him. 'I must say——' she began, but Ellie interrupted her.

'We can't stay behind the times, you know, Mother,' she said severely. 'And I don't suppose they would be allowed to fly the planes at all unless it was safe.'

But here Bart felt compelled to intervene.

'I don't know so much about that,' he said. 'If there's any danger you go into it with your eyes open. But that's not the point. The point is that in my opinion there is very little danger. Just the same,' he said, seeing a situation arising between Mary and Ellie which, if it was allowed to develop, would cast a shadow over the afternoon for all of them, 'just the same, there's something in what your mother says, Ellie. As far as we're concerned, anyway. After all, we have the whole of our lives ahead of us to do as we please. I suppose it wouldn't be a bad idea to wait and see how things develop. There may be a great improvement in aircraft within the next few years.'

But something had been stirred in Ellie, some obstinate daring streak that he was beginning to know so well and that he could not help admiring.

'If everyone were to take that attitude,' she cried, 'there wouldn't be much chance of it getting very far.'

'That's right too,' said Bart, unable to resist the admiration he felt for her courage.

But all the others were against them.

'I'd let someone else take the chance,' said Willie Haslip.

'Someone sick of life,' said Angie; 'someone who didn't care whether the plane crashed or not.'

'Is there anyone in the whole world that would feel like that?' asked Mary.

'I bet there are plenty!' said Larry suddenly, and at this cynical remark from one so young they all had to laugh.

'But seriously,' said Bart, 'I don't think the dangers are so great. It's really very safe,' he said, turning to Mary. 'It's surprising how few crashes there are; in proportion to the number of motor accidents—'

But here Willie Haslip interrupted.

'If you do have an accident, though, that's the end of you!' he cried.

Ellie turned and looked contemptuously at him.

'Some people set such value on their own skins!' she said.

'Ellie O'Grady!' Angie's pale face flamed.

What misfortune had made him mention the cursed planes at all, thought Bart? He had set the whole family by the ears. Here was Angie, the angel of the family, and never before had he heard such an acrimonious note in her voice.

'Oh, let's forget about it,' he said, putting out his hands as if he were soothing a crowd of children.

And then, unexpectedly, it was Mary herself who made the suggestion that altered everything.

'I must admit it would be very exciting to be up in the Park this afternoon. I suppose the whole world will be there; out of curiosity, to get a sight of the aeroplanes near at hand. I'd enjoy that myself. That's harmless enough. Why don't you all do that: go up to the Park to see the fun?'

'Will we?'

The same question was in every mouth.

'I don't see why you wouldn't,' said Mary. After the crossness she was glad to see them so happy and so excited. 'What will you wear, girls?' she asked. 'I'm sure it will be cold up there in the Phoenix Park.'

'It will be windy,' said Ellie. 'It's on such a height, you know,' she said, as she put up her hand to her hair. 'Do you think I ought to wear my hat?'

'And a veil? Why don't you wear a veil?' said Angie. 'That's what I'm going to wear.'

In a few minutes the two girls had veils tied around their hats and they were ready to depart. At the door they paused.

'Oh, Mother! Would you come with us?'

Mary drew back into the hallway.

'We'll tell you all about it,' Bart promised.

'So long, Mother!' cried Ellie. 'We won't be too late.'

Angie was the last to say good-bye.

'Where's Larry?' she asked. 'Is he coming?'

Mary laughed. Larry was not only ready, but he had preceded them, and was impatiently waiting for them a couple of hundred yards down the street.

Mary looked after them, but at that moment, over the tops of the houses on the other side of the street, far up in the sky, she saw one of the aeroplanes. It was like a tiny insect, a fly perhaps, but it made a hum that, although faint, was so insistent that over all the noise of the city it took, and held, the ear.

Mary looked at it, fascinated. Now it glinted and glistened. Now it darkened and grew leaden. It changed with every instant. She leaned out and gazed upwards. Now it was a silver cross, shining and shimmering above the clouds. Now as it passed under the clouds, it was a little black cross. And now, flashing out again into the open, it shone again like silver, until suddenly it passed like an arrow into the bosom of a great, soft cloud and then, although for a time she heard the drone of its engine, it was gone, and she could not see it any more.

She turned back to her work. Before the girls went out they had cleared away the remains of the midday meal, and carrying the used dishes into the scullery, they had washed and dried them with dispatch, and left them back upon the dresser. But Mary's eye fell upon the table that had not been cleared of crumbs. And what was that? Making a face, she rubbed her foot along the floor under the table. Sugar on the floor! That was one thing she couldn't stand. Really she would have preferred if the girls had left the kitchen the way it was, and gone out and enjoyed themselves without delay. She was always telling them that it was better to leave a thing undone than to do it badly. Her mind went back over the way they had cleared the table, carrying everything out to the scullery in one precarious tottering load, and then, dumping the dishes into the sink, they had set to work with a frightful clatter to wash and dry them. In a few seconds they had brought them back into the kitchen, and arranged them in their places upon the dresser. How could they have been properly washed and dried in that time? She would have to take down all the cups and saucers and examine them to make sure they were properly washed.

At last, however, having gone over all that the girls had done, perversely, Mary felt better disposed towards them, and putting on the kettle to boil, with a view to taking a cup of tea, she sat down at the kitchen window and gave herself up to thinking about them.

Perhaps after all it was a silly notion to go all the way up to the Park to see those aeroplanes, she thought. It would have been better to take a tram ride out to the sea, or out Rathfarnham way, where it was quiet and nice, and sit down on a bank somewhere and enjoy the sun. But of course, no one would have seen them if they did that, and there would be a big crowd of people up in the Park. That had to be taken into consideration. And there was no doubt about it, no one could blame them for wanting to be seen. She had never seen them looking so well. Blue suited them. Angie had looked a bit pale, as usual, but there was no need to worry about it. She used to worry about it at one time, but since the child had left school, and someone or other said it suited her to look pale, she had been reluctantly forced to agree it was true, and she had gradually ceased to worry about it.

I bet a few heads will turn to look after them, she thought, and, as she pictured the four of them, the two pretty girls, and the two strong healthy young men, strolling among a crowd of admiring strangers, she lost the last vestiges of her feeling that it was a foolish outing.

And there was no doubt about it that Larry would have the time of his life with them. He wouldn't have got much fun out of a tram ride, or a walk in the country. Probably they took that into consideration. They were very good to the boy. Every Saturday they took him with them, wherever they went. She could not say whether it was the girls who suggested it or the young men, but it was very nice of them all to consent to have him with them. A further wave of approbation for the absent ones washed over Mary. It wasn't every couple that would be bothered with a gawky young boy hanging after them everywhere they went.

Ah there, the kettle was singing. Mary took the teapot and began to pour a stream of water on to the tea leaves in her old earthenware pot.

They were good girls, both of them, and they deserved their good fortune in finding such nice young men. Bart in particular, Mary liked, although she hastily averred that Willie was just as nice as him, and suited Angie, they were both so quiet and so serious. But there was such life about Bart. He did her good, just by calling at the house for a minute.

She took a sip of tea. Was it really true, as Bart said, that aeroplanes would be as common as motor cars some day? Could it be possible that people would think nothing of crossing the Atlantic in them? She supposed indeed that they might. People stopped at nothing nowadays. She shook her head. And yet it was extraordinary how one got used to things. Take Patrick, for example. She had been so full of fear at the thought of his crossing the ocean, and yet he was no sooner gone than her fears for his crossing it were as nothing compared with her fears for how he would fare upon the other side of it.

She glanced at the calendar. He had already been gone three weeks and a day now, if she calculated correctly. They might soon expect a letter from him. He said he would write every week, and Patrick was not the kind to break his promise. Any day now she might hold in her hands a letter from him. A letter from Patrick!

And so as she sat there, a kind of wonderment came over Mary, and she saw that in some curious way her sorrow had turned into a source of joy.

And there was another thing—although she had dreaded his going, now that he was gone she found that with him had gone a host of small groundless fears about him that had troubled her rest ever since the moment she had given birth to him: a male child. Girls she had felt capable of handling, but a boy was a different matter. From the first, she had been oppressed by a heavy sense of her responsibility towards him. For one thing, it had been the terror of her life, from the time he was fourteen or fifteen, that he would come home to her some night with the smell of drink on his breath. Only now, looking back on it, did she realize how uneasily her ear had sought the sound of his footfall outside the door upon the garden path, and the sound of his hand in the letter box looking for the string that worked the latch. Was his footfall steady and firm? Was his hand quick to find the latchstring? It was; always.

Always, always, her fears had been set aside in a kind of shame, and yet she knew that they were not really shameful fears, for their source was not in her character, but sprang, natural as water welled in the earth, from the dark centre of her womanhood.

But even this fear about drink was, in itself, only a subordinate thing to the greater and more agonizing fear that she had felt for him, long before he had developed at all into his full stature as a man. And although it was part and parcel of her every thought of him, on nights when he was out late, after the others had come in and gone to bed, she had never let it become explicit in her mind, never exactly faced what it was that she feared. But what it was could be guessed in an instant whenever any scandal took place in the locality.

'I don't blame the man at all,' she said then, to the girls. 'I blame the girl. It is always the girl's fault.'

For Mary supposed her nature to be the nature of all her sex, whereas the nature of a man's was something dark and unknown to her, something that seemed to have no regard for time or place, character, principle, or anything else. And on many a night, as she lay in bed, listening to the last sounds that proclaimed the city laid to rest, she had recalled the way in which, at that hour in Tullamore, all living things would be gathered to safety within the homestead.

Up the lane, from the rushy bottoms, where they were at pasturage by day, would come the cows, with their calves running behind them, driven along more by habit than by the ambling youth sent out to fetch them home. And as they passed into the yard, the old working mare would be standing at the gate of the paddock, waiting only for it to be opened until she, too, rambled across the roadway into the stable yard, there again to come to a stand, this time outside her stall until someone opened the door and let her into it.

Already in the inner yard her mother would have gathered in her fowl, and shut them safely into the fowl house, and, having counted her turkeys, and given them their hot mash, shut them too into their house, being careful to hasp the door, and see that the wire mesh upon the window was secure and unbroken. And although the old collie dog they had was aged and feeble, and seldom stirred from the place, still at this hour of evening there was always a whistle for him, to make sure that he was within: to make sure that he was all right. And to this whistle he always replied by wagging his long shabby tail, that would hardly be perceptible by this time in the dusk were it not faded to so light a colour.

And the cats: numerous though they were, and though prone by nature to wandering, at this hour her mother always liked to see them all around the place, that none should suffer the loss of his share in the milk emptied into their bowl by the herd when the pans in the dairy were skimmed.

It was the hour of all the day most peaceful and blessed, when all, all, was laid to rest, and her mother lay down on her own bed secure in the knowledge that all things in her care were safe for that night at least.

And following her mother's example, in her own little home also, she too had made a ritual of setting the house to rest for the night. Last every night to go to bed, she went around the house securing and shuttering the windows, latching and locking the doors, dampening down the fires, and seeing that no trace of food remained abroad to draw forth mouse or cockroach. And the cat, though he might be let out for a few minutes into the yard, was anxiously watched until he returned and until he did so the back door was left partly open, no matter how cold the night. Whilst in summer, when dark fell late and dawn came early, the wire mat outside the front door, and the old iron foot scraper ever unused beside it, were always taken into sanctuary until morning.

But as time passed and the children grew up, although she never slackened in her nightly ritual, and locks and latches, shutters and fires, all got their proper attention, and the old yellow cat, the wire mat, and the foot scraper were all made secure and safe before she went to bed, still her head upon her pillow was often restless and uneasy. For where was the son of the house?

Oh dear!

In the middle of her thoughts, the sound of a letter being shot into the letter box, and, from it, falling with a flat slap to the floor, made her start to her feet with her hand to her breast.

Four o'clock. The afternoon post! She had no notion it was so late in the day. Standing up, she went into the hall with an indifferent step. Only the girls were excited about letters. For her they had long ceased to mean more than bills and advertisements. And even the bills had little interest for her, since she lived within the narrow circle of economies that had been dictated by their modest needs. The bills were as monotonous as they were regular. This was probably a bill now, she thought, although it made rather a heavy sound when it fell on the floor.

But instantly, as she caught sight of the long, glossy envelope, she associated it with the only other letters she ever got from America, from her Aunt Ella. But although her Aunt Ella had only written to her at most five or six times in twenty years, she had recently received a letter from her, acknowledging her own letter which told of Patrick's intention of going to America. There could hardly be a second letter from her: this must be from Patrick.

From Patrick! So soon! She hadn't dared to expect a letter before the next week, at the earliest. Eagerly, lovingly, she caught it up, and turning it over she examined it, back and front. Without opening it at all, the stamp, the postal imprint, the paper itself seemed all to have messages for her. It was a bulky letter, too. There was something in it besides notepaper. That was certain. Could it be possible that he had already sent her something: some money? It wouldn't be the first time she had dollar bills in her hand. When her own mother died, Aunt Ella had sent her a five-dollar bill with the request that she would buy a wreath, and lay it on her mother's grave, together with an inscribed card which had also been enclosed.

She had bought the wreath all right, and it had been sent down to Tullamore, with the card attached, as her relative wished, but Tom had paid for it out of his own pocket. For they had not known just how to go about changing the bill. And, for the time being anyway, it had been put aside carefully in the black tin box: and then forgotten. It was there still!

But what was this?

Out at her feet, from inside the envelope, there had fallen a little pad of paper, and before she as much as bent to lift it, she had seen and recognized not only that it was a little pad of bank notes, but that they were the familiar currency of the Bank of England. More than that, the very look of the little pad was so familiar, she got the immediate, unmistakable impression that she had had these very same notes in her hand at some other time.

Picking it up, she turned to the letter with a new and profound curiosity that steadied her, and made her read slowly.

Dear Mother,

I trust you will not be angry with me when I tell you that I did something you did not want me to do. But it is done now and cannot be undone, and I hope you will not be too upset. Well, after I left you all at the station I had a long ride in the train and plenty of time to think, and I began to say to myself that it was a great pity to spend so much on my passage when I could get over for nothing. So when I got to Queenstown, the first thing I did was to go straight down to the Cunard office and tell them how I felt about everything. The job in the purser's office was gone, of course, but they said that if I wanted I could still sign on for a free passage in another part of the ship. So I did. It wasn't as easy work as the purser's office would have been; it was a job as a deck steward, but as well as giving me my passage, they gave me some pay too. And that wasn't it all. I was always lucky, and my luck still holds. In the mess I met another fellow from Ireland, from Belfast, and he and I got talking together. He asked me what I was going to do when I got to the other side, and when I said I had nothing particular in view, this fellow made a suggestion. It seems he and his brother were going out to work in his uncle's factory, but the brother turned down the idea at the last minute. So after we were talking a while, this fellow suggested to me that I go along with him to Andover, that's the place where his uncle has the factory, and that he'd do his best to get me his brother's job.

Wasn't that a stroke of luck for me: I tell you, I jumped at it. The job isn't quite all I hoped it might be, but I've been here long enough to know one thing: that it doesn't matter what you do in this country so long as you get well enough paid. And that's what I intend: that's what I came over here for in the first place, because if it wasn't for that do you think I'd ever leave you all?

How are you all? When this reaches you I hope one of you will sit down and write me a long letter, because although I haven't had much time to be lonely yet, I don't forget what it used to be like in the evenings in the kitchen, when we all came in and got lectured for being so late.

This is a very long letter, but I often wonder what Mother would say if she saw so many drunks as I saw since I came over here. There is a thing called Prohibition here, which means you can't buy any intoxicating drink, liquor they call it, in the public houses, but all the same they get it somehow, and as I say I never saw so many fellows that were footless till I came here. They buy it in the speak-easies—that's what they call the places that sell the stuff illegally. But as far as I can see it's only the no-goods that go to those places. You won't catch me going near them. That's not the way to pile up the dollars.

Tell the two girls that they should see the girls over here! I never saw such style, but you'd need the earth to take one of them out for an evening, and I'll have better use than that for my money. How is Alice? Tell her I was asking for her.

This is only my second night here, but I think I've summed it up all the same, and you'll find that when I've got enough of the right stuff in my pocket, I'll be putting a few wads in a suitcase and taking a ship for home.

It's very late now, so I had better stop writing this, as I have to be up early in the morning. They get up at the crack of day over here. I suppose they're right. I bet you're all tired of reading this now, and wish I'd stopped about the middle.

Well, I used to find it hard to start a letter, but I find it hard to stop this one.

Here goes, good-bye,

> *Your loving son,*
>
> *Patrick*

P.S. I am sending back the passage money.

When Mary came to the end of the letter, she turned it around, and read it again from beginning to end, and it was likely that, after that, she would have read it once more, were it not that she knew she would have to read it aloud for the others when they came home, but in preparation for doing so, she found it necessary to glance through the letter again, and by anticipation she savoured this time, in addition to her own enjoyment of it, the various comments that would be made by the others. Bart was sure to know the whereabouts of Andover. And Ellie would surely take Patrick's part for having worked his way over after all. She would probably hazard a sly question about what was going to be done with the passage money.

At thought of the money, however, Mary stood up and went over to the old trunk out of which it had been taken not so long ago. It wasn't right to leave money lying around a house. She put it into the trunk and locked it securely.

But when she had locked the money away, her eye fell on the clock on the dresser.

It was five o'clock. How the time had flown. The others would be home any minute now, and before they came back, she wanted to have Rosie bathed and, if possible, in bed.

'Rosie!'

The child was playing in the backyard of the neighbouring house, and from the back door of her own house Mary was able to call to her.

'Rosie!'

It was a beautiful afternoon, the sky was rich with colour as the sun moved downward towards the golden horizon. There was no sound now of any plane, but there was a slight breeze in the air, and as she stood at the back door holding it open, somewhere behind her another door banged. A draught must have swept through the house and caused it to bang, because it was a little too early yet for the others to be back.

And yet, as she put her hands to her lips to call out once more to Rosie, whom she could see wildly running with a crowd of other children in the garden of the house next door, her hair flying and her cheeks flaming, all at once it seemed to her that behind her she heard her own name called.

'Mother!'

It was like a whisper, and yet it seemed to come from far away, from a place so very far that only a shout could have reached her, a shout that, when it came to her, had faded to a whisper.

And to make it still more odd, the voice that called to her was at one and the same time familiar and unfamiliar. At first she thought it was Ellie's, but almost at once she believed it to be more like the voice of Angie. It might even have been one of the others, Willie, or even Larry. How strange!

Turning aside from the doorway where she stood, she moved uncertainly into the middle of the kitchen. And then, again, unmistakably, there was someone calling out to her, and this time it was a voice almost stifled by heavy gulping breaths, as if whoever it was that cried out had been running and could only barely bring out enough breath for that one cry.

'Mother!'

'Larry!'

Mary's hand flew to her heart. Was it he, too, who had called to her the first time? If so, he must have been calling out as he ran down the street. He must have been running hard, too, because now she could hear the big gulping breaths that broke from him. Or was it something else—a sound of choking or sobbing?

'Mother!' He was running down the passage.

God in Heaven! What was the matter?

She flung open the door, but before he had thrown himself upon her, and buried himself in her outstretched arms, she had seen his face, and its terror and its pallor had struck her dumb. She could not ask what he had to tell; she could not ask what had brought him back, alone, without the others: she could only hold him convulsively in her arms, and stare past him through the open doors into the street beyond, to see if the others were coming.

As for Larry, all he knew was that he was home; that he was in his mother's arms. To her he had been running ever since the terrible thing happened. Too terror-stricken even to board a tram, where he would have been compelled to keep a certain composure, he had run all the way from the Phoenix Park. To her: all he wanted was to reach her. But having done so he was still in the same state of terror, and he stared up at her with his white face like a little demented animal. He had had no one to turn to in all the pushing, shoving crowds in the Park; in the thousands thronging the streets, he had only her, but after the first moments of blessed oblivion with his face pressed into the warm darkness of her bosom, his senses became calm again, and he remembered why it was he had run home. It was to her he had always turned for the truth in times of childish bewilderment. And so it was to her he turned now, also, for from her alone he thought he would get an answer to the agonized cry which face after face had denied him in the screaming, jostling riot in the Park. It was from her, only, he could get the truth.

'Mother,' he cried, his eyes wild and beseeching, 'it couldn't be them, could it? It couldn't, could it?'

He had drawn away from her with a jerk, but her arms, that had folded him, still rested upon his shoulders.

'It couldn't!' he cried again. 'Could it?'

But for the first time in his life it seemed that she was not able to answer him; there was no reassurance in the eyes that stared back at him. Instead, from moment to moment fear seemed to creep into her eyes too, until all at once, in her face he saw only the mirror of his own terror.

'What are you talking about?' she cried then, and her voice was harsh, and her hands upon his shoulders clenched so hard he felt the pain of their grip upon his flesh.

'What are you saying?' she cried. 'What is the matter with you,

Larry O'Grady?' and then, more urgently still, came her last cry, 'Where are the others? What happened? What brought you home alone?'

It was only then that he thought of her, and of the effect upon her of what he had to tell. For one moment he stared into her eyes; for one moment he made a frantic effort to withhold his words; but the habit of years, the habit that was life itself, was too great for him, and strike her to the heart as he might, the words were out of his mouth.

'One of the planes crashed!' he said.

One of the planes? One of those silver crosses she had seen high in the blue sky? So one of them had crashed. She knew it was a foolhardy game. But what had it got to do with her, or with him?

'What has that got to do with us?' she cried, her voice harsh and shrill. Now perhaps Bart and Ellie would see that she was right! she thought. But what was the matter with Larry?

'It couldn't be them!' he cried. 'It couldn't?'

And then, just as he had known he would, all at once Larry got his answer from her who had not stirred outside her little house in Ranelagh; the answer he could not get from any one of all the panic-stricken crowd that surged like a sea about him in the Park.

'It could!' She did not yet know what had happened, but from the depository of all her lifelong fears for them, she was able to give him an answer: a true answer. 'It could!' she said.

Ellie and Bart!

It was they who had come to harm. But how? They had only gone up to the Park for want of somewhere else to go. It was just out of curiosity they went. They had no intention of going in a plane. What then could have happened to them?

She looked at Larry. He was blurting out something.

'There were three planes——' Putting her hands to each side of her temples she forced herself to listen. 'There were three planes,' said Larry again, distractedly. 'The poster said there would be short trips only because the whole idea was to advertise travel by air.

' "You'd hardly be up when you'd be down again" said a man that got up on a platform and began to talk to us through a red megaphone. It would only be up in the air long enough to give you a taste for more, he said. But nobody made any move to go up. The man got kind of excited then. "Is there no one coming forward?" he said, looking around him on all sides. "Well, look here," he said then, "I'll tell you what I'll do. The charge is ten shillings a head, but just to coax along the timid ones we'll make it five bob for the first trip!" '

As he repeated the words of the man with the megaphone, Larry became more coherent; it was as if he had for the moment forgotten the outcome of the incident, and was caught up again in the excitement that they had all felt as they stood together on the ground listening to the fellow, and looking over the heads of the crowd, at the wings of the big silver beetle that was, in a minute, to rise and boom into the sky.

'Then Bart turned to Ellie,' Larry continued. 'He said, "Are you game?"

' "For what?" said Ellie.

' "To go up!" '

That was the whole conversation: not a word more, not a word less, and it was burned into Larry's brain, but as he repeated it he looked into his mother's eyes, and under her gaze he squirmed and dropped suddenly into his own way of speaking.

'I thought they were only joking,' he said, 'but the next minute I saw Bart put up his hand, and make a sign to the man on the platform.'

'Oh God!' Up to that moment there had been hope. Now Mary put her hands up to her own face and sank into a chair.

Then she forced herself to look at Larry again.

'Don't mind about that,' she said, as he began to say something about the megaphone. 'Tell me what happened?'

But at sight of her anguish, Larry's own anguish came back, and before his eyes there rose again a vision of the scene to which he had been witness: the sunny Park, and the crowded, jostling mass of people, the high platform from which the bald-headed man shouted at them through a red megaphone, and the big plane, crouched like a giant beetle on the ground beside them. He saw it all again; he saw it, and he heard again the noise of the engines turning slowly over to excite the nerves of the people. He even smelled again the odours that arose from the trodden grass. But clearest of all he saw Bart pushing his way through the crowd.

There was more after that; a lot more, but it was blotted out of his mind, for the moment, by the remembrance of how the plane soared. There was a cheer as it rose from the ground, and inside he could see Ellie looking down at the crowd. She was probably trying to see him, but he was lost in the mass of people. He waved, but it was no use, because in an instant the plane was high in the sky, going straight into the sun, it seemed: so straight it hurt his eyes to follow it. But very soon it was out of sight in the clouds, and although it could still be heard, the great roar with which it had risen from the ground had given place to a faint hum, not much more than the hum of summer.

And now, the crowd that had been so tightly pressed began to loosen, and here and there girls and boys began to make room for themselves to sit down; spreading coats on the grass, and taking chocolate out of their pockets, they unwrapped the silver paper, and began to laugh and talk together about other things. The aeroplanes were as good as forgotten.

And Larry too had turned aside and begun to wonder what he would do until the others came down again. But before he had even moved from the place where he had stood all the time, there was a stir in the crowd. The whole atmosphere of the day changed, and like a wind uprising at one and the same time from several points, the temper of the crowd altered, and it became tense again. People got hastily to their feet. They began to stare upwards, shielding their faces from the glare of the sun. And where they had been inclined to disperse, suddenly, once more, they crowded together in a dense mass.

And just beside him a young girl began to scream, and covered her face with her hands.

Where? When?

To either side of him, questioning faces looked at him for an instant, and turned away impatiently.

'I can see nothing,' cried somone beside him, and everyone, everyone on the crowded sward, stared upwards into the sky.

'What is it? What is the matter?'

In common with a thousand other bewildered people, Larry plucked at one sleeve and now at another. It was an old lady, jostled and irritable, who answered him.

'I don't know why they don't stay on the ground,' she said, 'where God intended them to stay. Serve them right; that's what I say.'

'What happened?' he cried, for the hundredth time.

'A crash!' said the old lady. 'One of the planes crashed!'

But now everyone in the whole crowd was offering information.

'Over the North Strand!' cried one.

'Over the Bay!' cried another.

And the next instant the crowd parted, and there appeared an ambulance, painted white, with a red cross on it, and with a man standing on either running board, like a fire engine, it dashed through the crowd.

'Go straight to the North Strand!' cried a man in uniform running alongside it and pointing with his finger.

But that was all Larry had waited to see or hear. It was then he turned and began to run. And now he was home.

'Oh, Mother!' he cried. 'Mother!'

With a whimper he threw himself upon Mary once more. But she pushed him aside.

'What about the other planes?' she asked, her practicality cutting through his hysteria like a knife.

'They came down,' said Larry, 'before the ambulance went out.'

'Did you hear anything more,' she cried, 'did you hear anyone say——' But the question she wanted to ask was too enormous, and she closed her eyes. She pulled herself together. She must get to them. She must see and hear all, even to the bitterest end of what was before her. The North Strand? That was the other side of the city.

'Oh, Tom!' A feeling of loneliness and helplessness came over her. If Tom were alive, or if she even had Patrick! But to whom could she turn? Suddenly something odd struck her. She turned back to Larry.

'Where is Angie?' she cried. For Willie Haslip would be with her, and although he was more like a girl than a man, he would be better than no one at a time like this. 'Where are they?' she asked, as she caught up her hat and her handbag. 'And Rosie! What will I do about Rosie?' she cried, but she settled this in an instant. Rosie would be all right: she could stay next door until they came back. She turned to Larry. 'Run out and ask them to keep Rosie until I come back,' she said. Then a practical idea struck her. 'Don't say anything about what happened,' she said. 'They'll know soon enough if it's bad news.'

Was it possible that she still had hopes? Was that why she was able to keep on her feet, so to speak; to think, to act?

'Well, what are you standing there for?' she cried, as Larry stood, rooted to the floor, making no effort to stir, and staring at her with the same desperate look that had been on his face when he first ran into the house.

Really, he was stupid! Oh, if only Angie were home, Angie and Willie!

'Did you hear me asking you a question?' she said irritably. 'Where is Angie? Why didn't they come back with you?' But even as she spoke she supposed that they had done what anyone in their place would have done, gone out to the North Strand. Or was that the right thing to have done? Doubts suddenly assailed her. How long ago was it since the ambulance had set out? It would probably be back now. Back to where? What was the use of going to the North Strand now? Oh, what was she to do? Where was she to go? Where was she to look for them now in this enormous teeming city that seemed to roar around her ears with the deafening roar of water.

'Did they not think of me?' she cried, meaning Angie and Willie.

'Wouldn't you imagine they'd have thought of me before anything, and come home to me?'

It was then that Larry, swallowing with a hard dry sound, brought out the words.

'I was trying to tell you,' he said, 'but you didn't let me.'

'Yes? Yes?'

'About Angie and Willie!'

Mary nodded vigorously.

'They went too,' said Larry. 'I was afraid to tell you at first until—'

But Mary heard no more.

~　　~　　~　　~

'Oh look,' cried Alice, when she saw Larry running up the path to the house. 'Look, Mother, there's something the matter with the O'Gradys. Here's Larry coming in our gate and his face is as white as a sheet.'

'In the name of God, Larry, what's the matter with you?' cried Mrs. Maguire, running to meet him, but she was halfway out of the doorway as she spoke, and she was by Mary's side and wetting a cloth at the kitchen sink to hold it to her head before she bothered to listen to Larry. But at last she turned to hear his story.

'Oh, God preserve us from all harm,' she cried then, 'you didn't tell that to your poor mother? Did you?' she cried. 'What kind of a boy are you? And what kind of a story is that you're telling? Sure you must be making some terrible mistake. The like of that couldn't happen in Ireland: it couldn't happen to people like us! Here—wet this again!' she cried, pushing the cloth with which she had dampened Mary's forehead into Larry's limp hand. 'Wet it, can't you,' she ordered, 'at the sink! What on earth is the matter with you? Do as I tell you, child, and don't stand there like a ghost.' Then she turned to Alice, who had followed her into the house, and she nodded towards Mary. 'If she doesn't come round quickly we'll have to get the doctor,' she said. 'But first we'd better get her upstairs to her bed. Run home, like a good girl, Alice, and see if your father is back, and if he is tell him to come over here at once.'

Then, settling a cushion under Mary's head, Mrs. Maguire stood up.

'There's nothing more I can do for her at the moment,' she said, and she went over to the fire, and taking the poker she began to poke at the dark embers. There was no sense in letting the fire go low.

'Is there any coal anywhere?' she asked, turning once more to Larry, but at the sight of his long, stricken face, that was ashen white, she began herself to look around for the coal. And after she had found it, when she saw that he still stood in the same spot looking at her, it annoyed her. 'What are you standing there for?' she asked impatiently. 'What good is that going to do anyone?' Because now that she had a little time to gather her thoughts together, it had begun to dawn on her that there might, after all, have been something in what the boy had said, although he had no business to frighten the wits out of people like that unless he was sure of what he was saying, and she for one wasn't going to give in to such a story until there was more proof than the word of a weed of a boy like Larry.

'Come now,' she cried, catching him by the shoulder, 'you'll find there is some mistake. If it was the aeroplane they were in that crashed, isn't it a wonder you were in such a hurry home? Wouldn't anyone think you'd have stayed there till you heard for certain what happened? It's my belief you didn't know the first thing about what happened, but when you heard there was some little accident some-where you got a notion it was their plane and took to your heels and fled home.'

Mrs. Maguire leaned on her hands on the table and faced Larry.

'Let me tell you,' she said, 'if that's the case you've a lot to answer for in the fright you gave your poor mother. You ought to be ashamed of yourself, do you hear me?'

She looked down at Mary again.

'What's keeping Alice?' she said. 'What's keeping Fred? He's surely home by now; it's long after six o'clock.'

It was after six all right. It was almost a quarter past six, and the newsboys should long since have departed from the streets, and gone back to their homes in the alleyways and lanes of the city. And so when, far away, but coming ever nearer, at that instant Mrs. Maguire heard the voice of a newsvendor shouting out something that was indistinct but compelling, she turned around and her eyes sought Larry's eyes with a look that was almost accusing.

'That's not a stop press I hear, is it?' she asked, but Larry only stared back at her.

'Is he stupid, or what?' said Mrs. Maguire audibly.

'Stop Press!'

Nearer now, the voice of the newsboy was unmistakable, and away behind him, going perhaps in a different direction, there was another voice, calling out the same thing. And if it was not an illusory echo, it seemed soon that all over the city and suburbs, minute by minute, there spread, like a great wave, the sound of the newsvendors' voices as they ran with their papers in their hands to impart some startling information to the unexpectant city. And in the next street now a voice was heard. In another minute it would be heard in their own street, accompanied by the sound of heavy footsteps running, and if the door were not quick to open, and hands quickly outstretched to clutch a paper and thrust forward a copper, gone for that evening was the chance of knowing what excitement was on foot.

'Oh, it's probably the result of some big match,' said Mrs. Maguire, but she fumbled for the coppers that surely here, on the top of the dresser, as upon the top of her own dresser, she could count upon finding, and she thrust them into Larry's hand. 'I hope I won't need these for the gas meter!' she said, in a last-minute effort to make light of the fears that had at last begun to flare up within her. But suddenly she snatched back the coins. 'Wait a minute,' she cried, 'I'll go myself. Keep an eye on the kettle, you, Larry,' she added, for the poker had raised a thin blaze, and over it the kettle had begun to sing. 'I just want to see what he's shouting about,' she said, as she ran into the hall. But coming towards her she encountered Alice, and with her the girl's father. And Fred put out his hand and barred her way.

'Wait a minute,' he said. 'You don't need to get the paper. Old Mr. Oakley got it—we just met him outside the gate.' He looked at his wife. 'It's true!' he said.

PART V

Larry

IT was three days now since the accident, and Mary was still unconscious. The doctor had come not once, but several times, and word had been sent to Tullamore. But Uncle John was not able to come to Dublin. A few weeks before this he had been hurt by a pedigree bull when he was feeding it in its stall. And so after all it was one of her Ranelagh neighbours who had to take charge of Mary and her household: Alice's mother.

To save time and energy that would have been wasted going back and forth between the two houses, the Maguire family had virtually moved into the O'Gradys' house, and although Mr. Maguire still slept under his own roof, he had all his meals with Larry and Rosie in Mary's kitchen.

But as the days passed and Mary's condition did not change, Mrs. Maguire began to find that her plan of organization had been too intensive, and she had after all very little to do beyond conducting in another woman's house much the same routine she would have conducted in her own.

And so, on the evening of the third day as she listened to Alice's whispered account of the inquest and the funeral, the good woman was experiencing the very common dissatisfaction of not being able to be in two places at the one time.

'Was there a big crowd?' she asked.

But when she was told of the huge numbers that followed the funeral she tossed her head.

'Most of them came to gape!' she said, but all the same she wanted to hear all that Alice had to tell.

'Where's Larry?' she asked suddenly, because she was worried about him. Ever since the accident he was like a wraith, slipping in

167

and out of his mother's room staring stupidly at her, and slinking away again, not to be seen perhaps until evening, when, as often as not, he got his own meal, cutting a hunk of bread from a loaf and devouring it in his hands, not even sitting down, but standing wolfishly in a corner.

'Oh, Larry is all right,' said Alice indifferently.

'He's a queer boy,' said Mrs. Maguire. 'He's not a bit like Patrick,' she said, but all at once she sprang to her feet. 'Isn't it odd that we never heard from Patrick?' she cried. For she had not forgotten in all the confusion to look up his letters to find his address, and she had sent him a cable. But there was no reply. 'I think I'd better write to him,' she said, and she turned to Alice. 'Just slip upstairs, Alice,' she said, 'and stay with the poor woman for a few minutes. I'll be up to you as soon as ever I can. There's no need for you to do anything, but just sit there.'

'All right, Mother!'

Obediently, like a child, Alice stood up and went out of the kitchen, and straight up the stairs to Mary's room. Only at the open door did she hesitate for a moment.

It was so still and silent; so unfamiliar! For her mother had ransacked Mary's cupboards for counterpanes and toilet covers with which she had so overlaid the old familiar furniture, that in the eyes of Alice the room had the strange appearance of a well-known landscape, keeping its broad contours, but having all its homely details obliterated under a fall of snow.

There was, indeed, in the atmosphere of the room something of the heaviness and weight that is in the air when snow is falling, and the white muslin curtains which Mrs. Maguire had unearthed and put on the window, covering it close to the glass, from top to bottom, filled the whole room with the curiously muted light that is found in a room when outside the window there is a mound of snow sash high upon the sill.

Yes: it was almost unbearably deathlike and silent, and Alice gave no more than a nervous glance, a dutiful glance, at the motionless figure on the bed and then went hastily across the room to the chair beside the window. There she settled herself, having first drawn the curtain to one side to give her a view of the street.

If it weren't for the people passing in the street, it would have been unbearable to her to sit in that room for a moment. Yet surely I am not afraid, she thought, and she forced herself once again to glance at the bed where Mary lay.

Poor Mrs. O'Grady! she whispered, a wave of pity coming over her at the sight of Mary. Poor, poor Mrs. O'Grady! But it was her heart that spoke, and from somewhere deeper and more mysterious within her there came almost at once a feeling of repugnance, and she looked away again.

What was keeping her mother? She had said she would be up in a few minutes. She shuddered. It was no consolation at all to hear from below, through the floor boards, the sound of her mother's voice, talking to her father.

She'll forget all about me, she thought in a panic. She'll leave me here all evening.

Where was Larry? The least he might do was take a turn sitting with his own mother instead of wandering about the streets like a big sheep! If it wasn't for the way he rushed in and frightened the poor thing out of her wits, she wouldn't be as she was now!

The fact was that since Patrick had gone away, Alice had found that little by little she had been drawn less and less to go down to see Mrs. O'Grady. That hitherto she had been going to the house in the hope of seeing Patrick she would have vigorously denied, and quite rightly so, since she went at all times of the day when she could have had no possible expectation of seeing him. No; it was for Mrs. O'Grady's own sake she went, and it had indeed been a pleasure to sit in her kitchen and watch her go about her work, and talk to her, and hear all about when she was young and when the children were small. She loved in particular to hear about when Ellie and Angie were small, and naturally also to hear about Patrick. But somehow since Patrick had gone away something seemed to have altered her relationship with Mrs. O'Grady. There did not seem to be the same opportunities for going to see her, nor the same desire to avail of them when they arose. And furthermore, on the few occasions recently that she had gone to see her, she felt that Mrs. O'Grady, too, felt differently about her. She had been inclined to be critical, and one or two things she said had been downright cross. And at least one thing she said was most peculiar.

'You always wear the same colour, Alice,' she said, looking at her and frowning.

Blue was always Alice's colour. Her own mother always bought everything blue for her.

'Don't you like it?' she asked in amazement.

'Oh, it doesn't matter to me!' said Mrs. O'Grady crossly. 'If your mother likes blue on you it's only right that you should please her. I was only just thinking that very few girls would go that far to please their mothers.'

And a few minutes later, as if she were still thinking along the same lines, she asked another queer question.

'Does your mother still select everything you wear, Alice?'

As if she didn't know that well! Sensing the criticism under the older woman's words, Alice altered her reply.

'Oh, not everything,' she said untruthfully, because a lie seemed more loyal to her mother than anything.

It hadn't been a success at all, that last visit.

Alice had parted from Mary in quite a stiff mood.

Well! she had told herself, she'll miss me more than I'll miss her. She can get someone else to take Rosie out for a walk!

For, curiously enough, she hadn't felt the same towards Rosie lately either. Rosie's fingers were always so sticky, and she was always hanging out of your arm. Only that very day she had taken Alice by the arm and left a big messy stain on the sleeve of her best dress. She made too free with Rosie, that was the trouble.

Ellie and Angie never let Rosie near them when they had their best clothes on. Not that she'd mind what they did: they were so stuck-up and vain!

Oh dear! For one moment she had forgotten the dreadful, dreadful thing that had happened. Oh, poor Ellie! Poor Angie! Alice was stricken with remorse. How could she have forgotten? And yet there was no doubt about it, she hadn't much reason to be fond of Ellie anyway. Ellie never went out of her way to be nice to her. Angie was different: but that was only because she was quieter, that was all!

For one defiant moment, Alice was prepared to face her memories of the dead sisters and defy them, but then the tears stole slowly down her cheeks.

And yet, even then, at the back of her mind, there still lurked a small resentment towards them. If they hadn't gone up in that aeroplane all this wouldn't have happened! And by all this, it must be admitted that Alice meant mainly the discomfort and inconvenience that she and her father were caused.

Oh, it's not fair, she cried, as she saw by the little watch on her wrist that it was nearly an hour since her mother had said she would be up in a few minutes. Disconsolately she looked out of the window.

It was then that she caught sight of Larry. He was coming down the street upon the opposite side, and just as she caught sight of him, he looked up and saw her.

Poor Larry!

All the unkind and hard things she had thought about him came regretfully back to her, and standing up she smiled out to him and waved her hand. A strange, warm feeling had come over her at the sight of him, and where she had been used to treat him as a child, she felt suddenly that he was no longer one.

He isn't a bit like Patrick, though, she thought, as, crossing the street, he passed out of her sight into the house. He's much thinner, she thought. He's taller too! And then, surprised at the way her comparisons were working out in Larry's favour, she had to admit that he was much more clever than Patrick, or so she had heard. The priests up at the College had a very high opinion of him, she had been told. You wouldn't think it to look at him, but then that was the way with most interesting people: you had to get to know them to like them.

I hardly know Larry at all, she thought, and a feeling of interest and liveliness suddenly pervaded the room. He must have got a terrible shock, she told herself, thinking back over the events of the week in a new light. It's no wonder he wasn't able to break the news: it's a wonder he didn't lose his head altogether. Instead of that, he had been deadly quiet and still, like a ghost.

A new interest came to life in Alice, and strangely enough she felt a return of her old affection for Mrs. O'Grady.

She would want us to be nicer to Larry, she thought, and when, at that moment, she heard his footsteps on the stairs, she sprang to her feet regardless of the fact that her chair scraped jarringly on the floor.

'Is that you, Larry?' she cried, opening the door and peering out into the landing, that was much darker than the room out of which she came.

There was only a muttered answer, but she knew his voice and recognized his awkward manner.

'Aren't you coming in to see your mother?' she asked.

'I was going to go in,' he said, slowly and haltingly, and then he said something else. 'I saw you at the window,' he said, but so low she hardly heard him.

'Is that why you changed your mind?' she whispered.

He only looked at her dumbly and shook his head nervously. Alice felt a strange excitement.

'Come in!' she said, and she stood aside from the door.

Oh, it would make such a difference to have someone with her, especially now that it was getting dark; but he hung back at the door.

'She's just the same!' said Alice, seeing that he was staring past her into the room, and leaning sideways as if straining to see across her shoulder.

'Alice?'

His voice was so intense, so urgent, and its appeal seemed to come so particularly to her, that her heart beat excitingly.

'What?' she whispered.

'Could you keep a secret?' he asked.

'Yes, yes!' She nodded.

She didn't know what he had to say. She didn't care. That he was going to confide in her was all she asked. It was as if it were for this she had been waiting all evening when the time had hung so heavily upon her, and she had been so restless. And beckoning him to come inside the door, she closed it quickly, secretively, even joyously upon him, shutting them both in with their confidences, in the dim and quiet room.

'You won't tell anyone, will you,' he cried, 'unless I say you can?"

'I won't! I promise!'

'You'll never tell her——' he asked urgently, gulpingly, and he nodded to where now in the twilight only the sheen of the flat damask counterpane showed the whereabouts of the bed. 'That is, you won't tell her if she gets well,' he said.

'Oh, she'll get well all right,' said Alice impatiently. 'What is it? What am I not to tell her?'

But Larry was staring at his mother's form which he could faintly discern, now that his eyes were accustomed to the dusk.

'She'd never forgive me for it,' he said.

'What on earth are you talking about?' Alice was beginning to find the situation growing tiresome.

'I was in it,' he said then, and his voice in the silence was leaden and portentous.

'In what?' asked Alice, angry at his obscurity; angry at her own obtuseness.

'The plane!' he said simply.

'The plane! What plane?' she said. Was he nutty? she thought suddenly. 'Not the one that crashed?'

'Yes,' said Larry. 'When it was on the ground, I mean,' he said hastily.

'And is that your secret?' she asked, unable to hide the disappointment she felt. It was just as if a mean trick had been played upon her. 'Is that all you had to tell me! Well! I must say——'

'But, don't you see, don't you understand?' cried the boy. 'I might have gone up in it too; I might have——' But here he put his hands over his face to blot out some terrible image. 'I might have gone up in it too!' he finished lamely.

'And why didn't you?' asked Alice, coming alive again to some interest in what he was saying.

'They sent me down out of it,' he said. 'It was a mistake. The man with the megaphone—that is, the man that was announcing everything about the planes and the fares and all that—he took the money from Bart and gave us all tickets, and we all got into the plane, but when we were inside there was no seat for me, and they said they'd give Bart his money back again, but that five was too many. Bart said I could sit on the floor, but the man said that wouldn't be any good: he said it was the weight that mattered.'

Alice was listening now with a certain amount of superficial interest in the facts.

'But why did they give you a ticket in the first place?' she asked.

'I don't know,' said Larry dully. 'I think they didn't know Bart was so heavy: that he was such a fine man——' A lump had come in his throat again. 'Bart!' The love and affection in his voice shook him all over. 'He wanted me to go,' he said. 'And when the man gave him the money back he gave it to me. "That's yours anyway, Larry," he said, as he gave me the five bob. That was Bart!' His voice broke. 'He was the only one that ever treated me like that! Patrick never treated me like that; or the girls! And then to think——' A great shudder passed through his body. 'Oh, Alice!' he cried in anguish, and he looked into her face.

Now, undoubtedly, Alice had felt let down in what she had expected to hear, but yet she felt a womanly vanity in having been the recipient of Larry's secret, even though as a matter of fact it seemed very small cheese to her.

'There now! Don't get upset, Larry,' she cried, putting her arm around his shoulder and patting him. 'I know how you feel, but you mustn't let yourself get upset. And anyway,' she added brightly, 'I think you're taking the thing in the wrong spirit. I do! If I were you I'd feel that I was jolly lucky: that's what I'd feel. I know how terrible it must have been when you heard what had happened, but all the same it wouldn't be human not to think you had a miraculous escape. Isn't that so?'

But instead of rousing him, she seemed in some way to have plunged him back into the abyss of his despair.

'That's what I did feel,' he said, 'at first, and when I ran home to her——' he nodded, but did not look, in the direction of his mother—'but, Alice——?'

She felt a new urgency in his voice.

'Yes?' she said, rising to meet it.

'That's what I want to tell you really,' he said, 'about how she looked at me when I told her.'

'How did she look at you?' asked Alice practically. 'I thought she fainted away at once.'

'Not at once,' said Larry, and he put up his hands to his face. He had begun to sob softly and uncontrollably. 'Oh, Alice, if you knew how she looked at me! Oh, why did I have to be the one to tell her? Why didn't I know that she'd always hate the sight of the person that would bring her news like that? Why didn't I know that? Why didn't I know it?' His voice fell. 'But I didn't know it; I wasn't thinking of her; I was only thinking of getting home: getting away from all the people that were shouting and running.'

He was talking so fast that Alice began to get frightened.

'Hush, ssh,' she said. 'That's nonsense. Why should she hate you? Your mother! Don't be silly.'

But her words were so facile and so shallow, he shrank away from her almost as if he had been betrayed.

'You don't understand,' he said. 'She'll always hate me, and that's why I don't like to come up here. I don't want her to see me when she comes to her senses. I know what she'll think, it's what I keep thinking myself all day long: she'll think how unlucky it was that it had to be me that was left, and not one of the others. It might have been, you know!' he cried. 'Bart wanted to let me go instead of him, and Angie—yes, at the last minute Angie wanted me to go in her place. I think she was a bit scared, but it wasn't altogether that, it was just because Angie was like that—always wanting other people to have what she had! Oh, why didn't I let her give me her place!' He turned suddenly, 'That's what I wanted to tell you,' he said. 'That's what I'll be thinking all my life. Why were they killed? Why wasn't it me?'

For the first time, as his voice grew loud and uncontrolled, Alice was recalled to her duty towards the sick woman.

'Ssh, ssh!' she cried again desperately. 'Oh, for heaven's sake!' she cried, because now he was sobbing again loudly and convulsively. 'For heaven's sake get out of here,' she cried. 'Are you out of your mind to make such a noise? If my mother hears you!'

With the help of the last threat, and catching him by the shoulders, she began frantically to push him towards the door which with one hand she managed to open, as, with the other, she tried to jerk him back to a sense of his surroundings.

'What on earth is all this noise?'

As Alice had expected, there was her mother at the foot of the stairs.

'What is the meaning of this?' cried Mrs. Maguire. 'Larry? Alice?' She had lit the gas in the lower hall, and from below, like limelight, it illumined their frightened faces.

But before anyone had time to say anything, to their utter astonishment another voice broke in upon the confusion: a voice that was low, and weak, but at the sound of it, the others stared at one another aghast, as if indeed it had been a voice from another world.

'My son,' said the voice again, and turning slowly around, they saw that the woman on the bed had leaned over the side, her hair hanging down in a cascade. 'My son,' she cried again for the third time, as she stretched out her arms to him. The next minute Larry ran blindly forward.

'Oh God in Heaven!' cried Mrs. Maguire, clutching at the banister rail and stumbling up the stairs. 'Oh, what is she saying?' she cried. 'Is she raving or what?' For the strain of going up the stairs with such haste caused her to breathe somewhat heavily and noisily, and she was unable to hear what was going on above her.

Having a tendency to avoirdupois, for Mrs. Maguire, going upstairs was something like going up a rope ladder, and she had to haul herself up by the banisters, her feet playing less of a part than her hands, and so when she got to the top of the stairs it was somewhat of a surprise to find Alice blocking the head of the stairway.

'What are you doing?' she cried. 'Why are you standing there?' and about to shoulder aside her daughter, she pushed forward. But Alice put out her hand and barred the way.

'Will you wait a minute, Mother,' she said irritably. 'Will you listen to me! You can't go in there: she doesn't want you!'

As she spoke, Alice nodded back over her shoulder, and looking past her, to her astonishment Mrs. Maguire saw that the door of Mary's bedroom was closed.

'You didn't close the door?' she asked accusingly, and again she tried to push forward. 'What nonsense are you talking? What do you mean: she doesn't want me?'

But this time Alice took such a grip of her arm she wasn't able to stir.

'Will you listen!' she cried. 'How can I tell you if you won't listen? You needn't go in there because she's after ordering me to get out.'

'Ordering what?' Mrs. Maguire's attention was at last secured.

'Ordered me out!' cried Alice.

But although this time she heard what her daughter said, Mrs. Maguire had not yet understood. Nevertheless she made no further attempt for the moment to press forward.

'Tell me what happened!' she said.

'Well,' said Alice, 'there's nothing te tell, but just that when she came to her senses, I heard her calling Larry, so naturally I ran over to the bed too.'

Mrs. Maguire nodded in impatient recognition of this most natural reaction on the part of Alice.

'Go on!' she said. Alice went on.

' "Oh, Mrs. O'Grady, are you better?" I said, and I was going to put my arm around her to support her, because she looked awfully weak leaning up, and holding out her arms to Larry.'

'Yes, yes?' said Mrs. Maguire.

'Well, that's all there is to tell,' said Alice, 'except that she just took one look at me, as much as to ask what was I doing there. "Who's that?" she said first, "Oh, it's you, Alice," she said then, and she looked impatient. "Would you please leave us alone, Alice," she said, as stiff as you like. If that wasn't ordering me out of the room, I don't know what it was!'

Mrs. Maguire said nothing for a moment. She was pondering her daughter's words.

'You're sure she wasn't wandering in her mind?'

'I'm certain she wasn't,' said Alice. 'The fact of the matter is that we're not wanted here!'

'After all we did for her?'

Mrs. Maguire could not understand such words, but at that moment Larry opened the door outside which they stood. His manner was excited, but there was also an embarrassed air about him.

'I'm very much obliged to you, Mrs. Maguire,' he said, 'and to you too, Alice,' he said, 'for all you've done for us; for Mother and me, and Rosie——'

'But is she all right, Larry?' cried Mrs. Maguire. 'Don't you want me to have a look at her? You know the doctor said that we were to let him know if——'

'I know,' said Larry. 'I'll call down to him later on.' But as a voice behind him in the bedroom recalled him to what he had to say, he hurried on apologetically, 'But just for the present,' he said, 'I think she'd be better if——' He halted; he stopped; he stammered. The

Maguires stood open-mouthed. 'I mean,' said Larry miserably, and getting hot about the neck—'I mean it was so good of you to spend so much of your time over here, I'm sure you must have a lot to do at home—I mean——'

'Do you mean,' said Mrs. Maguire, 'that you want to get rid of us?'

Well; that was not exactly how he would have put it. But how could it be better said? Larry was forced to nod his head.

Mrs. Maguire looked at Alice, and Alice looked back at her mother.

'Well, I like that!' said mother and daughter, both exactly together, and turning on the stairs, they began to go down, one after the other, Alice only pausing in the hall to call in to the kitchen where Mr. Maguire sat dozing; his feet on the range.

'Are you there, Father?' she cried. 'We're going home: are you coming?'

'Eh? What's that? What's that?'

But getting no answer, Mr. Maguire was obliged to take down his feet from the stove, and put on his shoes, and, without further explanation, to follow his womenfolk out of the house.

At the hall door he paused.

'Will I close this?' he asked of no one in particular, because Alice and her mother were gone out of hearing, but at that moment a light wind caused a draught to blow in from the street and, saving him the trouble of a decision, closed the door behind him with a loud noise that echoed through the house.

~ ~ ~ ~

After so loud a noise as was made by the door, in a house where for so many days all noises had been deadened, and all voices hushed, there fell a silence so great that standing on the landing outside his mother's door, Larry was at first paralysed by the awful stillness and silence that seemed to fall around him. But after a minute or two the small but perpetual noises of the house began to assert themselves once more, and he became aware of the thin ticking of the clock in the hall, the drip of the tap on the landing beside him, and not far away, the breathing of Rosie, like the chirping of a small bird, and suddenly nearer, and more normal than all, the sound of the bed-springs creaking in his mother's room. Only gradually was he able to realize it, but the nightmare was ending, the return to normality had begun. Were they really gone, those Maguires? In spite of the banging of the door he could hardly believe that the house was empty of them. Acting on a sudden impulse, he darted down the stairs and ran along the short passage that led into the kitchen.

It was empty all right. There were indeed many signs that it had lately been occupied by a number of people: there was a newspaper flung down upon the floor, there was a teacup with a spoon in it resting on the hob of the range, and on the table there were the littered remains of a meal. Those dishes would have to be washed, thought Larry, and in the back of his mind he knew that he would have to do them. And there were other things also that would have to be done, he thought, as his mind went back over the busy fussing of Alice and her mother, but all he could remember to do just then was to fill a carafe of water for his mother's room. From now onwards she would be able to tell him what she wanted.

And as quick as he had come down the stairs, he bounded up them again.

Minute by minute the energy that had been absent from him rose in his veins again, as the sap rises in grass that has been temporarily crushed under a heavy weight. On the landing only he paused for an instant.

The Maguires were the weight, he thought.

'I'm coming, Mother,' he cried, his voice joyous and elated, when, with his hand on the doorknob, he heard her call his name. He burst into the room.

'I filled your carafe, Mother,' he cried. 'Is there anything I can get you? Would you like a hot cup of tea?' He was filled with confidence; he felt capable and responsible.

In this moment, all that remained of the terrible feeling of loss that he had suffered for Ellie and Angie was the thought that they now, as Patrick had done to them some time previously, had passed on to him a heritage of responsibility. They had taken Patrick's place: he must now take theirs. He felt older, and if it wasn't a foolish thing to imagine, he felt taller.

He went over to the bedside, and Mary looked up at him.

'It hardly seems possible in so short a time, son,' she said, 'but you've grown taller!' And she pointed to his sleeves that had shrunk back to expose his narrow white wrists. 'And Rosie?' she asked anxiously. 'Is she all right? I suppose she's asleep now?'

Minute by minute life seemed for Larry to be returning to normality and sanity.

'Oh, Rosie is all right,' he said easily, happily. 'She's asleep. I'll go in and cover her before I go to bed,' he said, trying to sound casual, although as a matter of fact to do this had only occurred to him by chance. Everything was going well. Mary put out her hand.

'You're a good son, Larry,' she said. She was silent for a moment, but as he felt her fingers tighten upon his hand he got frightened once more.

'Don't feel bad, Mother,' he said. She wasn't going to cry, was she, he thought, and suddenly he began to feel very frightened. He remembered with panic that he had promised Mrs. Maguire to call the doctor.

Abruptly he detached his hand.

'Would you be all right, Mother,' he asked, 'if I went down the street for a minute: I'd be right back? I promise.'

She seemed surprised.

'But where are you going?' she asked.

There was nothing to do but to tell her. In the dark she groped for his hand and found it again, and with her other hand she patted the bed.

'Sit down, Larry, for a minute,' she said. 'I want to tell you something. I don't need the doctor. I'm not ill, son. I wasn't ill at any time, except perhaps for a little while after I first heard what you had to tell me. I think I fainted then: did I? But I wasn't unconscious all the time. It was just that I could not bring myself to face things again in the old way. I don't know what I thought would happen to me, lying here like this, not eating or speaking—Perhaps it was that I didn't care what happened to me. Or perhaps on the other hand I was ill, after all, and could not have acted any differently even if I had tried. But that is not the point; that is all past and done now. What I want to tell you is that when I heard your voice at the door, that time, when Alice Maguire was here, something stirred in me and I opened my eyes and saw you. My poor boy: you looked so pale and so frightened. And then I heard what you said! Oh, Larry, how could you have said such a thing? I felt so frightened at what I was doing to you, by lying here and leaving you in the hands of strangers.

'He needs me more than any of them, I thought, and after that I called your name. And now, son, let us not talk about what's past but think about what is to come. What time is it? Are the Maguires gone? If it weren't so late, I'd get up for a little while just to show you that I am not really ill, but perhaps since it's so late it would be better to wait until to-morrow. Besides I feel a little bit weak from lying here so long, and from fasting so many hours—Larry! Wait a minute! Where are you going?'

But Larry could hardly be restrained.

'I forgot all about it,' he cried. 'I ought to have thought of it long ago, Mother. You should have something to eat. Let me go downstairs. I'll get——'

At his eagerness she had to smile.

'Very well, son,' she said, seeing that it would have been hard to keep him, 'but all I want is a cup of tea. That's all,' she added hastily as he seemed inclined to doubt what she said. 'It wouldn't be good for me to take anything heavy after having eaten nothing at all for so long.'

'Is that right? Are you sure?'

He was so serious; so earnest! But so impatient. For the last words were hardly out of his mouth before he had rushed out of the room, and, as if it were a dark pit into which he flung himself headlong, he was flying down the stairs, his hobnailed boots striking the stair rods and making the whole house echo.

She held her breath, and the old pain of anxiety went through her heart.

'Careful, son!' she cried out, but her voice was weak, and did not penetrate beyond the room in which she lay.

She leant back helplessly. Would she never learn? In the light of all that had happened, had she not learned her own helplessness, and the folly of thinking that a warning cry, however deep it was wrung from the heart, could save a child from anything, from a fall upon the stairs, from a step in the dark, from——

But here a terrible shudder went through her, and she passed her hand over her face.

A few minutes later Larry's step sounded upon the stairs again. He was going slowly this time, with the exaggeratedly careful step of a person unused to his occupation: he was carrying a brimming cup of tea in his hand.

I must not think of it, said Mary almost aloud. And the next minute Larry was beside her, his face beaming, because he had not spilled more than a third of the tea. He no sooner looked at his mother, however, than his face fell, but saying nothing, he went forward resolutely. After all, he could not expect that she should be able to put everything out of her mind all at once.

'Here, Mother. Drink this nice cup of tea,' he said, putting the cup down on the table beside her, but beyond that he could say nothing more, and just stood miserably watching her.

Mary put out her hand, that was cold, and laid it on his hot throbbing fist, and with a stab of pain she noticed how thin it was, how grubby, and above all how passionately it was clenched. At once she began to unlock those fingers, and to smooth them straight upon the coverlet.

Their eyes met. Larry nodded at the cup of tea. Mary glanced at it.

'Thank you, son,' she said, but she made no attempt to take up the cup, and she made no attempt to sit up, but merely continued to stroke his hand and to look at him, her face softening, and then very softly she spoke.

'I cannot help thinking about them, son,' she said, naming no names, 'it would not be natural if I didn't. It would not be right. And I must talk about them too. And you must help me. We must talk about them——' And as she saw a frightened look in his face she hurried on to explain: 'Don't be frightened,' she said. 'I don't want to talk about——' she swallowed—'what happened, but I'd like to talk about other times, long before now, before they met Bart and Willie at all, when they were little girls.' But here she thought for a moment. 'Poor Bart,' she said. 'It isn't that I feel any bitterness towards him, or that I blame him for—for what happened: it's just that I'd rather forget all about him.' Here again she shuddered. 'And about Willie,' she said, but as she mentioned Willie's name, suddenly his pale and gentle face came before her mind. 'Poor Willie,' she said. 'Poor Willie.' And for the first time Larry saw the tears shining in her eyes, and he did not know what he should do; whether he should try to stop her from crying, or whether it was better to pretend that he did not see her tears.

He stood unhappily by the bedside, and as she spoke again, he felt still more bewildered, because it was of Willie she spoke again.

'Poor Willie!'

It was almost as if it were for him alone that her tears were falling.

But anyway, after another minute Mary wiped her eyes, and when she spoke again, to his great relief her voice was more normal.

'I wonder if they would have been married; I mean Willie and Angie?' she said.

And, with this question, another change seemed to come over her. And to her son's joy, a wan smile came over her face.

'Larry,' she said, 'I just thought of something. In another few months Ellie and Bart would have been married, and gone away from us. Not far, I know, and not—not for ever, but still it would have been a parting all the same. And just now, when I thought of Willie, a strange idea came into my head, and I thought that supposing Bart and Ellie had got married, as they planned, and that by some

change in circumstances Angie and Willie were married too—on
the same day; that they were married quietly—the way they wanted,
you know, and that they were gone away to their new homes. Supposing that was what happened, and not what did happen. That they
had gone away, for a short while, but that after a little time we would
see them again. Aren't we taught to believe that we must all sooner
or later be separated for a while, but that in a little while more will
be united again? Think of it, Larry. Think of it: one day we will all
be united again, your father and I, and Ellie and Angie. Those
meetings will come first of course, but after another little while the
rest of you will join us and we will all be together once more, and
never, never be separated again! Oh, Larry!'

Such a transport of joy seemed suddenly to possess her that she
raised herself up on her elbows and looked at him as if by gazing at
him she would set him aglow with her fervour. But as she searched
his face she saw that something in her words had only disturbed him,
and she sank back dispirited. As she lay back, however, she saw the
cup of tea beside her on her table. It would please him if she drank it.
So she leaned up again and putting the cup to her lips she sipped at
it. It was a little cold, but she continued to sip it, and over the rim of
her cup she anxiously watched Larry's face.

'This is just what I needed,' she said, indicating the tea, 'and just
the way I like it.' Then, because it really was a little cold, and in order
to strengthen her praise of it, she asked for more. 'Perhaps there is
another cup in the teapot?' she asked, and she was rewarded by the
childish vanity that shone in his eyes as he reached out eagerly to take
the empty cup.

'Oh, Mother!'

Such joy as there was in his voice, when, with her cup refilled, he
came up again to find that she was sitting on the side of the bed. She
smiled and, reaching out her hand, she took a few sips from the cup
and handed it back to him.

'I'm not going to wait until morning to see Rosie,' she said. 'Give
me your arm and help me across the floor. I want to take one look at
her.'

That was all she said with her lips, but her eyes said more. You and
she are all I have left now, they said, and the tears came into Larry's
own eyes.

I'll never, never leave her, he thought, and although he did not say
it aloud, as they went into Rosie's dimly lit room, he kept saying it
silently all the time that his mother stayed looking down at the
sleeping child.

I'll never, never leave you, Mother, he said.

Nor could he see any earthly reason why his vow should ever be broken.

~   ~   ~   ~

It was within a few days of the reopening of school after the long summer holidays. To Larry, as he wandered down the street in the direction of home, one September afternoon, the thought or returning to school was a pleasant one. It was not that he was a great favourite with the masters. Nor had he many friends among his fellow scholars, but yet he was happy at school. Perhaps it gave him a feeling of solidarity that he did not feel, even in his own family where he had been awkwardly placed between Angie, so much older than him, and Rosie so much younger. Anyway, for one reason or another he was always happier when he was at school than ever he was during the holidays. And at this particular time, unconsciously, he felt glad to think that he would soon escape for a few hours from the atmosphere of the house.

It was not that Mary had allowed her sorrow to make any difference in the daily life of the household; but all the same there hung over the house an atmosphere of imponderable sadness.

True to his fervent vow, Larry hardly ever left his mother alone, or only when he knew she was too busy to miss him; only when he knew she was occupied in some way that would not give her time to be sad. And yet, as the days passed he began to feel disheartened, and to think how much better, in his place, would have been any one of those that were gone. For he was unable to do anything but sit and stupidly stare at her.

This evening she said she was going to make bread and so he stole out for a few minutes. The thought that school would soon be starting again made him feel more lighthearted than he had felt for a long time, and he walked with a quicker and a lighter step, and even began to whistle a few bars of a tune.

It was as he rounded the corner of Appian Way, going in the direction of home, that he collided suddenly with someone going in the opposite direction.

'Oh, Father, I beg your pardon!' he exclaimed in confusion, his thin face reddening all over, as he saw that it was with a priest he had collided.

But the priest, although somewhat taken by surprise, was in no way confused. Being a tall man, he had not suffered the total eclipse that Larry had suffered in the first moment of the collision; and for the same reason he was able to recognize the boy before the boy recognized him.

'Well, Larry!' he said with ease and affability, two qualities that to Larry under the circumstances seemed almost divine attributes. 'It isn't often that you are going anywhere with such force and determination!'

The priest looked at him fixedly for a moment, and then putting out his hand he took a grip of Larry's arm.

'You're the very person I wanted to see, Larry,' he said. 'As a matter of fact I was thinking about you these past few days and intending to call to the house to see you.' Tightening his grip upon the boy he turned him around in the opposite direction. 'I'm going out to Clonskea,' he said. 'Walk some of the way with me!'

Father Dowling was an old friend of Larry's. It was he who had prepared him for serving Mass, and between them ever since there had been a certain friendship, although Larry was always in awe of the tall thin priest, with his spare frame and his thin lupine face. To add to his feeling of awe, he had heard that in the fervour of his early youth the priest had joined some austere Order, but that owing to bad health he was not strong enough to remain in it, and had to leave and become a secular priest. This was said to have embittered him. To-day, however, he seemed to be in good form and as he strode forward, it was all Larry could do to keep pace with him.

For some distance they strode along in silence. Then Larry's companion gave a sidelong glance at him.

'I'm glad I met you to-day, Larry,' he said, repeating what he had said at first, and he looked at the boy as if to see if this evoked any surprise in him. 'I intended to call,' he went on, 'but I thought it better to postpone my visit after——' Here he paused again, but this time he looked away from Larry altogether and it was clear that he did not wish to refer any more particularly to the accident in the Park. 'Not that I was lacking in any way in sympathy with your mother,' he said, after a minute. 'How is she?' he added, quickly.

'Oh, Father!' Larry was almost speechless with relief at the thought that here at last was someone to whom he could talk about his mother. It would be such an ease to his heart to tell Father Dowling about her: about the stony expression on her face, and the way she went around the house as if—'Oh, Father. She——' But Father Dowling interrupted him.

'I know: I know,' he said, rapping out the words like an admonition. 'It is not easy to carry our crosses.' Then, in a totally different voice, after a short cough he went on. 'Primarily of course,' he said, speaking slowly and now his first urgent stride altered to a slow measured pace, and it was almost as difficult for Larry to keep back as it had been to keep up with him, 'primarily it was to see you that I intended,' he said, 'or at least to talk about you.'

Now the pace was so slow that Larry had to concentrate largely on his own feet, measuring their stride, and matching them to that of his companion. A little acidly the priest saw this.

'Have you any idea of why I wanted to see you, Larry?' he said at last.

'No, Father.'

'I thought not,' said the priest, and there was something so odd in his voice that Larry looked up in surprise. Being unable to read the inscrutable expression on the priest's face he lowered his eyes again, and continued to walk along, staring down at his shabby black shoes. But the silence that fell between them made him feel ill at ease.

This time, however, it did not last for long.

'Tell me, Larry, how is Patrick?' said the priest.

'Oh, Patrick is very well, Father,' said Larry eagerly. 'We had a letter from him the other day. He is getting on well. He——' But Father Dowling did not appear anxious to hear too much about Patrick either.

'Is that so?' he said, once laconically. Then twice, sharply and incisively, he repeated the words. 'Is that so? Is that so?'

And this time, it was as if with two snaps of a scissors he clipped short all Larry had to say about his brother. Yet after a minute it was he himself who returned to the topic of Patrick.

'So he's getting on well?' he said. 'I'm not surprised. Patrick had ability. I never doubted that. I'm not surprised to hear he is doing well. Ambitious too! I don't believe he was much more than your age when he told me he was going to go to America one day and make a fortune! Yes, indeed. He was ambitious and determined, with a decisive mind, and an intransigent will.'

As he said the last words, Father Dowling was looking ahead, and Larry got the sensation that he had been forgotten. But the next moment the priest turned around to him just as if he were translating all he had previously said.

'Patrick knew what he wanted,' he said, 'and he knew how to set about getting it.'

And then, curiously, out of these curt words, aided perhaps by something in the priest's expression as he uttered them, an image of Patrick arose before Larry's mind. Yes, that was Patrick in a few words. Never had Larry seen him so clearly painted, but to his astonishment, these attributes of the first-born, that he had always vaguely apprehended, and which he had unquestioningly regarded as praiseworthy, seemed to have been named by Father Dowling in order to belittle his brother.

'Yes,' said the priest again, and this time he took no pains to hide his opinion. 'The world had a great glitter for Patrick,' he said, and he looked at Larry: a sidelong glance. 'There's a great difference between you,' he said, 'for sons of the one mother.'

And this time, under the sidelong glance, Larry felt uncomfortable, as if there were more meaning in the priest's words than he had understood. He felt that the glance was sizing him up, looking into his very soul.

'I don't think you have much ambition, my son?'

It was as if the questions that had circled vaguely in the air about him had narrowed suddenly. Larry felt a sense of imprisonment, almost of suffocation.

'You haven't thought much about what you are going to do with yourself; after you leave school, I mean?'

Ah! Larry was used to that question, but never before had it been put to him in quite the same way as now. Never before had it seemed to menace him for an answer.

He had to answer that question, if only with the unsatisfactory truth.

'No, Father!' he said, and he forced himself to look up into the searching eyes that were fixed upon his own. It was the priest who looked aside.

'No matter; no matter!' said the priest hastily. 'I've known many a man who made his mark upon the world, and who, at your age, did not know his own mind.'

They had come at last to Clonskea. To either side of them the lines of houses were broken, and fields showed between, poor littered fields, encumbered with delapidated hen coops, and discarded heaps of scrap iron—not the real country, and yet the air was purer and better than in the streets from which they had come, and as they came in sight of the River Dodder, there reached their ears the slow sound of falling water, very sweet to hear.

The priest stopped and glanced over a small wall that ran by the side of the little river. Into Larry's mind a strange peace seemed to be flowing. And the voice of the priest beside him seemed now to be as natural as the voice of the stream below them.

'Yes indeed,' it said, 'I have even known some priests who, at your age, were as unaware as you of the divine fire that burned over their heads. That, of course, is not usual, as you may imagine. From the very nature of his mission, chosen by God, the priest usually hears God's call at an early age. Take myself, for instance: I must admit that God in His infinite goodness made known to me at an early age the wonderful privilege of His choice. Yes, I was much younger than you, my child, when I first felt the stirrings of the divine will in my heart, or as someone once called it, "the still small voice"! Isn't that a wonderful expression!' For a moment the priest became silent, like one straining again to catch some echo of a diminishing sound. Then he spoke again softly.

'A wonderful expression,' he said. ' "The still small voice"! I think it has hardly ever been bettered, unless perhaps by the expression that I once heard on the lips of a young man. He was speaking of the time when he was still in the world, and he was trying to tell me how he had become aware of God's voice within him. It was, he said, like a little bird singing in the heart all day.'

As for Larry, as he listened something seemed to be altering, to be opening or unfolding in his own heart. He did not, he dared not, seek yet to know what it might be, it was enough for him to know that there was something extraordinary in the way the tall, taciturn priest was speaking to him—Larry O'Grady. In all his life no one had ever before spoken like this to him.

And then, suddenly, the priest altered his position and looked directly at him.

'Did you ever hear that call, Larry?' he said.

If the little river underneath him had swelled suddenly to a tumultuous flood and thundered in a mighty cataract around him, Larry would hardly have been more startled than he was at this question, spoken so softly and so quietly. It is doubtful if he even comprehended the meaning of the words.

Dimly—a faint gleam only—light threatened to break in the darkness of his mind and he began to grasp vaguely what was in the priest's mind concerning him. But almost at once the light was quenched.

For Larry had heard no call. The priest was speaking again though, and now his eyes seemed to search into the depths of the other's soul.

'No matter: no matter. Sometimes the call comes and a person does not hear it. I might even go so far as to say that sometimes it is the very virtues that God has implanted in his heart that make a boy slow to respond to His call.' As Larry looked bewildered, he smiled. 'Ah yes!' he said. 'It's hard for us at times to understand these things. It's what I call one of God's little paradoxes—in short, I mean that there are some people of such modesty and humility, that although they hear the call, they cannot comprehend that it is meant for them. Yes! Yes! So humble are they in their own eyes, so modest in their estimate of their own worth or ability, that it is difficult, nay, it is impossible for them to imagine that God could have any need of them; that He should single them out from among their fellows to be His ministers on this earth; His chosen few; His elect.'

At this point, having turned aside from him some time previously, the priest turned his eyes full upon Larry once more.

'With those people,' he said, 'it is necessary that someone who has had experience in the handling of souls should, as it were, make known to them God's will. I have known you now for many years, Larry, and I have watched you, and the more I have seen of you, the more I have felt that it was my duty to speak to you like this, and to ask you——'

But he needed to say no more. The light that had begun to break like a dim gleam upon Larry's mind now broke fully over it with a powerful, blinding radiance.

Instantly he ceased to be bewildered. Instead it was as if all his life, not knowing what he did, he had been seeking, and failing, to find this guiding light.

With a sigh, deep as the sigh with which the body yields up its life, he raised his eyes to the priest, who was still looking at him, but upon whose face there was now a curiously sad expression.

'*Deo gratias*,' said Father Dowling. '*Deo gratias*.'

Then immediately, in a different tone of voice, he spoke again.

'I will, of course, call to see your mother,' he said. 'In fact I intended to do so before speaking to you, as that is the more usual procedure, and generally considered to give more satisfactory results. But no matter; no matter. Things will work out all right. I will call directly, and then I will see you again shortly, because there are several matters to be settled, that is to say, assuming, as I suppose we may assume, that you will have her consent!'

His mother! For the first time Larry thought of her. How would she feel when she heard about this? A shadow fell on the brightness of his face.

And seeing this, although nothing was said about Mary, Father Dowling put a hand on the boy's shoulder.

'I'm sure we have nothing to worry about,' he said. 'I am sure your mother will not put any obstacles in your way.' He took away his hand. 'How wonderful they are; our Irish mothers.'

But the cold shadow that had fallen over Larry deepened. The priest was so detached, so impersonal, and not only that, but he seemed to attribute the same detachment to him—Larry.

A feeling of fear, of loneliness, came over him, and he was only able to obtain solace from it by telling himself that all this—this wonderful thing that was going to happen—would not take place for a long time. It would be years from now before he had to go away. He was still at school; only fourteen! And although it used to vex him, he remembered with joy that his mother sometimes said he was only a baby still! But as these thoughts passed through his mind, he heard Father Dowling speaking again.

'It is a pity I did not speak to you earlier,' he said. 'We have left things very late; there are so many things to be arranged, the first and most important, of course, being a choice of seminary for you.' Here he paused and looked at the startled Larry. 'You have no views on the choice of seminary, I take it?' he said.

Almost choking, Larry shook his head.

'No matter,' said the priest quickly. 'Perhaps it is just as well to leave that side of the matter to me. In any case I will have to get special permission for you to start in the middle of term, but I don't anticipate any trouble about this when I explain the exceptional circumstances.' As Larry looked dully at him, Father Dowling's voice grew sharper. 'The tragic occurrence in your family,' he said, and his voice was curt.

As for Larry, he was speechless. His mind was filled with questions, but he was afraid to ask them. In the past few minutes a great pace seemed to have been set up, and it was carrying him forward at a breakneck speed. He tried to speak, but the priest put out his hand.

'Leave everything to me, my boy,' he said. 'I will arrange all for you. There are, of course, certain financial matters which I cannot settle, but these can be settled by your mother. One thing however you can do, and that is to tell me when it would be most suitable to call to see her?' But after another glance at him, he seemed to think even this assistance too much to ask from the stunned Larry. 'No matter,' he said, 'I can call on chance. If I do not find her at home on one occasion I will upon another.'

The interview seemed to be terminating. Despair seized Larry. He must speak.

'Father?' In his own ears his voice sounded louder and more urgent than he intended. Father Dowling too seemed surprised at it. He raised his brows. Humbler, lowlier, but still determinedly, Larry forced out his words. 'I—won't have to go away soon, will I,' he asked—'not this month?' he said unbelievingly.

'This month? This week would be more like it,' said the priest with some asperity.

'But my mother——' To his shame, the tears had come into Larry's eyes.

For one moment it seemed to the boy that a compassionate look came into the priest's face, but it vanished at once.

'Do you forget the words of Our Lord?' he said coldly—' "Everyone that hath left . . . father, or mother . . . for my name's sake, shall receive a hundred fold, and shall possess life everlasting." '

The old familiar words, now so significant, fell upon Larry's ears with terrible finality.

'Are you putting your own feelings before the will of your Divine Maker?' asked the priest.

Humiliated, Larry bowed his head, but as he looked down at his shabby boots, which his mother always insisted on polishing for him in the morning to help him to get out for school quickly, a flame of revolt rose within him, and proud and vainglorious though it might be to think that he should pit himself against all the learned Fathers of the Church, from time immemorial to this present moment, he still felt that something had eluded these wise ones in their interpretation of God's works.

'I was not thinking of myself,' he said, 'but of her; my mother. After what happened! To leave her, now!'

But the priest looked coldly into his eyes.

'Is that to be your answer, so?' he asked. 'Is that to be your answer to your Lord and Saviour; that you cannot, you will not, answer His call?'

Torn, rent asunder, Larry looked back at him.

'Oh, no,' he cried in shame and in fear. 'It's only that I do not want to go away now, not just yet, not so soon after—after my sisters.'

For a moment they looked at each other, and then suddenly it was Father Dowling who gave way and looked down at his hands which, contentually, he crossed, the finger tips of each hand run up into the sleeve of the other hand.

'Do you suppose that I did not think of that?' he said, slowly, carefully. 'I thought of it all the time, but I knew that God's ways are not our ways. Sometimes when we think we have suffered all that we can endure, it is then that God asks us to suffer more. That may be His way of testing us, of trying our faith, of proving our love.'

Suddenly he put up his hand, and his voice changed. 'Put temptations aside,' he said. And then, again his voice changed. 'Meanwhile, leave your mother to me,' he said. 'It won't be the first time I had to deal with such a situation! But look here, in case I forget to tell you again, it isn't absolutely necessary for you to get a black suit: any dark suit will do as well for the first few months, as long as you wear black shoes and hose, and a black tie. Although, of course, where the extra expense is not too great a strain, there is no denying that black clothes are more desirable. But as I have said, it is not by any means necessary to procure a new suit for the first term.'

~   ~   ~   ~

It was late afternoon on the same day that Larry had his encounter with Father Dowling. Larry had not yet come home and Mary was in the kitchen alone. She was making bread, and her hands were deep in the big yellow bowl of flour which in the immemorial manner of countrywomen she was sifting by lifting it lightly in her hands and as lightly letting it fall again through her fingers. And as she stood there, in the stillness and quiet, a ray of deep golden sunlight from the scullery window moved slowly over the table until it enveloped her in its mellow glow.

In the blessed peace of that hour, and in the mellifluent warmth of that late yellow sunlight, her mind, for once, was at rest, when suddenly the stillness was shattered by a loud and imperative knock upon the hall door. Her whole body started, her hands in particular were so violently agitated that the flour scattered to all sides, and the yellow bowl tilted on its edge.

After the first startled instant, however, she steadied the bowl and pushed it in to the middle of the table.

'Who on earth could this be?' she asked herself aloud, wiping her floury hands in the back of her black dress, streaking it white.

If only Larry were here to answer the door, she thought. She always disliked answering the door. Even when she was first married she used to ask Tom to do it for her.

But there was no Tom now, and she did not even have Larry, although as a matter of fact he wasn't much use at that kind of thing, and so, throwing her apron across a chair, Mary hurried out to the hall. The next moment, when she opened the door, she was surprised to see on the doorstep a tall thin priest.

'Good afternoon, Father,' she said quickly to cover her surprise.

'Good afternoon, Mrs. O'Grady,' said the priest. 'I am Father Dowling,' he said. 'I am a friend of your son Larry.'

But Mary was hardly listening to what he was saying, because at sight of him, there on her doorstep she felt so happy. It was so like home to have a priest call to the house.

'Won't you come inside, Father?' she cried, and throwing open the parlour door she led the way into the room.

In the city the clergy did not seem to be very familiar with their parishioners, but then it was hard for them, with such big numbers of people, and some of them, like themselves, hardly ever going to their parish church, but going here and there all over the city to whatever Masses suited them. She herself had hardly been in the parish church three times. She usually went to seven o'clock, and sometimes six o'clock Mass in the little oratory round the corner, where the shadowy forms of the Poor Clares could be seen behind a brass grille at the back of the altar. And Tom, God rest his soul, always went to twelve o'clock Mass in a church near the carbarn. And the children, well, they went wherever it suited them; usually to Whitefriars Street because it was a short Mass with no sermon.

Ah yes indeed, it would be hard for the city priests to keep in touch with everyone in the parish. At first when she was a young bride, and later when Patrick was born, she missed the way in which the priests at home would call to the house just out of friendliness, but she understood how difficult it would be for priests to do this in a big city and she didn't blame them. They must be worn out, she had often thought, with sick calls and the like. That was why she used to argue with Tom about their dues. She thought they ought to send them in an envelope addressed to the parish priest, but Tom could be obstinate when he liked. If they want their dues, they can call for them, he said flatly, and from the first day to the last he stuck to his word; they never paid a penny in dues to any church.

Perhaps it was to collect dues that this priest had called? But as if he read her mind, Father Dowling gave an abrupt laugh.

'You don't need your purse so far as I am concerned, Mrs. O'Grady,' he said. 'Like a great many people, I suppose you think that all clergymen are beggars, as indeed we are forced to be on many occasions: beggars for Christ! But I am not begging to-day, or perhaps that is not quite right, because I have come to ask something from you, although it is not money.'

Here Father Dowling paused and looked closely at Larry's mother. Was she following him at all? Her face, although it had become more animated and coloured, had the same bewildered look that Larry's face had had when he first broached the matter to him.

Father Dowling coughed. Was he going to have the same trouble with the mother that he had with the son? A feeling of nervousness came over him.

This was not the first time that he had had an interview of this kind; but most mothers guessed immediately what was behind his words, and he needed to do no more than to throw out a few vague generalities about sacrifices that meant more than money; and they understood at once.

But this woman was different. Abruptly he decided to try a different method with her, and stepping over to the mantelpiece he took up the framed photograph of Patrick that stood upon it.

'Isn't this Patrick?' he said.

Mary did not appear to notice anything odd in his abrupt change of subject.

'Oh, did you know Patrick, Father?' she cried.

'I did,' said Father Dowling drily, 'but not as well as I know Larry.'

'Oh poor Larry,' said Mary, and with annoyance the priest noticed that there was a little disparagement in Mary's voice.

'What do you intend doing with him: Larry, I mean?' he asked sharply.

And this time to his intense annoyance Mary laughed good-humouredly.

'To tell you the truth, I don't know, Father,' she said. 'I'm afraid I haven't thought about the matter. He's never shown any aptitude for anything: not like Patrick, you know. Patrick was always making plans, but Larry is different. He's very young, you know,' she said then. 'He's only fourteen. There's plenty of time! There's plenty of time,' she repeated, to give herself confidence, because in the past few minutes a small worry had crept into her mind. Why was this priest so interested in Larry? Had he done anything wrong? But before she had time to say anything more, Father Dowling gave an exclamation.

'That depends!' he said, and although it was no more than an exclamation, Mary's heart began to beat violently, and something quickened in her mind as perceptibly and sensibly as life had quickened in her body long before he was born.

'Yes,' said the priest, 'there are some walks of life upon which one may enter at any time, although these, I may add, are the lesser ways. There are other paths, however, upon which it is never too early to set one's feet.'

Did she understand now? Was there a dawning of interest in her eyes?

Ah yes, there was. All at once, in the middle of her confusion, Mary became aware that this priest was trying to tell her something. It concerned Larry of course. But what could it be? Surely he was not thinking of the University for him. Larry would hardly aspire that high! But what else could he mean by these words about a lofty station in life!

She waited and held her breath, but she felt that something wonderful was about to happen, and her expectancy shone in her eyes.

Father Dowling lowered his voice.

'Did you never think, Mrs. O'Grady, that it was a strange thing for a young boy of Larry's age to be so indifferent to the future, to the world, if I might say so?'

Was she expected to answer this question? She could not, but her heart beat faster. It was as if through a heavy mist some light was threatening to break, but was itself as yet perceptible only in that it made the mist luminous.

'Have you never thought that God might have His own plans for your boy, Mrs. O'Grady?'

For a moment Mary stared into Father Dowling's eyes, and then with a cry she understood him.

As over her son's mind, so now, too, over her mind a light broke; a wonderful brilliancy.

'A priest?' she breathed, and then, without warning the tears rained down her face: tears of joy. 'Oh, how good God is to me!' she cried.

Perhaps at that moment the afternoon sun, that had travelled now towards its wane, flashed forth with its last rich rays, and slanting through the dark railway bridge had entered the little parlour, to flood it with its golden effulgence, for certainly at that moment the room, and all it contained, seemed to Mary to be transfigured with glory. Or perhaps the glory was in her own heart!

So great a glory! And to think that it was on Larry this great glory fell. Larry! The one alone among her children she had always least considered, in whom she had had least pride, and towards whom, indeed, she had always felt a kind of compassion, as if, in some unseen way, he were blemished or weak.

'Oh, Father!' she whispered. 'I never thought—I never dreamed—' But she finished neither sentence, and instead she trembled all over, so greatly did this revelation affect her. It surpassed anything she had experienced in her life, all that she had enjoyed, all that she had suffered.

As for Father Dowling, this was no more than he expected. He could not have been absolutely certain of the effect his words would have, for the world, alas, was changing, and the old simple faith was not to be looked for everywhere, nor found always where it was sought. But thank God this woman was of the old stock. He glanced at the clock. It was getting late, and his purpose was not complete.

Standing up, he began to walk up and down the room.

'Well, then, Mrs. O'Grady,' he said, 'I may take it that Larry would have your consent?'

Her consent! As well ask her consent for the sun to blaze in the heavens.

At this moment, however, there was the sound of footsteps coming up the little path to the house.

Mary's heart leaped. 'Here he is now,' she said.

But the priest hastily took up his hat.

'In that case I won't delay,' he said, and then he paused and looked solemnly at Mary. 'I know how my own mother felt when——

He paused. 'She died two years ago,' he said, irrelevantly, but something very deep and true to the moment lay under his words. 'So this is Larry!' he said then. 'I'm sorry I wasn't gone before he got home.'

But Mary could be quick at times.

'He'll go straight into the kitchen,' she said. 'You could slip out without his ever knowing you were here.'

'Perhaps it might be as well if I did,' said Father Dowling. 'I will call again of course. There are naturally a number of things to be settled, but we can leave them till later. Perhaps I might call again towards the end of the week. Meanwhile, of course, the boy could be getting his things together for the seminary. Oh yes, and in case I should forget to mention it again, I must tell you that it is not absolutely necessary for the scholastics to have a black suit in their first year; or at least not for their first term. Any dark suit will suffice. Black of course is to be recommended where it can be managed, but as I say there is no enforcement.'

For a minute after Father Dowling had gone, Mary stood in the parlour.

Beyond the thin partition she could hear her son moving about in the kitchen. But where she had first heard his step on the gravel with such joy, she now felt a curious reluctance to see him. She looked around her: the sunlight had passed from the room: it was filling already with the shadows of evening. And in the same way a shadow seemed to have come over her joyousness and gladness. It was then that she became aware of a slow dull pain somewhere within her breast, in her heart perhaps: the pain of a wound.

He never told me, she thought. Then she went over to the mantelpiece where pictures of all the family were arranged in different frames, but it was the photograph of Patrick that she took in her hands, and not the one of Larry. Only after she had stared for a long time at the face of her eldest, recalling all the hurt of his departure, did she take up the little frame that held a picture of Larry.

'And now you too!' she said, and lo! it was not a new wound at all that bled, but the old wound, still open—the wound made by Patrick.

Her lips tightened, and perhaps her heart hardened a little as she laid down the picture and went out to the kitchen.

~   ~   ~   ~

Finding no one in the kitchen when he came home, Larry had cut himself a slice of bread. And when Mary opened the kitchen door, whatever her feelings may have been beforehand, she felt a catch at her heart upon sight of him. He looked so like a small boy. And although she gave him a searching look, no words passed her lips. He would tell her now, and all would be well. She looked at him questioningly. But Larry said nothing at all.

The truth was that Larry was disconcerted at his mother's sudden appearance from the parlour. What on earth was she doing in that room, unused now since the gay company that filled it with laughter and music was gone. He did not think she was in the house at all. And there was no sign of tea.

After the exhilaration he had lately experienced, a feeling of lassitude and fatigue had come over him. He was hungry, too. So hungry in fact that seeing a loaf of bread upon the table he set about cutting a slice and plastering it with butter. When it was buttered, he paused for a minute to consider whether he should wait for his mother. She would be disappointed if he did not wait for her, and likely be cross with him for spoiling his appetite. But the thought of the large sacrifices ahead of him made him fasten the more tenaciously upon this one slice of bread, and so he bit into it. It was just as well to have something eaten before he encountered her. He would need to be in the best of form to tell her about his conversation with Father Dowling.

It was therefore a shock to him when his mother came into the kitchen, just as his mouth was stuffed with bread.

I can't tell her now, he thought. But seeing that she was looking at him with a curious, searching glance, he had to say something.

'Is tea ready, Mother?' he said.

His mother looked at him for a time that seemed eternity, then she turned away.

'It won't be long,' she said.

There was something odd in her manner, he thought. There was a strain between them. And acutely aware of it, he sat not knowing what to say. And in a few minutes she came over and set down a plate in front of him.

'There! That's something you like!' she said, and he saw that she had heated two crumpets and, splitting them, had thickly buttered them. But his appetite had gone. Nevertheless he began to eat them, without relish and without stomach, because he was afraid of worsening the situation by doing anything else.

Opposite him, Mary too sat down but he saw at a glance that she was as little inclined to eat as he had been. Indeed, pushing her plate aside after a few mouthfuls, she had put her cup and saucer directly in front of her, and taking her cup into both hands she leaned on the table sipping from it as from a bowl. And across the rim of the cup she was staring at him.

Why?

He did not know, but the atmosphere had become so tense he felt he could not possible tell her what he had to tell.

Where was Rosie? If only Rosie were to come in her presence might make things less awkward.

But when, almost simultaneously with his wish for her, his young sister burst into the room, throwing her coat to one side, her cap to another, although he did not know it, she was only to make matters worse.

Sensing something amiss in the air, Rosie looked first at her mother, and then at her brother.

'What's up?' she asked, but at that moment she caught sight of the two crumpets on his plate. 'You took two, you mean pig!' she cried.

'Rosie O'Grady: that's no way to speak!' said Mary. 'I have two more for you,' she said. 'They're in the oven.'

As she spoke, Mary was bending down to open the door of the oven, but her thoughts were of Larry. Perhaps he had no intention of telling her this evening? Perhaps he did not intend to tell her until he felt good and like it. How long had he known his own mind about the matter, she wondered? She hadn't thought of asking the priest that question.

If he had kept it a secret up to this there was no knowing how long he was going to keep it from her!

Well, he might be odd and secretive, but he couldn't keep it up for ever. He might keep his plans from her while it suited him, but he'd have to change his tune when it came to the time for paying out. Because although nothing had been said about money, it was hardly likely they were going to feed and clothe him in this seminary, and supply him with learning and books into the bargain, without getting something for it. And his clothes! Take that black suit, for instance, that the priest mentioned. That would cost something, wouldn't it? For naturally, if the other scholastics had black suits, she wasn't going to have it said that her son was backward in getting one. That was something that couldn't be put on the long finger.

Thinking of that suit, the old habit of authority took hold of Mary. He would have to see about that at once! She had given him his chance and he hadn't taken it. Very well, she'd let him see that she wasn't as backward as he thought.

The crumpets were ready. She came back slowly to the table with the plate, and set it before Rosie, and then she sat down again in her own chair, and after a minute she opened her lips. But although it was to Rosie she spoke, it was at Larry she looked.

'I must warn you, Rosie, you'll have to be careful what names you call your brother from now onward.'

Rosie had started to eat, but she looked up with her mouth full.

'Why?' she asked.

'Oh, never mind the why,' said Mary, still looking not at her, but at Larry. 'There are reasons, that's all. I'm not at liberty to tell you more. I'm just warning you to give up calling him names, that's all!'

What was the matter? Larry had no comprehension of her meaning, but he had wit enough to know that she was baiting him. He was the butt of her enigmatic words. For a moment he looked stupidly at her, and then dimly he recalled having heard the hall door close shortly after he came into the house. And his mother had come, not as he expected from outdoors, but from the parlour.

A divination of what had happened flashed into his mind. He started.

'Mother,' he said, 'who was in the parlour?'

Mary had started the chase.

'A visitor,' she said, speaking more easily now because she felt in a superior position to him.

'Was it——?' He couldn't finish.

He looked sharply at Rosie. Did she know anything about all this? But Rosie was eating away, unconcernedly. He looked back at his mother.

With some compassion she looked back at him.

'Yes,' she said cryptically, naming no names, 'it was him!'

'Oh!'

Just one exclamation; that was all that broke from his lips, but it spoke louder than a hundred tongues, and she knew that he had seen into the very depths of her heart.

For a moment they stared at each other, and then Larry's eyes fell, and he saw the incident of the past hour in a new light. It was as if in his hands had been placed some priceless unction or balm, that would have solaced her sad heart for all the suffering it had endured in the past twelve months; but he, clumsy fool that he was, had mishandled things. And why had this happened? He looked down at the remains of the unrelished, and only partly eaten meal in front of him. For this, he thought, for a few morsels of miserable food, he had lost the opportunity of giving her this wonderful happiness.

For a long time he continued to stare downward, and then the tears that he had not shed in all the nightmare of the past weeks gushed into his eyes and ran down his face.

But at sight of those tears, something welled up inside Mary too, and down her own face the tears began to stream.

'Oh, Mother!'

In a moment her arms were around him, and they were both crying, and after a few minutes they could not say if they were tears of sorrow or tears of joy.

As for Rosie, dumbfounded she stared at them, her mouth partly filled with unchewed food.

~   ~   ~   ~

As well as a new black suit, before they left Henry Street the following morning, Larry was provided with a new topcoat, several new shirts, and underwear, collars, and as large a number of black lisle socks as he had ever thought to possess.

'Well, I think that is about everything,' said his mother at last, as the shop assistant hovered around them, and added more and more articles to the large assortment of goods heaped on the counter to be delivered by special messenger next day. All except the suit.

'We'll take that with us,' said Mary. She was longing to see him in it. 'Can you think of anything else?' she asked then, turning to him.

But Larry wanted nothing more. He was upset enough at all the expense he had caused her already. To think that he had taken so much from her: he who could give her nothing in return, now or ever!

It was all very well for Father Dowling to talk of the inestimable treasures which he was bestowing upon her, but after they left the shop, minute by minute, like a measure of her bounty and goodness to him, the big cardboard box that contained his new suit grew weightier, until to carry it at all he had to keep shifting it awkwardly from one arm to another.

How much more would he cost her before he was finished, he wondered with a sickening feeling, as they elbowed and jostled their way through the crowds that surged around them in the streets?

But when they drew abreast again at the tram stop and he gave a sidelong look at her, his mother's face wore only a look of fatigue.

'Oh dear,' she sighed, 'we should not have let ourselves be caught in the rush hour. The trams will be packed!' She was concerned only with the problem of getting home.

Would they ever get home? Jaded, and footsore, they took their places in the long line of people waiting for the tram at the foot of the Pillar.

'Oh, if only we were at home,' Mary exclaimed, not once, but twenty times. Fortunately, however, here was their tram.

'We'll be home in a few minutes, Mother,' said Larry pathetically.

Yet, when at last they reached their destination and trudged down the street to their own door, Mary for once in her life felt no better at sight of it. And when the door of the narrow little house closed behind them with a flat melancholy sound, a shudder passed through her. Never had the walls seemed so narrowly to enclose her.

For the first time, perhaps in years, she recalled the way, long ago, she had hoped for a better house one day. She would never leave it now until she was carried out in her coffin. If only she could get around to having a bit of painting done, and fresh wallpaper put on the hall at least! Inside the door she stood and looked around her. She had hardly been aware of the way the smoke and dirt had settled everywhere, discolouring everything, so that it was no more possible to see what had been the pattern upon the wallpaper than it was possible to say whether the blackened ceiling was papered or plastered. Indeed so heavily coated were wall and ceiling and woodwork that the discoloration was itself like a palpable thing, a kind of fog or smoke or gloom that hung in the very air. It was like a kind of twilight: a perpetual twilight that had stolen into the entire house, that in Tom's time had shone with the gleam of early morning.

Mary sighed. She would have to do something about it, she thought, as she went up to her room, but now was hardly the time. Vaguely she tried to estimate how much she had spent altogether on Larry's clothes. And still more vaguely she wondered how much it would cost to bring him to the day of his Ordination.

Then, there was Rosie! She was getting so tall! Before they knew where they were, it would be time for her Confirmation. More expense! Mary sighed again. In Dublin there wasn't much fuss about Confirmation. The girls didn't have to wear wreaths and veils, and the boys wore dark suits, not like in the country where there was so much fuss and excitement.

Oh, such fuss as there used to be in Tullamore! Every house and shop in the town got a lick of paint on the windows and doors in honour of the Bishop's visit. And along the roads leading into the town, the cottages were all whitewashed. In the chapel the brasses were polished until they shone like gold, and there wasn't a garden in the whole town that wasn't emptied of flowers to decorate the altar. And then the procession: the children used to be lined up in the yard of the schoolhouse from ten o'clock in the morning, the girls in their white dresses with their pretty wreaths and veils, and the little boys too all in white suits, with red rosettes pinned on their chests. It was a sight to see them, coming across the yard to the church, walking two by two, and singing a hymn as they came. Such a pretty sight. Mary sighed.

Rosie would look so pretty in a wreath and veil. It would be cheaper to dress her up like that too, she thought suddenly. It would be a lot cheaper than it would be to buy her a new coat and hat. It was frightening to think of having to buy a lot of new clothes for the child so soon after spending so much on Larry.

Ah well! She had managed everything fairly well up to this, and she would manage all right for another while, she thought, as hearing Rosie, who had come in a few minutes after them, calling up to her from below, she stood up and moved towards the door. After all, it was likely that Patrick would want to do something for Rosie. She was his only sister now.

Patrick was getting on well in America. He was sending home an odd cheque now and then. And better still he was already beginning to talk about the day that he'd be coming home to see them.

What would he think of Rosie? She was only a child still, but she had a lovely face, soft and sweet, with all the promise of a bud.

A bold idea took hold of Mary.

Supposing, instead of going to a secretarial school, or commercial college like Ellie and Angie, supposing she went to the University?

It could be managed, she thought, particularly if Patrick was willing to give a little help. And even without him she might manage to do quite a lot.

Poor Tom: his pension had stood to her when he himself had gone.

She had done a lot on that pension, and please God she'd struggle along still further on it. But there was no denying the fact that it was good to think of Patrick in the background; Patrick and his occasional cheques, and better still, with his hints and promises of what they might expect from him when he came home!

When he came home! Ah, there was a glad note on which to end her sad reveries.

'I'm coming, I'm coming, children,' she called out gaily, as, thoroughly impatient by this time, Larry and Rosie together called up to her from below.

'I'm coming! I'm coming!'

Like a young girl she sang out to them as she went down the stairs, and hurried along the passage into the kitchen.

But one small fragment of worry remained in her mind, and she glanced at the clock. There should have been a letter from Patrick. It was due yesterday as a matter of fact. It ought to come to-day without fail, unless he was beginning to get careless about writing.

'Has the evening post come?' she asked, suddenly.

'Come and gone,' said Rosie lightly, carelessly, not thinking much of what she was saying.

'Oh!' said Mary, with a little sigh. 'No letter from Patrick this week either. How long is it now since we heard from him? It's two weeks, isn't it?'

But the young people hadn't heeded how much time had passed. They knew that she was disappointed, however, and they tried to gloss things over for her.

'Oh, it's not so long ago since you had a letter, Mother,' said Larry.

'It's probably delayed in the post,' said Rosie.

Mary looked from one to the other. They meant well, but just the same she felt her irritation against them. And at that moment she caught sight of the cardboard box that contained Larry's new black suit.

That suit! If it were not for Patrick and his money she might not

have been inclined to buy that so readily. All at once she turned on
Larry.

'Do you mean to tell me you didn't take that expensive suit out of
the box?' she cried. 'Do you mean to say you left it there to be
destroyed with creases?'

There now! She had satisfied it; the spleen that had been rising in
her for a long time and which, like the twilight of smokiness and
drabness that had settled upon the walls of the house, was settling
inside her heart. Why? She did not know. She had spared neither
toil nor sweat nor sacrifice, and yet life, that had been as sweet as
milk and honey, was souring, hour by hour.

PART VI

Rosie

O N an afternoon some eight years after Larry had gone away to the Seminary, Mary was standing at the hall door, looking anxiously up and down the street.

She had got word from him that morning that he was coming up to town to attend the dentist, and that he might have time to call to the house for a little while to see how they were—she and Rosie.

It was to see if there was any sign of him that she had gone to the door. But that was not her reason for remaining there, with such an anxious look upon her face, for Larry had put in his appearance almost at the same moment that she had appeared at the doorway to watch for him, and he was at that moment sitting down to the table in the kitchen as she had bid him.

'Go in to the kitchen, son,' she said, after they had greeted each other. 'Rosie is watching for you all day. I think she has something in the oven for you, but I'm not supposed to know about it.' And giving him a pat on the shoulder she squeezed back to let him pass into the hallway.

'But what about you, Mother?' Larry asked. 'Aren't you coming in too?' And taking out of his pocket the big silver watch she had given him on a recent visit to the Seminary, he consulted it. 'I won't be able to stay long, you know,' he said, with a slightly admonitory tone, because from the way she was leaning forward, and scanning the street like that, he more or less guessed what was keeping her at the door.

'Oh, what's your hurry!' said Mary absent-mindedly. 'Isn't there train every other hour?'

'Every two hours,' said Larry, in a tone calculated to be still more admonitory. 'I have to be back before seven,' he said. 'You know that, Mother. We have Divine Office at seven-thirty and——'

But clearly his mother was preoccupied.

'Oh, what difference would it make to be late for one night?' she said.

Larry stared at her, and he was about to say something else, but thinking better of it he laughed instead.

'You wouldn't make a good scholastic, Mother, I'm afraid,' he said, and he passed into the house.

As he went into the kitchen, however, he was frowning and when Rosie looked up with a pleased exclamation he could not return her smile.

'Was there no letter from him since?' he asked.

There was no need to mention their brother's name. The smile on Rosie's face faded.

'No,' she said simply, and sitting down she let her hands fall into her lap, a dispirited look coming over her face that had been gay and happy. 'It must be months and months now since she had a letter,' she said.

'It's a change from when he first went away, isn't it?' said Larry. 'Do you remember that day when we went downtown to buy my black suit, and when we came back Mother was so upset because he had gone a few days over the week without writing? She felt so bad! I often think of that day. Do you remember it?'

Rosie nodded.

She remembered it all right. But she might well be forgiven for confusing it in her mind with the many similar evenings she spent afterwards when he, Larry, was safely out of the house and far away from its gloom and depression.

For, after that first failure on the part of Patrick, there had been more, and still more, disappointments until there was often a month and longer between his letters. Rosie endured some bad days then.

As a matter of fact it was better, somehow, when at last things slackened so much that there was hardly one letter in three months. Then her mother got used to the new situation. Indeed, she gave Rosie to understand that it was to be accounted for in some way that did not take from, but rather added to, her elder brother's filial devotion.

'That boy is under a great strain,' Mary said, 'working his body by day, and his brain by night. It's a great strain.'

Exactly in what way her brother was working his brain Rosie did not know, and as far as she could make out, neither did her mother. But she gathered that he had some scheme for getting rich quicker even than he had calculated when he first went out there.

'Patrick always had a great head for figures. It's no wonder he hasn't much time for letter writing.'

The day after this was said, there was a letter from him. And there was some money in it too, but here again, although Rosie gathered it was something less than usual, it appeared that her mother was satisfied. Exactly how this should be Rosie did not fully understand, but she accepted it. Oh well, if her mother was satisfied, that was all that mattered. Indeed, if it came to that, all that mattered to Rosie was that there had been a letter at all; money or no money.

If the letters were to stop altogether!

But this dread never had time to settle for long upon her, or not, that is to say, until just recently. However, on the day that Larry was coming home for a few hours she was prepared to hide her gloom. And this would have done had he not brought it down upon himself by his first words on seeing her.

'Just how long ago is it since the last letter?' he asked.

How long? Rosie tried to think. Five, six—was it six months? Was it seven? She could not say, but sat staring into the fire.

'I'm trying to think,' she said, as Larry moved his feet in a way that made her know he was irritable with her for her silence. 'I'll be able to tell in a minute,' she said, to gain time, because in the uneventful days that made up their lives since he too went away from them, she ought, by thinking hard, to be able to remember when they had last had occasion for cheerfulness and good spirits.

Ah, what was that? Like an echo of that last joyful occasion, the voice of their mother at that moment broke upon the two young people in the silent kitchen.

'Children!'

From the open door, where it was rendered indistinct by the sounds from the street that mingled with it, her voice called out gaily to them.

'Children! What do you think?' she cried again, as she burst into the kitchen. 'Patrick is coming home! Yes!' she cried, as Rosie and Larry stared at her, their mouths open. 'Yes,' she cried, 'can you believe it! Your brother Patrick!' she said. 'Such a surprise!'

This was more than anyone could have hoped. And yet as her children looked at her, they saw on her face a flush that they did not like. It was different from the habitual flush that Patrick's letters brought to her cheeks. It was as if it had been bad news instead of good that she had heard. Rosie and Larry sprang to their feet, and Larry dragged a chair across the floor.

'Sit down, Mother,' he said alarmedly, before he allowed himself to think at all.

Gratefully Mary sank into the chair, the letter in her lap.

'Thank you, son,' she said, and she looked at them, a slightly bewildered look in her face. 'Isn't life strange?' she said. 'Ever since he went away, I have been dreaming of the day when I would have a letter like this, and now when it comes I don't know how I feel—I felt so queer in the hall when I opened it and read the first few lines. It's a kind of shock, I suppose. My own mother used to say long ago that it didn't matter whether news was good or bad, it could give you a shock either way, if you heard it suddenly.' She looked at them and tried to smile. 'I suppose I startled you too?' she said. 'Although of course it's different for you. I suppose you almost forget him!'

'Indeed we don't,' murmured Rosie. But she spoke without conviction. Without conviction Mary accepted the correction.

'All the same it is a long time since you saw him,' she said. 'I suppose he'll see a lot of changes here,' she added after a minute.

Over her face there came a faint but familiar shadow. And knowing that the shades of Ellie and Angie, at that moment, hovered near to her, on their ghostly white wings, Rosie hurried to distract her.

'I wonder what he will think of Larry?' she said, and then with a quirk of humour she looked at her brother. 'He may see a few changes he won't like!' she said saucily. 'He probably thinks we'll still be kids, glad to run messages for him, for the sake of a penny! Not that I wouldn't consider doing an odd message if he raised the price a bit; but that won't be the way with Larry.' She looked more intently at her brother. 'Do you remember, Larry, the way he used to ignore us? It will be a different story now.' She looked at Mary, and hoping to make her laugh, she nodded her head in Larry's direction. 'Indeed,' she said, 'I shouldn't be surprised but that our big brother will have to take a back seat to Father Lawrence here——'

'Rosie, please!'

It was a sore point with Larry that ever since he had begun to wear the black clothes of a scholastic, Rosie had given him this appellation.

'Oh sorry,' said Rosie, 'I keep forgetting.' And on her face there was a contrite look, but it only lasted a moment. 'I always thought the clergy were not superstitious,' she said, and there was a twinkle in her eye again.

At the word 'clergy' Larry winced once more.

'It isn't a matter of superstition,' he said, 'it's just a matter of respect——'

'Ah, there you are!' cried his sister. 'That's what I meant! I wonder how our Patrick is going to like all this respect he'll have to have for little brother Larry.'

Seeing, however, that Larry was getting genuinely upset, and that Mary was not entering into the fun, Rosie dropped her teasing manner.

'Well, I hope he'll be as good as his word anyway,' she said. 'Do you remember he said he wouldn't come home till his pockets were well filled? Do you think he'll throw his money around a bit? Wouldn't it be awful if he turned out to be mean?'

Mary stared at her. It was as if she was talking about a stranger, she thought, and more than anything else Rosie's careless words made her realize how long a time it was since Patrick went away. Her thoughts strayed for a minute or two, but when they returned the others were still talking about the possibility of their brother having plenty of money to spend.

'I suppose the first thing he'll do after he arrives is to go down to see you at the Seminary,' said Mary.

'I'll tell you what he'll do!' cried Rosie, her face aglow. 'He'll hire a car and drive us all down.'

Mary smiled. This was the kind of talk she liked. But Rosie's shoulders slumped down suddenly.

'Like everything else,' she said, 'I suppose we'll be let down. I mean that he'll say he's coming, and he's coming, and he's coming, but that's all there will be to it!'

But here Mary straightened up, and her face brightened.

'Oh no,' she said, 'I forgot to tell you; that's the best of it all: he's coming almost immediately; right away! In fact——' and here she rustled the letter that all this time she held in her hand, not looking at it, not giving it to them, but just rustling it towards them, as if by shaking it she would cause it to exhale its suggestions—'it sounds as if he is sailing almost at once, any day now; he may be on the sea at this moment.'

On sea—Oh, how much better now than hitherto she felt about that vast and fathomless ocean! What a shining, blue expanse it was now, sun-rippled, and foam-dappled, not for a moment to be compared with the dark and stormy sea over which he had to sail when he first went away from her!

'Any day now?' Rosie's voice broke in upon her thoughts. 'On sea! But didn't he know the day he would be sailing? I thought those things had to be settled!' She put out her hand for the letter, but Mary instinctively drew it back.

'Oh, I didn't tell you,' she said, 'the letter isn't from Patrick at all; it's from your Grandaunt Ella!' And then, realizing that letters from that source were rare enough for those two, the youngest of her children, not to have heard of this person, she hurried to explain what she meant. 'My Aunt Ella,' she said, 'your grandaunt that lives in New Jersey.'

So that was why she had held the letter like that in her hand, so unregarded: that was why she had hurried in from the door, and had not stayed out in the hall, reading it over and over again, as she usually did with letters from America. Above all perhaps that was why she had not been as elated as they had expected; why that little flush on her face had not been of a kind to reassure, but rather, to disturb them.

Once again the brother and sister looked at each other.

'But I didn't know——' Rosie was going to say something but she stopped.

Mary, however, seemed to know what she had been about to say.

'I didn't know he saw much of Ella, either,' she said. 'He went to see her when he first went out there, of course, but I didn't think he saw much of her after that. He didn't care for her family or something like that. He told me but I forget exactly what it was. I know he hadn't much fault to find with your aunt—he said she was very kind to him, and introduced him to a lot of people, and that kind of thing, but I often thought myself that he'd find her a bit opinionated. Patrick was so sure of himself; he had his own opinions about things, you know.' She sighed, and then she looked down at the letter in her lap. 'But it appears from this that Ella has seen him a little more frequently lately. In fact he seems to have been staying with them, or to have been staying near them.' She looked at the letter. 'Or perhaps he is staying with them at present, I can't quite make out from this.' She looked at the beginning of the letter again. 'I think he must be staying with them at the present time,' she said, 'that is to say if he hasn't already sailed!'

'Already sailed!' Once again Rosie stretched out her hand for the letter that had such astonishing news.

'Just a minute, Rosie.' Her mother withdrew it again. 'I'll give it to you in a few minutes, but I want to read it again,' she said. 'I only glanced through it, and when I saw what she said about Patrick coming home, I hardly read what came after—I only skimmed through it to see that everything was well with them all over there——'

'And was it?'

No one noticed that this was the first time Larry had spoken for a long time, but Mary did notice a queer note in his voice. And what a queer question for him to ask!

'Oh yes, of course!' she said, and standing up she went over to the dresser and felt along the top shelf with her fingers. 'Did you see my glasses anywhere, children?' she asked. 'I want to read this again thoroughly.'

Larry and Rosie exchanged a look of exasperation and amusement. Mary's glasses were a family joke. With wonderful eyesight that could outdistance theirs at any time, Mary had recently purchased a pair of cheap, steel-rimmed spectacles which were kept for the specific purpose, or so Larry said, of helping her to concentrate. For, as in this case, it was usually for a second reading that she wanted the spectacles.

'Now where did I put those glasses?' she said in exasperation a few minutes later, having failed to find them where she had searched. 'Why, what on earth are you doing, Rosie?' she cried, because all at once Rosie had darted over to the window sill, and snatching up something from it, had rammed it recklessly into her pocket. 'It's not my glasses you're treating like that?' she cried in consternation.

But it was.

'I won't break them,' cried Rosie, 'but you're not getting them, Mother. You're not going to read that letter again until we've had our tea. Look, the kettle is boiling!'

For a moment Mary looked as if she did not know what to say. Then she smiled.

'Very well, dear,' she said, and feeling tired all at once, she sat down again.

In a way she was just as well pleased at being prevented from perusing Ella's letter again. In spite of her assurance to the contrary of there not having been anything wrong, and even in spite of a particular message of reassurance with which the letter had ended, she still felt a vague uneasiness, and had indeed felt it from the first moment of seeing her aunt's handwriting upon the envelope.

Why, in the first place, had Patrick himself not written? Granted that if, as Ella said, arrangements were being made for his sailing in a few days, he would without doubt be very occupied, but still—a few lines? Surely he could have written a postcard? That would have been enough for her, and it would have been so reassuring. That wouldn't have taken much of his time no matter what was his hurry! Although why he should be in such a hurry was another thing she found hard to understand. Why was he coming at such short notice? This, however, was something about which it was foolish to wonder. There could be so many good reasons for it. He might have been able to manage a few weeks' holiday at this time, that he could not manage again, although somehow it didn't sound as if he were coming for a short holiday. With a piece of bread halfway to her mouth, she paused. Didn't Ella say something that would give one to understand that he was coming home for a fairly long stay?

Feeling in her pocket for the letter, she itched to take it out again, but Rosie's eyes were upon her. Not indeed that she wouldn't be delighted to have him home for as long as he could stay. For of course, he would be going back eventually. There was hardly any likelihood of his coming home for good just yet. And still, Ella had said something about missing him, and that didn't sound as if she expected him back again. It was strange. Abruptly she stood up.

She had to go over that letter again. In particular she wanted to read a paragraph she had only skimmed through in her anxiety to see what was said about Patrick; it was something about the big failure of the Stock Exchange in the autumn. She had been reading about it in the papers. It seemed extraordinary that such a thing could happen; that people could lose all their money like that, overnight you might say. It would be interesting to see what Ella had to say about it. But just at first, when she opened the letter, she was naturally more interested in news about Patrick. All at once an uneasy thought entered her mind, but she put it aside. Patrick would hardly have had any money in stocks. What would the like of him know about the Stock Market? And if he had lost money, wouldn't Ella know about it; wouldn't she have said something about it? Instead of that she only told them what they could have read for themselves in the paper; about all the big men that were ruined, yes, that, and the fact that Sumner, her husband, had lost a considerable amount of subsidiary capital, whatever she meant by that! Not a word about Patrick having lost anything. Not Patrick! Not him! How silly she was to have entertained such an idea for a moment. Why! Was it likely that if he had lost money that he would have chosen this particular time to take a trip home, a trip that would cost so much more now than when he had first gone out there, and this in spite of all they said about improvements in travelling? Hardly, And yet—And yet?

'Come Rosie. Enough is enough. Give me my glasses! I don't like to see anyone fooling with things that are breakable.'

Yes indeed. She wanted her glasses badly. Although in her mind she had gone back over every word of the letter, although every word of it was seared into her brain, desperately still she wanted her glasses, or any other aid of which she could avail, in order to snatch from the stiffly worded letter its secret; its deep, disturbing secret, that no-where, nowhere seemed to come so near the surface as in that part where it purported to be the most reassuring. For towards the end of the

letter, after she had said how they would miss him, Ella had expressed
the hope that they would find him looking well on his return. And
why not? As she said in the very last line of all, he was in perfect
health. Mary had to read that line aloud.

'Listen, children,' she said. 'I'll give you the letter to read for
yourselves in a few minutes if you'll have patience, but just listen to
this line at the end. "He is in perfect health: I never saw him in better
physical condition." Why should she say that? I wonder? I suppose
she wanted to end the letter with something nice. I suppose it's to
reassure us; don't you think?'

But already, before they said anything, she saw that Larry and
Rosie were as ill at ease as she was. And all at once she felt unable to
hear what they had to say. To keep them from talking she had to talk
herself, ever so quickly, about anything that came into her head.

'I suppose they don't often see a man as fine as Patrick over there,'
she said. 'Oh, you can't beat the Irish! I was told one time that during
the war when the Irish Brigade marched through Belgium the women
wept all along the streets, they were such fine men. And those Belgians
weren't softhearted, I can tell you, after all they suffered. It was just
that they never saw such fine men; such shoulders and such limbs.
Like Patrick, you know. Patrick was a fine man, even when he was
leaving here. Do you know, I used to see people turn around in the
street to stare after him, I did! Do you not believe me?'

But it was not in reference to her rambling, lightheaded talk that
Larry was nodding his head. And as if she had never started her story
at all, he put out his hand, as Rosie had done.

'Give me the letter, Mother,' he said. But he said it so differently
from the way Rosie had said it. Oh, so differently. There was no
withholding it from him. Handing it to him, Mary saw that her hand
was trembling. And while he ran his eyes over it she hardly dared to
draw her breath.

Yet when he came to the end at last he only shrugged his shoulders.

'What kind of a woman is this Aunt Ella?' he asked.

He could make neither head nor tail of what she had written.

~   ~   ~   ~

'A dance?' Mary exclaimed.

'Only a practice dance, Mother,' said Rosie hastily. 'It's not like a
real dance you know. Outsiders aren't admitted; it's only for ourselves. We got it up ourselves, you see!'

'Ourselves?'

Rosie flushed.

'Well, Violet Esmay for one, and myself for another. You heard me mention Violet, didn't you, Mother? She's in my class.'

'Yes, I heard you speak of her,' said Mary curtly. She was very much taken aback by this talk about a dance; Rosie was barely eighteen. Mary was, of course, familiar with Violet Esmay's name. She had often heard Rosie speaking about her, particularly of late, and she knew that the Esmays lived in Raglan Road, but she did not know that Violet and Rosie were such friends. Slightly mollified at the thought that the girl had such a fashionable friend, she persuaded herself to at least hear what was to be said about this practice dance. That wasn't saying that she had any notion of letting Rosie have anything to do with it.

'Where are these dances to be held?' she asked cautiously.

'Oh, I thought I told you,' said Rosie, becoming more lively. 'There is a hall at the back of Esmays' house in Raglan Road.'

'I see,' said Mary. She was still cautious. 'Will there be any boys at these dances?' she asked.

'Oh no,' said Rosie in a faintly shocked tone of voice. 'That is to say,' she added, 'there won't be any strange boys, but of course you couldn't expect Violet's brothers to be kept out, could you, when the hall is practically at the back of their house? They are admitted, naturally, them and a few other boys, but those others are brothers too, of the other girls, I mean; brothers or else cousins; relatives anyway, I mean!'

How was it mothers were always so slow to understand! Rosie puckered her brow.

'At any rate, they're subscribers,' she said, somewhat sulkily. 'They wouldn't be admitted otherwise. They have to pay their subscription just like the rest of us. They aren't outsiders. There are no outsiders!'

But Mary was not ready to capitulate so easily.

'So there is a subscription too?'

'Only sixpence!' said Rosie eagerly.

'Hmm!' said Mary. 'It can't be very select!'

'Oh, Mother!' Rosie's pride was hurt. 'The sixpence is only to pay for the hire of the piano. It doesn't mean that everyone who pays sixpence will be admitted. As a matter of fact everybody's name has to be put before the committee. Just think: if Larry wasn't going to be a priest, and if he wanted to join the class, he'd have to submit his name to the committee, and he'd have to get someone to nominate him. I'll have to be nominated too,' she added seriously. 'Even though I'm Violet's best friend I will have to have someone to nominate me before I'm allowed to join.'

Surprisingly, Mary was ruffled at that.

'I don't suppose it will be hard to find someone to do that!' she said drily.

'Oh, I don't know,' said Rosie dejectedly. 'Violet is on the committee, of course, but she is only one person. And some of the girls are frightful snobs from Aylesbury Road and Clyde Road, and they're awfully stuck-up about themselves. Violet isn't like that at all: she's not a bit stuck-up, although——'

'Although what?'

'Oh, nothing,' said Rosie, but at that moment, perhaps indeed unconsciously, she looked down at her old school dress, which was not too bad, and only slightly faded and stained, but which was very decidedly getting too small for her, particularly in the sleeves.

'I see,' said Mary coldly. 'You want a new dress, I suppose?' As well as looking for her consent, Rosie wanted a new dress. 'Well, we'll see!' she said, intending to convey that there was still some doubt in her mind about the whole matter. But Rosie's face was beaming with smiles.

'I'll want it for Saturday evening!' she said.

~   ~   ~   ~

It was Saturday afternoon, and Mary and Rosie were walking home after buying the new dress. Perhaps they should not have started to walk home, but the evening had been so soft and mild, with a pale glow in the sky towards the west, the way in which they were going, that they never gave a thought to the tram. Rosie indeed felt that she could at that moment have set out to walk to the ends of the earth. But before they were less than halfway home, her mother, who had been chatting freely, became more silent.

'Are you tired carrying that dress box?' she said then unexpectedly.

Unsuspecting of what was to follow, Rosie only laughed.

'Is it this?' she cried airily, swinging the box that contained her new dress backwards and forwards by the pretty striped string that was looped around it, just indeed as she always did with her satchel coming up the street every day after school.

Perhaps something in the way she did so reminded Mary, too, of the satchel, which on many occasions she had seen Rosie fling down on the floor of the hall the minute she came in from school, oftentimes, indeed, giving it a kick as well.

'Look what you're doing,' she exclaimed crossly, and she frowned at the dangling box. 'If I had sense, I suppose I'd have left it where it was; itself and its contents,' she said, suddenly.

'Why, Mother!'

Shocked, taken bitterly by surprise, Rosie stood stock-still in the middle of a stride.

'Why, Mother, what do you mean?' she cried.

But Mary was walking ahead. Perhaps at that minute she was sorry she had said anything. There was no use taking the good out of a thing once it was done.

'Oh, never mind what I meant,' she said. 'Come on: I want to get home if you don't.'

But as Rosie drew abreast of her again she saw that her mother's face was troubled. And all at once, perhaps because she, too, was tired, Rosie turned around.

'If you grudge the money you spent on me, why don't you let me do as I want: why don't you let me get a job, and bring a little money into the house instead of all that's going out of it these days, on one thing and another? I told you a hundred times that I don't want to have my nose stuck in books for the rest of my days. I hate them! I'm only living for the day when I'll see the end of them. And then you keep talking about college and university, and the like of that. Me! At the University!' She gave a short laugh, but her face was unsmiling, and out of the corner of her eye she stole a glance at her mother.

Mary's face was very white and still looking. She was listening in a kind of shocked silence.

'You passed all your examinations up to now,' she said, after a few minutes.

'Maybe I did; but how? By the skin of my teeth! But I've got to do my Matric yet, and that won't be easy. Wait till you see how I'll do in Matric. I know I'll fail!'

Mary, however, was accustomed to talk of this kind. Hadn't Ellie put her through tortures every year before her music examinations, and in the end she always sailed through them with flying colours.

'You're only saying that!' she said.

Noncommittal, Rosie shrugged her shoulders. They had come to the end of their own street, the far end, but nevertheless they were almost in sight of home, and so, not wanting to carry the argument over the threshold of the house, they paused in the street.

'I can't describe it to you, Mother,' said Rosie, throwing out her hands with a sudden vehemence, 'but something comes over me lately when I see you handing out money for this, or that, and I doing nothing. Why, in the shop, when you took out your purse to pay for this——' she dangled the dress box in front of Mary—'you don't

know how I hated to see you having to pay for it. I thought if only
I had the money to buy it for myself—and not only that, but to buy
something for you, Mother, after all you spent on the lot of us;
and not one of us ever did anything for you; except Patrick, of
course,' she added hastily, because he used to send money home one
time.

But she had no sooner mentioned her brother's name than she
regretted it. It was a sore point with her mother that ever since the
letter they got from Aunt Ella, there had been no letter or explanation
from him. He had not come: that was all.

And after a few weeks Aunt Ella had written a note to say that she
had misinformed them about his plans. He had been ill, it seemed,
and she and her husband, Sumner, thought it might have done him
good to return to Ireland. But he had been disinclined to do so. He
was now back at work, she said. But her letter was somehow unsatisfactory, and ever since she got it, Mary had been unsettled.

What possessed me to mention his name, thought Rosie, and she
began to talk again, excitedly about her own concerns.

'Just think how wonderful it would be if I was working too. Think
of all the things I could buy for myself; and for you too, Mother. And
all I could do for you! And the house: we could get something done
to it, and keep it looking nice again like it used to be long ago.'
Covertly she glanced at her mother to see the effect of her words but
Mary's face was stolid. She had begun to walk forward again. 'Well,
at least I wouldn't be a burden on you any more!' the girl cried,
moving slowly after her.

Mary stopped dead.

'Have I ever complained that you were a burden?'

Rosie bit her lip. For a moment she felt beaten. Then she burst out
again.

'I have eyes, haven't I?' she cried. 'I can see that it's not easy to keep
everything going.'

Mary, who had been about to walk on again impatiently, suddenly
turned around.

'Perhaps it's just as well we had this talk, Rosie,' she said. 'And I
suppose I should be glad that you were unselfish enough to see that it
hasn't always been plain sailing keeping the house going nowadays.
But what you didn't see apparently was that I had set my store on
you, Rosie. Yes! My store! I never spoke much about the past to
you, or to anyone for that matter, because what is the use of talk?
And I'm not going to say anything now either except this: that
you're all I've got now, Rosie; you're all I have left, and no matter

how much it costs me, or how hard it is to do it, I want to give you a fair chance in life, and the only way to do that is to give you a thorough education. Your father intended you to have a good education too. When you were all growing up he used to look at you, and he used to say that by the time you were grown-up we ought to be able to do well for you: to give you a better chance than we were able to give the others. He meant that by the time you were grown-up we ought to be in better circumstances. Well, as you know, we're not, but I made up my mind that that wasn't going to make any difference, and that I was going to give you as good a chance in life as you'd have got it your father was still alive. And not only that, but I often felt that your father was looking down at me and approving of what I was doing for you.'

Rosie shivered. She didn't like this talk of the other world.

'If Father was looking down he would have seen what you didn't see,' she said.

'And what is that?' said Mary, rasped.

'I told you already,' cried Rosie. 'That I have no brains! It's true!' she cried, as her mother frowned. 'Father knew that too,' she said suddenly. 'That's one of the things I can remember about him. He used to take me on his knee when he came home from work and he used to look at me—"Your face is your fortune," he used to say.'

That was true. Mary had often heard him say it. But not just to Rosie.

'He used to say that to all of you,' she said sharply. 'And he didn't mean it the way you think. He was always saying that to people. It was his joking way of paying a compliment. He used to say it to me too.'

'To you, Mother?'

With a little glance of surprise, Rosie looked at her mother. And all of a sudden she remembered an incident that had happened on the previous Sunday.

'That reminds me, Mother!' she said. 'Do you remember last Sunday, when we were on our way to Mass? Do you remember we passed a girl and an elderly lady, and—and a young man?'

What had this to do with what they were saying? Only vaguely did Mary recall an encounter with some people, and among them a young man who raised his hat to them, but at the time she was more concerned about being in time for Mass than she was about anything else.

'I cannot say,' she said shortly. 'I may have seen them.'

'Do you know who they were?' said Rosie, somewhat dampened.

'No,' said Mary, unenthusiastically.

'Violet and her mother,' said Rosie. 'You know Violet Esmay?'

'Well, what about them?' said Mary. Surprisingly to herself she suddenly recalled having seen these people, and in particular the young man who was with them and who had stared at her particularly she thought at the time. He was good-looking. Who was he? she wondered. 'You said there was a young man with them?' she said.

'That's right,' said Rosie, voice and face once more eager and bright. 'Violet's brother; his name is Frank.'

'I noticed him,' said Mary shortly. For all his good looks he hadn't the kind of face she admired in a man.

'He noticed you too, Mother,' she cried. Her face was all bright and glowing. 'Do you know what he said?'

It was on the tip of Mary's tongue to say she neither knew nor cared, but seeing the eager glow on Rosie's face she said nothing. Taking silence for interest, Rosie rushed ahead.

'He said it was no wonder I was so good-looking! Now, Mother! What do you think of a compliment like that?'

But Mary was too tired to be tactful.

'I think he must be a poor judge of looks,' she said crossly. Not only was she tired, but it annoyed her to see the way Rosie sparkled and glowed. Surely she didn't admire that kind of young man, or pay heed to that kind of talk?

The young man must be impertinent, she thought. And as for his sister: it was probably she who had put all this nonsense into Rosie's head about leaving school and taking a job. She would like to hear more about these Esmays.

'Who are these Esmays anyway? Why don't you bring Violet to the house sometimes if you are such great friends?'

But almost as soon as she asked the question she regretted it, because she saw Rosie's face flush with shame.

'Well, perhaps it's just as well you didn't bring her,' she said hastily, repentantly. 'When Patrick comes home we might make some changes. At least we'll get the parlour papered.'

When Patrick comes!

How Mary's face altered when she said those words: how it too glowed with eagerness and love. But Rosie had heard those words a bit too often of late.

'If he comes at all!' she exclaimed impulsively.

'Oh, he'll come all right,' said her mother, easily and confidently, but suddenly she turned around. 'Why did you say that?' she asked urgently. 'Had you any reason for saying it?'

'Oh no,' said Rosie. 'I hadn't, honestly, Mother, I hadn't.'

'Larry didn't say anything, did he?' she asked.

Rosie frowned. Oh, why had she drawn all this down on her head? She hated talking. You never knew where a conversation would end, or into what pitfalls a simple word might lead you. Could she lie?

'Oh, I wouldn't mind Larry!' she said defensively.

So he had said something? Mary felt her heart turn over. Would she never get used to her children talking behind her back?

'For goodness' sake, Mother! Don't look like that! Larry was only afraid you were setting your whole heart on seeing him; seeing Patrick, I mean.'

'I am,' said Mary faintly.

'I know,' said Rosie. 'But I suppose Larry felt that you never can tell with Americans. They're always changing their minds!'

'But Patrick——'

She was about to say that Patrick was not an American, until it occurred to her that that was how he would appear to Rosie, who had been only a youngster when he went away. An American! She had to smile.

How would he look when he came home? she wondered. He couldn't have changed much in nine years, or could he? But her thoughts seemed to have grown as heavy as the heavy shoes upon her feet.

'We shouldn't have walked the whole way, Rosie,' she exclaimed suddenly. 'I'm very tired.'

Yes. She was tired.

'It's these shoes that are making me so tired,' she said then, looking down at her feet. 'I shouldn't have worn them when I was going into town, and when I did, I should have known better than to walk home.' She looked up at Rosie. 'Why did we walk?' she asked. 'Why didn't we take a tram? I'm jaded.'

So jaded was she indeed that when just then they came in sight of the house it did not occur to her to wonder at the hackney car that stood just outside their own door. She was in fact looking down at her feet that ached with every step.

'Mother, look! Is that taxi outside our door?'

Rosie had exclaimed without thinking of the start she might have given her mother.

'Oh, I don't think it is at our door after all,' she cried, trying to undo the harm she had done. 'And anyway it's probably only a breakdown or something.'

But it wasn't a breakdown. There, on the opposite side of the street from them, but only a hundred yards away, was the taximan, standing on the pavement, scratching his head, and looking up at the houses as he tried to make out the numbers over the fanlights. And there, standing beside the taxi, was a man with a big suitcase in his hand.

He's not giving the taximan much assistance! thought Mary, staring at the man with the suitcase. It's wonderful how some people can be content to leave everything to others. For although the taximan was experiencing great difficulty in finding the house he wanted, and had traversed the same piece of pavement several times without success, his passenger just stood beside the taxi without moving hand or foot to assist him. It takes all kinds to make a world, she thought, and she turned back to Rosie.

'My heart is beating. You ought to be more careful, Rosie. You gave me such a start when you exclaimed that time. Do you know what I thought when you said there was a taxi at our door?' She laughed self-consciously. 'I thought for a minute it was Patrick!'

But Rosie didn't laugh.

'That's what I thought too,' she said. She was staring steadily ahead of her at the taxicab and the tall man standing beside it. Although the light was failing, she could discern that the taxi was parked exactly outside their door. 'What did you say, Mother?' she asked.

'I said he wouldn't have come like that, you know, without sending us word, no matter what Aunt Ella said.'

'I suppose he wouldn't,' said Rosie halfheartedly; then, pointing not at the taxi but at the tall man who stood so heavily and motionlessly beside it, she exclaimed:

'That man! Do you see his overcoat? He looks like an American.'

In an instant all that Rosie had tried to say was clear to her mother.

'Patrick!' With a gasp she brought out the word. At once Rosie's arm went around her.

'Easy, easy, Mother!' cried Rosie, as her mother went to run across the street in front of a bicycle that was coming towards them without a light in the dusk. 'Easy, Mother! It may not be him at all. After all, if it was him, wouldn't he have known the house? He wouldn't be standing there letting a stranger look for the number!'

'I thought that odd too,' said Mary, but what did any unlikelihood matter in the face of that familiar form, still with its back to her, but which in a minute she would have reached. In a minute she would be by his side; he would have turned: they would be face to face. And——

But first there was the taximan, and breaking free from Rosie's arm, Mary crossed the street.

'It's all right,' she cried to the taximan. 'We're here! I'm sorry you had such trouble looking for the house. It's hard to see the number on the fanlight when there's no light in the hall. Just a minute and I'll have the door open. You can carry in the bags and leave them in the front garden!'

Seeing that the taximan was more bewildered than ever, Rosie smiled at him.

'It's my brother,' she said, nodding her head at Patrick. For Patrick it must undoubtedly be, because her mother, after her hysterical words to the taximan, had run forward and flung her arms around him. 'It's my brother,' she said again, although for some reason this time she had a feeling of shame in saying it. But looking again at the tall stranger in the big broadcloth coat with astrakhan on the collar who was going up the path to the house in her mother's footsteps, she felt better. 'From America!' she said proudly.

The taximan pushed back his cap from his forehead, revealing a head of curly hair. He was young.

'It's a good thing you came along,' he said. 'I didn't know what to do with him.' Another thought struck him. 'What would I have done if you hadn't come?'

'Wait, I suppose,' said Rosie. 'We'd have come back some time.' She smiled.

But the young man didn't smile.

'He was in no condition to wait,' he said, and jerked his head in the direction of the hall door of the house, which Patrick and her mother had now reached.

But Rosie was not paying much attention to what he said. She was glad, however, to stand thus, apart with him, for a few minutes at any rate, and so avoid intruding upon the other two. Although of course they wouldn't be saying anything of much importance to each other until they were in the house, and just now as a matter of fact it was only her mother's voice she heard. Their first real look at each other; their first real words to each other would come when they got inside. She didn't want to intrude upon those looks, those words. But on the other hand she could not stay out here for ever. And the taxi driver, after plunging into the depths of the taxi and dragging out a big portmanteau with brass handles on each side, was now making his way up the path to the hall door. Slowly she began to follow him up the path to the house. Midway up the path, however, he came to a stop. And looking up to see why he stopped Rosie saw that the other two were still outside the door.

'Oh dear, what did I do with that key?' her mother cried, as she ransacked her bag for it in the dusk.

'I suppose you're not long living in this house!' said the taximan to Rosie, putting down the luggage and looking at her.

'Oh, I've lived here all my life,' said Rosie.

The young man seemed surprised.

'And what about him?' he said, nodding towards the dark doorway, and she knew he meant Patrick.

'Oh, we were all born here,' she said, 'every one of us.'

And then she saw what was in his mind. He was thinking it odd that Patrick hadn't known the house.

'He's been away a long time,' she said.

'Oh yes, I know that,' said the young man. 'Nine years!'

'Oh! Was he talking to you?' asked Rosie, and for some reason she was surprised.

'Who—him?' Again the driver nodded towards the doorway. 'Oh, he never said a word to me: never opened his mouth. It was the other gentleman told me that.'

Rosie stared.

'Yes, the gentleman in the train. The one that gave me the envelope with the address on it.' At this he began to fumble in his pocket, and then, failing to find what he sought, he looked vaguely around him on the ground. 'I must have lost it,' he said.

Rosie stared at him. What did he mean? What gentleman was he talking about? What envelope? Didn't Patrick tell him the address?

There was something odd about the whole incident, but for the moment Rosie did not concern herself about it. All that mattered was for them to get into the house quickly, and not be standing like this in the dusk outside the door.

Oh, what was the delay? What had become of the key? Ah, thank goodness! It was found. There was the sound of it turning in the lock. The taximan took up the portmanteau once more. But there was another delay. Rosie looked up anxiously.

'Just a minute,' said her mother. 'Don't come inside until I give you some light.'

Did she imagine it, or was her mother's voice false? Was it unnaturally bright and gay? And oh, why didn't she hurry? Why didn't she put on the light? It was dreadful standing here in the dark in this silence. Because the chatter of the taximan meant nothing. It was just like the ticking of a clock in an empty room; it emphasized the dreadful, the queer, the uncanny silence of the other figure, hardly discernible now, except as a heavy form hunched against the doorway.

Oh, thank God, there was the light. And there was her mother standing in the doorway, framed all around by its sane white glow. And her voice when she spoke was as true as a flame.

'Come in!' she cried. 'Come in, my son.'

Rosie turned abruptly to the taximan.

'Give me that case,' she said. 'I'll carry it the rest of the way.'

But although the young man yielded the portmanteau to her at once, he made no move to turn away, and she recollected that he probably had not got his fare.

'How much do you want?' she asked harshly, but immediately she was ashamed of her unkindness.

Without offence, however, he answered her simply.

'The fare is four shillings,' he said.

'Just a minute,' she cried, 'I'll get the money,' and she darted into the house, leaving the door open.

Just as she plunged into the passage, however, at the other end of it, the kitchen door opened and her mother came out.

'What are you doing?' she asked, fussily, and without waiting for an answer she ran upstairs.

I won't ask her for the money, thought Rosie. I'll get it out of her bag and tell her about it later.

But the next moment she regretted that she had not followed her mother. She had not expected to find her brother in the kitchen: in the parlour, perhaps, or already gone upstairs to see his room, but not sitting here in the kitchen alone.

Stopping on the threshold of the door she stared at him.

Had he not heard her? Well, perhaps that was not surprising, because under his weight, the dry and decayed osiers of the old wicker chair in which he sat were creaking loudly.

He was still in his overcoat. And he had not taken his hat from his head.

How heavy he was; how heavy, and big, and yes, how awkward! He seemed to fill the whole kitchen. And to her it seemed that there was no room in it for anyone else: that the space had diminished, and that the tables and chairs were huddled together like furniture in a secondhand shop. Thank goodness she did not have to press her way between those chairs and the table, for so far as she could see there was no sign anywhere in the kitchen of her mother's old purse.

Ah, thank goodness, there was her mother now. She turned eagerly. But Mary was frowning.

'Why isn't that door closed?' she asked, feeling the cold draught from the hall door upon her back. 'Isn't it bad enough that we were out all afternoon, and the fire dampened down, and the kitchen as cold as a tomb, without you leaving the outer door open into the bargain——'

Into Rosie's eyes came tears of vexation at the undeserved rebuke. As if she would knowingly have done anything, at that moment, to make things more difficult!

'The taximan is at the door, Mother,' she said. 'He's waiting for his fare.'

'Oh!' said her mother, and she was taken aback, but then without much alteration in the tone of her voice she asked the amount of the fare.

'Well, why doesn't he get it?' she asked irritably. 'Attend to it, can't you? I have enough to do, goodness knows!'

Get it? Where?

'Will I ask Patrick for it, Mother?' she said timidly, and in a whisper.

'In the name of goodness, what are you saying? Why are you whispering?' asked her mother irritably. But whispered or not, she had heard what was said. 'Do no such thing!' she exclaimed. 'Get my purse, you'll find loose change in the inside pocket of it.'

'But where is your purse?' asked Rosie, desperately.

'How do I know?' said her mother. 'I had it in my hand at the door. Find it, can't you! I threw it down somewhere when I came into the kitchen. How do I know where it is?' With an irritable expression on her face she was about to turn away but something in Rosie's face made her turn back again. Then suddenly she stretched out her own hand. 'Don't pay any heed to me, love, if I speak a bit cross. I'm so fussed. Such a surprise! And I'm so unprepared. Thank goodness I have plenty of food in the house, but as to his room—I haven't a thing aired, and I'm not at all sure if we'll have enough blankets to put over him; they have got so thin. I meant to get a pair of new ones, but I thought I had plenty of time.'

As she spoke, her voice lost its tense high note. It had done her good, this small colloquy; two women together faced with the care of a troublesome male.

'That's where I was now,' she said, 'up to put the bedclothes in the hot press so they can be airing while we're getting his supper. And, Rosie, when you've paid the taximan, you might run up and light a little fire in his room. It will take the dampness out of the walls. There now: hurry up like a good girl.'

Her mother's voice was so normal now that Rosie wanted to cry with the feeling of relief that flooded over her. Why had she had those foolish fancies outside on the path, and again that time when she stood at the door of the kitchen? But at that moment over her mother's shoulder she caught sight of her brother once more, still stiting in the same place; still so silent.

'Mother?'

'Yes, what is it? Don't delay me!' said Mary.

Is he all right? There's nothing wrong with him, is there? That was all she wanted to ask, but the words would not come, and when she said nothing her mother began to move away impatiently.

'We'll talk later,' she said. 'I told you I can't delay now. That poor boy must be dead for a cup of tea. He's worn-out. He must have been travelling since seven o'clock this morning. He looks dead out; he can't speak he's so jaded.'

Was this an answer to her unasked question? Rosie looked upwards. Her mother was running up the stairs, and her steps were the light, quick steps of a young girl. Would she be able to move so youthfully if she had anything on her mind, any trouble or worry? Rosie took comfort from those small feet that tapped so lightly on the linoleum.

Near the top of the stairs, however, her mother came to a halt and looking down she leaned over the banister.

'I wouldn't make him talk if I were you, Rosie,' she said. 'Just let him sit quietly till his meal is ready. That's what I told him to do: I told him he ought to close his eyes if he felt like it. You know a doctor once told me that there is as much rest to be got from sitting for five minutes in a chair, as there is to be got from a full night in bed. It's all a question of knowing how to relax. Let your body go slack, he said, and try not to think about anything. I told Patrick that just now, so don't be surprised if his eyes are closed. Just slip in and look for my purse; but don't speak to him unless he speaks to you. Hurry now!'

Whether it was because she expected that his eyes would be closed or not, Rosie could not say, but when she went into the kitchen again, she felt a curious tension in her body at finding that the heavy man slumped in the chair had his eyes wide open, and indeed fixed upon her with a still and unblinking stare.

Her mother's injunction came into her mind, but shouldn't she say something to him when he was looking at her like that?

'Hello, Patrick!' That would be the normal, the natural thing to say, but as in a dream the words stuck in her throat, and all she could do was to swallow awkwardly.

For one terrible moment she was afraid that, as in a dream also, she would not be able to go into the room, to stir her limbs at all, to put one foot before another. And all the time, the heavy sombre eyes of her brother were staring at her, and she at him.

At last she tore her eyes away and, as she had done before, she looked around the room for the purse. Ah! there it was on the floor underneath one of the chairs. Only a few paces would take her to it. Surprisingly her feet seemed to be freed. It must have been the sight of the old familiar-looking purse, out of which had come every penny she had ever held in her hand, since she was a small, small girl, that steadied her and made her go forward to pick it up. And not only her feet, but her tongue too, seemed to have been freed.

'Mother's purse!' she said, holding it up, and forgetting all about her mother's cautions, but her voice faltered away as her eyes met once more the stare that had met her when she came first into the room. And as for what she had said, he seemed to have paid no more heed to it than he had paid to anything since he came into the house. Then suddenly she saw that he ceased to stare at her, and that his heavy gaze had dropped to the old worn purse in her hands. And she felt that he attached some significance to it, beyond her power to imagine. Suddenly he stood up.

For a moment he loomed so tall in the small kitchen that his shadow behind him was cramped and, striking the ceiling, it bent towards her so menacingly that she almost screamed. As for the man himself, however, he took no notice of her at all, except to push her aside, and without speaking he went into the hall. Yet she had nearly screamed! What was the matter with her? For now that he was gone out of the room she felt differently about him, and she was able to interpret his sudden movement. He didn't want anyone to pay the fare of the taxi for him. It had annoyed him to think that he had forgotten it. That was all. And when, at that moment, she heard him talking with the taximan she felt still more at ease; except for one thing. It had given her a little start of surprise to hear him speak at all.

But he had spoken: she was certain she had heard two voices.

And her mother had heard them too, for she had come to the head of the stairs and was calling down.

'Is that you, Rosie?'

'No, Mother!' she cried. 'It's Patrick!' For in spite of having heard his voice at the door, somehow she did not expect that he would answer their mother, his silence had become to her such a part of him, like his unblinking way of looking at her. 'It was Patrick you heard, Mother,' she cried again, as her mother began to come down the stairs,

What was keeping him at the door anyway, she wondered, but almost as quick as her thought he appeared in the kitchen doorway again. And how had he come down the passage so quietly? Instinctively she looked at his feet. He was in his stocking feet.

'Now children!' It was Mary's voice from the hall. 'What about supper? Is the kettle boiling? Is the table set? What are we going to have? What would you like, my son?'

Oh, how welcome was that voice, and that unsuspicious face! If there was anything wrong wouldn't Mother be the first to notice it?

'The kettle is boiling,' she cried, 'and I won't be long setting the table.'

The next minute the kitchen was filled with those sounds which alone perhaps take the place of words to women: the clatter of china, and the singing of a kettle. And only once or twice did Mary address herself to her son.

'You must be fainting with the hunger, son,' she said once.

'I suppose you're thinking we'll never be ready, Patrick,' she said another time.

But as he made no reply, she gradually ceased to address him further, and addressed herself instead to Rosie, as if indeed he were not there at all.

'I'm going to send him straight to bed as soon as he's had his supper,' she said. 'And I think also that we might let him have his supper in peace, and while he's eating we'll attend to his room.'

At last, however, she had to address herself directly to him.

'Come now, son,' she said, 'your supper is ready.'

Oh God, make him say something. All at once, Rosie's fears, founded or unfounded, came down upon her again like a dead weight, and she clenched her fists. Did he hear what was said to him? Or was he not going to come to the table at all? And if he didn't what were they going to do with him?

Oh, Mother, poor, poor Mother, cried her heart. This was so different from what she had dreamed when she used to look forward to his coming home, and when she used to tell them how wonderful it would be to have him back again. Oh, how could she stand it? Out of the corner of her eyes Rosie dared to steal a glance at her.

To her surprise her mother did not look troubled. She was equal to everything, it seemed, and although for a minute she stood looking at him, she said nothing more to him, but turning instead to Rosie, she nodded her head; so calm, so wise.

'Give me a hand with this, dear,' she said, and she caught the table by the edge nearest her. 'Don't stir, son,' she said, 'we'll move

the table over near you, so you won't have to leave your chair; so
you won't have to move from the fire.' As if those were the reasons
why he hadn't stirred; why he hadn't spoken!

'Come now, Rosie,' she said, moving towards the door. 'We'll
leave you to have your meal in peace, Patrick,' she said, 'while we
make your room comfortable for you. You can get to bed then as
soon as you like. Come, Rosie!' And she went towards the stairs.
At the foot of the stairs, however, she paused with her hand on the
banister rail. 'Perhaps you ought to close the kitchen door,' she said.
Why did she say that? Rosie looked sharply at her, but already Mary
was halfway upstairs. 'It's such a pity we happened to be out,' she
said, 'isn't it? It takes the house so long to get warm again when the
fire goes low.'

Still on the bottom step Rosie stared upwards. Not by one word,
not by one single word did her mother show that there was anything
unusual in the situation. Well: Rosie shrugged her shoulders. Then
she walked down the passage. Would she say anything as she closed
the door, or would she just close it quietly without looking into the
room at all?

There was no need to have been agitated. As she came to the
door she saw with relief that her brother had altered his position.
He had got up from the wicker chair and was sitting on a straight
chair drawn up to the table. She could not help noticing, though,
that he was not sitting at the place that had been laid for him, but a
the other end of the table altogether, so that his back was towards
the doorway in which she stood. He had pulled over the food, and
just then he was bending forward to grasp his knife and fork.

Silent and unsuspected, Rosie stood a moment in the doorway and
looked at him. But as he began to eat the food hungrily, and even, it
seemed to her, voraciously, she shivered, and putting out her hand
softly she drew the door towards her until it closed without a sound.

But she did not at once move away, but stood outside it, musing
at a curious impression she had had while she stared in unseen at the
great hulk of a figure. For where up to that moment she had felt
timid, and even frightened, by his heaviness and his size, just then, as
she stood in the doorway, looking at him, unsuspected, she had felt,
small as she was, in some way vastly more powerful than the huge
man with bent back leaning forward over the table; almost as if he were
in some manner a victim, over whom anyone, even she, his sister,
so slight, so frail, had yet some terrible advantage. Shivering again,
she put the thought aside and hurried up the stairs after her mother.

Mary was in Patrick's old room; the room where he used to sleep with Larry. She had begun to make the bed, and when Rosie came into the room she shook out the cold white sheet to her.

'Here,' she said, 'catch one end of this, Rosie.'

'All right, Mother,' said Rosie, and then unaccountably she stepped around to the other side of the bed and gave her mother a little push. 'I'll take this end,' she said, 'you go to the other side.'

But after they made the change, when she saw her mother standing where she had stood, with her back to the dim landing beyond, she was filled with compunction, the more so since at that moment a cold draught came up from the stairhead. Why had she made such a change? What was the matter with her? She lowered the sheet.

'Mother!' she said imperiously. 'Are you keeping something from me? Is there anything the matter with him?'

Her mother looked at her steadily.

'He's tired, child,' she said.

'Oh, I know that,' said Rosie impatiently. 'But you'd think he'd make more of an effort to act right on his first night home.'

'Now, now, child, don't be disappointed,' said Mary. 'I know it's too bad for you, but think of the terrible journey he's had. And think of me! Think of how disappointed I am at not hearing all about everything, about my Aunt Ella and all. But there will be other evenings. That's a good girl! Try not to let him see we're disappointed. Come now: take up your end of that sheet, or we'll never get this bed made.'

Rosie lifted the sheet but let it fall slack again.

'Mother!' she said. 'I wanted to tell you something. The taximan said a queer thing to me.'

'Was it about Patrick?'

Rosie nodded.

'I suppose he thought him a bit quiet,' said Mary. 'I wouldn't mind that! He was dead tired after his journey. That's why I want to get this room ready, so he can come up to bed. That's the main thing now. What he needs is a good sleep.' She turned and looked at Rosie. 'He's home; that's the main thing.'

They looked at each other. Dimly then Rosie understood that in that sentence lay the explanation of her mother's attitude. If she had noticed something odd about Patrick, she had pinned her faith to one thing, and that was that no matter what was wrong with him, she had him at home. He was home: safe between the walls of the house where he was born, within sight, within call, within reach of her arms.

Perhaps her mother was right. Perhaps he would be all right, now that he was with his own, but she sighed at the thought of the task before them. She was just about to release this sigh in a long breath when suddenly she held it, afraid to expel it, and her eyes flew to the door.

Some expression in her eyes, some catch in her breath, made Mary turn around also.

'Oh, Patrick!' she exclaimed. 'You startled me! We didn't hear you coming up the stairs. Did we?' She looked at Rosie, her cheeks burning a little with embarrassment. 'You frightened the wits out of Rosie,' she said. 'Look at her, she's like a ghost!' Then, to change the conversation she laughed, a brittle, forced laugh. 'Well!' she said. 'Do you like your room? I'm going to put a hot bottle in your bed.' She gave Rosie a nod. 'Go and get the hot water bottle, dear,' she said. But as her mother fussed about the bed, Rosie stood, reluctant to leave the room.

'Is he coming down again?' she asked, unable to speak except in a whisper.

'I don't know,' said Mary quietly, and then she looked at Patrick. He was still standing in the doorway, although she saw with relief that he was looking around the room. 'It's your own old room, son,' she said. But he made no reply. For a moment Rosie thought that it was the last straw, and that her mother was going to break down; to burst out crying, or run from the room. Instead, biting her lip for a second, she forced her face into a smile.

'Perhaps you'd like to stay up, now that you're here, son?' she said. 'Perhaps you'd like to get into bed at once? Don't mind us, if that's the way you feel. We'll have plenty of other nights to talk.'

Was it possible that he was not going to answer even now? Rosie stared at him. Then Mary spoke quietly, oh so quietly, oh so gently.

'Well, son?'

Ah, at last he answered her, in a kind of way at least: he put up his hand and began to unfasten his tie.

Then Rosie looked down at his feet, and after staring a minute, she put out her hand softly and quietly and pulled her mother's dress to draw her attention to his feet. He was still in his stocking feet. Wasn't that queer? Wasn't that unnatural? What would her mother do now?

Her mother, however, seemed to take no notice of this any more than of anything else.

'Very well, son,' she said quietly, as if in answer to something he had said. 'Have a good sleep. You'll feel better in the morning.' Then she motioned Rosie out of the room and began to follow her. At the door she stood. 'Everything will be different in the morning, son,' she said. Then, they went downstairs, she and Rosie.

'Well, he had a good meal anyway,' said Mary, a few minutes later, when she went into the kitchen, and saw the empty plates on the table. 'There's nothing wrong with his appetite anyway.'

But Rosie was staring more particularly at the table. Every plate was empty: the side plate, the bread plates, the meat dish, the butter dish, the jam dish. Impelled by more than curiosity, she leaned over the table and looked into the sugar bowl: it too was empty. Then she picked up the salt cellar and looked into it.

'Mother! Did you forget to leave him salt?' she asked.

'I don't think so,' said her mother absent-mindedly. 'At least I hope not,' she said more alertly, and she came over to the table. 'Did I?' she asked anxiously, but seeing the little glass salt cellar on the table she turned away. 'Oh no, I didn't forget it, I remember filling it.'

Rosie laid it down; she said nothing. The saltcellar, too, was empty. There was a drumming sound in her ears, and her knees felt so weak she had to sit down abruptly. Her mother, she noticed, had taken up a pillow that had been airing by the fire.

'I only gave him one pillow,' she was saying, as she thumped it to make it softer. 'I think he would like another one, don't you?'

Weak as she felt, Rosie got to her feet.

'I'll take it up to him,' she said, reaching out her hand for it.

Mary hugged the pillow against her breast.

'I had better take it myself,' she said.

'Well, I'll go with you,' said Rosie doggedly.

They looked at each other.

'Very well,' said Mary then, and they went towards the stairs. Midway up the stairs Mary paused.

'He won't want you going into his room if he's undressing,' she said triumphantly, and running up the rest of the stairs she went to the door alone. There she stopped. 'Oh, you're in bed!' Rosie heard her exclaim in surprise. Standing on the stairs she too also exclaimed, but under her breath. They had only been a few moments downstairs. How could he have got into bed in such a short time? Unable to stay below, she followed her mother up the remaining steps.

Had he undressed at all, she wondered, but as she came to the open door, before she glanced at him at all, there at the foot of the bed, on the iron rail, were his clothes laid out neatly and orderly. Then before she had time to draw her glance away, her mother had taken her by the arm.

'Ssh!' she said. 'Ssh! What do you make of that? I told you so! I told you he was played out; dead to the world.'

Rosie looked where her mother pointed. It was hard to believe it, but her brother was asleep. With his arms spread down to either side of him, over the coverlet, breathing deeply, he was in a profound sleep.

Mary raised her eyes to the holy picture over the bed.

'Thank God!' she murmured.

Like his appetite, and his great physique, so much greater now than when he left home, this deep sleep into which he had fallen so quickly, and so easily, was to her the manifestation of health. She was hardly able to tear herself away from the sight of him lying there in his own bed.

'Don't you remember,' she whispered exultingly, 'what Aunt Ella said: that he was never in better health—do you remember?'

Rosie wanted to remember. She wanted desperately to remember. But she couldn't recall the words of that letter. As far as she could remember, however, they were not exactly as her mother had repeated them.

'What did you do with the letter?' she asked, on an impulse.

'Oh, I put it somewhere,' said Mary lightly, uncomprehendingly. She was still looking at Patrick's sleeping form on the bed, but at last, stepping backwards, she lightly closed the door. 'We mustn't wake him,' she said.

Outside in the hall she laid a hand on Rosie's arm.

'In the morning we must try not to make noise with the dampers,' she said, 'because he needs all the sleep he can get.' They began to go downstairs. 'We'll bring up his breakfast,' she said, as they got to the bottom of the stairs. 'Indeed, for that matter,' she added, as they went into the kitchen, 'we ought to try and make him stay in bed for the whole day if we can possibly manage it.'

Only when her eyes fell on the remains of Patrick's meal did her spirits threaten to fail. But even then her dejection was only momentary.

'And now we must get our own meal,' she said.

Looking at her mother, Rosie remembered that they had eaten nothing since noon. And she remembered with astonishment the tired look her mother's face had worn on their way home from the city. How was it that now, so many hours later, having fasted so long, and endured so much, she could look as she did: so animated?

PART VII

Patrick

IT would be hard to say when exactly Mary began to experience her first vague fears about Patrick, or when Rosie began to define the nature of hers. Not for some days, probably, because for the few days after his return, Patrick O'Grady stayed in bed, and, for most of the time, he slept.

'I wouldn't mind that at all,' said Mary, when Rosie showed uneasiness. 'A person could not get enough sleep.'

This had been a part of Mary's philosophy since the early years of her marriage, when, month after month, she had not known what it was to sleep for more than a few hours at a time without having to get to her feet to attend to one of the children.

Sometimes a frightened cry in the night would bring her on to the floor only to find that the child that had cried out was asleep again, with no need for her comforting presence. And there had even been times when she had found herself on the cold floor, in her bare feet, awakened by an imaginary cry. In those years, she had come to think that of all God's blessings, the blessing of sleep was greatest.

'I tell you he couldn't get enough sleep, Rosie,' she repeated, when it was already past noon, and they had heard no stir in his room. All the same she went over to the door, restless and dissatisfied. 'I only wish we had some way of knowing when he wakes,' she said. 'I wouldn't want him to be lying up there awake without our knowing it.'

It had become such an accepted thing; his silence.

'I was thinking last night I'd give him a walking stick to keep beside his bed, and if he wanted to let us know he was awake he could rap on the floor and we'd hear him. There used to be a walking stick belonging to your father, somewhere in the house, but it will take me a little while to find it, I'm afraid. In the meantime he might be awake. You'd better run up and give a glance at him, Rosie.'

Rosie was not at school. There had not been any suggestion that she should stay at home, but on the other hand it had not been suggested she should go.

'He's awake!' Almost before Mary knew she had gone upstairs, Rosie was down again with this information.

Mary did not ask if he had said anything. Instead she went over and began to take from the oven the plate that had been put there to keep hot. It was Patrick's breakfast.

'It's tasteless, I'm afraid,' she said.

It was.

'You'll see he'll eat it all the same,' said Rosie.

It was one of the things that irritated her, that no matter how long he fasted, he would never call their attention to the fact that he was hungry, and yet when food was brought to him, he devoured it.

'Isn't it great he has such an appetite?' retorted Mary. 'There can't be much wrong with him.'

Rosie glanced sharply at her. This was the first time Mary admitted that there was anything at all unusual about him, but she did not seem to be deeply disturbed.

'We'll see what Larry thinks of him,' she said, almost light-heartedly. 'We'll see what he has to say.'

'To think he had to be on retreat this week of all weeks!' said Rosie. It wasn't the first time she had longed to see her young brother.

'He will be out of retreat to-morrow morning,' said Mary, 'and your letter will be waiting for him. It's likely he'll get permission to come home as soon as possible, don't you think? He may be able to get up for a while to-morrow afternoon.'

To-morrow: to-morrow afternoon. What an eternity it seemed until then. Yet the day dragged along, and evening came in course, and when it came it found the mother and daughter sitting by the kitchen fire, in much the same attitudes as those in which they had sat that morning.

The house had begun to darken. Without, the sky was still bright, but only because the westering sun had cast a last rosy beam upon the high, far clouds. Nearest to earth, the clouds were unillumined, and seemed to smudge the sky.

'Ssh!' said Mary, raising her hand once. 'Did you hear anything?'

Rosie only heard her own heartbeats. She shook her head from side to side. But suddenly she shivered.

'I wish it was this evening Larry was coming,' she said.

Mary sighed.

'It's a pity he couldn't get permission to stay home for the night,' said Rosie after a few minutes.

Mary looked up sharply.

'I suppose he could get permission all right if we wrote and told the Superior about Patrick.'

'Told him everything, you mean?' said Rosie, startled.

'Oh no,' said Mary immediately. 'We might have mentioned that Patrick wasn't very well, perhaps, that he wasn't just himself as it were, but it wouldn't be right to make out there was anything very wrong, just for the sake of getting Larry home for a night!'

There was silence. Mary looked into the fire.

'Oh dear, oh dear,' she said then, 'what on earth has come over Patrick?'

It was, for Rosie, the saddest hour of all they had lived through in the whole three days.

Poor Mother! She wanted to run over and throw herself down at Mary's knees, but that wouldn't help matters. Was there nothing else she could do?

'I wonder if there would be any use in me trying to coax him to get up and come downstairs,' she said. She got to her feet.

'I wouldn't try to force him to get up against his will,' said Mary, slowly and reluctantly, and obviously with something else yet to say. 'Don't forget,' she said then, in a low voice, 'he'll have to shave if he's coming downstairs.'

That was another thing: the very day after he came home he had shown the need for a shave. Mary herself had been the first to comment on it.

'He won't look so bad when he shaves,' she said, after Rosie came down from his room with a frightened look. She had gone up to bring down a tray, but she hadn't gone beyond the door of his room.

'Well, I wish he'd hurry up and shave then,' Rosie answered crossly.

'None of that, now, Rosie,' said Mary sharply. 'What need is there for him to shave if he's going to stay in bed all day? I often think it must be a great rest for a man once in a while not to have to shave. I know your father used to say that was the only reason he'd like to live in the country; that he wouldn't need to shave every day. How I used to laugh. I used to tell him that my father, that's your grandfather, was the exactest shaved man I ever saw in my life.'

That was the second day after Patrick's return. By the next day he was almost transformed by the great uncouth growth of hair on his face.

After seeing him on that day, Rosie was almost hysterical.

'You'll have to say something to him, Mother,' she said. 'He looks terrible.'

'But I did say something. I spoke about it this morning first thing,' said her mother.

'How did he take it?'

Mary hesitated.

'He didn't seem to take it very well! A kind of a frown came over his face.'

'I'll tell you what we'll do,' said Rosie suddenly. 'We'll open his portmanteau, and get out his shaving things, and we'll set them out on the table beside the bed, ready to use, and we'll see what he'll do then.' She stood up. 'I'll have to make some excuse for going to his suitcase, but I was thinking last night that we ought to unpack it anyway, and hang up his clothes. So I could tell him I was going to do that, to unpack his clothes, but at the same time I'd take the opportunity of getting out his shaving things. What do you think of that?'

Mary didn't know what to think. She had misgivings, but at the same time anything seemed better than the inaction of the past few days.

'Well?' she asked eagerly some time later, when Rosie came back into the kitchen, but Rosie put up a finger to her lips. Her face was all animated, and her eyes were almost feverishly bright. Mary felt her heart begin to pound against her ribs.

'He didn't like to see me going near the case,' said Rosie in a whisper.

'Oh, I hope you didn't touch it so!' cried her mother.

'Don't be silly!' said Rosie. 'I paid no attention to him at all. I just went right ahead and opened it, and took out his things. Oh, Mother! If you saw his things!'

Only at this point did Mary realize that it was due to some pleasurable cause that her daughter was in such a fever; such a glow.

'Yes, yes?' she cried eagerly.

'Oh, you should have seen into that case!' cried Rosie. 'Such ties! I never saw anything like them, and so many pairs of shoes: I must have counted ten! As for gloves and handkerchiefs: if you just saw those handkerchiefs! They all had his monogram done in red silk floss. And he has two other suits besides the one he wore the night he came home. If you saw them! There's one dark one, with a small stripe in it, and it's as light as a feather, and the other one——'

All at once Mary lost her patience. Rosie had changed towards Patrick since seeing his clothes.

'Never mind about his clothes,' she said drily. 'What about his shaving things?'

It was hardly fair to throw cold water upon such animation. In Rosie's face the light quenched.

'That's what I came down to tell you,' she said then, dejectedly. 'I couldn't find them. You didn't take them and put them anywhere, did you?'

Mary answered her with one look.

'I knew you didn't,' said Rosie, still more crestfallen. She looked at her mother. 'Do you think he didn't bring them with him at all? How did he manage on the boat?' But before her mother could say anything, she was talking again. 'I forgot to tell you about the way his clothes were packed; you never saw anything like it.'

'What is remarkable in that?' said her mother. 'It was probably Aunt Ella who packed for him: she was always as natty as an old maid.'

'In that case,' said Rosie, 'isn't it odd she didn't put in his shaving things?'

'Oh, for goodness' sake, Rosie,' said Mary, standing up, 'I wish you'd stop this nonsense. You're always making mountains out of molehills. There's some simple explanation: you'll see.'

Rosie shrugged her shoulders.

'Explanation or no explanation, he'll have to have the barber come in to him; he won't be fit to go out in the street if he goes on like this much longer,' she said. 'Even by to-morrow he'll look pretty terrible.'

And to-morrow, or so they hoped, Larry would be home.

'Perhaps if I mentioned to him that we were expecting Larry it might stir him to do something about it,' said Mary after a little while.

Rosie did not reply at once. She was thinking.

'Do you know, Mother,' she said then, 'I'd just as soon Larry would see him the way he is.'

'Listen!' For the second time, Mary put up her hand. 'Did you not hear anything that time?' she asked.

'Oh, don't be so jumpy, Mother,' said Rosie, but almost as she spoke, she heard a distinct sound on the ceiling overhead. Then they both heard a step on the stairs.

'He's coming down,' cried Mary. and instantly all her fears were dispelled. Elated she got to her feet. 'We're here, son!' she cried.

Rosie stared at her. Her mother's face was transfigured with happiness, and after hearing that step, her first thought had been to drag over the old wicker chair to the fire. When, however, the footsteps seemed to go not towards the kitchen at all, but in the opposite direction, she called out again.

'——in here, son!'

But the steps did not alter their course, and the next thing the two women heard was the clap of the hall door.

Together they waited a moment, looking at each other, and then Rosie ran into the parlour, and pressed her face to the window. A minute later she turned around.

'Oh, for goodness' sake, Mother, don't do that!' she cried. 'What good will that do?' Because her mother had begun to sob.

'Oh, where has he gone?' she sobbed.

Where indeed, thought Rosie? But her feelings and Mary's were different.

'Oh, Mother! Please! Please!' she cried, putting her arms around the convulsed figure that crouched so despairingly against the wall. 'You'll see,' she said, 'he'll be back in a few minutes.'

Would he? Was it true that she thought he would come back? Rosie did not know, but as she felt her mother's sobbing grow less violent, a dreadful, dreadful thought passed through her mind. Perhaps it was a sinful thought, but as it blazed through her brain it was bright and beautiful as a comet. And yet, how could she have let such a thought enter her head about her own brother! What kind of a creature could she be to have given countenance to such an evil thought; such an evil wish! For she had wished—yes; she, his sister, had wished——

Ah! Sinful it may have been, that wish, but the enormity of it seemed, like all sin, to be the greater for being vain and ineffectual when, only a short while after they had heard the door close behind him, from the parlour window they saw him coming up the path again.

'Look!' cried Mary, for even in the dusk they could see that he had been shaved. 'I'll open the door,' she said, springing to her feet. Then she looked back at Rosie. 'He must have spoken to the barber,' she said. 'He couldn't have just walked in and said nothing, and sat down and expected him to know what he wanted.'

Rosie too had thought of the same thing, but it made her nervous to see her mother delaying at such an important moment.

'Are you going to open the door or not?' she said, testily, making a move as if she herself would go to the door.

At that minute, however, they heard the sound of fumbling at the letter box, and the hall door opened. With a last victorious glance cast back at her daughter, Mary rushed into the hall.

'So you didn't forget the string on the latch!' she cried.

~   ~   ~   ~

He had spoken.

From the parlour, Rosie heard him and gasped. Then she, too, like her mother, ran into the hall to meet him.

To say that, for a moment, his mother and sister did not know him would perhaps adequately express the startled feeling with which they beheld him. But taken literally the phrase would have been quite untrue, because, in that moment only, for the first time since he lurched into their lives, did they really seem to know him, really to recognize in him the person they might have expected: the son; the brother. Yes, indeed, here at last was Patrick O'Grady come home to his mother and sister. And here, if you like, although somewhat more robust, somewhat less youthful, here, too, was the young man of the photograph in the parlour.

And what had he said that had wrought this change in everything? Only a few simple words, uttered quite casually as, with a gesture equally casual and natural, he took off his hat and coat, and hung them on the rack inside the door.

'Well!' That was the first word; a mere exclamation. And then he repeated it. 'Well!' he said. 'The old street hasn't changed much!'

That was all; only a few words, ordinary and commonplace, yet by them Mary and Rosie were lifted up from the depths into a region of blinding light and happiness.

For it was so exactly, oh but so absolutely exactly what, things having been different, he might have been expected to say on that first night of all when they had come, all three of them, into the kitchen, and the door had shut upon the darkness without and upon the sound of his taxi driving away into the night.

'I just stepped out to get a shave,' he said then, speaking again because Mary and Rosie were in truth too astonished as yet to say anything. But neither of them failed to notice the naturalness of the way he stroked his chin with the thumb and forefinger of his right hand. It was a gesture so absolutely true and universal.

Brighter and brighter shone the light about them; the whole world was lit again. And as, accompanying them into the kitchen, he looked at them attentively, it might well be that he was bewildered at the radiance of their countenances. Rosie in particular held his eyes. And impetuously he put his hand under her chin.

'Say! I didn't expect to come home and find you such a beauty,' he said. Then he turned back to his mother. 'She's just like you used to look in the photographs in the old album you used to give us on wet days, the one with all the old-fashioned pictures; do you remember?'

Mary remembered, but she could only nod her head for fear the tears of joy that filled her eyes would brim over and roll down her cheeks.

As if she had forgotten one minute of that past, that precious past into which she was always ready to wander!

'I remember,' she said, but she made no attempt to linger over the scenes he recalled. The past still shone as golden and beautiful as ever, but to-night the present was sufficiently beautiful for her.

So she only smiled, and pulled up a chair for him at the fire.

'Where did you go for your haircut?' she asked, brightly, briskly, because as she looked at him in the light she saw that in addition to being shaved, he had had his hair trimmed.

Patrick sat down.

'To Oakley's, where else?' he said, quite as if he had never set foot in any other barber's shop in all his life.

Old Mr. Oakley was the local barber whose premises were just on the other side of the bridge from the O'Gradys' house, and he had had the patronage of the O'Grady family since Tom got his first haircut after they settled into the locality.

'I'm glad you went there,' said Mary.

'Yes, it was like old times,' said Patrick.

Rosie meanwhile said nothing, but she looked at the others blissfully. Was it not enough that they were sitting there talking, and that in every word they said, commonplace though it might be, there was a glow of warmth and light?

'Did you see old Mr. Oakley himself?' she cried at last, because she was aching to enter the shining circle of the conversation. 'He was always asking about you! I never could pass without being stopped for news of you!'

Patrick smiled.

'I saw him,' he said. 'The old man didn't change one bit. I'd swear he looked the same as the day I last saw him.'

'And he knew you?' asked Mary. 'I bet he knew you right away!' For looking at him as he now was, she had begun to forget the strange heavy man that lived in his place for the past four days.

'Of course he knew me,' cried Patrick. 'The minute I walked into the shop!' And at this they all looked at each other with satisfaction.

'Did you see old Mrs. Oakley?' asked Mary then.

But here Patrick put up his hands defensively, and they all laughed. They knew Mrs. Oakley.

'Thanks be to goodness, no!' he said. 'Mr. Oakley wanted to go upstairs and get her down, but I managed to stop him; I managed to get away, with a promise to call again.'

It was all very well to laugh, but Mary wasn't so sure that that was the way she wanted her son to behave.

'Oh, you'll have to call again, son,' she said. 'You wouldn't want to hurt their feelings.'

Patrick turned to her and smiled; a broad, heart-warming smile.

'Feelings?' he exclaimed. 'There's a word I haven't heard for years. I know I'm home again now that I hear that word. In America people don't waste much time upon feelings.'

Again he smiled, but perhaps not so broadly this time.

'Did you like America, Patrick?' Rosie had taken courage, and asked another question. 'What is it like?' she asked eagerly.

'Well now, that's a big question, Rosie,' said her brother. 'I say, the best thing you can do would be to go out there for a spell. You'd get your answer then. You'd get it at first hand.'

Something in his gaze made Rosie feel good, and she smiled back at him, in a smile that matched the brilliance of her eyes, which shone with a lovely lustre. Looking at her, with more and more conviction that she was very pretty, her brother spoke more soberly.

'That's what they want over there, I can tell you; girls like you!'

By now, however, Rosie was blushing so much that Mary felt bound to intervene.

'Did you see anyone else you knew while you were out for your walk, Patrick?' she asked. 'Did you meet anyone you knew in the barber shop?'

'Not a soul!' Reluctantly Patrick withdrew his eyes from Rosie. 'I suppose most people go down town nowadays when they want a decent shave.'

'Oh, I don't know. Old Mr. Oakley is supposed to be pretty good. Your father always went to him,' said his mother, a little aggrieved.

Patrick laughed.

'All I remember clearly about my dad is that he always had the worst haircut I ever saw. Say! If old Oakley was in America he would have been put out of business twenty years ago. They have no time out there for anything but the best.'

'Is that so?' said Mary a little coldly. 'He seems to be doing fairly well. Didn't you see the new shop front he had built: a new show-board and all?'

'Was it new? I thought it was the same old one.' He laughed. 'Waste of time and money,' he added abruptly, and when Mary seemed about to say something else, he put up his hand to forestall her. 'What did he do but tear down a few rotten old boards and put up a few more that will be rotted again before long?' he demanded. 'Well?' he challenged, leaning forward. 'What more did he do? I didn't see behind the shop, but I caught sight of the stairs, the same old wooden stairs with the brass tips, so I suppose that he did nothing to the inside at all. It's a new front, but inside it's the same little box of a place as ever; cramped, and dark as a vault.'

'They were going to do something to the inside, I thought,' said Mary, looking questioningly at Rosie.

'They were going to get the whole place done from top to bottom,' said Rosie earnestly, 'but they put off doing anything more for the time being.'

Patrick laughed.

'For the time being,' he said, repeating her last words. 'Another indication that I am at home. Why, if that was in America they'd have pulled down the whole shack and built it up from the bottom. That's America!' he said proudly. 'We pull down the old century and put up the new.'

A little bewildered, Rosie stared at him. But wasn't that what she had expected, after all, that she would be bewildered, nay, more, that she would be dazzled by him, and by all he had to tell them? For, had it not seemed to her, a while ago, that when he came home, there still must play around him some flashes from that glittering world across the ocean?

Mary too was bewildered, but not quite in the same way as her daughter. It was thinking about the Oakleys that had bewildered her. Where would the Oakleys go while all this was being done, she wondered, and a feeling of nervousness came over her. In her mind, she saw a new building, slim, white and virgin, and a feeling of pity came over her at how awkward poor Mrs. Oakley would feel in such surroundings. She would have to keep out from the walls when she moved about the house, and not rub against the wallpaper; and she would have to give up tilting her chair and leaning her head back against the wall, when she took a bit of a rest behind the counter in the evenings, because it would never do at all to get the new walls all marked with patches of grease.

It didn't matter so much with the old walls, because the wallpaper had an all-over greasy look anyway, and as well as that the pattern hid the stains a bit, being a big sprawling pattern.

But what was that Patrick was saying? She had missed something he said, although she had not missed seeing that he was enjoying himself more and more every minute. Just now he was answeri g a question put to him by Rosie.

'Sure!' he said. 'And do you know how long it would take to put up the new building? About two months! Figure that out: How long do you think it would take in this country? About ten years, I'd say, if I remember rightly the easygoing ways of the people here.'

But suddenly, in the midst of his excitement, he sank back in his chair.

'Easygoing!' he said again. 'But maybe that's why it's so good to be back home.' Turning deliberately to her, he stared his mother in the face.

Her crown! He had at last produced and placed on her brow her rightful crown.

Never, for many a long year, had Mary felt so proud. But she was not going to be foolish; to cry or to exclaim. She was going to keep on talking naturally and normally.

'Did Mr. Oakley have anything new to say?' she asked.

'That depends on what you consider new,' said Patrick gaily. 'If you call it new to sit and listen to the everlasting praise of Floss and Minnie, then——'

But just as he was about to say something else, Patrick became aware that Rosie had glanced at her mother: quickly and nervously.

Then he remembered.

Minnie and Floss Oakley had been to school with Ellie and Angie. They had all been about the same age, and although they hadn't much in common when they grew up, they used to play together when they were little girls, and so now Mary never saw them without a pain in her heart, never heard their names without a catch at her heartstrings.

And that, of course, was why Rosie had flashed a glance at her.

But it was too late. Mary nodded her head sadly.

'They're both married now,' she said. 'Minnie was married the year——'

But how quick Patrick was! How sensitive! He was almost like a woman. For in a flash he had guessed in what year Minnie Oakley had been married, and he did not allow Mary to say anything more.

'I know,' he said quickly, and leaning over he took their mother's hand in his. 'I know. Don't think about it, Mother! I wish I hadn't mentioned them at all. Don't distress yourself, Mother!' Then patting her hand softly, he sighed himself. 'Who knows,' he said, 'everything happens for the best, they say. From what I gathered, Minnie's life isn't all a bed of roses.'

Mary lifted a corner of her apron, and dried the tears that had escaped.

'That's right, son,' she said. But she spoke without conviction. It was just that she wasn't going to give way: she wasn't going to spoil his first night at home. For it seemed to her now that it was indeed his very first night among them. It was enough that she had his sympathy; his understanding. Some other time she might unlock her heart to him. But not now!

'I'm all right, son,' she said, withdrawing her hand from his. 'I don't feel so bad—now. It's only at times it all comes over me; but it passes again. Now that you're home I'll have no excuse to be going back over things that are past and done, and can't be undone.'

He patted her knee.

'That's right, Mother,' he said, and his face took on a pleased boyish look.

Seeing it, Mary could not help repeating the sentiments that had given him pleasure.

'It will be different now that I have you back again.'

But Patrick was hardly attending this time to what she said, or else he put a different interpretation on her words, for looking around the dingy kitchen, he exclaimed suddenly.

'I'll say it will be different,' he said, and he waved his hand at the walls. 'Wait till you see all the changes I'm going to make around here.'

A little dazed Mary looked around her also.

'Is it the walls you mean?' she said. 'I meant to have them papered before you came home but I let it slip. I was so used to your father doing all that kind of thing for me that——' Pausing suddenly she was unable to understand how it was that she had let the place get so neglected. 'It's very bad, isn't it?' she said, struck with shame.

Rosie too was ashamed.

'I told you long ago it was a show,' she said, turning accusingly to Mary. 'The whole house is a show if it comes to that. The parlour is a sight.' She looked hard at Patrick, and remembering his foulard dressing gown and his pigskin gloves, she felt angry in case he might think she had been content with her lot, that she had not seen how poor and wretched their house had become. What her mother might feel at her words she did not wait to consider. 'It's a rotten little house anyway,' she said. 'I'm always saying that.'

But Mary was hurt; deeply hurt.

'That's all very well for you to say, Rosie,' she cried, 'but you never saw this house as it was in your father's time. But Patrick remembers it, don't you, Patrick? Don't you remember how nice it was then? People used to love to come into it. And our parlour—do you remember the way it used to look, with the lamp lit and a big fire roaring up the chimney, and everything so bright? Do you remember, son: so bright; so bright!'

As she repeated those words—'so bright, so bright'—a spark seemed to kindle in Patrick. Ignoring Rosie, he looked back at his mother.

'I do!' he cried. 'I do! Many and many a day I thought of that little parlour.' Standing up, he walked over abruptly and opened the door that led into it. At once a faint odour of damp, and even of stale dust, wafted out to them; yet he, when he turned around, was all aglow.

'It's not so bad at all,' he said. 'It wouldn't take much to make it the same as it was always!' Closing the door he came back into the kitchen, but this time he did not sit down. A new energy and anima-tion had taken possession of him, and walking around the kitchen he critically examined the walls. 'The walls are sound enough,' he said. 'It's only paper and paint that's needed, and that's a small job. I'll have it attended to right away. A few pounds ought to put the whole house to rights.'

But as he spoke, a shadow seemed to fall on him for a moment. And seeing it, Mary's heart trembled.

'You'll want your money, son,' she said, in a low voice.

For a terrible moment, Rosie thought he was not going to answer. Then, rubbing his hand across his forehead, he seemed to brush aside whatever had shadowed his mind.

'That's true for you, Mother,' he said practically, and even cheer-fully. 'But why pay anyone to do what I can do myself as good as anyone? You say Father used to do it! Well, why wouldn't I do it?' Eagerly he looked around him. 'I'd do this kitchen in one night!' he cried. 'I would!' Stepping up on a chair suddenly, he pulled off a piece of paper that was hanging loosely down. 'Have you a step-ladder?' he asked. 'No! Well, never mind, a big packing case would do me as well, and I'll get that easily enough somewhere.' Still on the chair, and as if reluctant to step down, he looked at them. 'Why,' he said, 'this will be child's play to some of the things I've done in America. I'd do the whole house inside a week!'

And then, as if to silence their protestations by seeking bigger things to do, he stepped down from the chair, and going to the back door he opened it and looked out.

'I'll do the outside of the house as well,' he said. 'The outer wood-work is pretty bad. As a matter of fact, I think I'll start on the outside of the house,' he said, when at last they persuaded him to sit down again by the fire. 'The front in particular looks very neglected.'

So he had seen that too? Even in the fading light he had seen the dilapidated look of the outside of the house.

'Yes! I will certainly start with the front of the house. I have half a mind to begin to-morrow,' he said. But then another thought struck him. 'It's a wonder the landlord doesn't see to it,' he said. 'I thought the tenant was always responsible for the inside, and that the landlord had to do the outside. Isn't that the law, or am I thinking of America?'

'You must be thinking of America,' said Mary, 'either that or else our landlord got into the habit of leaving it to us to do, on account of the way your father was always beforehand in doing it. He never could wait for any landlord: he loved tinkering with pots and paint.'

Patrick was hardly listening.

'What about the rest of the people in the street?' he asked. 'They don't all own their houses, do they? I may as well tell you that I couldn't help noticing, as I came along from the barber's, that our hall door was the shabbiest in the whole street. What do the people in the other houses do? Who paints their door and windows; them-selves or the landlord?'

But what did Mary know of such matters? She had always been vague about such things, and without curiosity. But she did remember that a solicitor had called and explained something to her a few years back. Now what had he told her? Something about the terrace having been sold, and that the houses were no longer all under one landlord, but that some were bought by one man and some by an altogether different man. And—oh yes, she remembered now: most of the tenants had bought out their own interest.

'You mean they own their own houses?' asked Patrick, and then he nodded. 'Something like that came into my head, mind you,' he said, 'as I was walking along. I noticed that the hall doors were all different colours, whereas long ago they used to be all the same. I can remember them well; all the same dull green, all, that is to say, except ours,' he added, 'ours and Maguire's.'

How sharp he was to have noticed a little thing like that, when he was so young, and to have remembered it all those years. Mary's pride in him increased.

'That's right,' she said. 'The old landlord used to send one man around to do all the hall doors, and he always did them the same, and the windows the same too: all except ours and Maguire's: ours because your father was so impatient, and the Maguire's, of course, because they had bought their house years ago; before we ever came to live here at all.'

'I remember,' said Patrick again. 'Their door used to be a dark green, much darker than any other door in the terrace.'

For a minute he was silent, as if he were thinking of that distant past, and then surprisingly, by his next words they saw it was of the present he had been thinking.

'And it's just the same still,' he said. 'I stood outside the gate this evening for a full minute looking at it. It's the same; exactly the same: the same colour on the door, the same shine on the brasses, and the same curtains on the windows. It made me smile. Even the front garden! As neat as ever: newly dug, and ready for planting. And I could just imagine that in a few months the same old wallflowers would bloom in the beds under the window. And I suppose it's the same inside as it is outside. I was nearly tempted to open the gate and walk up to the hall door and call to see them. But I thought I'd better not. I thought I'd better ask you about them first. Are they all well? How is old Maguire? I hope he's still alive? And poor old Mrs. Maguire, still sitting inside her lace curtains, I suppose, and watching out at the world. Do you remember what I said a few minutes ago about poor Mr. Oakley's place, and how, if this was America, it would be pulled down long ago? Well, when I was standing outside Maguire's, I thought to myself there are some things stronger than progress. You can't tear down Mrs. Maguire's lace curtains. But tell me: are they all well? I must go in to see them. To-morrow, perhaps?'

At the thought of the visit, his face again wore the exceedingly youthful expression that they already had noticed once or twice, but as he looked at Mary for her approbation of his plans, his expression altered.

'They're still living there, aren't they? The Maguires, I mean?' he asked suddenly. 'The second house from the end of the row?'

'Oh yes, they're still there.'

It was Rosie who answered although it was to his mother Patrick had turned. And as she answered, she too turned to Mary.

Why hadn't her mother answered such a simple question?

'Yes, they're still there,' said Mary then, quite as if Rosie had not answered at all. Did Rosie imagine it, or was her voice dull? And did Patrick notice it?

If he noticed it he said nothing.

'Old Mr. Maguire has got a bit feeble,' said Mary after a few minutes. 'He doesn't go out much now at all; he's been getting his pension for years, of course. You knew that? He hasn't been working for a long time, but he used to be very active in the garden. Now he's hardly ever out of doors.'

'Mrs. Maguire is very well, though,' said Rosie, volunteering the information quickly because there seemed to be a strain in the atmosphere ever since those Maguires were mentioned. 'She looks the same to me as she always did,' she added, for want of something to say.

To her astonishment, her mother seemed to resent what she said.

'Why wouldn't she?' she demanded angrily. 'Isn't she all the time sitting in an armchair reading novels? It would take a great deal to worry that woman!'

Rosie stared, but to her relief Patrick laughed.

'You never forgave her for only having the one ewe lamb, Mother,' he said, 'when you had a houseful of us, plaguing you at every step you took, under your feet all day, and keeping you out of your bed at night with all the darning and mending you had to do for us! Very little time you ever got for reading! Isn't that so, Mother? Come now; tell the truth,' he said, and this time there was such a note of excitement and elation in his voice that, looking at him, it was almost impossible to believe that this was the man who, an hour before, had been so silent and morose.

Such a change! And all brought about by those two stuffy old people down the street. Why was he so interested in them? Rosie wondered. Then she noticed something. He had not asked for Alice; wasn't that odd? A faint memory came back to her. Wasn't Patrick great with Alice, one time, long ago, or wasn't she fond of him, or something? Then why didn't he mention her name? She looked at him. Ah, that was it! He was hoping that they would speak of her first. But didn't he know——

Uneasily she glanced at her mother. Patrick, however, could wait no longer.

'And Alice?' he said, his voice almost uncontrollable in its excitement.

Without taking her eyes away from her mother's face, Rosie waited. What would her mother say?

Suddenly she felt that a game was going on between these two; a game she didn't understand.

'You never mentioned her in any of your letters,' said Patrick more quietly.

'Didn't I?' said Mary, dully.

Gradually the light was fading from Patrick's face.

'She isn't married, is she?'

As Mary hesitated to answer, and Rosie saw her lips moving, she thought for a moment that her mother was going to tell a lie—to say that Alice was married.

To her relief Mary did not lie.

'No, she's not married,' she said.

'Ah-ha!' Patrick's face lit up again. More than that, he began to laugh joyously, youthfully, like a boy, as if he longed to shout, to throw his arms into the air. 'I knew you'd have told me,' he cried, looking at Mary; and then he turned exultingly to Rosie. 'Alice used to be my sweetheart,' he cried.

It was then that Mary stood up. She could bear no more.

'Sweetheart!' she said bitterly. 'Very little notice you took of poor Alice.'

'Poor Alice! Why so poor?' Patrick too stood up, but only because his excitement had increased. Pacing up and down the floor he began to talk furiously. 'She would have been a lot poorer if I had not kept my head in those days. What would she have done if I had spoken my feelings for her then? Waited for nine years for me? Or come with me and been dragged——' Suddenly, unexpectedly, in the middle of a sentence, he stopped, and a shudder passed through him, but almost at once he began to pace up and down again. 'It's better this way,' he said, and he leaned forward. 'Isn't it a funny thing, I often thought of her. I often wondered if she were married, or if she ever thought of me after I went away.'

'She thought of you all right,' said Rosie, suddenly remembering other things out of the past, but Mary intervened sharply.

'What do you know about it?' she said crossly.

Silenced, Rosie shrank back.

'Isn't it funny,' said Patrick again, 'when she was a kid I used to think she was plain-looking: her hair was so straight but it wasn't so much that her hair was thin as that it was fine and silky.' He paused. 'And as for her face—I never saw a face like it anywhere I went,' he said solemnly.

But he couldn't be solemn for long.

'I must call and see them!' he cried again, as if it were a line of a song that broke from his throat involuntarily every few minutes. But then another thought occurred to him. 'Does Alice know I'm back?' he said. 'It's a wonder she hasn't been in to see me. She used to be in and out all the time, in the old days. Isn't that so?'

Mary nodded.

'Isn't it the same now?' he asked.

But at that moment he remembered Minnie and Floss Oakley, and how his mother had felt when he mentioned their names. Perhaps it was the same with Alice.

'I'm sorry, Mother. I suppose things are not the same since—since the girls——' He could not say any more. 'I keep forgetting. It isn't as if I was here when it happened. I just imagine they're out somewhere, and that they'll be back any minute. All the same,' he said after a minute, 'I'm surprised at Alice! I thought she'd come in oftener after that to try and take their places. I'm disappointed in her,' he said.

'Oh, don't say that,' cried Mary. 'Poor Alice. She did all she could. She couldn't have done more. Don't say anything against her.'

Slightly puzzled, Patrick looked at his mother. Then he turned to Rosie.

'Alice Maguire was very fond of you, Rosie. If I remember rightly, she nearly reared you and Larry.'

Larry? It was the first time he had mentioned him. Rosie and Mary both looked up with a start. They too had forgotten all about him in the past few hours.

'You didn't ask for Larry at all, son,' said Mary, and she seemed to grasp eagerly at the opportunity of changing the conversation. 'He'll be home to-morrow, we hope,' she said.

'Good!' said Patrick. 'That's good. I was afraid I'd have to go down to the Seminary to see him. I didn't fancy that.'

'Oh, but it's a lovely place,' said Rosie.

'Maybe,' said Patrick, 'but I don't like institutions, and that's all I want to hear about it. See! Tell me more about Alice,' he said, abruptly, and ignoring Mary this time he spoke directly to Rosie, keeping his eyes so fixedly upon her that she was unable to look away; unable to seek her mother's eyes and find guidance or counsel in them.

'I don't know much about her,' she floundered. 'I haven't heard much about her lately.'

'Heard? She's not gone away, has she?'

The urgent look on his face almost paralysed her.

'I thought the old couple never let her away from them; don't tell me she's broken loose and taken a job?'

Rosie shook her head.

'Well, where is she, then?'

Wrenching her gaze free of those terrible eyes, Rosie almost ran over to her mother.

'You tell him, Mother,' she cried, but the next minute when she saw those terrible eyes fixed upon her mother's blanched face she felt still more afraid than ever.

What would her mother say?

'I thought I told you in a letter, Patrick.' That was all her mother could say at first, and with a sinking feeling, Rosie heard the false note of fear in her voice.

'Told me what?' said the voice of the man, flat, hard, utterly changed. 'You told me nothing,' he said, accusingly, menacingly, and he moved nearer to them both. 'What was there to tell? What are you keeping from me?' Although he hadn't come any nearer now it seemed to Rosie that his face had come so close up to theirs that she could feel his hot breath breaking over her in gusts.

Unable to bear the strain another minute, she stepped in front of her mother.

'That she had to go away for a while!' she cried.

At once his face was thrust towards her. To fend off that face she would say anything.

'To a sanitorium,' she cried.

For one, long, paralysing moment her brother's face was so close to hers that she couldn't see his features but only the dark flush of his flesh, and then—then he was sitting in a chair, slumped down, and the air flowed free again, and she was able to breathe. But something had happened.

He's going to stop talking, she thought; he's going to be silent again. He's not going to speak to us any more, ever! A great pity for him came over her. But suddenly he started up.

'Is that the truth?' he said, and it was Rosie he addressed.

No longer afraid she answered him.

'It is,' she said. 'It is. Yes, Patrick.'

'Do you swear it?'

'Why should I say it if it wasn't true?' she said quietly.

'Are you sure it's nothing worse?'

What could he mean?

'What could be worse?' she cried.

'You swear it's a sanitorium? Only a sanitorium?'

Only a sanitorium! What kind of talk was that? Her pity for him vanished. And the next minute she heard her own voice lashing out at him.

'What could be worse than that?' she cried. 'She's in the wing for incurables. I went to see her. I saw her. Oh, it was awful. Her hair was all grey, and her cheeks were sunk in her face! You'd think she was about forty instead of only——'

'Only twenty-six,' said her brother. Then he sat back in his chair. And silence came down upon them all.

The tears were raining down Mary's face. In Rosie's heart a cold despair had settled. He won't speak. He'll sit there for ever and he'll never say another word. Oh, what will we do, she thought? Things are worse than ever now.

But once more, to her joy she was wrong. He had spoken; he had said something else, though so low she hadn't caught it.

'Did you say something, Patrick?' she said gently, oh so gently.

But her voice could never be as gentle as the voice that whispered back at her.

'Little Alice! Little Alice!'

~   ~   ~   ~

Larry came home next day.

'Here he is at last,' cried Mary, as a foot sounded on the path outside the door. 'Now, Rosie, I beg of you not to rush out, and frighten him. We agreed that it would be better not to tell him anything, but to let him judge for himself after he has been upstairs.'

For Patrick had sunk back into the condition in which he had been at first. He had not come downstairs all that day.

'Now, don't be obstinate, Rosie,' said Mary, as she saw the set of Rosie's lips.

'Very well, Mother,' said Rosie coldly, but she came back from the door towards which she had rushed so eagerly at the sound of the footsteps. 'Very well so,' she said, 'but you'd better meet him yourself then: I'd blurt out everything.'

'Ssh!' said Mary.

For Larry was upon them; he was coming down the hall.

'Ssh!' she said again. 'Ssh!'

And yet, after all, it was Mary herself who broke down, or perhaps that is not the right word to use. Perhaps the change that came over her was attributable to the change that had come over Larry himself since she had last seen him.

And how long ago was it since they had last seen him? Only about ten days before they had been down to see him at the Seminary. And yet, it seemed to Mary when he opened the door that in the time that had intervened an incalculable change had come over him.

Was there some change in what he wore? Taking him in from head to foot, Mary was surprised to see there was no change in his attire. It was something about the way he walked; she almost expected to see that he wore some loosely flowing garment like the black petticoat that the priests in St. Mary's wore when they walked in the chapel garden, saying their Office, while they were waiting for the Mass hour to come. But it was only a mistaken impression, because Larry was wearing his usual clothes, and indeed they were getting shabby, and the sleeves were beginning to fray. Then she saw his hands, and a curious feeling came over her, because she would hardly have known them. She who had washed them and scrubbed them, and cleaned the fingernails, and pared them and filed them, and painted them with bitter aloes to keep him from biting them: she, his mother, would hardly have known them, they were so white, and so well cared for, so smooth. They were priestly, she thought, and as he stood in the doorway, so tall, so thin, and so pale, that was what he looked too: priestly. And suddenly, under some impulse, flinging herself forward, she stretched out her hands in supplication, not to the son in him, but to the priest.

'Oh, thank God you've come,' she cried. 'We're nearly out of our mind. We didn't know what to do. He's up there——'

'Patrick?' said the cleric. 'There's something wrong with him?'

Incisively, but without probing the wound too much, he wanted to get to the heart of the trouble.

Rosie nodded miserably.

'He's up there on the bed, and he doesn't say a word to us.'

'I knew there was something wrong,' said Larry. 'I read between the lines of Rosie's letter. And then the minute I opened the door and stepped into the house, I felt there was something——'

'Yes,' cried Rosie—'the silence! You'd notice it the minute you set foot inside the door! It presses down on you!'

She put up her hand to her head with a frightened gesture.

'He doesn't talk, you say? Did he say anything at all?'

'Oh yes.' Mary had recovered. Something in Rosie's gesture of pressing her hands to her head annoyed her. 'Oh yes,' she cried. 'Last night he went out for a little while, and when he came back he was all talk: for a while anyway.'

'I see!' Larry's face was stern: so stern. 'Has anyone seen him?' he asked.

'Anyone?'

Larry was impatient. 'A doctor, I mean,' he said sharply.

This, however, was going too far.

'Oh, there's no need for a doctor,' cried Mary.

She wasn't going to hear of a doctor being brought into the house. A thought of Alice flashed capriciously across her mind, and of something she had said to the child years ago. Leave doctors alone, she said, as long as you can. You never know what you'll be led into by them.

Since he had come into the kitchen, Larry had lost some of his sacerdotal qualities, and when at that moment he swung his leg upward and sat on the edge of the kitchen table, she felt once more that he was her son: her own son.

'This isn't a case for doctors,' she said. 'If that's all the help you're going to give us, you could have stayed where you were!'

Was he listening to her? He was listening all right, but at the same time she did not feel that her words were touching him. He's changed, she thought. He's not one of us any more. But she had to keep talking.

'It's only something or other that has got on his nerves,' she said. 'I was reading your grandaunt's letter again and I took note of what she said about all the people that lost their money, and I was thinking that perhaps she was trying to break it to us that Patrick might have lost his money; or some of it. He certainly has not got much money with him because Rosie and I looked in his pockets when he was asleep and all we found was a few pounds. And you know,' she looked up at him—'if that was the case it would be enough to depress anyone, especially Patrick, who always set such store on making money. That's it, I'm sure. That would explain everything. A thing like that, happening to a person like Patrick, could be the cause of terrible depression.'

Larry nodded his head.

'Yes,' he said. 'Melancholia!'

'That's right,' said Mary eagerly, not having grasped the technical meaning of the word, and taking only a loose meaning from it. 'That's it,' she said again, but after an instant she looked up with a frightened look on her face. 'What word did you use?' she asked. 'Melancholy, did you say?'

'Melancholia!' said Larry again. 'It's a disease,' he said then dully.

'Oh well then, it's not what I mean,' said Mary quickly. 'There's nothing like that at all, is there, Rosie?' She appealed to Rosie. 'There's nothing at all like that the matter with him. It's just like your aunt said in the letter, his health was never better. If you saw him you'd hardly know him: he's got so heavy and so strong.'

For confirmation of this, Larry looked at Rosie.

'He's very stout, all right,' said Rosie, but she shuddered.

Mary saw the shudder.

'Stop acting so ridiculously, Rosie,' she said. She could have slapped her. She turned to Larry. 'He's perfectly normal and natural,' she said, 'only just that he won't talk.'

It was then that Larry put out his two hands, and pressed her arms to either side.

'But, Mother,' he said, 'how can you call it natural and normal for a person not to speak?' Then, as if she were a cracked vessel, that by pressure might still be made to hold together, he pressed her arms still tighter to her sides. 'I'll go up and see him,' he said, 'and then afterwards we can see what is to be done.'

~   ~   ~   ~

What was there to be done? That was the point. Even after Larry came down again with his lips pursed, and shook his head to show that he, too, had failed, they had that question still to face.

'It has to be faced, Mother,' said Larry. 'What I suggest is that you get a doctor, right now, this afternoon, while I'm here.'

'Oh yes, while Larry's here, Mother,' cried Rosie, and her eyes were wide with fear.

'Oh nonsense,' said Mary. 'If you think, Larry, that we ought to have a doctor, we'll have one, but there's no need to get hysterical over it: there's no need to get one to-day. After all, look at how normal he was last evening. He may be the same this evening. It's my belief it's only a fit of melancholy that came over him and he can't help it.'

'He can't help it; that's true,' said Larry. 'But that's all the more reason why he should have medical assistance.'

'He didn't have any medical assistance yesterday evening!' said Mary.

'Maybe not,' said Larry, 'but last night may only have been another symptom.'

'A symptom of what?'

'A symptom of his disease,' said Larry. 'Sometimes the patient struggles to get clear of it, but he only succeeds for a short spell, and the thing comes over him again.'

Rosie's eyes widened. The thing: it was like as if it was something tangible that closed over him, smothering him. She put up her hand to her throat. At the thought of him she felt as if she too were smothering.

Mary sat down.

'My poor Patrick,' she said softly. Then she raised her voice, and standing up again she moved over to the window. 'You're against him, both of you,' she cried. She looked particularly at Larry. 'And to think that I was counting on you to give us some help,' she said. 'Instead of that——' Wearily she looked at the clock. 'Here it's five o'clock already,' she said, 'and I suppose you have to get the five-thirty train. I'll make you a cup of tea before you go back.'

But Larry put out his hand to stay her as she went away.

'I don't think you realize the seriousness of this, Mother,' he said. He paused. Then, taking a deep breath, he seemed to come to some decision: a decision of some moment, too. 'I'm not going back to-night,' he said then slowly. Without looking he saw Rosie's hand leap with relief to her breast. 'I'll send a telegram to the Rector, They'll know it's something serious, and I'll explain to-morrow, or by letter if I can't go back then, either.'

'But——' Mary started to speak and stopped. It was impossible to deny that her heart too had leaped at the thought of having him with them, but she was worried about his staying away without leave.

'Will they say anything to you?' she asked, like a timid child.

Would it do him any harm, she meant: would it interfere with his progress; would it retard his ordination? Things were bad enough without making them worse, she thought wearily.

For the enormousness of their situation seemed by implication to have been increased a hundredfold by the enormity of Larry's proposed transgression.

'I don't think there's any need for you to stay at all,' she said suddenly. 'I think it's most imprudent for you to take it on yourself to stay out without leave. How do you know but that they'll send you home altogether?'

'They won't do that, Mother,' said Larry quietly. 'They'll understand when I explain. And even if they don't understand, what alternative have I got!' he exclaimed. 'Here, Rosie,' he said, and he put his hand into his pocket and drew up a coin, 'run out to the post office and send a telegram for me. Just say that I'm unavoidably detained.

Rosie didn't need to be told a second time. She was already out in the hall.

'Don't go out like that in the cold air,' said Mary mechanically. 'Throw a coat over your shoulders.' Then she turned back to Larry. 'I think this is most unnecessary,' she said. 'And where will you sleep? There isn't a room ready for you or anything.'

'Don't worry about that,' said Larry. 'I wouldn't sleep anyway. I'll probably stay down here. I can sit in that chair.' He pointed to the wicker chair.

Mary looked at him. Was he making things easy for her, or had he some reason behind this suggestion too? He seemed so reasoned and cool.

'I never heard such nonsense,' she said. 'How could you sleep in a chair?'

Larry looked at her.

'I wouldn't sleep, Mother,' he said levelly. Then, seeing that she did not grasp what he meant, he altered his voice. 'Now! Mother,' he said, 'I know it's worse for you than for us, but you'll have to face it. I want to talk to you—that's why I sent Rosie out with the telegram. If you're not thinking of yourself, you must think of her. Didn't you see her face? Didn't you see that she was trembling all over from head to foot? She's terrified. And I don't blame her! Three days and nights of that!' he said, glancing up at the ceiling over their heads. 'I don't know how she stood it. She certainly wouldn't stand another night of it.'

One word was all Mary deigned to utter.

'What's that?' said Larry.

She repeated it.

'Rubbish!' she said.

But it brought a flush of anger to the face of the cleric.

'Look here, Mother,' he said, 'I care about Rosie if you don't. Do you want her to go out of her mind too?'

Ah! Was it a sigh or a sob that escaped from Mary's lips? Then their eyes met: mother and son.

'Come to the foot of the stairs, Mother,' said the son, and he took her by the arm. 'Listen!' he said, and he inclined forward. 'Do you hear anything?'

Hearing nothing at first, Mary bent forward also. Then she bent her head still more.

'I hear it,' she said at last. 'What is it?' It was the sound of scratching. 'A mouse?' she said, inconsequently, without relevance, even foolishly, it seemed to the cleric.

He shook his head. Looking around him his eyes fell on the carpet of the stairs; a hard, much-worn material, in texture not unlike the texture of the counterpane on his brother's bed. The next minute he stooped down, and drew his nails across it, once, twice, three times.

There was a scratching sound exactly the same as that which, more faintly, was coming from the room at the top of the stairs.

'Don't you see?' he said. 'It's gone beyond us to do anything for him, Mother.'

He looked at her. Mary looked back at him.

For a moment he rose up in front of her in the narrow hallway, tall and strange in his priestly black; decisive and fateful in his reasoning. And for a moment she was about to yield to him. Then an old mannerism betrayed him. He ran his hand through his hair, and in that hesitant, worried gesture he became again her son, her younger son, the least considerable of all her family.

'Come into the kitchen,' she said curtly, and she turned her back to him and walked down the passage.

Not quite realizing for the moment that he had failed Larry followed her, and so was unprepared when, upon reaching the kitchen he found her waiting for him with her eyes blazing.

'Shut the door,' she ordered. Then when he had done so, she came nearer to him. 'Very well!' she said, and to his utter amazement her eyes were savage in their expression. 'Very well: bring in your doctors! But what will they do for him? Answer me that!'

Into those fierce eyes he gazed helplessly. She leaned closer to him.

'I'll tell you something,' she said. 'I'm not blind, do you understand! You and Rosie making signs at each other, and throwing looks at each other behind my back! Did you think I had no eyes in my head? And all this time, since he first walked into the house, did you think I noticed nothing; that I was content with him? Did you think I saw nothing wrong? Do you think that anything could be wrong with any of you, let alone him, and that I wouldn't know it? That I wouldn't notice it first of all, before anyone in the world; that I wouldn't know it in a flash!' Her voice dropped. 'Do you know the lines of the Gospel: "Not a sparrow shall fall——" Well, I often thought to myself that it was like as if Almighty God was looking into a mother's heart when He said those words, because I always used to think that not a hair could fall from your heads, any of you, but I'd feel something in my own heart fall with it. Why! when you used to be playing in the street, long ago, the lot of you, and one of you would fall and cut your knee, or get your hand scratched, I often used to think that it wasn't when I heard you come running in to me that I knew you were hurt, but that I knew it before I heard a cry at all. I'd be washing the dishes, or standing at the fire, stirring a saucepan or something, and my breath would sort of stop for a minute, and a minute after I'd always hear one of you crying, or calling me. It might be only one drop of blood that would be drawn from a little scratch, but it would take a drop of blood from my heart along with it. That's the truth! I used to think when you got bigger and too old to cry if anything happened to you, you'd only have to come to the door and I'd know there was something the matter with you. I'd stretch out my arms to you. Isn't that right? Don't you remember that?'

Larry nodded miserably. Her words were true, but he didn't altogether see what was coming.

'You do!' Mary was triumphant. 'Well then, how is it that you thought I didn't know there was anything wrong with Patrick? Patrick that——'

She didn't finish, but he knew what she had meant: that Patrick was more to her than any of them.

'One look at him was enough for me!' she said, and her voice weakened again.

'But——'

A great pity for her grew within Larry's breast, but all the same he did not see how this altered the situation, or made any difference in what they would have to do.

'But——' he began again.

Mary looked into his eyes: she read his puzzle.

'Oh, it's all very well for you,' she said, 'you and Rosie. What is he to you but a brother? A brother!' She sneered. 'What is a brother?' She thought fleetingly of her own brother, John, who had been only a young man when she left Tullamore, and who was now an old man, and whom she had only seen once in the last ten years, and hardly more than three times, in all, during the past thirty years. Brother—— What did the word mean: nothing! What was the man upstairs to them: the man on the bed, restlessly clawing at the counterpane? What was he to these younger children of hers, but a stranger.

But he is my son! My first child! She looked at Larry. Did he not understand what that meant? 'Did you think I wasn't going to fight for him?' she cried. 'Did you think I was going to let anyone take him away from me?'

So she knew all there was to be known. She knew only too well. Larry was somewhat taken aback, but he quickly resolved to make the best of the matter.

'Now, Mother,' he said soothingly, 'you're letting your imagination carry you away. You don't know what the doctor would say! Things mightn't be too bad at all. He might only need a little treatment: a little rest. You'd never know: a good sedative might be all he needs.'

On account of the elementary course in biology that he had taken the previous term, Larry felt confident to speak in this manner, but as he felt his mother's eyes on him he faltered. And when he raised his own eyes he felt his face redden because she was looking at him with contempt.

'How soft you are!' she said. 'Don't you know as well as I do that there's only one thing the doctor would say? Don't you know that? Is it a cut or a bruise he has, that a bit of bandage would heal it? Is it something the matter with his inside that a bottle of pills will cure? Is it even a thing that could be cut out of him with a knife?'

She bit her lip to steady herself.

'Don't look at me like that!' she cried. 'I know what I'm saying: there's nothing any doctor can do for him. I don't need anyone to tell me that. No! If anything can do him any good now it is to be here, in his own home, in the house where he was born. And let me tell you this, Larry, that's where he is going to stay! Do you hear me?'

Larry heard her. Further than that, he saw her; and not alone with the eyes in his head, but with a deeper vision. At this moment he realized she was not a person; she was a force, against which he felt powerless to contend. Before her he felt as helpless as he had felt when he had stood beside the bed of the man upstairs and called his name, again and again, and known that, although his voice was heard, it prevailed nothing. Nevertheless, the habits of reason and logic held good. He would try another approach.

'Look at it this way, Mother,' he said briskly. 'Supposing we are wrong. Supposing instead of poor Patrick, that it is ourselves who have got things a bit muddled: that it's we who are nervy and highly strung? How do we know but that a doctor would laugh at us; that he'd tell us we are making fools of ourselves and——'

'Stop!' cried Mary. And then in a lower voice she went on. 'I want to hear no more talk like that,' she said. 'That was the way they talked to him in America; that was the way they got around him.'

'In America?' He did not follow her.

'You weren't here,' she said, seeing that he did not understand. 'It was something he said last night. I didn't tell you about it. We were talking about poor little Alice Maguire. And he said something. I heard him, and I knew what he meant, but I don't think Rosie heard, or else she didn't understand as well as I did.'

'What did he say?' said Larry, deliberately calm, although a feeling of fear had begun to stir in him for the first time.

Mary sank down on a chair.

'There's no need to go over it word for word, but the meaning was clear to me,' she said, 'and I've my mind made up to one thing! What strangers did to him won't be done to him by his own!'

'Do you mean—do you mean that in America they had him——'

Ah! That made a ripple in the water. With a curious satisfaction

Mary saw that the cleric was shaken by what she had revealed, but the next moment she was sorry she had been so abrupt because she saw that she had not furthered her designs. On the contrary, Larry's own designs seemed to have acquired a new urgency. He looked over his shoulder.

'Why don't you light the gas?' he said, and there was a querulous note in his voice that up to this she had never heard in it.

Then, as the light struck him in the eyes, he looked dazed. He sank down on a chair.

'I don't understand,' he said. 'If what you say is true, how did he come home?'

Mary shook her head.

'God is good,' she said.

'God!' As if it were a Name he had never heard, he stared at her. Then he sprang to his feet again. 'Oh, Mother, how can you be so blind? If what you say is true, you've got to take some action: you can't just leave him lying up there.'

'Why not?'

Why not? Wildly he sought for some answer to this outrageous, this preposterous challenge.

'It's not right,' he said at length lamely. Then words came freely to him. 'He's not himself, Mother. It's not fair to him to let him stay there. If he got worse; if he did any harm! Have you thought of that? If he did any harm!' He shuddered. 'Didn't you hear that terrible sound of scratching with his nails, as if he—as if——'

'Do you think I'm afraid?' cried Mary, and her words rang out like a bell.

But was she pretending, he wondered? Was it for some cunning purpose of motherhood that she was hiding her real feelings?

'His own mother!' she said.

Larry was at a loss for words, but just then he heard Rosie's footsteps running up the path to the front door.

'Ah! Rosie!' he exclaimed. 'Have you forgotten her? You're not being fair to her. Even if nothing happened it is not fair for her to be living in terror, in mortal dread. And that is what she is doing. The minute I came in the door this afternoon, if I never got any warning, I'd have known there was something terrible the matter from the look on Rosie's face.'

Rosie was in the hallway by this time. Larry lowered his voice and spoke more quickly.

'Here she is now,' he said. 'I won't have a chance to say any more to you. The poor kid, she's had enough already without terrorizing her any more. But think of her, Mother, I beg of you. You've got to think of her. She's your child, too.'

It was his last, his supreme argument, but it failed.

'Do you think I forgot her,' she cried. 'Do you think when I lay awake, every minute of every hour, for the last three nights, that it wasn't of her I was thinking too: my little Rosie, the last of you all, the only one I've left to me! But my way of thinking about her isn't the same as yours. I had to look deeper than you, and farther. And that's another reason why I'll let no doctor into this house.'

'I don't understand?'

She was caustic.

'Just because you've put certain things behind you,' she said swiftly, 'is no reason to ignore the fact that Rosie has her life to live in the world.'

Sometimes when he was a boy she had complained that Larry at times could look so stupid he was like a half-wit. Well, that was how he looked how: half-witted.

'I don't understand,' he said again.

'Can you be so stupid?' she cried. 'Think! What would her chances be if it could be said that she had a brother who had to be put away? How would that sound, do you think? How would that appear? Do you think that would benefit her with any of the nice friends she's made? Let me tell you something, Larry. Rosie has made more than any of you of her opportunities—and I'm not going to let obstacles be put in her way.'

Larry was not certain that even now he understood what his mother meant.

'But she's only a youngster,' he ventured.

'No matter,' said Mary. 'People have long memories.'

It was such a new argument: such an unforeseen factor thrown into the contention that he was taken by surprise. Furthermore, Rosie herself was at the door. They had to change the conversation.

'Well, did you send the telegram?' he asked, as at that moment she appeared in the room. 'Did you ask what time it would be delivered?'

'Oh, I didn't think of that. Does it matter?'

Her cheeks were flushed, and her face looked the same childish face that was so familiar to him, but under the bodice of her blouse, though he quickly averted his eyes, he had not failed to see that her breasts had budded. She was indeed already a young woman. And with the concern and anxiety of a woman, the first thing she did on coming into the kitchen was to inquire for Patrick.

'Is he all right?' she asked. 'Do you think that I ought to slip upstairs and have a look at him?'

To have her out of the way for one more minute, in which he would make a last plea on her behalf, Larry nodded his head in approval of her suggestion.

'I don't see how anyone could hold anything against her,' he said, when she had passed from the room. 'It isn't as if it was hereditary,' he said vehemently, and then suddenly, a shaft went through him. 'It isn't, is it, Mother?' he cried, his eyes as well as his lips speaking for him.

'Of course not, my son,' said Mary. 'Of course not,' and she came and stood by his side, overwhelmed suddenly with softness towards him. 'Poor Patrick!' she said. 'Something came over him out there in America. I've heard of such things happening before to other people, and I often thought it was as if America was a great big wheel, always spinning around at top speed, and on which some people manage to keep their hold, but upon which there are others who are not so well able to keep their hold, and who, when the wheel begins to go fast, are all of a sudden shot off from it——'

Since she had come nearer to him, and while she was speaking, Mary had put up her hand and begun to smooth back her boy's hair, where he stood in front of her. It was the old soothing caress, that had scared away the bogies of many a childish nightmare, and under the soothing strokes Larry longed to close his eyes and forget everything, but after a minute or two he straightened himself.

'We can't leave it at that, though,' he said. 'We'll have to come to some decision.'

At that moment, however, Rosie came back into the kitchen. She had only gone midway up the stairs when she turned back. Her face was ashen.

'What's that noise upstairs?' she asked.

Mary and Larry sprang to their feet.

'A kind of scratching,' said Rosie, and then she faltered. 'I thought I heard it last night too, in the middle of the night.' She looked from one to the other. 'Do you hear it?' she whispered again, urgently.

But her mother and Larry had relaxed.

'We heard it: we heard it,' said Larry impatiently. 'It's nothing,' he said, but he looked at Mary. She too was looking at him. Their eyes questioned each other. Each wondered what thought had leaped to the other's mind; each wondered what could have caused the other to spring up with such dilated eyes and strangled breath.

'What will I do?' said Rosie then. 'Is it all right to go up?'

It was Larry who answered her.

'Go up,' he said impatiently. 'You're not a child, are you?' But after she had gone into the passage again he called after her kindly. 'Aren't we here beside you?' he said.

When Rosie had gone, Mary stood looking at the fire. Then she turned around. Something had happened. She was changed.

'In any case,' she said, and her lips trembled, 'how could we make him consent to see a doctor? How could we break it to him that there was a doctor coming to the house?'

Larry stared in astonishment. How quickly in the end she had capitulated.

'I'll attend to all that,' he said, glib in his relief.

But it seemed he would never understand her, for this did not please her at all. If anything, it displeased her.

'No,' she said. 'If he has to be told, I'll tell him.'

~   ~   ~   ~

Patrick was ready at last.

They were only waiting now for Larry to come with the cab. Dressed in his best suit, that Rosie had admired so much, he was sitting waiting with his pigskin gloves laid across his knees. He was carefully shaved, too, although there had been a good deal of indecision over whether he would shave himself or go to the barber.

Was it safe to let him do it himself, alone in that room? On the other hand, was it wise to let him go out of the house?

But in the end, everything was accomplished, and now there was nothing to do but sit, like this, and wait for the cab: Rosie and her mother down in the hall; Patrick upstairs on the side of the bed.

But what was keeping Larry? Why wasn't he here with the cab? Why this awful delay?

'I think I'll go upstairs again, Rosie,' said Mary at that moment, and she stood up stiffly, and began to mount the steep dark stairway.

Rosie continued to sit where she was, still turning over in her mind all that had happened in the last twenty-four hours, and trying to feel that they were lucky that everything had been brought to an end so easily after all.

For all this, she thought, looking around at her brother's luggage in the hallway, and looking at the wide-open doorway through which they watched for Larry and the cab, all this had after all been accomplished more easily than anyone could have believed possible.

Patrick, of course, had helped. It was, in a way, all due to him that things were going so nicely, and without fuss. He had behaved splendidly. That was what her mother said, when she came downstairs after talking to him.

'What do you mean by acting splendidly?' said Larry sceptically. He thought she was still trying to evade the issue.

'I mean,' said Mary, 'that he has consented to see a doctor.'

'So he spoke?' Both Rosie and Larry had exclaimed with surprise. But Mary's own surprise was still greater.

'Well, what do you make of that!' she cried. 'Just fancy! I never noticed anything strange about it when he answered me.' Wide with surmise, her eyes sought Larry. 'That might mean he is getting better?' she cried. 'Perhaps we won't need the doctor after all?'

But Larry was adamant.

'He may have another good spell,' he conceded, 'but as long as he gave his consent to see the doctor, it would be a mistake to lose the opportunity of sending for him.'

Mary's face fell.

'It was awful. When I went into the room he was lying there looking at nothing, but when I went over and stood beside the bed he moved his eyes and looked at me.' As if those eyes were still fixed upon her, she shivered. 'I don't know what I said,' she went on, 'but I suppose I must have said something about being worried at the way he was behaving, and I suppose I managed to mention that we thought he should see a doctor, because all of a sudden he spoke.'

'What did he say?'

But Mary's mind had strayed from what she was saying.

'Can't you imagine how upset I must have been when I never thought it strange that he should answer me!' she cried. 'It must be an answer to my prayers,' she exclaimed, her face radiant.

Inexorably, however, Larry pursued her with questions.

'What did he say? Tell us!'

'Yes: tell us,' cried Rosie, but more than she wanted to hear what Patrick had said, she wanted to hear what her mother had said. 'What did you say, Mother?'

But Mary put up her hand to her head.

'I don't know,' she said. 'I don't know what I said.'

'What did he say?' asked Larry. 'You didn't tell us.'

'Oh, didn't I?' Mary looked vaguely at him.

'No,' he said sharply.

'Well,' said his mother, 'I can't be expected to remember every word.'

'Try!' said Larry. He felt sure that his brother had not spoken so many words that she could have forgotten any of them. 'Go on,' he urged.

Cornered like this, Mary had to tell the bare facts.

'He asked what doctor we were going to get,' she said. 'He meant what kind of a doctor.'

'Yes, yes? What did you say?'

For a minute Mary stared dazedly in front of her. Now that it was over, she could hardly believe that she had had the strength to do as she had done, to say what she had said.

'I told him,' she whispered, 'I told him out straight that we were going to get a nerve specialist.'

In spite of herself, Rosie gasped.

'Hush, Rosie!' said Larry. This was very important. 'How did he take it?' he asked urgently.

But from here Mary could hardly proceed any further. Softly at first, but getting louder each minute, she had begun to sob. Only by inclining their heads could the other two catch anything of what she said.

But they gathered enough to reassure them and give them cause behind their mother's back to exchange a look of relief and satisfaction.

It would seem that Patrick had been agreeable to whatever was suggested.

'Whatever you say, Mother.' That was what he had said.

'And after that,' said their mother, anxious now to tell them all, 'after that he sat up in bed and said something that nearly broke my heart. "If they had told me the truth in the first place," he said, "things might have been different, but they tried to trick me. Aunt Ella tried to pretend that the doctor she brought to me was only a physician: that all I needed was a good tonic. And then—" But I didn't want him to think any more about what happened after that. "Don't distress yourself, son," I said, and changed the conversation. "What are you going to have for your supper?" I said. It was the first thing that came into my head. I was so confused and upset I forgot he was only after getting a cup of tea. He didn't forget it, though. "It's a bit soon after that nice cup of tea you brought me!" he said.'

And here Mary had thrown out her hands.

'Doesn't that show you that he's perfectly normal again? What is the need now in bringing a doctor to him?'

'Although he practically asked for the doctor?' said Larry.

'How do you make out that he asked for him?' asked Mary.

'Well, he gave his consent, didn't he?' said Larry. 'God help him,

I suppose he is as frightened as any of us. All that scratching and clawing at the counterpane, I suppose that means something——' He paused and then he looked at his mother. 'God help you, Mother,' he said. 'How will you ever forgive yourself if he comes to any harm after asking for help and you having refused to get it for him.'

'Any harm? To himself, do you mean?'

A startled look had come on their mother's face. How was it that among all the terrible things she had imagined, she had never, at any time, thought of that? In horror her hands flew to cover her face.

'Oh no,' she cried. 'That couldn't happen!'

~   ~   ~   ~

Two hours later the doctor was in the house. And when he went away again everything was settled.

And now, not twelve hours later, they were waiting for the cab that was to take him to the Home. And so far everything was satisfactory. It was still very early, and that was a good thing: there wouldn't be many people in the street yet and the neighbours weren't likely to be in their parlours at that hour.

If only Larry would hurry.

Ah there! He had come! Rising hastily Rosie went to the foot of the stairs to call her mother. Was that Patrick's voice she heard again?

Oh, how she hoped nothing would be altered now. Anxious not to lose a minute, she listened no longer.

'Mother! The cab is here!' she cried.

But just at that moment, just as she had feared, the door of Patrick's room opened, and her mother rushed out on the landing.

'Where is Larry?' she cried. 'I want to talk to him.' But seeing no one on the landing, or in the hall below, only Rosie, she began to run headlong down the stairs. The next minute she was in the street. 'Oh, Larry,' she cried. 'We don't need the cab after all. He spoke to me again. Oh wait till I tell you. It wasn't just a few words like the other times: it was altogether different. He's better: I know it. He couldn't have spoken as he did unless he was well.'

By this time Rosie had come out into the street also. Her mother turned to include her.

'Rosie will tell you,' she said. 'You must have heard the voices, Rosie?'

'I heard some talk all right,' said Rosie.

'There!' cried Mary. 'You see!'

Patiently Larry listened to her, and then he took her by the arm.

'Come inside, Mother,' he said, leading her back to the house. People were beginning to stare at them. 'You can tell me when we get into the house,' he said.

'But the cab?' cried Mary. 'Tell the cabby that he can go away.'

'Just a minute.'

To Rosie's dismay, Larry ran back to the kerb where the cabman was standing holding the reins of his horse. But at the gate he turned and winked at her, and she knew the cab would not go away. In fact, looking back she saw that the cabman had seated himself on the box and had taken out a newspaper and begun to read it, unfolding it leisurely.

Then, closing the door, she turned her attention to her mother.

'——it was about Alice,' said Mary. 'Alice Maguire. And oh, it was so sad! I had just gone up to his room for a minute to look at him, and it was so unexpected to have him start to talk to me like that. And about Alice of all people.

' "Is she bad, Mother?" That was the first thing he said. He didn't mention any names of course, but I knew at once who he meant. And then he said something else. He looked hard at me. "You didn't want me to go to America, Mother," he said. "Did you?" "I couldn't stop you, son," I said. At that he nodded his head, but I could see that there was something running through his mind and that it concerned himself and Alice. "Did Alice say anything about me?" he asked then. "When?" I said. "At any time," he said, but before I had a chance to answer that he asked me something else still stranger. "Mother," he said, and he looked at me so sadly, "Mother, I want to ask you a question. Is it true that if a young girl that has consumption gets married when she's still young, say before she's thirty, that the consumption often leaves her, and she may get as strong as anyone?" Oh, I guessed at once that it was Alice he was thinking about, but I didn't know what to say. "Is it true?" he said again. "You ought to know. Do you remember you used to tell us long ago about a girl in Tullamore that was almost dying with consumption but she got married and after that she never ailed a day in her life." I didn't remember, but I said I supposed that I might have heard of some such case and told it to you one day. "I know I often heard that a woman could be cured of it in childbirth," I said, but that I'd be afraid that might mean she passed it on to the child. "Ah," he said then, "that may be so." And all at once he seemed happier.'

As she told them all this, Mary had been obliged to speak slowly in order to recall all that she related, but coming to the end of it her voice became more excited.

'Don't you see?' she cried. 'He may have been worried all the time about Alice, but what I said eased his mind. And so——' imploringly, supplicatingly, she threw out her hands to Larry—'he couldn't be as bad as we thought,' she cried.

But at that very moment a heavy step sounded on the landing overhead, and turning around, all three of them saw Patrick starting to come down the stairs, heavily, bringing both feet together on each step, in the manner of a child. At the foot of the stairs, he came to a stand.

'I'm ready,' he said then, simply.

The next moment Mary was swept aside, and Larry and Patrick were in the cab, which almost at once began to drive away from the door.

Rosie closed the door abruptly.

'We'll look out the window, Mother,' she said, because she, at any rate, felt awkward standing at the door.

From the window she could still see the cab.

'It's just like as if they were only going away for a bit of a holiday,' said Rosie. Then suddenly she swung around, as if a load had been taken from her shoulders. 'That's what people will think,' she cried. 'They'll think he's going back to America.' But the next moment she looked frightened again. 'But what will we do if they question us?' she cried. 'What will we do, if they ask us straight out where he's gone?' And with this she burst into tears. 'Oh, what will we say then?' she sobbed.

PART VIII

Rosie and Frank

THE cab was out of sight at last.

'What time is it? Is that nine o'clock I hear striking?' said Mary.

'Oh, it must be later than that,' said Rosie.

'Hush, listen! I knew I couldn't be mistaken,' said Mary.

They were still standing at the parlour window where, until the cab had gone out of sight, Mary had stood looking after it, her face a stone. That her mother's first words should have been so commonplace stunned Rosie.

'You're not going to make me go to school to-day?' she cried suddenly. 'You're not going to stay here alone, are you?'

'I don't mind being alone,' said Mary dully. 'And Larry will be back—after a while.' She turned away from the window. 'I don't want you to miss any more of your schooling,' she said decisively. 'You've missed too many days already. I was worrying about that, as well as everything else, all the week.' Catching Rosie by the arm she gave her a jerk. 'Hurry on,' she said. 'Get your coat. Get your satchel!'

Rosie hung back.

'Couldn't I stay home until to-morrow?' she pleaded. 'I don't want to leave you alone. Larry wouldn't like it.' But after a minute the truth came out, and the tears rushed into her eyes. 'What will I say kept me at home?' she cried.

But her mother had neither sympathy nor patience with her.

'Say whatever you like!' she said shortly, and she turned to go back to the kitchen to clear away the remains of Larry's uneaten breakfast. The next minute there was the sound of dishes knocking together in the sink.

279

Rosie stood in the middle of the parlour for a few minutes longer, then she moved towards the hall reluctantly to look for her satchel. If she had to go to school there was no use making things worse for herself by being late. But as she looked around the hallway half-heartedly, she still hoped to find some pretext for staying home.

Perhaps she would not be able to find her satchel?

But the satchel was hanging from one of the pegs of the coat rack, and when she took it down and slung it across her shoulder it seemed there was nothing more to keep her, and she went down the hall to the front door.

At the foot of the stairs, however, she paused and glanced upwards to where, upon the landing, the door of Patrick's empty room stood open wide. Well! He was gone now. He would trouble them no more. And there would be no more occasion to worry about him, or about themselves, she thought. Yet, as she looked up at the room in which he had lodged for the terrible days and nights that he was in the house with them, she could not say that she was happy. Indeed, she began to think uneasily about her own share in the business of getting him away, and she began to wonder how much her mother, and more particularly Larry, had been influenced by the way that she had behaved. All that trembling and starting up at a sound? Was it all genuine?

With a feeling that was like guilt, she recalled her brother's face as she had seen it when he passed her in the hallway on his way out to the cab with Larry. It was so sad; so sad! Could there have been any mistake, she thought in panic? And hoping perhaps to be reassured in some way that they had all acted for the best, upon an impulse she ran up the stairs, and walked into the empty room.

But the first thing that met her eyes was Patrick's breakfast tray, and with a stab at her heart she saw that, like Larry's, Patrick's breakfast was uneaten. It was so normal; it was so much what one would have expected if it had not been for the voracious, inhuman appetite with which up to then he had devoured all that they had set in front of him, that Rosie felt her heart turn over. Poor Patrick! How did he feel? What did he think? The first real feeling she had ever felt for him swept over her, and she began to cry. For the first time too she began to wonder what her mother must feel. What would she feel when she came up to this room, to strip this bed, and to take away this tray?

Ah! There was something she could do! How had it not occurred to her sooner? In a minute her satchel was unslung, and thrown upon the floor. In a minute she was pulling the blankets from the bed, and folding them into neat piles, and bundling the sheets together she stowed them into a cupboard. And the tray? What was to be done with the remains of the food upon it?

It was only when Rosie heard ten o'clock strike that she realized the way in which she had disobeyed her mother. And she stood still in the middle of her work with fright. The next minute, however, she felt better. For after all this room was just over the kitchen. Her mother must have heard her feet moving overhead. She must have known that she was still in the house. Why then had she not called up to her long ago, and reminded her of the time?

Ah! She was calling her now. But with what a gentle voice!

'I'm here, Mother,' she said, humbly and contritely, and as she heard her mother's footsteps coming up the stairs she went out to meet her with a frightened look on her face.

But her mother's face, when they met upon the landing, wore a look of tenderness, and her voice when she spoke was like the voice with which she used to speak to her when she was a child.

'Poor little girl!' she said. 'Poor little girl. You got out of going to school to-day, but what about to-morrow? To-morrow you will have to face all that you were afraid to face to-day. Did you not think of that?'

Rosie had not thought about it. Nor did she think about it now. For her mother's face had a look she had not seen since she was very small; a vulnerable look. It was a chance that should not be let slip.

'Oh, Mother!' she cried, and she threw out her hands beseechingly. 'Why do I have to go back at all? I didn't think I'd have to go back after—after what happened. After all,' she said, raising her eyes, 'there isn't any point now, is there, in my staying on at school? I won't be going to the University, will I? I mean, now that Patrick——.

But something in Mary's face silenced the words on her lips.

'I'm sorry, Mother,' she said, apologizing for those unsaid words. 'But I don't see what is the use now, of my doing my Matriculation. Do you?'

'Rosie, look at me!'

Her mother's voice was still tender and loving, but there was a compelling note in it, and Rosie looked up.

'I never told you before, Rosie,' said her mother, 'but although things have been hard on me at times, all the same I managed to save a few pounds from time to time. And I still have the passage money that I gave Patrick when he was going to America, and that he sent back to me. It's not a great deal of money, but I think it would be enough to put you through the University if only you'd make up your mind to it, and stick to your books. Oh, Rosie, you're all I have now! Can't you see that? Can't you see that I want to do all in my power for you, Rosie? I want to give you all that——' she hesitated, and a shadow passed over her face that was otherwise so ardent—'all that I wasn't able to give the others,' she finished, more soberly.

Behind Rosie's eyes the tears burned. She knew so well how her mother must feel. That money, which had been given to Patrick and sent back by him, might have been spent on Ellie's wedding, or part of it at any rate, because some would probably have been put aside for Angie's wedding. But the money wasn't needed by Ellie or Angie, any more than it had been wanted by Patrick.

It was almost as if it wasn't lucky, that money, she thought, but the thought was somewhat forced and wilful, although there was no doubt about it, that if it was to be the means of keeping her with her nose buried in books for the rest of her life, it was certainly not lucky money for her.

But what about Larry? Had her mother forgotten him? Animated anew, she looked up at Mary.

'What about Larry, Mother?' she cried. 'Don't you want to keep the money for his ordination? I thought you'd have to buy him vestments, and all kinds of things.'

What else would a newly anointed priest need, she wondered, in a fever to make the ordination expenses seem more formidable. But her mother remained strangely calm.

'Larry's ordination is a long way from now,' she said indifferently, so indifferently indeed that Rosie stared at her. Why, it was almost as if her mother doubted that Larry would ever be ordained.

'You don't think——' she cried in alarm.

'Of course not,' said her mother at once. 'What put such a thing into your head?'

But the fact that she had known, from an unfinished sentence, what had been in Rosie's mind was enough to show that, say what she might, her mother had some misgivings about the future of her younger son.

But surely she was mistaken.

'I think Larry was cut out to be a priest!' Rosie averred defiantly.

At first Mary appeared as if she did not intend to answer. Her lips were pressed tight together and her eyes were enigmatic. Then the pressure of something on her mind became too great, and she made a remark that Rosie could hardly connect with what had gone before it.

'I hope his superiors think the same as you,' she said.

What on earth did she mean? A frightened look came into Rosie's face. And seeing it, Mary's own face grew less stony.

'Don't look like that, child,' she said. 'And don't mind what I said. It's only that I'm a bit worried. I'm not at all sure that we did right in letting him stay at home last night without getting permission from his superiors. You'd never know what view they might take of his having done the like of that!'

'Oh, what view could they take but a sensible one,' said Rosie impatiently. They had enough troubles already without looking for more, and she went over to the wall where, upon coming downstairs, she had hung her satchel upon a nail, and from its jaws, that sagged open, she drew out a ragged remnant of a book, and bringing it over to the table she slapped it down ostentatiously on the oilcloth covering. 'If I have to go back to school to-morrow, I'd better start to make up for lost ground, particularly if I have to do this examination,' she said, and she sat down and opened the book.

Without looking, she saw that her mother was taken aback. In spite of her repeated pleas to her to keep at her books, Rosie knew that her mother hated the silence that fell upon the house at such times as she started to do her lessons, for in order to make anything out of the miserable books at all, it was necessary for Rosie first of all to put her elbows up on the table, and clasp her head between her hands in a gesture more usually betokening ache or anguish of the body than of the mind, and then, having assumed this stricken attitude, it was necessary that she should have not only absolute silence, but absolute stillness as well. At her peril did Mary break that sacred silence. And if she did, it was to incur the most caustic exclamations.

'For heaven's sake, Mother! How can I work if you keep making all that clatter!'

And caustic though they were, these exclamations were as milk and honey compared with the glances that accompanied them.

On this particular morning, then, when as Rosie had indeed rightly divined, there was something oppressing her mind, it was with a sinking of the heart that Mary saw her daughter take out her book and proceed to bury her head in her hands.

Now she regretted the way she had bottled up all her worries and fears for Larry, instead of pouring them into Rosie's ears when she was patient and ready to listen to them. Was it too late now?

'Did you start yet?' she asked suddenly.

Rosie took down her hands from her head.

'Why?' she asked.

Mary faltered.

'Oh nothing,' she said weakly. 'I'll tell you some other time.'

'Well, I like that!' said Rosie bitingly, and with a look of withering contempt. 'I must say if you are going to keep interrupting me for nothing, you can't care much about your three guineas!'

'Three guineas! What are you talking about? I heard nothing about three guineas, or about any guineas at all. What about them?'

'Oh, didn't I tell you?'

For a moment, but only for a moment, Rosie was genuinely disconcerted to learn that she had omitted to inform her parent of this important item in connection with the forthcoming examination, but almost immediately she saw an advantage in the omission. Meanwhile her mother had come over to the table.

'What three guineas?' she repeated.

Very quietly Rosie answered.

'That's the fee!' she said.

'I didn't hear about any fee,' said Mary. 'There wasn't any fee for your other exams. There wasn't any fee for your Intermediate!'

'Oh, that was set by the State,' said Rosie, 'by the Department of Education!'

'And all those other exams you did?'

'Oh, they were only preliminary examinations. Matric is different. Matric is set by the University.'

For a minute there was silence.

'Are you sure about this?' said Mary then, slowly.

Rosie disdained to answer this question, or rather, her next remark answered it for her with exquisite pertinence.

'And what is more, it has to be paid before the first of June!' she said.

The first of June! With alarm, Mary looked around for the calendar. She had an oppressive feeling of being driven into a corner.

Three guineas might be a small sum compared with what she would no doubt be called upon to expend when it came to the regular fees for entering the University, and the fees for lectures and books, and goodness knows what, but all the same there was something about this three guineas that put her astray in her calculations. To all that she would have to expend in the future she was more or less reconciled, but there was something irreconcilable about the three guineas.

'And if I fail,' said Rosie suddenly, 'I have to forfeit the money.'

For a moment there was silence.

After a minute or two, however, her mother stood up, and going across the kitchen she took up the morning paper that lay unopened on the table.

Rosie said nothing, but passing behind her mother's back, she saw with satisfaction that the paper was opened at the page which contained the advertisements, and that in particular her mother's glance was travelling down the column announcing vacant situations.

~   ~   ~   ~

'Well?' cried Mary, opening the kitchen door and going up the passage to meet Rosie. 'How did you get on?'

Partly serious, and partly in fun, Rosie had gone out that afternoon to answer an advertisement for a job she and her mother had seen in the paper the previous day. The job was that of assistant in a small library on the north side of the city.

'That would just suit me,' said Rosie.

'I thought you didn't like books,' said Mary sarcastically, but all the same she had consented to discuss the matter, and the result of this discussion was that next day Rosie had gone for interview.

All that afternoon Mary had waited for her return with pleasurable curiosity, and indeed with a good deal of amusement. Who in their senses would give a job to a girl like Rosie, so lightheaded, and with no training or experience? But you never could tell.

'Well: how did you get on?' she cried again, but as they came face to face in the hall she came to a standstill. 'You didn't get the job?' she cried, incredulous.

For Rosie's face was glowing, and her eyes were shining.

She also stood still.

'Guess?' she cried.

There was just a faint note in her voice that Mary did not like; a note of overconfidence.

'I don't have to guess,' she said drily. 'I can see you're satisfied with your day's work.'

Abruptly Mary turned back towards the kitchen, but back in the kitchen her curiosity was too great to conceal.

'Well, tell me about it,' she said.

Rosie was eager enough to tell her story.

'Wait till you hear!' she cried provocatively, as she pulled her cap from her head, and began to drag her arms out of the sleeves of her jacket. 'I thought I'd never get home quickly enough to tell you all about it. I ran all the way down the street! And my shoes were hurting me, too!' Kicking off her shoes she sat down at the table.

'Would you like to put your feet into a basin of cold water?' asked Mary.

She was longing to hear about the interview, but she knew what it meant to have aching feet.

'Oh, they're not as bad as all that,' cried Rosie, taking one foot between the palms of her hands and massaging it.

'Well?' said Mary. 'So you got the job?'

'What did you think?' challenged her daughter. 'I knew I'd get it.'

Her voice was still arrogant, but it was less excited. Her eyes began to move over the cups and saucers on the table, and then she glanced sharply at the fire.

'Is the kettle boiling?' she asked. 'I'm starving.'

Mary had sat down also, on the opposite side of the table, but she stood up at once.

It was the same old story, with Rosie as well as all the rest of them. They came in, radiant with their adventures, but before they told her about them, they remembered they were hungry, or that their feet were tired. And the radiance grew dim. Yet for another instant Mary remained expectant.

'I have everything ready. I have only to pour the water on the teapot!' she said.

And she stood—waiting.

But Rosie began to examine her foot again, and when she looked up and saw her mother standing in front of her, she was impatient.

'Well! What are you waiting for, Mother?' she cried. 'I can be telling you while I'm eating; you don't seem to realize I'm starving. The north side of the city is on a great height, you know! The air is altogether different up there from what it is down here. It would give you an appetite I can tell you! I felt hungry the minute I got there. And the library is on the top of a big hill. Did you know that, Mother? You can see the whole city from it. I could see as far as Kingstown. And that's another thing! It's a long walk from the tram up to the library. I can't be walking that distance two or three times a day. I'll have to get a bicycle!'

Where now was the radiance, the glow? Something had slipped from Mary's grasp; something had been lost. She would, in time, hear all that there was to hear about the whole episode, down even to the smallest details, but gather them up as best she might, they would be nothing more than the facts. But that did not mean that Rosie was in any way to blame.

'I'll wet the tea,' she said.

'Oh do!' cried Rosie, and she pulled her chair in to the table, and taking a piece of bread she began to butter it. 'Well, in the first place,' she said, feeling more disposed to talk now that she saw some sign of her meal being ready, 'in the first place, I was the last to arrive for the interview. I need hardly tell you that I was almost late. You know me! And so when I saw about ten other girls there in front of me, I nearly lost heart and turned around to come home. But instead of that I went along and stood at the end of the line. Of course I thought——'

But at this point the bread was buttered and Rosie had to stop talking while she took a bite of it.

'Of course I thought——' she began again, but one bite of bread doesn't go very far, and no more of the sentence had been completed than at the previous attempt, when she had to take another bite.

'Of course——' she began again—

But the interruptions had begun to get on Mary's nerves.

'Don't talk with your mouth full,' she said irritably.

'I can't help it, I'm starving,' said Rosie, also irritable. 'Do you want to hear it or do you not?'

'If you mean while you're eating, No!' said Mary.

'There's nothing to tell, really,' said Rosie at length, when the last of the bread was eaten, and just when Mary indeed was afraid she had been sulking. 'There's nothing to tell, except that I have to start work to-morrow!'

'To-morrow!' Mary started.

Rosie laughed. A little excitement crept back into her face.

'Yes,' she cried. 'I'll have to send word down to the school. They'll get a surprise, won't they? I'd just love to let them know that brains aren't everything.'

'How do you make that out?'

'Well, I told you there were five or six others ahead of me, didn't I? And that I was the last to arrive? Well, I didn't tell you what they were like: the others! If you saw them! They were bulging with brains, every one of them. Oh, don't ask me how I knew. I just knew. In the first place they were all plain-looking, and then most of them had glasses, and that pale, sickly look of people that are always humped over a book! Oh, I could tell the minute I saw them that they all had ten times more brains than me!'

Here, however, Rosie jumped up and ran over to the mirror, where after one anxious, intent peer at her own reflection, she turned back reassured to Mary.

'And yet, Mother, see the way I was picked and they were all sent about their business! As a matter of fact, Mr. Young—that's the name of the librarian—Mr. Young told me that he noticed me the minute I came into the library. He must have taken a fancy to me, I suppose.'

I don't wonder at that! thought Mary involuntarily. Never had she seen Rosie so pretty: so vivacious. But suddenly she was on her guard. Should this strange man have spoken like this to Rosie?

'What kind of a man is this Mr. Young?' she asked.

'Oh, he's not the kind of person you think,' exclaimed Rosie, reading the look upon her mother's face. 'Why, he's going thin on top! But all the same he's a dear. I was thrilled when he said that he thought I'd suit him. And when he asked me when I could start work, I said I could start any time. "Would you like me to stay and give you a hand now?" I said.'

'I hope you weren't too forward,' said Mary. 'And shouldn't you call him "sir"?'

'Oh, he wasn't as old as all that!' said Rosie.

For a moment Mary was silent. In the past few minutes she had formed two totally different impressions of Mr. Young, and both apparently were wrong. Now she hardly knew what to think about him.

'Perhaps I should have gone with you,' she said. 'I hope he knows that you have a mother!'

'Oh, he knows all about me,' said Rosie. 'He never stopped asking me questions, and making remarks. He thought I was from the country at first, he said. And when I said I wasn't he said that he bet my mother was from the country!'

'What did you say?'

'I said you were: what else would I say?' said Rosie in surprise.

'Why didn't you say I was from Tullamore?' said Mary.

'Now, Mother, I wasn't going to give him my whole family history, was I? He'll find out soon enough anyway, because I never knew anyone to ask as many questions as him. "It's a wonder your mother didn't try to keep you at home for another year or two," he said. "It seems too bad that a girl as young as you should have to begin to battle with the world." '

'That shows he was interested in you,' said Mary proudly. 'He seems to be a very nice man.'

Something in the way her mother said the last few words made Rosie glance at her with a sudden suspicion. It was almost as if her mother were drawing comparisons between Mr. Young and some other person. But who could be the other person? It wasn't as if she could have heard any of the foolish talk that went on among the girls at school. It wasn't as if she could have heard the ridiculous messages that Violet Esmay brought to her, pretending they came from her brother Frank. For Violet could only be pretending. Surely, no young man would send such sentimental messages to any girl? At the thought of them Rosie blushed, and feeling her mother's eyes upon her, she became still more uncomfortable. But just then she saw her mother give a slight start.

'Oh, I forgot to tell you, Rosie,' she said. 'I had a visitor while you were out!'

Rosie swung around.

'Not Violet Esmay?' she cried, in dismay. 'What brought her here?'

There was such a stricken look on her face that Mary almost regretted the abrupt way she had told her about the visitor. On the other hand it irritated her to see how little attempt Rosie made to disguise how ashamed she was of the house.

'What did she want, Mother?' she asked almost in a whisper, and then on top of that question more urgently she asked another. 'Did she stay long?'

'I don't know how long she stayed,' said Mary sharply, 'but I know one thing: she stayed too long for my taste; and I can tell you another thing too: she took in all there was to be seen. I never saw anyone stare around so rudely.'

There was silence for a minute after this.

'What did you think of her, Mother?' asked Rosie then, her voice still hardly more than a whisper.

But Mary felt no inclination to whisper.

'I thought her very silly; if you want to know!' she said.

As a matter of fact, although Mary had forgotten it until this minute, she had been considerably annoyed at something that Violet Esmay had said. It was about her brother. 'He's "gone on Rosie." Didn't you know that!' That was what she said. And she tittered. Oh how Mary disliked her.

Rosie's friend was certainly a forward, brazen piece. And although Mary had given her no encouragement she started to tell her all about this Frank, and how fond he was of girls, and how hard he was to please and a number of other things about him that were all equally distasteful to hear. They were all too young to be talking like this about being 'gone on' people.

And she said so.

'You're only children, the whole lot of you!' she said, but Violet only smirked.

'Frank is no child, I can tell you!' she said, and there was some double meaning in her words that made Mary dislike her still more.

'I thought her more than silly,' she said, recalling those words of the girl's about her brother.

And then, having given Rosie her opinion of the sister, Mary's tongue burned to make a reference to the brother as well, but she decided that it would be beneath her dignity to mention him. Yet, as she looked at Rosie, she fancied that Rosie's lips burned also to ask if Violet had said anything about him.

She would talk about something altogether different, Mary thought. And she fastened on Mr. Young. It could hardly be possible that two coxcombs should rear their heads in the one day.

'Tell me more about Mr. Young,' she said.

~   ~   ~   ~

In the beginning it may have been an unconscious antagonism to Frank Esmay that made Mary take sides with Hubert Young. But as well as that, she liked what Rosie told her about him from time to time, and also, for a long time she did not regard him in any other relation to Rosie than that of a kindly, good-natured employer.

On the other hand, from the very first, she had had an instinctive feeling that Frank Esmay could be a disturbing influence in her daughter's life. And against this influence she was glad to set up the bulwark of Hubert Young.

'I'd like to make the acquaintance of Mr. Young,' she said once or twice when Rosie recounted something more than usually favourable about the young man. But instead of becoming acquainted with the admirable Hubert, Mary was to become acquainted instead with the charming Frank.

It was a Saturday afternoon, and Rosie had gone over to Raglan Road to spend the afternoon with Violet.

It had been a great disappointment to Mary to find that Rosie and Violet, instead of drifting apart when the former left school, had become still faster friends than ever. And whereas previously she had heard very little mention of the name of Esmay, lately she seemed to hear nothing else but it.

'Will you be back for your tea?' Mary asked, as she stood at the door with her.

'I will, of course,' cried Rosie reproachfully. 'I wouldn't stay out to tea without telling you, Mother.'

Pleased by those last words, Mary remained a few minutes at the door looking after her as she went down the street.

Perhaps she should not have exacted that promise from her that she would be back for tea, she thought, as she went into the house. And when, at about five o'clock, out of a blue sky it suddenly began to rain, she reproached herself still more.

Surely she will use her own judgment, she thought. Surely if they want her to stay until the rain is over she will use her common sense and stay.

All the same when she began to lay the table, she set places for two people.

'But I won't wait longer than six o'clock,' she said, speaking aloud as she moved around the kitchen.

If it were not for her distrust of those Esmays, how pleased she would have been to see Rosie setting out to spend an afternoon with young people of her own age, who lived in such a nice locality. For she had seen the Esmays' house. It was a very big house. Rosie had shown it to her one evening when they were out for a walk.

It was dusk, and Rosie had not said where they were going until they were just opposite the house, and then she had pointed it out to her.

'They only rent it, of course,' said Rosie, somewhat apologetically, as Mary exclaimed at its grandeur. 'There is no use in their buying property until they know just how they stand.'

Mary had not understood what she meant.

'Oh, I don't understand either,' said Rosie. 'Violet explained it to me several times, but I couldn't make head or tail of what she was saying. It's something about a lawsuit that's been going on for years and years, and about some old aunt that won't sign something or other. I can't make head or tail of it. But they understand it themselves, of course, and Violet says they'll have lots of money some day. She says they are entitled to it now, but that this old aunt did something or other that delayed them in getting possession of the money. So you see that's why they have to rent a house instead of buying one.'

'I see,' said Mary, but that she did not see very far was clear from her next remark, as she stared across the street at the tall four-storied house, with its large windows and its high arched doorway. 'It must take a nice penny to pay the rent of that house,' she said.

'Oh, they can get all the money they want for things like that, for rent, and clothes, and for Violet's education,' said Rosie, 'They have only to go to the solicitor and get it, but they can't do anything foolish or extravagant.'

'Hmm!' said Mary, looking back at the house once more. 'I

suppose there's no danger that things would go against them?' she asked. 'That they'd have to pay back all they got some day?'

'Oh good heavens, no,' said Rosie. 'It's theirs, you know; it's only just that they haven't a legal claim to it yet. The case cannot be finally settled until they get around the old aunt and get her to sign those papers, whatever they are! She must be a spiteful old cat not to sign them when it means so much to Violet's mother, and to Violet, and all of them, and it can't mean anything to the old aunt herself, because as Violet says she has one leg in the grave already anyway.'

'What will happen if she dies without signing?' asked Mary.

But Rosie thought there was no fear of that happening.

'They'll get around her,' she said. 'Violet is always soft-soaping her.'

'I see,' said Mary again.

Less and less did she like the sound of the Esmays. But this afternoon, listening to the sound of the rain falling so heavily, like them, or not, promise, or no promise, she hoped that Rosie would stay to tea with them, and not come home in such a downpour.

It was just as she formed this wish, however, that she heard Rosie's voice in the hall. With mixed pleasure she got to her feet, but almost at once Rosie was in the kitchen, with the door closed behind her, and her finger on her lips.

'Ssh, Mother!' she said, and for a minute she was able to say no more, because of the way she was panting.

'What's the matter with you?' said Mary, not troubling to lower her voice. 'Were you running?' She looked critically at the girl. On her head was a coloured scarf that was unfamiliar to her and from it came a curious scent.

'Oh ssh!' said Rosie frantically, putting her finger to her lips again. 'He'll hear you,' she cried. Her mother looked at her in amazement. 'Frank Esmay!' said Rosie petulantly. 'You know! Violet's brother. He's waiting for me in the parlour!'

'In the parlour!' Mary looked so startled Rosie laughed.

'It's all right, Mother: he won't break anything!' she said. 'And anyway we'll be going in a minute. I only ran home for a second because I promised I'd be back to tea. But the Esmays insist on my staying to tea with them and I have to give in to them. But I told them I'd have to run home first to tell you, so you wouldn't be worrying about me, but that I'd be right back; although indeed I know they thought it queer that you didn't trust me to stay out for a little while in a friend's house. Mrs. Esmay said that she always trusted her children: not that she wasn't very nice to me, In fact it was she who insisted on Frank coming back with me. "If you're such a ewe lamb I'd better have Frank walk over with you," she said. And now——'

'And now the young man is sitting in the parlour,' said Mary.

Well, there was only one thing to do. Putting her hands behind her back, Mary began to unfasten the straps of her apron. It was the old, familiar gesture that betokened warmth, welcome, and hospitality.

'Are you going to speak to him, Mother?'

'Don't you think I ought?' said Mary.

'Oh, Mother: you are an angel!' Rosie ran over and put her arms around her mother and pressed her face against her mother's cheek.

'I didn't want him to come, Mother,' she cried. 'Honestly, I didn't. I tried my best to stop him. The house is so awful,' she wailed suddenly. 'If you could only see their house: if you could only see the inside of it, I mean. They have so many rooms: I haven't seen a quarter of them. There's a dining-room downstairs, and a drawing-room upstairs——' She stopped. 'I was so ashamed of our parlour. I only just opened the door and shoved him into it. I felt so awful. My heart was jumping out of me. That's why you thought I was running.'

Mary's heart melted.

'I know, child,' she said. 'We must do something about getting the place done up. but the parlour isn't so bad, you know; it never got the usage of the rest of the place. But if you don't want him to see any more of the house, you'd better go in to him, or else he'll wonder what is keeping you and come out here looking for you.'

'Oh, if he did that I'd die,' Rosie pressed her hands to her cheeks. Then she caught the handle of the door. 'I'd better go back to him,' she said. But before she opened the door she smiled disarmingly. 'I won't be late, I promise!' she cried. 'And probably Frank will see me home anyway. I must say I don't know why they're so particular about me!' she added, as she opened the door to go out.

She appeared to have forgotten that Mary had undone her apron to go in and meet the young man. But at the door she stopped and looked back at the table set for two.

'Poor Mother!' she exclaimed. 'You'll have to have tea alone.' Then she glanced at the clock. 'Oh my goodness, how late it is! I said we'd only be ten minutes! I must fly!'

Still she paused. Something more was wanted. What?

Darting back, she planted a kiss on Mary's cheek.

'Don't be too late!' The words rose naturally to Mary's lips.

'Oh, I promise I wont!' cried Rosie.

But there was still something wanting in the situation.

'Oh, I forgot you wanted to speak to him!' she said, and she looked at Mary with a startled face.

Put like that, Mary hardly recognized her own impulsive suggestion.

'Only if you wanted me to do so,' she said, and it was impossible not to be a little cold.

'Oh, Mother, please!' Rosie stepped back into the kitchen and, closing the door once more, stood with her back to it. 'I didn't mean anything! I was only thinking of the delay. I'd love you to come in and speak to him, only we wasted such a lot of time up to now, and I do so want not to keep Mrs. Esmay waiting. I said we'd only be a few minutes. Oh, please understand, Mother?'

'I understand,' said Mary.

But Rosie was not satisfied.

'I know what I'll do!' she cried. 'I'll bring him in to see you to-night, Mother, when he leaves me home. It will give you time to do a little bit to the parlour. I don't suppose he'd take anything at that hour, but it would be nice if we had a fire, wouldn't it? It would be a good idea, don't you think?'

Impatient to be away, Rosie's main idea was to please her mother. It was with surprise that she met Mary's cold stare.

'I don't think it's necessary to bring him into the house at all to-night,' said Mary. 'I think you had better say good night at the door.'

Just then, however, there was the sound of a cough from the parlour, and Rosie started.

'All right, Mother,' she said. 'I suppose you know best.'

And she opened the door, but before she closed it she put in her head again. 'You might have a fire in any case, Mother,' she whispered. 'He'd see it from the door, and he'd think we sit there at night, and not in the kitchen—like we do.'

Like we do! There was something about that little phrase that struck Mary in particular.

'We'll see,' she said.

Rosie smiled. The next minute she was gone. There was the sound of voices in the hall, and then the outer door banged.

I won't look out of the window. Firmly Mary made her resolve, and resolutely she turned towards the table and began to remove Rosie's cup and saucer. But, with a cup in one hand, and a saucer in the other, a few moments afterwards she was standing at the window.

They were almost out of sight. In another moment they would have gone under the arch of the railway bridge. Indeed she had only caught a glimpse of them, and then they were gone. She turned back from the window.

She hadn't looked at all at the young man. It was at Rosie she looked, for all the world as if she hadn't seen her for a twelvemonth, because in fact she had been carried away by how tall the girl had grown, how tall and how stately she was, and how coolly she comported herself.

But she's only a child all the same, she thought.

And yet she had two young men, no less. If she began like this, how would she end? Partly in dismay, partly with a feeling of pride, Mary turned back to her work. The great thing was not to take things too seriously; this Esmay business least of all.

And yet, before she took her own tea, there was a fire beginning to kindle in the parlour grate, although it had been slow in lighting. Nowadays, she thought, getting up from her knees, the fires always went against her. She never had trouble with them in the old days, although she was fitter then, than now, for kneeling and stooping, and, as she straightened up she got, again, the same strange shaft of pain in her shoulder that she had got once or twice of late. Not that she attached much importance to it. She couldn't expect to go for ever without pain or ache, and the years were gaining on her now. Anyway, it couldn't be very serious. The shoulder was a harmless enough place to have a pain, or an ache, for it was more of an ache than a pain, now that she had got to her feet and was able to rub her shoulder with her hand.

I'll feel better after a cup of tea, she thought. It was a long time since she had broken her fast. Still, before she went back to the kitchen, it seemed more sensible to go upstairs and tidy her hair a bit, and put on her black satin dress, because there was no knowing when they might come back.

It was a long time since Mary had put on her best dress for an evening at home. She had worn it once or twice under her coat when she went down to the Seminary to see Larry, but she could hardly remember when she had last worn it in the house. It was a mistake not to wear if oftener, because it was a bit creased from being stuffed away at the back of the cupboard. And the neck looked a bit bare. There was a bit of lace somewhere in the house if only she had the energy to look for it. But she hadn't the energy. Nevertheless, as she caught sight of herself in the mirror on the landing she felt exhilarated, and she realized that she was looking forward to the return of the young people. For in spite of what she said to Rosie, she intended, when she heard their voices at the door, to invite the young man to come in for a cup of tea.

But I don't want it to become a customary thing, she said to herself, as at last she looked into the parlour to see if the fire had lighted well.

In the firelight, the room looked as it used to look. She felt better and better.

For Rosie's sake, it would of course be nice to have a little fire in the parlour every evening, even if there was no one coming to the house at all.

She glanced at the clock. How time flew! It was after nine o'clock. And she had not had her own cup of tea yet. No wonder she felt that pain. Pressing her hand to her shoulder, she went back to the kitchen.

Ah dear! That was always the way with a woman's work. No sooner was one thing done than there was something else undone: the kitchen fire was out. No matter; there would be plenty of time to boil a kettle on the parlour fire before the young people came back.

As she knew would happen, after a good hot cup of tea the pain had vanished; but while it lasted it had been a bit more severe than usual. Poor Tom! She thought with sadness of the way the sweat had broken out on his forehead the night he died. That must have been something like what you'd call pain. Poor Tom! It was some months now since she had visited his grave in Glasnevin. A shudder ran through her. How she hated that cemetery, with its cold grave slabs, set side by side as close as paving stones, with nothing to take from their bareness but the cold glass domes of pallid immortelles. The little cemetery at home in Tullamore was so different. It was like a meadow, with the graves, and even the gravestones, lost in the rich wild grass, or tangled all over with dog rose and briar. Some people would call it lonely, but then there were people who would say the country was lonely anyway. As if there could be anything more lonely than the city streets! Sometimes she used to think she could not be more lonely in her grave than she was in this vast city.

Ah, but she should not let her mind run on such things. The children, Larry and Rosie at least, wouldn't like it if they knew she was letting thoughts like that take possession of her. She went back to her chair by the fire.

What had she been thinking about before these gloomy thoughts assailed her? Ah yes! She was thinking about Tom. She sighed, and as she glanced at her hands, they seemed very thin and wrinkled. She held one up and examined it. She hadn't noticed it before, but there were little brown flecks on the backs of her hands. like freckles, only where would she have got freckles at this time of year? She was slightly puzzled and stared at them until a memory came to her of the hands of an old priest who used to call to see them at home long ago. His hands were like that too, spotted here and there with brown marks. She rubbed them kindly. They were just the marks of the years, she realized with a sigh.

She sat staring into the fire.

Perhaps it was not right for her to be so opposed to Frank Esmay. Perhaps she ought to be glad that this young man, so apparently well-to-do, or at least in easy circumstances, had taken a fancy to Rosie. Perhaps there was more in it than she had let herself think. It was all very well for her to tell herself that Rosie was only a child. Angie had been younger than Rosie when she first met Willie Haslip. Perhaps when she met the young man she might feel differently about him. She threw another lump of coal on the fire, and glanced once more at the clock.

They couldn't be much later now. She looked around the room. Was there anything she could do to make the room look better? Her eyes fell on the torn cover of a cushion. Would there be time now to put a stitch in it? One stitch would hold it.

Too late! That was the click of the gate. They were back. She listened. Yes: there were voices, she could hear them, just faintly. Hastily she put the cushion back on the chair, trying to turn it so that the frayed side would not show. But it was torn in more places than one. She caught it up again. It wasn't needed at all. If she could stow it away somewhere, out of sight entirely! Vainly she looked around her for a place of concealment in the small square box of a room.

Meanwhile the voices continued outside. But why weren't they coming inside? With the cushion pressed against her breast, Mary went closer to the window. Could she have been mistaken? No. Just outside the window, it seemed, there was a subdued murmur of voices, and then to take away all doubt, she heard Rosie laugh, a suppressed laugh, and it was followed by a man's laugh, and a low, a very low voice; barely to be heard at all.

The voices made her uneasy. Why didn't they come inside, she thought again, and unable to move away, she remained at the window. Then she remembered something. It was she herself who had told Rosie to say good-bye at the gate: but she hadn't meant this kind of thing—this talking and laughing in the darkness outside the door. Suddenly throwing down the cushion, which fell on the sofa with the torn side uppermost, Mary went into the hall and opened the front door.

'Is that you, Rosie?'

'Yes, Mother.'

It was hard to see into the darkness of the night, and there were no stars. Rosie and a young man were sitting on the garden seat, but Rosie started up at once, and seeing her in the shaft of light from the hall that fell upon her, Mary felt more at ease. The young man had not stirred.

'Is that Mr. Esmay with you?' asked Mary, after a moment or two of embarrassed hesitation.

Why hadn't he come forward of his own accord? Was he shy, or was he awkward? Mary felt impatient. But at that minute, upon hearing his name, Frank Esmay stepped into the beam of light beside Rosie.

'Good evening, Mrs. O'Grady,' he said, and his voice and bearing, far from being gauche, were perfectly poised and assured. He was almost too poised, and standing there in the flood of light from the hallway, Mary thought there was something theatrical about the way he turned to Rosie. 'Aren't you going to introduce me to your mother, Rosie?' he said.

Rosie, however, was her own plain person.

'Oh, Mother knows who you are,' she said carelessly.

How proud Mary was of her in that moment. How much she approved the robust ordinariness of her words. That's the way to treat him, she thought. But, of course, as an older person, she herself would have to behave differently.

'It was nice of you to come home with my daughter,' she said, not too warmly, but not too coldly either. 'And it was very nice of your mother to invite her for the evening.'

'Oh it was a pleasure,' said the young man, and there was something free and easy in his own manner that struck Mary as unsuited to the occasion. Moreover, although he had evidently addressed his words to her, in reply to her own words to him, while he was speaking he looked, not at her, but at Rosie. It was almost impolite. But that was hardly a reason for her to be impolite in return.

'Aren't you going to come in for a few minutes?' she said.

Frank Esmay looked at the watch on his wrist.

'Isn't it a bit late?' he said.

Mary wanted to say it was a bit late for standing outside the door in the dark, but she did not say it.

'Come inside you, Rosie, anyway,' she said, trying not to be sharp. 'You're shivering.' And when Rosie had stepped inside, she still held the door open. 'Well, is it too late?' she said.

Frank Esmay was looking at Rosie.

'Is it?' he asked.

Rosie may have noticed the way he ignored her mother. Anyway she looked uncomfortable.

'I don't know,' she said. 'Come in if you like; stay out if you like! Only make up your mind. I'm freezing. And so is Mother. We want to shut the door.'

For a moment the young man gave Mrs. O'Grady his attention.

'What do you make of a girl like that?' he said. 'Is it any wonder she'd drive a man wild?' But so saying, he stepped into the hall. 'Allow me!' he exclaimed, as Mary went to close the door.

'It's all right, thank you. The lock is broken. You'd need to understand it,' said Mary, and she contrived to close the door unaided.

When she had succeeded, she found that the young couple had gone into the parlour. She was glad of that because the hall was no place for them to delay; it was the worst part of the house, with its greasy walls, with no room to turn without hitting into the hall stand or the butt of the banisters. But there was no need for them to close the parlour door after them.

A feeling of loneliness came over her. It was silly, but she had so recently been thinking of Bart and Willie, with their warm ways and their friendly manner. They were country boys, with country ways, and she had always felt at ease in their company. With this young man she had felt as if she were superfluous. She recalled the way he had addressed Rosie as if she were not there at all. But believing that this might be some unusual manifestation of nervousness, although she was reluctant to do so, she opened the parlour door.

'You'll have to excuse——' She was going to apologize for the cushion, but when she looked at the young man he was looking at Rosie, and he seemed as if he were unaware that she was in the room at all.

Rosie on the other hand was painfully aware of her.

'Where are you going to sit, Mother?' she asked. And when she turned back to Frank she was irritable with him. 'As long as you're here, you may as well sit down,' she said.

'May I?'

This time he looked at Mrs. O'Grady, and as he sat down he

turned towards her as if about to address her. Feeling that she might have been unfair towards him, and wishing for Rosie's sake to give him every chance of appearing in a more favourable light, she determined to ignore the way he had slighted her at first.

'Did you have a nice evening?' she said.

'Did we?' Immediately Frank turned away from her, and looked at Rosie with a peculiar expression.

Once again Mary had the desolate feeling that she was not wanted, but more than ever she was determined to ignore it. One thing she could not bring herself to do, though, and that was to address Frank Esmay. So she turned to Rosie.

'How about a cup of tea, Rosie?' she asked. 'It would warm you up,' she added impulsively. 'You look cold.'

To Mary's surprise, the young man showed an immediate concern.

'Oh, she's cold all right,' he said, but when she turned around to him gratefully, she saw that he was looking into Rosie's eyes as he spoke, and there was a look in his own that gave a meaning she did not understand to his words.

To break the spell of that look, against her will Mary spoke directly to him.

'Would you care to stay and have a cup of tea with us?' she asked.

But he continued to look into Rosie's eyes.

'It's very kind of you, Mrs. O'Grady,' he said, still without taking his eyes from Rosie. 'It's kind of you to ask me to stay, but I don't know how your daughter feels about it. I don't know whether her heart is as kind. I fancy she'd just as soon turn me out in the cold.'

Exasperated, Mary addressed Rosie.

'Will he have it, or will he not?' she asked.

Rosie was hardly listening to her.

'How do I know?' she said, with a toss of her head, but Mary knew that she was not serious, and the next minute behind the young man's back she nodded her head vigorously in approval of the suggestion.

Mary stood for a moment, not knowing what to do.

'You'll have a cup anyway, Rosie,' she said. 'I'll get the kettle. We'll have to boil it in here, I'm afraid,' she added, looking nervously at Rosie, but Rosie didn't seem to mind, or else she had not heard her. At the door she paused. 'I won't be a minute,' she said, the nervous phrase falling from her lips before she realized that they were hardly likely to appreciate her return.

In the kitchen she had a lot of things to do. As well as filling the kettle, she had to set a tray.

I should have had this ready, she thought, but the next minute she corrected herself. I should have sent Rosie out to do it, because somehow or other she felt uneasy about having left her inside alone with that Esmay fellow. Only a thin wall divided her from them, but all the same she was uneasy.

Why were they silent? Or was it that they were speaking very low? She could see no reason why they shouldn't talk out loud—that was, if they were talking at all.

'I'm coming,' she called out, and she rattled the things on the tray. What else did she need? She looked vacantly at the cups and saucers. Then she gathered her thoughts together. They would like a few biscuits.

'I'm nearly ready,' she called out. If only she could have left the door ajar between the two rooms, but the kitchen was such a sight she couldn't possible let it be seen.

She should have had the tray ready: that was the mistake. And now she wasn't thinking properly. Twice she had been on the point of going in with the tray, when she noticed something lacking. Once it was a spoon, and the second time it was the plate of biscuits.

And that wretched little pain. It was nothing to complain about, just a little dull ache, that was all; but it was disagreeable. At last she was ready. Everything was on the tray. She would have to make a second journey for the kettle. She would send Rosie out for it, only the danger would be that the young man might offer to go for it. She laid down the tray once more to open the door.

Ah, that was better: as with the tray in her hands she elbowed her way through the door that led into the hall, she heard their voices; they were talking quite normally. Rosie's voice was as clear as a bell. Leaving the tray on a chair she opened the door of the parlour.

'Was I long?' she asked. 'Were you getting impatient?'

Then she saw that Rosie was alone. At the same time she became aware of a cold breeze from the hall.

'What is the matter?' she cried. 'Why is the door open? He hasn't gone, has he? You didn't have a quarrel?'

Rosie only laughed.

'Of course not,' she said gaily. 'He's just gone. Why are you so surprised? Look at the hour it is!'

Mary looked down at the tray that seemed suddenly so heavy that it was dragging her arms out of their sockets.

'But I thought he was going to have some tea?' she said bewildered.

'Oh, you needn't mind him!' said Rosie.

Mary supported the tray with her knee.

'Well, I wish you'd let me know that before I got the tray ready,' she said. She seemed now to be so tired that her body ached all over. 'If it was only for you and me, I wouldn't have gone to this trouble.'

Contrite, Rosie took the tray from her arms.

'Oh, Mother, I'm so sorry,' she cried. 'But we'll have it ourselves, just the two of us. It will be nice to use the good cups and have a tray cloth, just for once.' She lifted the lid of the teapot. 'Oh, the tea isn't made yet?' She yawned. Then she recalled something her mother had said about boiling the kettle on the fire in the parlour. 'Oh, I forgot we had to boil the kettle,' she said, and she looked around the hearth for it, sleepily, and without much enthusiasm. 'Where is it?'

'It's in the kitchen,' said Mary.

'Oh, don't stir. I'll get it,' cried the girl. 'Sit down, Mother, I'll make the tea too. I'll do all the rest. Only for goodness' sake give the fire a poke so the water will boil quickly. I'm fagged out. I'm dying to go to bed.'

'Perhaps you don't want the tea at all?' said Mary.

Rosie paused.

'It might keep me awake all night,' she said, and she yawned again. 'But you'd like it, wouldn't you, Mother?'

'Oh, don't mind about me,' said Mary. 'I don't care one way or another.'

'Honestly?'

Mary nodded.

'I have to be up so early in the morning, you know!' said Rosie.

'I know,' said Mary. It was hard to wake her, too.

At the door Rosie hesitated.

'What about the tray?' she asked. 'Wouldn't you like me to put the things away for you?'

'No,' said Mary. 'Go up to bed at once. I'll put them away, or else I'll leave them till morning.'

'Oh, that's an idea; leave them till morning,' cried Rosie. She yawned again. 'Well, I'll be off,' she said. 'Leave them till morning, Mother. Promise!'

And she was gone.

Mary looked at the fire. Was it worth while making tea for herself alone? Rosie had not brought in the kettle. It was hardly worth while going out for it.

But I'll put away these things, she thought, and she stood up to put away the tray, but her mind was still occupied with thoughts of Frank Esmay.

I don't like him, she thought, and I never will.

She recalled the way he had looked at Rosie. He didn't see anything but her: the room or anything in it. She need not have worried so much at its condition. Yet she was sorry to think the place had not looked better for him.

~   ~   ~   ~

'How can you say that, Mother?' cried Rosie one day, when Mary had unwisely let fall a few words that were unfavourable to Frank Esmay. 'You hardly know him,' she added.

Mary said nothing, but her lips tightened. She did not often make the mistake of speaking ill about Frank Esmay. Indeed, it was only with reluctance that his name crossed her lips at all. On the other hand, she was always talking about Hubert Young, of whom she had formed a very favourable opinion.

Rosie had been over a year working with Mr. Young, and from little things she had said about him from time to time, Mary had developed a strong regard for him, although she had never made his acquaintance. She knew that he admired Rosie, but the knowledge did not disturb her in the way that she was disturbed by the attentions showered upon her by Frank Esmay. This may have been because the advances of the older man were steady and prudent, and above all so slow, that it looked as if it would be years before he need be regarded seriously as a suitor.

With Frank Esmay, on the other hand, there was no knowing what reckless impulse he might take, or what recklessness he might inspire in Rosie.

Since the first evening that he had accompanied Rosie home, he had called several times, until in recent months his calls had become almost regularized by their frequency.

Mary, however, after the first evening that she felt so uncomfortable in his company, declined to see more of him than the demands of propriety made necessary. Hence therefore came Rosie's accusation.

'You never come into the parlour to speak to him,' she said. 'It's not fair to form opinions of people without knowing them.' She looked at her mother with a sad look, a pleading look. But as Mary still said nothing, the look changed. 'It's the same with Hubert Young,' she said bitterly. 'You made up your mind about him too, without knowing him: without ever meeting him!'

This time Mary turned around.

'It's not my fault that I didn't meet Mr. Young,' she said.

That was true.

Several times she had suggested that Rosie should invite the young man to call to the house; but Rosie never seemed anxious for him to do so. Once or twice, when they were working late at the library, Hubert had left her home, but he only came as far as the gate with her and no farther.

'I don't know why you didn't bring him in one of those evenings when he came home with you,' said Mary. 'You know I'd like to meet him. I've often told you that I would have no objection to his calling; that I'd be glad to make his acquaintance. I'd like a little warning of when he was coming, of course, if it was possible, so that I could have something in the house. I'd like to have a few biscuits, or a piece of cake, or something, in case he'd take a cup of tea.'

Rosie was listening, but impatiently. How tired she was of hearing Hubert's name.

'If you want to know the truth,' she said, suddenly, cruelly, 'Hubert wouldn't come. Not that I wanted him indeed, but I had to ask him out of common politeness those times when he came all the way over here with me, right up to the door, you might say! But he wasn't having any!'

Looking up to see how her mother took this information, she was exasperated to see from her face that she was silently attributing Hubert's conduct to some gentlemanly scrupulosity or delicacy.

'Indeed, you might not think so much of him if you heard what he said about our house,' she cried. ' "Why don't you come inside?" I said, one night. He looked up at the house, and shook his head. Then after a minute he took my arm. "I don't like to think of you living in such a mean little house!" he said. There now! I didn't intend to tell you, but you're always throwing it in my face that I don't ask him to come inside.'

Once again she looked at her mother, but this time she was frightened at her own vindictiveness. For an instant her mother had the look of one that had got an unexpected hurt, but her words when she spoke showed no sign of it.

'I wouldn't mind that,' she said. 'It only shows what a high opinion he has of you, Rosie. And isn't he right about the house?' she added after a minute. 'It is a mean little house; he's sincere anyway.'

'I suppose that's a dig at Frank!' flashed Rosie.

'It's a dig at no one,' said Mary tersely, 'but it you want to know my mind I'll tell you. It's a funny thing to me that a dandy like that Esmay fellow can take so little heed of your surroundings. You'd think it would cool his ardour a bit to see the condition of the house where you live.'

Rosie could hardly believe her ears. She stared at her mother.

'To think that you could say that!' she cried. 'My own mother. It's me Frank comes to see; not the house. He hardly takes his eyes off me from the time he comes in the door till the time he has to get up and go home.'

That was true. He always acted as if there were no one in the room but Rosie. It was one of the things Mary disliked about him. A shiver went through her, inwardly, but Rosie's eyes were on her.

I must not show my feelings, she thought. Instead, she picked up the dress she had been sewing.

'There's no need for you to get vexed with me, Rosie,' she said, as evenly as possible. 'What does it matter what I think of one young man or another? I expect to see a great many young men, of all kinds and all sorts, before you bring home the right one. When you were small, I used to say you were like your Grandaunt Ella. And I think you still have a look of her at times. You probably take after her in more ways than one, and she had twenty-four proposals before she met your uncle, Sumner. He was an American, you know, and he was in Tullamore on a visit when he met Aunt Ella. And the next thing that we knew, there was Aunt Ella, who was afraid to go out in a rowing boat, and——'

'Oh, I know, I know.' said Rosie impatiently. 'She was afraid to go out in a rowing boat, and yet she crossed the Atlantic with him! You told us that a hundred times. I don't see what it has got to do with Frank and me.'

For a moment, Mary could not see what it had to do with them either, for she had become entangled in the skein of her reminiscences, and she could not immediately extricate herself from it.

'He was a very good match for her,' she said. 'But as you say, that's not the point. Now what was it I wanted to tell you? Oh yes! I wanted to tell you about all the proposals she had as a girl——'

But here Rosie interrupted her again impatiently.

'Oh, those days are gone,' she said. 'Men aren't so simple nowadays. They're not so ready now to come to the point.'

'Is that so?' Mary could not keep a note of contempt out of her voice. How could one so young, so innocent, speak so heartlessly? 'Is that so?' she repeated. 'Well, if that's the case, the girls have only themselves to thank for it, with their cigarettes and their brazen manners, and their skirts up to their knees.'

Now Rosie did not smoke. And her manner, although independent, could never have been called brassy. Unfortunately, however, the dress she was wearing at that moment was a new one, it was moreover the first that she had bought with her own earnings, and she had chosen it without Mary's help. Undoubtedly also, it was a bit short. Rosie sprang to her feet.

'I hate hints,' she said.

Genuinely bewildered, Mary stared at her. Rosie was looking at herself in the mirror.

'Frank said this is the smartest dress I ever wore,' she said.

'Did Mr. Young see you in it?' asked Mary.

'Oh him!' cried Rosie.

She was sick and tired of this duet between herself and her mother. Whenever she mentioned Frank, her mother was sure to strike a note for Hubert Young.

'If Hubert had his way, my dresses would be down to my ankles. If he had his way there wouldn't be much fun in the world. He'd like to do away with dance halls, he said—altogether. Oh, you should hear him! "I'd like to take you to a nice concert," he says. Think of that! Can you imagine me at a concert!'

'I can't!' said Mary promptly. She meant to be disparaging, but she was disarmed by the way Rosie swung around with a smile.

'You see!' she said, and she began to pat her hair at the sides, making the large heavy waves deeper and softer. 'He's not my type at all.'

'More is the pity!' said Mary flatly. 'I don't see what harm it would do you to go to one of his concerts with him, if it made him happy. When I think of all the times I went to Croke Park with your father, just to please him, without knowing the first thing about football, and in the middle of winter too. I used to be perished with the cold. But those concert halls are well heated, I imagine. I'm sure the seats are very comfortable too, and if you didn't like the music you could close your eyes and have a little rest. And you never know, you might enjoy it. In any case it wouldn't be more than an hour or two until it would be over and then you'd be glad of the pleasure you gave Mr. Young by going with him. I know I never regretted anything I ever did to please your father, although I don't mind telling you——'

But here Rosie interrupted her.

'I don't see the comparison between you and Father, and me and Hubert Young,' she cried. 'I don't see why I should put myself out for him. If it was anyone else! As a matter of fact I've done lots of things with Frank that I didn't care much for doing, but that's different! I'd nearly go to Croke Park with Frank!' she ended with a laugh.

Frank Esmay: always Frank Esmay. There seemed to be no getting away from him.

'I don't think there's any danger of your having to go to Croke Park with him,' said Mary sarcastically. 'I don't think the simple amusements that interested your father would have any interest for your smart Mr. Esmay. Talk of comparisons! There may not be much comparison between Mr. Young and your poor father, but you never heard me making any comparison between Frank Esmay and him. No, and you never will hear it. One hair of your father's head would be worth the whole of Frank Esmay. Tell me: did he get a job yet?'

'I told you, Mother——'

'I know! I know! He's coming in for such a big heap of money one of these days there's no need for him to stir a finger. Well! Take care that he's not let down in his big expectations. There are others who have not half his boasting, who might be better able to give a girl a secure roof over her head, if things were put to the test.'

'Meaning Hubert again, of course——'

'Meaning no one,' said Mary shortly. 'As a matter of fact, I don't know why we're talking like this at all. Many a girl older than you hasn't spoken to a boy in her life!'

Mary spoke crossly, but Rosie laughed.

'Indeed, there are some people who think I should still be playing with dolls!' she said. 'Hubert Young makes me tired with the way he goes on about my age. "Wouldn't you like to attend night classes?" he says. And he's always asking about my music! "I hope you keep up your music: there's nothing like the piano," he says. "You should practise." Did you ever hear the like? He said he'd let me home early to practise. You'd think I was about fifteen. As a matter of fact he was saying the other day that that was all I look: fifteen. Fifteen!' she repeated, and she smiled, a curiously tender little smile, as if at the recollection of some other little thing that had been said to her which she did not choose to divulge. Then she seemed to put the recollection aside deliberately. 'Frank's another: he's always giving me sly digs about my age.'

The look that Mary's face had worn when the conversation concerned Mr. Young faded at once.

'What does he say?' she said crisply.

But Rosie had turned aside.

'Oh, he's always at it,' she said vaguely, and she averted her face, but chancing to catch sight of the girl's reflection in the mirror, Mary saw why she had turned aside. In her cheeks two pink spots glowed. And at the sight, momentarily forgetting the cause of those blushes, Mary held her breath. She was so lovely.

'Well, I must be going,' Rosie cried at that minute, and running into the hall, she snatched her hat from the hall stand, and ramming it down upon her head carelessly, she called back something else, indistinct, but most likely unimportant, and the next instant she was gone.

~   ~   ~   ~

In the past, whenever Tom was working late, Mary used to sit up and wait for him, no matter how much he protested against her doing it. Usually when the house grew still and quiet, she fell asleep sitting by the kitchen fire, and when he came at last, his entry, however gentle, always made her leap to her feet in fright.

'What way is that to come into a room?' she used to exclaim in confusion at having been found asleep.

And so, one evening that Rosie was working late, Mary, partly perhaps from habit, fell asleep while she was waiting for her to return. But in this case when she woke with a start at Rosie's entry, her mind was more than usually cloudy and confused.

'Oh, it's you, is it?' she said, after a minute, seeing Rosie standing beside her in the light from the fire. Almost, she had fancied—oh but she must surely have been asleep!

'Who did you think it was?' asked Rosie in surprise.

Who indeed? Mary rubbed her eyes. She felt curiously tired, although she must have been asleep for a long time.

'Don't put on the light for a moment ' she cried, groping for her shoes, which she had kicked from her feet, and putting up her hand to her hair. She felt so disarranged, and even disassembled, that she shrank from being seen even by Rosie, in the glare of the light.

But Rosie did not understand.

'Why not?' she cried impatiently. 'You know that I hate to see you sitting in the dark, Mother; it gives me the creeps.'

But she had another reason for wanting to put on the light.

'Hurry up, Mother,' she cried, waiting for the word to illumine the room. 'Hurry; I have something to tell you; you'll die laughing when you hear it.'

Although she felt cramped, Mary rose to her feet. The next minute, the light was on.

And she saw that Rosie was laughing.

'It's Hubert,' said Rosie, and she laughed again. Then, a look of mock seriousness came over her face. 'After what I was telling you the other day,' she cried, 'about his saying I was a child! Oh, men are all alike; they are all the same!'

'What on earth are you talking about?' cried Mary, although she had at once guessed what had happened.

'I told you,' cried Rosie. 'It's Hubert! As Violet would say, "He's been and gone and done it." '

The expression was not minted by Violet. It was as old as the hills. Mary had heard it when she was a girl in Tullamore. But it was only used by a certain kind of person, and she had always considered it common and ugly. To hear it upon the lips of Rosie was very disagreeable to her, and applied to a person like Hubert was downright distasteful.

And so not only was her daughter's meaning unmistakable to her, but as well as conveying the fact that Mr. Young had proposed to her, it conveyed also what had been Rosie's reaction to the proposal.

Feeling as if an imponderable weight had suddenly been placed upon her, Mary sank back into her chair. This is a calamity, she thought, but at the same moment, another thought came involuntarily into her mind.

How is it, she thought, that although I only went to a national school, in the heart of the country, and Rosie went to a convent in the city, she speaks in a way I never spoke, or never heard my parents speak, although they were only small farming people, mixing always only with their own kind, not like her with her fancy friends from Raglan Road?

'What are you talking about?' she said suddenly. 'Why can't you speak plain English?' But the next minute she betrayed herself. 'I hope you kept your head?' she said.

'Oh, I was as cool as a cucumber,' said Rosie happily. She had been afraid that her mother had not understood what had happened. 'It was poor Hubert that was flustered. I told him not to be a donkey!'

For Hubert's sake, Mary winced.

'I hope you didn't give him an answer there and then,' she cried. 'I hope you showed some consideration for him. I hope you told him you'd think it over and give him an answer later.'

'I told him no such thing!' said Rosie. 'Why should I?' Suddenly the fun had gone out of the incident. 'Why should I keep him in misery?' she demanded. 'That's not what I'd call consideration for a man. He may be an old donkey, but he's mad about me, I can see that, and what would be the use of dragging things out for him, keeping him in suspense, when the answer would be the same in the end anyway. It was much better to put him out of pain at once.'

Mary pursed her lips.

'I don't know so much about that,' she said. 'You have very little experience, Rosie. A time might come when you would think differently from the way you think now. A girl ought to think twice before throwing away a good match like that. Not that I want you to get married. I don't—not for years anyway, but I often heard that it wasn't lucky to turn down the offer of a good honest man, when you had nothing against him. You had nothing against him, had you?' she asked anxiously.

By now, however, Rosie was exasperated.

'Of course not,' she cried. 'What a question to ask. I told you hundreds of times that he's a dear. Of course I have nothing against him. If only he didn't look at me with such sheep's eyes. But it's funny you should ask me if I had anything against him, because he asked me the same thing himself to-night. He thought, too, I had something against him: the poor old duffer! "You've nothing against me, Rosie, have you?" he said, and he was almost crying. I kind of pitied him. "Not a thing in the world," I said. "Then why won't you give me some encouragement?" he said.'

'What did you say to that?' asked Mary, dully.

'Oh, what could I say?' said Rosie. 'I said enough if you ask me. If I said any more I'd have let the cat out of the bag. As a matter of fact unless he's stupid, he'll have guessed——'

'Guessed what?' All of a sudden Mary became alive. 'You didn't let him think there was anyone else, did you?' she said, and her cheeks not often red nowadays, were bright with anger.

For the first time, Rosie looked frightened. For the first time she was visited by some sense of seriousness in the situation.

'Why not?' she said defiantly, her own colour rising.

'Because it's not true: there isn't anyone else. Oh, there's no need to look at me like that, Rosie. I know what I'm talking about. I know what's in your mind about that Esmay fellow, but you're making a mistake if you place any reliance on him or the like of him. I know him!'

'How can you say that? You don't know him. You only met him two or three times, properly speaking.'

'It was enough. Before I ever met him at all, the first day his sister called here looking for you, I judged him by her. Didn't she as good as say to me that he was a rag in every bush?'

Rosie's cheeks deepened in colour.

'That may have been true then,' she said, 'but it's different now.'

'Since he met you, I suppose you mean? I'm glad you have such confidence in yourself!' said Mary, and her voice was acid.

But it might well be that the young man had changed since he met her, she thought. She looked so pretty. I wish she was plainer, she thought suddenly. Her looks are a danger to her. She thought of how she had nourished those looks from the earliest years of the child's life, brushing her hair unfailingly every night, even on nights that she was hardly able to hold the brush in her hand with fatigue, and not content with that, after the brushing, she used to rub down her hair with a piece of old silk because she had heard that silk would bring out the gloss on it. And as for her skin—never once had she washed her face or hands in anything but soft rain water. She thought of the way she had contrived to save water from the eave shoots and the slates, in every old canister and bucket she could collect, making the back yard a sight.

Now she saw those efforts in a new light. Now she saw herself suddenly as Rosie's enemy.

'I will tell you another thing!' she exclaimed. 'You'll have to look out for another job now. You can't continue to work for Mr. Young under the circumstances.'

But Rosie only laughed; and there was a slackening of the tension.

'Oh, for goodness' sake, Mother, don't be so old-fashioned. People don't behave like that nowadays. As a matter of fact, that was one of the things Hubert insisted on: that it wouldn't make any difference between us, that we'd still be good friends; like always.'

Mary looked hard at her; then she turned away. She sighed. How hard it would be on him, she thought, looking at her day after day, and cherishing the feelings he had for her without hope of ever having them returned. He must be a very exceptional man, she thought, unless of course he had some secret hope of her changing her mind.

And might there not be hope of that? She looked up suddenly. If Frank Esmay got tired of her one of these days, as she believed would happen, then Hubert might get his chance. If only the affair with Esmay did not drag on too long! Because she well knew that it would not help matters for Frank to take his departure unless he did so soon, before he had done any more damage to the girl's feelings and sensibilities.

If only she could put an end to it! If I could see him alone for five minutes, she thought, I'd soon tell him what I thought of him; I'd soon send him about his business.

'Are you going to be home this evening,' she asked suddenly, 'or are you going out?'

'I'm going out,' said Rosie.

Was it Mary's fancy, or did the girl look at her suspiciously?

'With whom?' asked Mary.

Rosie shrugged.

'What's the use of telling you,' she said, 'if it will only annoy you?'

Mary pursed her lips. So it was with Frank Esmay!

'Is he calling here?' she said then, tensely.

'Yes, why?'

Mary hesitated.

'At what time?'

'Seven.'

Mary glanced at the clock.

'In that case,' she said, 'you'll have time to do a message for me beforehand.'

'What?'

Incredulously Rosie stared. Since she had gone to work, a kind of tradition had grown up that she would not be asked to do any more messages.

'I'm sorry,' said Mary shortly. 'But it's important.' That sounded lame, but she couldn't help it. It was the best she could do at a moment's notice.

'But Frank will be calling for me in less than half an hour,' cried Rosie, glancing at the clock in dismay. It was after six then.

Mary's hands had begun to tremble, but she put them behind her back.

'Don't worry,' she said, 'you may be back before he gets here. Punctuality is not one of his virtues, if I remember rightly. And if he comes while you're out I can keep him company.'

Rosie stood up.

'Well, if I have to go I may as well go at once. It's a wonder you didn't mention the matter earlier. I could have been back by now. What is the message?' she asked suddenly.

The message? Mary was taken aback. To get the girl out of the house had been all that concerned her. Then all at once she had an inspiration.

'I want to have a Mass said for your father. I want you to go down to the chapel with the offering money.'

Rosie's eyes flew to the calendar.

'It isn't his anniversary, is it?' she asked in surprise.

'I should hope I'd get a Mass said for him more often than once a year,' said Mary.

Rosie said no more, but stretched out her hand.

'Give me the money,' she said.

'Just a minute,' said Mary. 'I'll have to get an envelope.'

'I think you might have hurried,' said Rosie crossly, when she came down a few minutes afterwards with the envelope in her hands. 'Now I'll have to run most of the way.'

Mary handed her the envelope.

'If you do that, you'll be more foolish than I thought,' she said. 'Let me tell you no man's opinion of a girl was ever lessened yet by being kept waiting a few minutes for her. Take care would you run! Think of your appearance! You don't want the man to see you all hot and red in the face, do you?'

'Oh, I wouldn't mind how Frank saw me,' said Rosie. 'I expect he'll see me looking worse than that before we're much older.'

Was it a meaningless remark, or was there more between them than she thought? Mary did not know. But I'll soon know, she thought, as she closed the door after Rosie, and turned and went upstairs again to change into her best black dress. The better her appearance, the better this Esmay fellow would see that she was a person with whom to reckon. As she dressed, however, the trembling that had come in her hands came over her whole frame. This, that I am going to do, she thought, is the hardest thing I have ever had to do in my life. But her determination to do it did not in any way slacken.

All my life, she thought, I have suffered things to happen to me without protest. This is the first time that I ever tried to take things into my own hands.

In a few minutes she was ready. She was dressed. And, as if blown by a favourable wind, from the window of her bedroom she saw Frank Esmay coming down the street.

'I'll let him see,' she said aloud, 'that he's not going to philander with my daughter.'

Only once, on the stairs, as she went down to open the door to him, did she have any misgivings about what she was about to do; she was daunted at the thought of what Rosie would say when she came back to find that he was gone. But she took heart again at the thought that she could not be unhappy for long about him once he was shown up in his true colours.

For that she knew what Frank Esmay's true colours were, Mary did not for a minute doubt.

~ ~ ~ ~

'Speech from the bridegroom!'

'Speak up now, old man! What have you got to say for yourself!'

'Speech from the bridegroom!'

In the crowded room of the hotel, where the wedding breakfast was being held, the guests had become boisterous, and drumming with their glasses upon the table, with one accord they called upon the bridegroom.

Frank Esmay rose to his feet.

'Ladies and gentlemen!' he said, and he flashed a smile at all the company, including the slightly dishevelled waitresses who squeezed their way between the backs of the guests' chairs and the soiled walls of the hotel dining-room, serving out the remains of the collapsed jellies, and the unlabelled bottles of wine.

'Ladies and gentlemen!' he repeated, and he laid his hand on the shoulder of his bride. 'I wish to convey my thanks, and the thanks of my wife here'—at this point there was some laughter at the end of the table—'for the kind tributes which you have paid to us. As for myself, I am afraid that those of you who spoke so highly in praise of me were making a bit of a mistake, but I hope it will be a long time before Rosie here finds out her mistake.'

More laughter greeted this mild sally.

'I would like also to thank you all,' went on the bridegroom, 'for having showed up here to-day at our wedding.'

Mary listened to her new son-in-law with mixed feelings. There was no mistaking his suavity, or the accomplished way in which he was acquitting himself at that moment. Indeed, as he had risen to his feet there was a stir in the company, and a look of expectation came over the faces of the guests, and although most of them were friends and relatives of the Esmays, even her own few friends, to whom he was a stranger, seemed ready to be swayed by his charm. He was certainly at his best. His self-confidence and poise, which on another occasion had caused her to mistrust him, were on this occasion the attributes of success. It wasn't every young man who could appear so much at home in his first morning suit, and that a hired one. But far from suffering any eclipse of his faculties, Frank did not forget when he spoke to make a discreet number of gesticulations with his hands in order to show off his cuff links, which were of rolled gold.

It was understandable that a young girl would find it hard to resist him, thought Mary; but further than this she was not prepared to venture an estimate of one about whom, not six months earlier, she had made such a false calculation.

At the thought of that disastrous evening when she had hoped to put an end to his relations with Rosie, Mary's cheeks began to burn.

It was just at that moment, when she was least prepared to meet it, that looking up she found her son-in-law's eyes upon her with a mocking gleam in them.

He had just said something that she had missed through her inattention, but the laughter it had caused still rippled through the company.

'And now, my friends,' said the bridegroom, waxing more confident with every minute he held the floor, 'I want to propose another toast, but before doing so, I want to take you into my confidence, and to tell you that this happy occasion to which you have so kindly lent your approval and approbation would never have taken place were it not due to the efforts of a certain person! In short, ladies and gentlemen, it is entirely due to my mother-in-law that we are gathered here to-day at this festive board.'

At this point there was something like a gasp of surprise from the company, particularly those of them who were intimates of either family, but the next minute, either from embarrassment or from a feeling of confidence in the bridegroom, there was a laugh, which, once started, became almost an uproar. Never, outside of vaudeville or the hippodrome, it seemed, had such an outrageously comical remark been made at a wedding.

But just as the laughter became almost hysterical, Frank, who had kept his eyes fixed on Mary, raised his hands to quell the hilarity.

'Don't mistake me, my friends,' he cried. 'I think there is a misunderstanding! In fact, you have only to turn your heads in the direction of my mother-in-law in order to realize the extent of your misunderstanding. For contrary to what you may have thought from my innocent words, it was with the greatest reluctance that Mrs. O'Grady permitted me to become her son-in-law! But I will tell you the whole story! It was like this! One evening, about six or seven months ago, I called down to the house of my friend Rosie here—oh yes, that was all she was to me at the time, and who knows but that might have been all she was ever intended to be were it not for a certain turn in events that night. But I mustn't run ahead. As I say,

I was going down to see her this evening as usual, to take her out for a bit of a walk, and the like of that, with no other notion in my head I assure you. I suppose it crossed my head once or twice, like it will cross the mind of any young fellow, that there would have to be some kind of an end to an affair of that kind some day or another, but I didn't know Rosie long enough at this time to let that worry me, and so, as I say, I went sauntering down the street to her house. Now I must tell you another thing at this point. It was nearly always Rosie herself that opened the door to me on those occasions, and I don't suppose I had met my mother-in-law here on more than a half dozen occasions. I think she wasn't any too well disposed to me at any time!' Here there was some laughter at the end of the table, but it was quickly silenced by those at the top who were eager to hear the rest of the story. 'So,' said Frank, 'it was a kind of a shock to me when instead of Rosie it was Mrs. O'Grady here that came to the door on this evening. But of course I never let on but that I was glad to see her. "Good evening, ma'am," I said, as civil as you like. "Is Rosie at home by any chance?" I said, casually, as it were, although of course I knew she was expecting me, and I thought she was only upstairs putting a few finishing touches to herself or the like of that. You can imagine my surprise when Mrs. O'Grady here said she wasn't in the house at all. "As a matter of fact," she said, "I sent her out on a message." "Oh, that's all right," I said, and I was wondering ought I to suggest waiting for her, or ought I to go away, when all of a sudden I got the shivers at the way she was looking at me. "Mr. Esmay," she said, and there was a look on her face I didn't like, "will you step inside for a minute. I want to have a few words with you."'

There was such a comical look of consternation upon her son-in-law's face as he repeated the words of their interview that even Mary had to join in the laughter that broke out all down the table this time, and threatened to drown his voice.

'Well, my friends,' Frank continued, 'I don't know if any of you have had an experience of this kind, but I can assure you that a chappie feels pretty weak about the knees at a time like that. He feels the noose tightening, if you know what I mean, and his thoughts are filled with visions of poor little gambolling lambs being led to the slaughter.'

Here again there was a loud burst of laughter, but Frank put up his hands appealingly for attention.

'Wait a minute,' he said. 'I see you're all making the same mistake I made myself. As a matter of fact I nearly bolted off down the street, but if you please the next thing I realized was that instead of wanting to know my intentions in regard to her daughter here, my brave mother-in-law was trying to give me my walking papers.'

But here there was such a deafening outburst of laughter and drumming of feet on the floor that particles of the icing on the cake fell down upon the plate, and the dregs of the wine in the glasses rocked.

Frank Esmay looked down at Rosie. And at the sight of her blushing face, raised half fearful, half smiling to his, he, too, laughed. Then his glance flashed over their guests again.

'Well, my friends, I had to let it be seen that I wasn't going to be shown the door like that!' he said, and then, lifting his glass, Frank Esmay looked directly across the table at Mary. 'And so, my friends,' he said, 'here we are: Rosie and I, and all of you! And I think you will agree with me that we ought to make some acknowledgment to Mrs. O'Grady for the part she played in bringing us all together here to-day! Ladies and gentlemen! I give you another toast: my mother-in-law!'

PART IX

Larry

ONE evening in the middle of Lent, as dusk was falling, Mary was standing in the parlour window looking out into the street.

Surely that is not Larry, she thought in alarm, as she became aware that in the dusk there was someone standing at the gate, and staring straight at the house. It was just Larry's height, and Larry's build, but yet there was something unlike Larry in the way this person leaned as if for support upon the railings. Larry's bearing was so erect and purposeful.

How could it be Larry anyway in the middle of Lent? And Lent or no Lent, if he had happened to be in Dublin, he would long ago have left the house to catch his train back to the Seminary. Indeed, at that moment, in the distance her ear caught the whistle of his train as it pulled out of the station. Except for that one defection on the night they were so frightened about Patrick, in his ten years at the Seminary he had never once failed to leave the house in good time for that train.

All the same, the person at the gate who still stood there looking inward was extraordinarily like Larry, and hoping to see him better, she ran to the door, but as she opened it, turning up his collar against the heavy drops of rain that had at that moment begun to fall, the person who had stood at the gate, whoever he was, turned and walked rapidly down the street.

She knew it could not have been Larry, but her heart was beating irregularly, and her face was flushed. She was glad to stand at the door for a few minutes and watch the blessed rain that soon was falling heavily.

All over the city it fell, and in the little railed plot in front of her

321

own house if fell soundlessly into the long neglected grass. But every now and then, as she listened, from the broken eave over the parlour window, a heavy drop fell with a clear treble note upon the gravel below.

It was settling down to be a cold, wet, miserable evening, and with one last look into the darkness, Mary turned back to the house. In the darkness and the driving rain, she had not seen, inside the gate at the end of the garden, the big yellow suitcase that stuck out from under the bushes, through which, already, a few drops of rain had fallen, pocking and spoiling the surface of the leather.

She had not seen it, but had closed the door, and gone back into the warm kitchen.

All the same, as she sat down and listened dejectedly to the rain outside, she was troubled by thoughts of the person who had stood at her gate, and stranger though he might be, she felt for him. It was a bad night to be wandering about the streets.

It seemed to her now that the resemblance to Larry had been unnatural, and her mind was invaded by tales she had heard, of visitations and apparitions.

If Larry were anywhere else but where he was that night, she would indeed have been disturbed at this visitant that had come to the gate in his likeness.

How thankful to God she ought to be that she knew where her boy was this night. It was even some solace to think of the high walls that enclosed Patrick, and gave him sanctuary. But oh, the happiness of thinking about Larry, and of knowing how near he was to his ordination. For there had been dark hours when she had feared that something would come between him and his goal.

Ever since she stood at the window and watched the back of the cab that bore the two of them out of sight on the morning that Patrick went away, some shadow had hung over her mind. Had she not heard of a young boy in Tullamore who was sent home from the Seminary because of something his superiors had found out about some member of his family?

She couldn't remember exactly what it was that people had whispered at the time, but she imagined that it might have been something the same as had happened to poor Patrick, only in Patrick's case it was not hereditary; it was only bad luck. But in the other case they must have been afraid that it was a weakness in the family and that it might declare itself again in the poor fellow that was going for the priesthood. So they sent him home, and his people tried to pretend that he was in bad health, but everyone knew that there was nothing at all the matter with him. It was very sad to see the young fellow going about the roads for years in his black suit, because his people didn't see the sense in his not wearing it out as long as it was in good condition.

If Larry had had the misfortune to be sent home like that, she would never have let him suffer the humiliation of going about in his clerical clothes, although she had bought him a good many clothes now since that first black suit they had bought together. Only lately she had bought him a heavy black overcoat, and any number of scarves and cardigans and gloves, but of course there was no need to worry about him now: it was nearly two years since poor Patrick went away, and in that time his superiors had had plenty of opportunity to find out all about him, because, of course, right at the beginning Larry had to tell them about him, to explain his behaviour on the night he stayed at home without permission. What other excuse could he have given?

Oh, how she had worried at that time, and how she had lain awake, night after night, regretting that she had let him stay at home, because only for that it would not have been necessary to say anything at all about Patrick.

But it might have been worse if he had said nothing and they had found out for themselves. They must have realized that it was only misfortune that had upset poor Patrick's balance. They must have seen that Larry was as sound as a bell, because there was never any further mention of the matter after the first day Larry told them about him. She knew that because she had questioned him closely the next time she saw him, although for his own part he didn't appear to have any anxiety at all in the matter. In fact he found it hard to understand why she should be worried about it. And so gradually her fears had been set at rest, and as time passed and his ordination drew near, she had all but forgotten that she had ever been disquieted about him. For every time she saw him it seemed to her he was in every way more sanctified and more priestly. And not only that, but it seemed to her sometimes that his present sanctity cast an illuminating light over the past, and even explained the way that, as a child, he had differed from her other children. She used to think that he was lacking in some way, and God forgive her, she used to think at times that there was an almost vacant look on his face, but now she knew that it was vacant only of worldliness.

He was the least worldly person she had ever known. Even as a child, he had always been ready to deny himself in order to give to others. And when the girls had met with their sad fate, had she not heard him saying to Alice Maguire that he wished he had been taken in their place! Even then, he was already eager for sacrifice, eager to suffer, for others. The tears rushed into her eyes. If he was her son a hundred times, she felt sure there was not another boy in the Seminary with his sanctity and his holiness. And even if his superiors had not been told, or had misunderstood in any way, the nature of Patrick's illness, in the face of such spiritual aspiration, how could they ever turn him aside?

But still, as she sat listening to the rain, she was unsettled and ill at ease. And several times she thought of the solitary figure who had stood in the street outside the gate. She even went to the parlour window and looked out, half thinking that he might again be standing there. God help him, whoever he was, and give him ease and shelter.

God help all poor wanderers and wayfarers, she prayed, and all those who are homeless this night, and desolate.

For a time she stood there at the window, looking out; but she still did not see Larry's suitcase at the end of the dark garden, nor was it likely now that she would, for it had by this time become so sodden and discoloured that it was hardly to be discerned from the saturated earth around it.

And Larry? What of him? In all his misery, and desolation, it was of his big new suitcase that he thought when he felt the first drops of rain falling upon his face as he walked, not knowing where he was going, into the darkness of the night. His mother was so proud of it when she bought it for him the day before he left home. He was proud of it too, although he didn't want her to spend the money on it; he could have made up his things in a parcel, or borrowed an old case from the Maguires. But she insisted, and when he was walking up the avenue to the Seminary, he couldn't help being proud of his big yellow case; solid leather, with brass locks. And now it was lying out under all the rain with no protection but a few miserable bushes.

If only he had put it in some sheltered place, where this terrible rain would not fall upon it and spot it all over and spoil it. If only he had thought of leaving it in the station, or in some of the little shops he had passed on his way home. But his mind had been so confused when he got out of the train that he walked along in a kind of trance until he found himself standing outside the gate of his mother's house. He hadn't meant to go home until he gathered his thoughts together, and prepared what he was going to say to her, but as he stood outside the gate looking up at the house it crossed his mind that there was no place else for him to go.

Not yet though, his heart had cried. He could not face her yet.

He could not bear any more than he had already had to bear. He could not bear her sorrow until he was more accustomed to the burden of his own. It had fallen upon him with so little warning. That morning he had taken his place in the choir; he was still in his soutane and surplice, when the superior called him into his room. Just a few words about Patrick, that had seemed quite natural to him, and then a few questions about his own health that seemed of no consequence, and to which he had been able to give satisfactory answers. And then there had followed what was almost a monologue, to which he had hardly attended at all so little did it seem to concern him, although towards the end he was disturbed by the penetrating way the older priest was staring at him: he forced himself to listen more intently.

'You see, my son, the religious life is an arduous life,' said the priest. 'It imposes a great strain upon all those of us to whom God gives the health and strength necessary to persevere. I think I need hardly tell you that spiritual aspiration alone is not sufficient; there is need of a strong physical constitution, and great stamina of mind and body. Indeed it might be said of the priesthood that the greater the spiritual zeal of the aspirant, the greater need there is for those in authority over him to see that he is not imposing too great a strain upon himself: that he is not, in short, taking too much upon his shoulders. For we have a duty towards God in regard to our body, as well as the duty we owe Him in regard to our souls. God does not want us to strain ourselves beyond out capacity, or to give of ourselves beyond our resources. And if there is any latent weakness in ourselves or in our family it is necessary that we face up to the fact that we may not have the necessary qualities for the work which we have undertaken, and nowhere is this as necessary as in God's ministry. For what voice shall come forth from the broken reed? And how shall such a voice proclaim His Gospel?'

There was a pause then, and the superior had looked at him steadily.

'Do you understand me, my son?' he asked. But he had been as stupid then as he had been ten years before that, on the banks of the Dodder. And it had been no harder for his obdurate mind to understand God had called him, than it was now to understand that He was dismissing him.

'I see you do not understand, my son,' said the superior, and he sighed. 'I must tell you, my son, that those of us who act as agents for God in the election of His ministers, we do not always find it an easy task to make His will clear to others. It is not without great awe that we give the word to go forward. Nor is it without compunction that occasionally we have to put out a staying hand and draw a young man back from what he desires. But you know it is one of the endearing things about our religion that God left us so many of His own words and sayings to be our solace in times of adversity. And so to these young men I say, as I say to you now, the words of God Himself, Many are called but few are chosen.'

That was all; a few words, and at last he knew what was required of him. At the door the superior had put out his hand and patted him on the shoulder.

'These things are best done quickly when they have to be done at all,' he said.

Those last words were true anyway, and it was they that helped Larry to pack his things, and walk down the avenue, and get into the train. It was they that compelled his feet towards home, too, until he reached the gate. But there he had come to a stand. He could go no further. He could not open that gate and walk up the path to that house into which he would bring such disappointment and sorrow.

A spoiled priest: it was all very well for them to say in the Seminary that there was no such thing, and that it was a phrase coined by ignorance. Those were the words that would come into his mother's mind the first minute she set eyes upon him standing in the doorway with his suitcase in his hand.

And there and then he had thrown the case over the railings into the little garden in front of the house where it fell partly on the long grass and partly under cover of the bushes, and taking a last look inward over the gate, he hurried away.

He had to have time to think; he had to have time to plan what he would say to his mother: and what he would do to make up to her for the cruel blow that his return would be to her.

But his mind was in turmoil, and at first all he could do was think about his beautiful new suitcase which he had left exposed to the rain that was falling heavily now, and saturating him to the bone as he walked along the streets.

But what would happen if his mother happened to come out to the gate for something? If she should happen to see the suitcase, what would she think?

In the abject terror that seized him at this point, he came to a standstill, and as he did he felt the hot sweat rolling down the hollows of his armpits in exactly the way in which the chill cold drops of rain ran down the back of his neck from the brim of his saturated black hat. Would he be in time to prevent her from making such a discovery if he ran back now at once to the house, he wondered, but the next minute he began to walk forward again into the rain. For what better way had he devised of telling her what had happened to him? Might he not just as well let her find the case, and spare him the anguish of having to tell her in words what the sight of it would tell her in an instant?

Oh, poor Mother, he thought. To think that I should be the one to wound you deepest of all! I that would have done anything on earth for you; I who loved you so much more than anyone—Patrick or Ellie or Angie or Rosie!

He stood again for a minute and stared unseeingly in front of him, trying to get his thoughts into order. How was it, he wondered, going back to the beginning of things, that he who had vowed never to leave her had let himself be led into a course of action so different from what he intended?

I'll never leave you, Mother: never!

Those were the words of the vow he had made in silence, and in secret, but with the truest fervour of his heart, and yet, within a few days of making it, he had left her and gone away from her, as they both thought for ever. But although his mind was in turmoil, and one thought mingled with another in confusion, he felt that in some obscure way it had been for her sake that he had allowed himself to be taken from her side. It was as if clumsily and stupidly he had held out to her all he had to offer, when someone had come along and whispered to him that his store was greater than he dreamed. And after that, intoxicated with the notion that he, the least of all his family, should have so great a happiness to give her, he had rushed blindly and headlong forward.

But no matter how she may have hidden it, she must have felt a pang at parting with him, just as he too had felt it, if only when the moment came to say good-bye to her.

Well, he had been sent back to her now, he thought bitterly, and if their parting had wounded her lonely heart, his return now would only cause it to fester into a lifelong sore. A spoiled priest!

Father Dowling had said that it was the hope of every Irish mother to see one of her sons become a priest. He said nothing of their dread of having a spoiled priest in the family!

It was with a curious feeling of irony that at this moment Larry became aware that the sound of the water running in the gutters was not the only sound in the darkness, but that, somewhere below the road in the darkness, there was the sound of other waters flowing— very sweet to hear.

It was probably some unconscious irony of events that had led him to Clonksea, to the banks of the River Dodder, to which he had been led by Father Dowling on the evening it had first been intimated to him that God's ways were not man's ways. God's paradox: those were the words Father Dowling had used to convey to him that those who least suspected it were often the ones God chose for His elect.

Oh, how had he been so stupid as to believe those words! To think that he, Larry O'Grady, who was always so backward and slow-witted, and unambitious, should be chosen by God Himself to enter His priesthood?

But that was what he had been deluded into thinking, and then, seduced by the thought of the happiness it would give his mother to see him ordained, he had never once looked backward, or considered there could be any obstacle in his path. It is true that almost at once he was taken by the scruff of the neck and thrown into seas of theology, and philosophy, and mounting waves of metaphysics, but he had managed to keep his head well above water. He had not fallen short of his class-men, and when it came to examinations he had done better than most of them. In other ways too he felt that he was making headway, and although self-denial was not encouraged in the Seminary, there were times when he felt that the rule of life was not severe enough to satisfy his aspirations for sanctity. His soul at such times seemed to fly before him, eager to embrace the sacrifices ahead, and he thought that the day of his ordination would never come, so earnestly did he long for it.

And yet, in spite of all his yearning, and all his aspiration, were there not times when he had been daunted by the way in which those around him had increased in suavity and subtlety, while his soul seemed always to have remained as dull and plain as when he was an uninstructed boy out in the world?

Oddly enough those who inspired him with a sense of his own inferiority were those who at first had been manifestly more backward and undeveloped than him; many of them when they had first come up the avenue to the Seminary had been raw-looking individuals, their few belongings made up in paper parcels, and their accents and appearance no more uncouth than their manner. But still, they had progressed in ways in which he had either stood still or fallen back. And so he began to feel the old sense of inferiority that he used to feel at home among his brothers and sisters.

Why did he always feel different from other people; marked out from them in some way, and set apart, solitary always, and lonely?

Why?

With the force that it entered his mind, this question scattered to all sides the confused thoughts that had made such turmoil in his brain, and he came to a standstill. All his life he had been a misfit; and yet it had never occurred to him until now to ask why this should be the case? Was it natural? Was it normal? Or was there perhaps something in what his superior had hinted: that there might be in him, as in Patrick, some latent weakness that would not bear too great a strain upon it?

Perhaps it was true that he might not have been able to bear the burden of the priesthood. Not that any sacrifice would ever be a burden, nor any service or devotion to God's creatures, but was it not true that in his innermost heart he had flinched at the thought of the responsibilities that would be laid upon his shoulders and from which never in this world would he ever again be freed? And even when his soul would at last be loosed from his body, to make its way to the judgment throne of God, would it not still be weighted down in its passage by the sins of others for which, not now the sinner, but he, their priest, their confessor, was answerable?

Even before he went away at all, whenever he strayed into one of the vast city churches, so dimly lit and so silent, it gave him a feeling of disquietude if he heard far behind him in the recesses of the transept the sound of a shutter being drawn back as some penitent entered the confessional. And a strange feeling of terror used to come over him at the thought of the figure in black that sat solitary inside that confessional, listening—to what? At the thought of what things must be whispered in those dark recesses, his face had flamed, and standing up, he hurried out again into the streets.

That was years ago: that was before he went away at all, but more recently a small incident had occurred that had awakened the old disquietude. He had stepped inside the doors of the Franciscan Friary on the Quayside, one Saturday afternoon, to say his Office in the calm and quiet of the oratory, when he had heard the door of a confessional near at hand opening to admit some penitent. And raising his head, he had been just in time to see that the penitent who at that moment stooped his head to enter the box was his own brother-in-law, Frank Esmay.

Surely there was nothing unusual in that? Frank was not a bad sort. Rosie said he went to the Sacraments regularly. And yet, at the sight of him entering the curtained alcove of the confessional like that, with his head stooped, he, Larry, had felt a return of all the old feelings of his boyhood. What power was there in the person of the confessor before whom the bland, the debonair, the smiling Frank would kneel to seek counsel and guidance? And out of his life of abstinence and continence, what guidance would the priest within the box give to this subtle and sophisticated soul?

That day too he had hastily risen to his feet and left the church. And yet he had not examined his own conscience even then, nor wondered if he were a fit person for the ministry to which he still aspired.

But his superiors had watched him, and they had not failed to find out his weakness, even though it was buried in the secret depths of his being. They had seen the place where, with the slightest strain upon it, the crack would come, and the edifice would fall. 'God does not want us to strain ourselves beyond our capacity.'

How clear those words now seemed: how reasonable.

He began to walk forward again, but slowly now, his steps matching the measured pace of his thoughts.

The rain had ceased, and the sky was high and clear, and white with stars. Gazing into those starry meads he became aware, as once before, of the small sweet voice of the little stream that ran under the bridge he was about to cross. He paused. It was here he had stood with Father Dowling on the night that he had first been led to imagine that his God had need of him.

He leaned over the parapet. But as he gazed downward at the stars that had fallen into the stream and now lay upon the sandy bottom his heart was filled with an aching sadness for the boy who had been so ready to forsake the world.

What place was there for him now in that world?

God's ways were not men's ways.

The words came back into his mind insistently, as if they had been spoken aloud.

Was there yet some message in them for him that he had not heeded in all the times that he had heard them voiced by other voices?

They told him to come and he came, and then they told him to go and he went. But what were these voices to which he had listened but the frail voices of men?

Why had he been led so far astray from the pathways of men that he would never again find his way back to their earthly dwellings? Was there no design in God's mind for such as he who seemed to have no will of his own, but put his trust in others and let them lead him where they would?

God's ways were not men's ways.

Was it not possible that God still had a use for him, not such as men had ordained for him in the Seminary, but in some other field, far, far away, perhaps far from this city, or any other city, among peoples so simple that they needed neither suavity nor subtlety, but only a simple shepherd to lead them into the Fold?

It was getting late. A light wind had risen and just then once again it wafted with it the voice of the little stream. It was a voice very clear and sweet to hear, and so; too, after the clamour of many voices, is the voice of God, when for the first time it strikes into a grown man's soul.

~   ~   ~   ~

It was after midnight when Mary heard footsteps outside the door, but she knew at once that they were Larry's footsteps, as deep in her heart she had known all the time that the solitary figure who had stood at the gate had been her son.

But oh, what had happened to him that he should have turned aside from his own door to wander in the city streets until this hour?

No matter what had happened to him, he should have come home to her, she thought, but instead of pity for him, as she stood staring at the door, her heart was filled with bitterness, and bitter words rose to her lips.

He was always odd and different from the others; and from the time he was a child he had mismanaged everything he had ever undertaken. Was he a fool, or what? she thought harshly.

But then the door opened and he entered the room.

'Why, son!' she faltered.

For never had she seen such a look of peace and happiness as radiated from his shining countenance. Something had happened to bring him home to her like this in the middle of the night, but whatever it was, it did not signify failure.

She rose to her feet, unable to say anything more. And he came forward towards her with his hands outstretched.

'Mother, I want to ask you something,' he said quietly. 'Would it make you happy to know that I was a priest even though I might be ordained in some far place, so far away that you could not come for my ordination, or be with me, or perhaps ever see me again?'

'Oh, son!'

A great feeling of weakness came over Mary, but it was not the shock of what he had said that made her sink down on the chair beside her, but the shock of relief that she felt to hear him speak like that of his ordination, so confidently and calmly, as a thing to be taken for granted. A few minutes before she thought that he had been sent home to her; a spoiled priest. Ah, what did anything matter so

long as that had not happened to him, or to her? She hardly took in
what he was saying at first, so great was her relief, but after a minute
she looked up at him with a startled face.

'I am going on the Foreign Missions, Mother.'

Ah now, she might well put her hand to her heart, for this time
there was nothing to divert her mind from the plain statement of the
fact: that, as he had said, he was going far away from her, and that
in this life they might never meet again. All at once her faculties that
had been dulled became active and alert. When was this parting to
take place?

'But when?' she cried. She didn't know where he was going either,
but that mattered less than when their parting must take place.
'When are you going?' she cried.

For a moment he hesitated.

'My suitcase is outside,' he said then.

'Outside?'

'It's at the end of the garden, inside the gate. I put it there early
this evening, under the bushes.'

He had answered her question, but she did not realize this for a
minute, and the habits of a lifetime of care for creatures and things
made her start to her feet.

'Not your good new suitcase?' she cried. 'It wasn't out in all that
rain?'

But even before he put out his hand to stay her, telling her the rain
was over and that anyway the harm was done, she had come to a
stand, and turned back with a glance that pierced him through and
through.

'They sent you home from the Seminary?' she said.

It was the moment he had dreaded. As if they were threatened by
some physical danger, he put out his hand to steady her; to steady
them both.

'It was not they who acted, Mother,' he said, 'but God Who acted
through them. It was God's way of showing me my true path in
life.'

While he spoke Mary stared at him. On his face there was again
the same expression of radiance that she had seen when he had first
entered the house.

But there was still one thing she had to find out even if it was to
put out the light of the world for them both. She turned around and
putting her hands upon his shoulders as she used to do when he was
a little boy, she looked him steadily in the eyes.

'Are you sure it's not for my sake you're doing this?' she asked.

He was taken so completely by surprise that for a moment he could only stare at her.

Was it not due in some part to her that he had made his decision? Was it not from dread of facing her that he had walked the streets in the driving rain until he came to the little stream where he had at last found peace? And was it not a solace to him that she would be spared the pain of having him come home to her, a failure? It was, but he knew that his motive was good in God's eyes.

Whatsoever ye do to one of these my least ones, ye do unto Me.

And what did it matter anyway what it was, or who, that had caused him to turn his face towards those Mission Fields; those burning golden fields where the harvest was so heavy for the sickle, and the labourers were so few.

He turned and looked at her, but he knew at once that he did not need to give her any answer. She had looked into his heart, and what she had seen there had filled her with love and compassion, and a feeling of awe.

PART X

Mary and Rosie

WHY should she worry about them? Young couples always had their difficulties, or so she had heard. Just because she and Tom got along so well together, right from the start, was no reason to think that all marriages were the same.

Such were Mary's thoughts one evening. Rosie was eight years married now, and although a various times her mother had been vaguely worried about her, of late her fears had become more real. Yet surely, now too, her fears were foolish? What grounds had she for thinking there was anything wrong between them? Frank was always in the best of humour when they came to see her. He'd hardly be always ready to laugh, and make jokes, if there was anything wrong with their marriage? She thought not; but still Rosie of late had been nervous and irritable every time she came to see her. The very last time she came she was almost unbearable.

It was early one morning of the previous week. Mary was in the yard when she heard a step in the kitchen. Who could that be, she wondered, because it didn't seem likely that it could be Rosie, for it was her wedding anniversary, and she and Frank were both coming to see her that evening. They were only going to spend the earlier part of the evening with her, because afterwards they were going to Esmays' to play cards.

But it was Rosie. Then next minute her harassed face appeared at the back door.

'There's nothing wrong, is there?' Mary cried.

Rosie frowned.

'Can't I call at the door without being questioned?' she said. 'I thought I'd just look in to see how you were.'

'But aren't you and Frank coming to-night?'

'We are!' said Rosie shortly. 'Is that any reason for me to pass the door without coming in?'

'Oh, not at all, Rosie,' said Mary. 'I was only surprised, that's all. Wait a minute, and I'll come inside,' she said, and she began to wipe the clay from her hands.

With restless, bitter eyes, Rosie looked around the yard. Of late, Mary never set foot in the real garden beyond it, which had always been wild and unmanageable, but which latterly had developed into a rank wilderness, the gateway leading into it being permanently closed, like a sluice, against the tides of weedy greenery on the other side.

In the small cemented inner yard, still at her disposal, however, she had collected a large array of old buckets and basins, canisters, and cracked crockery, and even a few old pitted enamel saucepans, which she had filled with clay, and stuck all over with slips and shoots that surprisingly enough continued to grow, and even to flourish, in their strict confines.

In summer, the O'Gradys' back yard was a bower of roses. And at such times the nature of the receptacles that contained the plants was hardly discoverable in the profusion of them.

But it was not summer now. And the sight that met Rosie's eyes was a collection of pots and pans, one more cracked and battered than the other, and all filled with a hardened grey clay from which stuck upward, like pins in a pincushion, a few sticks of dead wood.

'For goodness' sake, Mother, why don't you get rid of this rubbish?' she cried. 'What must people think of it? I never saw such a yard.'

Mary was less concerned with what was said to her than she was with the querulous tone of her daughter's voice.

'Oh, it doesn't look well now,' she said, 'but wait till you see it in the summer.'

Rosie looked around her indifferently.

'If you ask me, it looks like this always. I wonder the neighbours don't make complaints.'

'Complaints!' Mary was listening now. 'Complaints?' she repeated. 'Only this morning Mrs. Maguire was talking about the two lovely buds I sent down to her last summer to take to Alice in the sanatorium.'

Restlessly Rosie turned back and looked at her mother.

'How is she? Alice, I mean?' she asked, but as at that moment, suddenly from the grey sky a heavy raindrop fell, she turned and went back towards the house. 'Oh, it's going to rain,' she said. 'Come on into the house.' She wasn't, at heart, any more interested in Alice than in the plants.

There seemed to be something on her mind that interfered alike with her interest in the sick girl and her interest in the condition of the yard, but as they went up the narrow cement passage at the side of the house, and she had to squeeze past a large wooden crate on which there was another array of pots and basins, she stopped short.

'Is this more of it?' she cried. 'Really, Mother, you've let the place get into a shocking state. It's too bad of you to let it get into this condition! Thank goodness Frank never has occasion to come out here. If he ever got a glimpse of this, he'd surely say——'

Suddenly, however, she thought better of her sentence, and stopped midway.

'What would he say?' asked Mary, but as the rain began to fall more heavily, with another shiver, Rosie stepped into the house, and drew up the collar of her costume.

'Well, I'll be going,' she said.

'But you're only after coming!' said Mary in surprise. 'Won't you sit down for a minute? I'll make you a cup of tea.'

'No thanks,' said Rosie. 'I've got to be going.' But still she lingered.

'It wouldn't take me a minute to wet a few grains of tea,' said Mary. 'Look, the kettle is just boiling!' She went over and stirred the kettle to make certain that what she said was right. After a minute, however, getting no answer from Rosie she looked up.

Rosie was standing at the door, her mouth tightly set. Then her lips parted.

'It's a great wonder you don't press me to take something stronger,' she said.

The words were utterly incomprehensible to Mary, but she recoiled at the look on Rosie's face.

'Why, Rosie, what do you mean?' she asked, weakly.

'Oh, you know very well what I mean,' said Rosie. 'You're not in such a hurry to put down the kettle in the evening, when Frank is with me—I suppose it's easier to put a bottle of wine down in front of him.'

Oh, Rosie: how could you be so cruel; so unjust? That was Mary's first thought. Her next was one of pity. Poor Rosie! she must have been sorely hurt, by someone or something, to make her so blind to the way she was hurting another in her turn. But what was the meaning of her accusation? Slowly an explanation dawned upon her.

'But, Rosie,' she protested, 'it was because of what you said, that I offered it to him in the first place. When did I ever have any liquor in the house, unless in a case of sickness, and, even then, I was always reluctant to give anyone alcohol unless the doctor ordered it in particular. Oh, Rosie! You know that! You know that I would never have offered it to Frank of my own free will. I thought it was very strange of you to suggest it, too, and although I didn't say anything at the time, I didn't approve of it, but, like many another thing you did that I didn't approve, I told myself you were old enough to know what you were doing. Besides, I decided that you knew him better than I did. But to think that you should turn around and blame me! Oh, Rosie, how could you do such a thing?'

How indeed? As she saw the truly stricken look that had come on her mother's face, Rosie had in fact been taken aback, and if she was not altogether ashamed of her words, she certainly saw the inconvenience of having uttered them.

'Oh, don't take it to heart so much, Mother,' she said, but she said it impatiently, and without feeling. She wanted desperately now to get out of the place. 'I'll see you this evening, Mother,' she said, putting out her hand to grasp the knob of the door, but Mary put out her own hand, and with it she kept the door pressed tight.

'You are not leaving here, Rosie, until you take back those words,' she said, 'until you admit it was you who made me get wine for him. You can't have forgotten that? It was one of the first evenings you brought him here after you were married. It was a warm evening; I remember it well, and he said he was thirsty. So naturally I offered him a glass of lemonade, and he took it too, but afterwards you came into the kitchen to me and you were furious. You said that he'd think I was a fool; offering him lemonade, like as if he was a schoolboy. You said he'd think we didn't know anything, or never went anywhere, and you told me about the way his mother always had a full decanter on the sideboard to offer to anyone that called. Oh, Rosie: you can't deny that, can you? The only pity is that I listened to you. Well, I've learned a lesson, that's all.'

Taking her hand away from the door, she stood aside to let her pass.

But Rosie lingered. Her mother's words had cut her to the heart. She too remembered that evening as if it were yesterday.

'I remember,' she said sadly, but the next minute her mouth hardened. 'He made a laughing stock of me when we were going home. Lemonade!' The sound of the word seemed to infuriate her. 'Lemonade!' she cried again. 'What on earth made you suggest lemonade in the first place? That was the cause of all the trouble. It was all the fault of that lemonade.' She opened the door.

Sadly Mary looked at her. She saw that she was in a bad nervous condition.

'I'll come as far as the gate with you, Rosie,' she said, and she followed her down the hall.

Was Frank drinking, she wondered? But even if he were, it would not explain Rosie's nervous condition. Besides, although she did not care much for him, she would say that Frank was one of those young men who could take a drink or two without causing too much concern to those belonging to him. Tom, although he never took a drink in his life, used to say that no one objected to a man taking a drink so long as he knew how to hold it.

If she was any judge of Frank Esmay, he was too vain to let himself be seen with a sign of drink on him.

They were at the gate. The rain had passed over.

In the strong light out of doors, Mary saw with concern that Rosie did not look well. She said good-bye to her with reluctance.

'I'll see you to-night,' she added.

But Rosie had not gone more than a pace or two when, irresistibly, she turned back.

'There's another thing I meant to tell you, Mother,' she said. 'For goodness' sake don't do all the talking this evening—like you do most evenings. Let someone else get a word in for once. You don't realize, Mother,' she went on, talking now in a hysterical way as if, having started, she could never stop, 'you probably don't realize it, but you are always talking about the one thing: about us when we were children. And it sounds so ridiculous to others; particularly to outsiders who cannot possibly be interested. Like Frank, I mean, a man who isn't interested in children at all.'

'Frank? But I thought——'

Whatever Mary thought, however, she had to keep to herself, because, with that, Rosie turned and walked away.

For a minute Mary looked after her with sad and perplexed eyes. Then her expression changed. There was something about Rosie's back view, and about her gait, as she walked away that took her mother's attention. She was so thin, and her gait was so, so—Seeking for a word, Mary was surprised at the word that came to her mind: spinsterly. Rosie's walk was spinsterly.

And so too is her attitude to the little stories I tell them in the evenings, thought Mary.

And in another moment, she understood all.

Poor child, she thought, with another ache in her heart. So that was what troubled her, and made her so restless and unhappy? But why did she not confide in someone, she wondered.

Why did she keep her disappointment locked up in her own heart? Why, above all, did she begin to despair so soon?

For eight years after all was not so very long for a couple to be without a child. Years ago it might have caused their relatives some concern, but nowadays plenty of young people put off rearing a family until they were several years married. Plenty of young women refused to accept their responsibilities in the matter until they had a certain amount of enjoyment out of their marriage. Not that she approved of that kind of thing, or even understood exactly how these smart young people conducted their affairs, but it would be consoling for Rosie to be reminded of such people. And apart altogether from such people, there were plenty of women who did not have their first child until they were married for nine or ten years. And they always maintained that they never gave up hope at any time! It was ridiculous to despair after eight years. There was a woman in Tullamore——

As Mary's thoughts reached this point, however, she realized that Rosie had not taken her into her confidence, and that she could not, therefore, proffer her any help or consolation, so dejectedly she turned back towards the house, and a feeling very like despair settled on her heart. If they had no children, how would it affect their marriage?

All at once she felt terribly tired: tried and aged. If Rosie's marriage was a failure, what would she do?

All day long her thoughts were upon them.

Even if they never had children, surely that was not enough to break up their marriage. Someone had told her one time that childless couples were oftentimes more united than other husbands and wives. They went around together a lot, and there was not the nervous strain in the home that there always was with children. Then, too, women who had no family were able to look after themselves better than women with children. They were able to keep their good looks, and they were able to give time to dressing themselves and doing their hair. They might well be better tempered, too, never being kept awake all night, nor harassed all day, like women with young children to mind. And there was Mrs. Maguire who had told her one time that Alice hadn't been born until she was married for ten years— and that Mr. Maguire was annoyed when he discovered her condition! She said he didn't want a child in the end. She said he was jealous of Alice!

But there wasn't much use in putting any reliance on what Mrs. Maguire said because Mr. Maguire on another occasion had told her quite plainly that Mrs. Maguire was nothing but a fool.

Mary had to smile at the thought of what Mr. Maguire had said, but the smile soon vanished, and her thoughts were centred on Rosie again.

She had altered so much in the eight years of her marriage. She should only be in her prime now, but instead of that she was beginning to have a thin, dried-up look, not only in her face, but all over her body, as if something were fretting her, wearing her to the bone.

I should speak to her, she thought, but remembering their recent encounter, she shrank from the thought of doing so. It is to Frank I should speak, perhaps, she thought, not to her at all, but a feeling of embarrassment and humiliation came over her at the thought of the only other time, eight years before, that she had endeavoured to speak to him upon a serious matter.

Most likely he would not take her seriously now either, but would blandly dismiss her worries as imaginary.

Were they imaginary, she wondered. And she let her mind wander back to the past. She used to worry then, too, but as she remembered the old worries of her early motherhood, a shudder passed through her. The things she had worried about had not come to pass, but had not worse entirely come about? Worrying had not helped. It had only marred the harmony of days that were as near to being truly golden as any days in her whole life.

I should have enjoyed them while they lasted, she thought regretfully. And now, with Rosie, what good would worry do either? Things would probably settle themselves in the long run. God was good: they might yet have a family. And if not, they would probably settle down to their situation in time. One way or another, a few years would make a great difference.

A few years? What did that mean? To them it would mean less than to her. That was certain. With less and less confidence nowadays could she count upon the future to solve anything for her. The thought of death did not dismay her now as it did when she was a young woman, but all the same she felt that she could not die in peace if Rosie was unhappy.

Once, long ago, at the time that one of the children was born, Rosie perhaps, the thought that she might die had filled her with anguish. And how she had prayed to be spared; believing her prayers to be selfless prayers of a mother for her children! For what would happen if she had to leave them, she thought, her children who were so young and helpless? If, after all the pain and suffering of bearing them, the weariness and strain of rearing them, she should be taken from them suddenly before she had a chance to see into their futures that had promised so well! Ah, how that promise had deceived her. Would it not have been better, a thousand times, if she had died then, long ago?

The children would have fared all right. Tom would have been a good father to them while he was spared to them, and even if he were taken from them, there would always be other people who would have taken care of them: Tom's people and her own people. Her brother John, for instance, would most likely have taken them to live with him in Tullamore. He was almost an invalid now, since the time he was hurt by the bull, and they would have been a help to him about the place.

They would not have been petted so much perhaps, but they might not have been any the worse for that. They might indeed have been better fitted to face the hard side of life. And Patrick, for instance, when he went into the world, might not have gone under so quickly. Rosie, too, if she had grown up in Tullamore, would never have met Frank Esmay, or anyone like him.

But ah, how useless it was to think like that. The past could not be undone.

It was well for Tom, she thought suddenly. He had been cut down in the middle of life, when his hopes were highest. He had known nothing of the sadness and disappointment that was in store for them.

She thought of him lying in Glasnevin; at rest: at peace. And she thought of the day when she would once again lie by his side.

But once more, as she had done long ago, she prayed that she would be spared yet another while. This time, however, the prayer was pure and selfless, and no tenacity for life dictated it, for now no golden hopes lit the horizon. It was indeed because the skies were dark above them that she did not want to leave them, those of her children that were still in the world. For now, more a thousand times than when they were young, they needed her. Who now, but her, cared anything for them, grown men and women, without the appeal of youth, alone and unfriended, except by each other, in a hard and cruel world?

And of the three of them, Patrick, Larry, and Rosie, she felt that Rosie needed her most.

For a long time it had been Patrick that had seemed most in need of her, and about him she felt so bad at one time that she used to pray that God would take him to his rest before her own turn came.

But time went on, and as she visited him, month after month, and saw that he was healthy and strong, she realized the falsity of her hopes that she might survive him. Indeed, not long after he went into the Home, one of the attendants told her that he was the strongest man in the men's ward. There was no reason why he would not live out his normal span, entombed within the great grey walls that were so high at one side that upon one part of the yard the sun never shone, and the grass never grew, but wall and ground alike sprouted with a viscous green lichen.

In that place who would visit him if she were gone? Rosie and Larry might do so in duty at certain times, but only his mother would be faithful to the monthly visits to him, which meant something to him she knew, even in the beginning when he had refused to speak to her sometimes, and she had had to go away, as she had come, leaving the little presents she had brought with her to one of the warders to give to him when she was gone.

When his nerves improved, of course, there was no mistaking his pleasure in seeing her. The same nurse that had spoken of his fine physique told her that towards the end of the month, he used to hurry out to the grounds after his midday meal to get possession of a certain seat there, from which the entrance gates could be seen. At first he used to pretend that he did not see her coming, but as he became more normal, he gave up this childishness, and a time came when he would put up his hand and wave to her as soon as she came into sight.

Then one day he asked her to bring him a calendar so that he could know to the day when she was due to visit him. That was so normal. At the time it had made her so happy. She had even begun to think that he might be let home to her one day. Yet, one day, when one of the doctors, whom she encountered in the grounds, said something about his progress, a terrible feeling of fear had come over her.

'How do you think my son is getting on, Doctor?' she had asked, almost gaily, because the visit on that day had been almost pleasurable to both of them.

The doctor too was in good form. He looked back to where Patrick was standing by the entrance door of the refectory, waving to them.

'He's making excellent progress,' he said, and he began to walk across the grounds with her, pacing his footsteps with hers.

It was a beautiful sunny afternoon, and the air was balmy with the fragrance of the lime trees on either side of the short avenue. The young doctor was on duty, but it was agreeable to persuade himself that pacing up and down like this, with Mary in the bright sunny air, constituted a legitimate part of that duty. It might not have been so pleasant to converse with the relative of another inmate, but the O'Grady man was rapidly getting back to normal.

'Excellent progress,' he repeated. And Mary smiled.

But then he said something else.

'We could let him go out of here any time now if he wanted,' he said.

But no sooner had the words passed his lips than he had seen the change in her: had seen the look of fear that had come into her face. For of course he had interpreted it as fear when she had started at his words and given a little cry. Yet it was not so much fear as a feeling of utter weariness. Her mind had grown accustomed to the idea that he was settled for ever in this place, and whatever her views had been upon the matter in the beginning, now she was too tired and too wearied to be able to visualize him in any other place, least of all in the home he had quitted so many years back. For the few tragic days that had passed between his return from America and his departure for this place were now almost faded from her mind.

'Oh, Doctor?' she cried, and her knees seemed hardly able to bear her, as she came to a stand and looked up at him. But the doctor had laid his hand on her arm. His momentary lapse had had unexpected consequences, and he was once more the alert young medical, able to probe to the quick of the mind, whether ill or in health.

'But you see, he doesn't want to come out,' he said quickly.

It was then that she was frightened; not until then.

'Oh, why is that, Doctor?' she cried, and she began to rack her mind to see if anything in her manner made Patrick think that he was not wanted at home; made him think that he would cause them embarrassment or confusion by his return?

'Oh, Doctor, why is that?' she repeated.

But the doctor had reassured her. His kind eyes had shown that he had understood all the terror in her heart, now and all the time, just as he knew the poor warped minds of his patients.

'We cannot answer that question,' he said quietly, 'except by saying that he was not influenced in any way, by anyone, not by anything that was said to him or by anything that was done to him. It is just an involuntary reaction that has occurred in consequence, perhaps, of some trait in his nature; some obstinacy or some vanity, which even in health he may have possessed in some degree.'

'You mean he would feel humiliated at meeting people, Doctor?' she asked.

The doctor nodded his head.

She had said nothing for a few minutes, then she had forced herself to ask a last question.

'Is there anything we could do,' she said, 'to make him feel differently?'

The doctor had looked into her eyes, into her very soul, it seemed to her.

'No!' he said then, quietly and with conviction. 'It is probably wiser to leave things as they are. According to medical standards he is as normal as ever now, completely sane and untroubled by whatever temporarily deranged his mind, but in this department of medicine, we have still, unfortunately, to rely to a great extent on guesswork and intuition, and while there are no positive indications or symptoms of disease, we cannot altogether neglect the patient's reaction to his own state. Indeed, it is often our surest guide to his true mental state.' Here he bent towards Mary. 'And so the fact that your son doesn't feel inclined to leave here may be a sign that he isn't ready to leave. After a number of years in here, it might be hard to take up life in the world outside, especially when it has proved a bit stormy. After all, he knows he is safe here and you know it too—safe in haven.'

How differently she felt that day as she went out through the big gates and looked back at the high walls that, up to then, had seemed so terrifying. All at once they seemed to her to be, as the doctor had said, the staunch walls of a harbour, within which, safe after the storm, her boy sat smiling in the sun.

Yes, she was reconciled about Patrick.

And as for Larry, although he sent home pictures of the little straw huts in which the missionaries lived, surrounded by great flats of sun-baked clay, she seemed always to think of him as striding through golden fields, as golden as the fields of grain in her own old home in Tullamore. And she felt that the happiness that had shone upon his face the day he went away still shone upon it, as constant as the burning African sun.

If it were only Patrick and Larry that she had to consider, she might truthfully say that she was ready whenever God chose to call her!

But there was Rosie. How could she think, with anything but despair, of leaving Rosie, knowing that things were getting worse and worse between her and Frank? Let it be God's will, she prayed, to allow her stay a little longer, until she could do something for Rosie. But what? For it filled her with dread to think of Rosie coming back home. She looked about the house.

It was bad enough before Rosie left it, but since she went away it had become like a tomb. Small as it was, there were rooms she never went into nowadays, and they had a peculiar smell, partly composed of dust, and partly of damp and darkness. How could Rosie face the thought of coming back to it after having had her own bright airy flat for so many years? Yet where would she turn in her trouble if this house were once gone? Bad as it was, it would be a refuge for her. Yes, for Rosie's sake she beseeched God to allot a few more years to her.

But if it wasn't for Rosie, would she care much about her life? She had gone out into the yard again, and unconsciously she moved over to where she had been at work with a big metal spoon, loosening the clay around one of her precious cuttings in an old blue enamel saucepan, and delving her hand into the deepest part of the clay, she deliberately thought of death.

It gave peace to her soul of late to think of it, although she had not always felt like that about it. Nor had she this curious love for the clay of the earth, that soothed her hot fingers.

The day after Tom died, it had rained; and it had rained steadily all the next night, and she had lain awake listening to the sound of that rain, falling on the ground and beating into the clay, and she had been reminded of the grave, as she had seen it when they were lowering the coffin into it, and at that thought a sweat had broken out on her face, where she lay alone in her bed, until at last the thought of that cold, wet clay, sodden, and black, and heavy as lead, she could bear her thoughts no longer and she had to light a candle and go out to the girls' room and wake them.

And it was not only that one night alone, but on many nights, she had wakened in a kind of nightmare, where the touch of the cold sheets upon her body had made her think of the cold clay of the grave.

But now—she felt so different—deeper and deeper she delved her fingers into the clay. Now it held no terrors for her, but like the thought of death itself, it filled her with peace.

There was only one thing that disturbed her, and that was the thought of where Tom had been laid to rest. If only he had been laid somewhere else besides Glasnevin. That was something she had regretted fitfully ever since the day of his burial, but she had been so inexperienced at the time, and everything had been carried out so quietly and so well by Patrick, that she had not ventured to interfere. If only she had had him brought home to be buried in Tullamore! But it had not occurred to her to do so at the time. It was a wonder her brother John hadn't thought of it. It would have cost a great deal of money, of course, but that wouldn't have mattered.

I will have to be buried in Glasnevin too, she thought. If only it could be Tullamore! The cost of the journey would not matter now at all. The money for it was in the black tin box, untouched; the money that was to have been spent on so many things: on Patrick's passage; on Ellie's wedding; on Larry's ordination; on Rosie's education—and which still lay unused in the tin box. It had accumulated during the years too, because she had thrown a few shillings into it from time to time. Indeed, she could not say exactly how much money there was in it now, but there would be more than enough to pay for her last journey to Tullamore if she wanted to go there.

I'd be going home at last, she thought. But she knew that she could not do that to Tom; leave him to lie all alone in Glasnevin. And the girls? For a moment she had forgotten that they too were laid to rest in Glasnevin. How could she have ever thought of going elsewhere? Where they lie, I belong, she thought. And where I belong, I shall go. When I meet them, I want to have nothing to regret.

When I meet them!

At first when they were taken from her, the worst of her pain was to think that she would never look upon their faces again. But now, like a child in the womb, her faith leapt within her. And the shorter life's remnant seemed, the surer it seemed that in another life they must all one day meet again. They would be united in that place where there was neither pain, nor any thought of pain. Those were the words she had learned at Sunday school years and years ago, when she was a little girl. And she had become so used by this time to the pain in her shoulder that she wondered what had put those lines into her head just then. She was almost unaware that the pain had grown more severe than usual. But after a little while its severity became insistent, and she put up her hand to try and ease it.

I should not spend so much time in this damp yard, she thought, looking at the humid walls, and she turned to go inside the house, but like a golden lantern she carried her thoughts into the dark house, and as she sat down in Tom's old chair by the fire, her eyes were dazzled by visions of the heavenly fields through which she would wander to meet her lost ones.

I wonder what will be the first thing we'll say to each other? she pondered. And then, with a sudden feeling of guilt that she had not prayed for them as often as she might have done, she felt in her pocket for her Rosary beads. But for each bead she thumbed, it was a thought, not a prayer, that formed in her mind.

And after a little while, her fingers ceased to move from bead to bead, and closing her eyes, she gave herself up to dazzling dreams of those heavenly fields of light; fields that were something like the fields at home in midsummer, but lit with such radiance that as they advanced towards her, the figures of her dear ones that she sought so eagerly were indistinct as in a mist. But understanding this mist to be the nimbus of their own glory around them, she tried not to be disappointed at not seeing them with familiar earthly clearness. And perhaps the clearness would come later when she became accustomed to the dazzling radiance? She opened her eyes. After this dark kitchen it was hardly to be wondered that she would be blinded for a while by such great light.

It is a wonder that I never thought more about the next world, she mused. Like everything else, it was only lately that she seemed to have the time to sit down and think about anything. And even now, she thought, glancing around her, there were a number of little things to be done to prepare for Rosie and Frank, who would be coming to see her that evening. But she was reluctant to stand up, and just then a new wonder came to her.

My own mother, she murmured. I'll meet her again also. And my father! I will see them both again. So great a wonder was hardly to be borne, and as if the thought, like a vision, might disintegrate, she was almost afraid to breathe.

Oh, Mother, she repeated, Mother! And this time, vaguely, she knew that she was speaking out loud, but an unreality had come over everything, and it did not seem to matter.

Mother! The name that had signified her own being for so long suddenly took on the meaning it had in the distant, golden past, and before her eyes she seemed to see her own mother. And oh, how clearly she seemed to see her; her stout figure, and her full, placid face, her hair parted so plainly and severely, and her calm steady eyes: a true countrywoman.

That was how her mother used to look when she herself was a child: that was how she liked to think of her, instead of as she was in later years on her rare visits to Dublin, an elderly woman, uneasy in the company of her young son-in-law, and already ailing, though her daughter did not know it, of the illness that was to take her from them. That tired elderly woman was almost a stranger to her. It was not this tired old woman that she wanted to see in the other world. She wanted to see her in her prime, standing perhaps at the kitchen door with her apron tied around her waist, and an old, cracked enamel basin in her hand, filled with yellow maize which she threw in handfuls to the hens that gathered about her feet.

That was the way they used to see her, she and her brother John, when they came running up the lane on their way home from school. And if it were indeed to be Heaven, that was the way she wanted to see her in the next world. And at the thought of their encounter, a feeling of such bliss swept over her, it was like being again a child, and instead of feeling, as she had for years, that she was being slowly drained of all the good that was in her, she felt instead as if she were drawing in some beneficence. That was the way she used to feel as a young girl before she was married; before she had responsibilities. And for a few minutes in fancy she savoured the taste of those carefree days. Then, with a stab of remorse, she thought of her children. She had forgotten them. She, from whose mind they had never been absent before for an instant, had for that moment completely forgotten them.

To think that her mother had never seen any of them, except Patrick, and even he had only been a few months old when she saw him.

But they would meet in Heaven, she thought, with an ever growing wonder at the way the joys of the hereafter multiplied minute by minute.

To think that she would one day be showing the children to her mother. In particular, she wanted her to see the girls, because her mother loved a pretty face. Yes: for all her practicality and plainness she loved a pretty face. She'd love Rosie in particular. Mary could just picture how she would bend down and catch the child in her arms.

But was she dreaming? Mary rubbed a hand over her eyes. Had she fallen asleep? She had been thinking of Rosie as a small child— Instead of that, with a chill feeling, she recalled the fretful woman that had taken the place of that sunny child.

She didn't want her mother to see Rosie like that! She wanted her to see her as she used to be when she was a child, or a growing girl.

Don't look, Mother! In anguish the words rose to her lips. Don't look! she cried. And when the next moment behind Rosie the heavy somnolent face of Patrick appeared as out of a mist, she felt that she must scream. I don't want you to see them like that: I want you to see them as they were when they were small. Don't look! Don't look! she screamed.

It was her own scream that woke her. Then she sat up with a start.

Oh, such a dream, such a terrible, terrible dream! For a few minutes it was hard to feel that it was only a dream, but when she attempted to rise from the uncomfortable position into which her body had slumped when she fell asleep, the pain in her shoulder was like the thrust of a knife, and her heart beat with such violence she could not discern whether it was the pain or the terror of the dream that was causing it.

It could hardly be the dream. It must be the pain that is causing it, she thought, putting her hand under her breast. For how could a dream upset a person sufficiently to bring on palpitations like this? And yet, although she did her best to dismiss it as nothing, fragments of the dream still ran through her mind, and filled her with disturbing thoughts.

How will people appear to each other when they meet in the next world, she wondered? Will they be as they were when they died? Will they meet again in the form in which they had last seen each other on earth?

Oh no! Not that, she cried out, dream becoming thought, and thought becoming prayer.

Not like that, oh God! If I am to see the children again, let them be as they were long ago; let them be as they were when they were small.

But if this prayer were granted, and the children were to be perpetually young, how could her own mother be as she, her daughter, remembered her in her own childhood? When Patrick was born, her mother was already aged, already ailing. If she had lived until Rosie was born, she would have been an old woman.

And how would she, herself, appear in the irrevocable moment of meeting her loved ones, to be united with them for ever and ever? An image of her own tired face came into her mind. Would she be like that for all eternity? So far as the children were concerned it would not matter; she did not mind their seeing her like this; because except for Patrick, it was unlikely that any one of them could remember her as anything but an elderly woman, a woman full of cares. But her mother had not lived long enough to see any great change in her. She was a young woman when her mother died, although she was already the mother of several children at the time.

Her mother would have been proud of her then, and for many a year after that as well, if she could have seen her. Even as a widow she had kept her appearance. The black clothes became her, and she carried herself well, and looked active and erect.

But if her parents were to see her now! Oh, how could it be Heaven for them if they saw her condition now?

The radiance and glory of her vision had faded. Her mind was clouded with doubt.

But all these things would be solved in some mysterious way. I suppose we will only meet as spirits, she thought after a little while, and with this thought the last rays faded from the heavenly fields, and her eyes filled with tears.

It was only one more disappointment. She would never see them again in the old familiar way. The old heartache that she had felt in the days and nights immediately after Tom's death, and again more keenly still after the death of Ellie and Angie, returned with tenfold intensity.

If it was to be Heaven in earnest, why could we not meet again in earthly, in bodily, form?

~ ~ ~ ~

'Mother!'

How many million times had Mary raised her head at that call: at that name.

From their earliest years no matter where they had been, no matter if they had only gone out of the house a moment beforehand, no sooner did her children open the front door on their return, than they called out to her from force of habit:

'Mother!'

At times she was not able to tell to whom the voice belonged.

But now it could only be Rosie who called.

'Why, Rosie, I was just thinking about you,' she said.

'Is that so?' said Rosie dully. She stood in the doorway. 'I don't suppose your thoughts were very pleasant,' she said bitterly.

'Now, why should you think that, Rosie?' said Mary, without looking up, for she was endeavouring to get to her feet, a task that was not easy nowadays when she had been too long seated. When she got to her feet, however, she saw there was a distracted look about Rosie.

'Is there anything wrong?' she cried.

Now that she looked closely at her, she saw that her face was unusually pale, and that her hat was pulled down on her head without regard for how it looked. Her lips too were in a hard line.

'That depends on how you look at things,' she said. 'I consider that I have done something right for the first time in eight years.'

Mary calculated quickly.

Eight years: the term of her marriage. For it was not much more than a couple of months since their wedding anniversary, a date Mary had good cause to remember because on that evening Rosie had been more irritable than ever before, and since then, day after day, she seemed to grow more and more strained and distraught.

But now things seemed to have come to some sort of head, for all at once Rosie went to pieces.

'Oh, I know it is hard on you, Mother,' she cried. 'Only for you I'd have left him long ago! But when I used to think of having to come back here, and having to tell you, I used to try to put up with things for another while. But I'm finished now.' Her face quivered. 'I've done it now,' she said, 'and I can't go back on it.'

Mary had managed to get to her feet.

'Sit down,' she said, and she pushed the chair from which she had risen towards Rosie.

But Rosie still stood—at bay.

'Don't you understand?' she cried. 'I've left him! I've left Frank!' Her voice was high-pitched and hysterical.

To gain time Mary had to say something.

'There's no need to shout,' she said.

It was the first thing that came into her head, and she said it, because she wanted to find out more about the situation before she said anything else. But Rosie's nerves were unstrung.

'Don't look at me like that,' she whimpered. 'I've left him, I tell you. I've left him for good and all.'

Mary sighed.

'I suppose you had good reasons for whatever you did?' she said at last.

It was a question, or so she intended it to be, but to her surprise the fretful ravaged face in front of her was suddenly wet with tears. Could it be possible that she was so starved of kindness that those grudging words had meant something to her?

'Oh, Mother; do you mean that?' she cried. 'You don't blame me? You don't think it was my fault?'

A little disconcerted at the way her words had been misinterpreted, Mary hardly knew what to say.

'Tell me all there is to tell,' she said.

But Rosie's dejection had returned.

'What is there to tell?' she said, dully, then almost the next minute something flared up inside her again. 'If only you knew all I suffered,' she cried. 'Perhaps you did know?' she asked, as her eyes met the penetrating gaze of the older woman. 'I tried to keep it from you, but I suppose you guessed there was something wrong. Didn't you?'

Miserably Mary nodded her head.

'Oh, but you couldn't have guessed how bad things were,' cried Rosie. 'Oh, Mother, if you only knew what I've gone through since I left you: if you knew how he'd treated me——'

But here, as if she read something in Mary's face, her own face hardened.

'For God's sake, don't say you could have told me this would happen,' she cried. 'It would be the same no matter who I married. I'm unfortunate, that is all, unfortunate!'

Mary stared at her. It was true that she had been thinking of how she had opposed the marriage, but she did not see how things could have turned out the same if she had married someone else.

'What do you mean?' she asked in bewilderment.

'I mean that we're an unlucky family; that's what I mean,' cried Rosie. 'Some families are unlucky—I heard that but I didn't believe it. Now I know it's true. Look at all that happened to us! Look at Father, dying when he did, in the prime of life. Look at Ellie and Angie—the way they were killed, and Bart and Willie with them. You'd think that that was enough trouble for one family. But look at Patrick! And now look at me!' Here her voice broke into a wail. 'Look at me!' she cried. 'Did you ever know anyone as unlucky as me?'

'Rosie O'Grady!'

As if she were a young woman, Mary drew herself upright, as straight as a blade, and her eyes were ablaze.

'No more of this talk!' she cried. 'How dare you say such things! It's true that I've had my sorrows, but I was reconciled to God's will. And I'll have no talk about bad luck, if you please. That is pagan talk, and I won't listen to it. Your father was spared a lot by being taken when he was taken, and who knows what the future might have held for your sisters? As for Patrick——' She hesitated; it was harder to find something that mitigated the sorrow they had suffered on Patrick's account. 'Patrick is not to be pitied,' she said lamely, 'he's well and happy. But you!' With a look of scorn she met Rosie's eyes. 'I don't want to be hard on you, Rosie, and God knows I never had much opinion of him, but it may be your own fault that you and Frank cannot agree. He has his faults, I know that: I knew them before you did, but many a woman has had to put up with worse in a man and yet made something of her marriage in the end. I'm not saying that you should do that, or that you have the strength to do it, but I won't have you blaming God for your failure—which is what you are doing.'

For a minute Rosie sat docilely enough, as if she were thinking over what had been said to her. Then she looked up, and her eyes were once more wild and distraught.

'I'm not blaming anyone,' she cried. 'But why didn't I have a child? Is it my fault that I didn't? Is it? Or is it, what I said—bad luck?'

It was out at last, the admission of what had made her so bitter for all those years. Time and again, Mary's heart had ached to have her confide in her. Yet now some perversity made her give a sharp answer.

'I thought you didn't want a child,' she said.

'What else could I say when there was no sign of us having one,' said Rosie sadly. 'I wasn't going to have people pitying me.'

'And Frank?' said Mary. 'You said he didn't like children.'

'Oh, they all say that until it's too late, and then they have a different story,' she said.

'Was he ugly to you about it?' asked Mary, her heart beginning to pulse irregularly.

'About my not having a child?' asked Rosie, and she shrugged her shoulders. 'Oh, if that was all!' she said. 'That is only one of the things he has against me: in fact lately he's been saying it's a good job I didn't have a child.'

'A good thing you didn't have one?' Mary could only repeat this incomprehensible remark in astonishment.

But as if she had been upon the point of disclosing something that she had not intended to disclose, Rosie became confused.

'Oh, what's the use of going over everything!' she said, hurriedly. 'I suppose I just made a mistake: that's all.' But here her voice dropped. 'It's not that I didn't love Frank,' she said, 'but we started wrong. We should have waited to get married until he got a job.'

'But I thought he had plenty of money,' cried Mary. 'I didn't think you wanted for anything——'

'I didn't either!' said Rosie. 'Can't you wait and hear what I have to say, Mother, and not be always interrupting me! We had all the money we wanted, or else Frank was able to get more when we hadn't. I told you that long ago. I told you before we were married at all. He only had to go to the solicitor, and ask for it any time he wanted it, and the same with Violet and Mrs. Esmay, although as a matter of fact once or twice lately Frank didn't seem as anxious as usual to go to him, but I dare say there was some explanation for that; he may have had a bit of a difference with him, but I don't think it could be serious, do you?' She looked up. 'Do you?' she insisted, as Mary said nothing.

But one thing was enough at a time.

'You can talk about that later,' said Mary. 'Go on with what you were telling me.'

'What was I telling you?'

With a distracted air, Rosie ran her hand through her hair. Then she remembered.

'Oh yes I was talking about his having no work,' she said. 'Well, it wasn't a question of money. I'd imagine you'd have sense enough to realize that, Mother. If it was only that, things might have been better. If he had no money to give me he would have had to get it somewhere, because he was as proud as Lucifer. That was one of the things I admired about him; the way he liked everything to be first class. But of course it wasn't easy to have everything looking ship-shape all the time, particularly when he was about the house all the time. That was another thing—having him about the place all day! How could I ever get the flat cleaned up when he was always there, walking around the place, or maybe just sitting down watching me? And there's another thing: he never wanted to see me any way but well dressed and looking my best. As if I could be like that all day long.'

But as if a memory of some particular scene or incident returned to her mind at this point, Rosie suddenly buried her face in her hands and began to cry softly.

'Do you mean to say that was what upset you?' asked Mary, and it was impossible for her to keep a dry note out of her voice.

'That was the beginning of it,' said Rosie tearfully, but seeing that her mother was looking at her in a peculiar way, she hurried to defend herself. 'Oh, it's all very well for you,' she said, 'you don't know what it's like to have a man around the house all day. I often thought of the way Father used to go out to work——'

'You were too small to remember that!' said Mary.

'Well maybe I was, but I used to think of the way other men go out every day, and it began to get on my nerves to think of Frank inside in our room. You see he used to stay in bed until nearly dinner time, and then maybe when I'd have the dinner ready, he'd get up and dress himself, and say he didn't have any appetite, or else he'd say he had to go out to call on the solicitor. At first I used to believe him, about the solicitor anyway, but after a while I knew he couldn't be calling on the solicitor every other day. It was only an excuse; an excuse to go out and have a few drinks.'

'You don't mean he took drink in the middle of the day?' Mary wondered was Rosie imagining things. 'I never saw him with the sign of drink on him in the daytime,' she said. 'And at no time did I ever see him the worse for drink,' she added sharply. She might not have much regard for him, but you had to be fair to everyone. 'As a matter of fact, Rosie,' she said, 'you know I'm not one to say anything good about liquor, and no one belonging to me ever took a drop of drink inside their lips, but I told you before all men aren't alike, and it's my opinion you may be too hard on Frank. If you knew what some women have to put up with! If you saw some men!'

'What use is talk like that?' cried Rosie. 'What do I care about other women—or other men? To think that Frank could turn out this way! Frank!'

Something in the way she said his name made Mary's heart turn over. She was fond of him still; that was clear. But whether this was a good thing or a bad she could not wait to consider.

'He never——' She didn't know how to say what was in her mind. 'He didn't ill-treat you, did he?' she asked then, bluntly.

Rosie looked with a bewildered look which was rapidly replaced by an angry one.

'Oh, you didn't think that! You don't think he'd lift his hand to me,' she cried. 'Oh, how could you think such a thing? And what do you take me for? Do you think I'd have stood for that?' Some of the old fire had come back into her eyes.

Mary was perplexed.

'Oh, you don't understand,' said Rosie helplessly. 'He's not the kind to use violence. It would be better if he did, instead of goading me the way he did, with his sly looks and his sly remarks. People all think he's so charming, with a smile on his face all the time. Oh, how I hated that smile! I used to long to take up something and hit him in the face!'

Mary stared at her flushed face, and slowly a dark, purple flush came over her own face.

'You don't mean to say that——'

She could not finish the sentence, but Rosie understood what she was trying to say.

'If I did, he drove me to it!' she said.

Mary stood up.

'When did this happen?' she said, in a voice as heavy as stone.

Rosie shrugged her shoulders.

'Oh, ages ago!' she said.

'You don't make a practice of it?' she said.

Rosie said nothing. Mary could not interpret her silence, but she looked hard at her.

'If you did,' she said, slowly and deliberately, 'I can only say it's a great wonder to me that it wasn't him that ran away from you. Oh, Rosie, how could you lose control of yourself like that? I feel so ashamed! How can I ever look him in the face again!'

'You forget you won't have any occasion to look him in the face again,' said Rosie shortly, but after a minute she seemed to recall something about the incident that was less unpleasant than the details she had related. 'At first he did not mind at all,' she said, her face reflecting the shallow happiness the recollection gave her. 'He only laughed,' she said, musingly, and as if to herself. 'He called me a little devil! But he often called me that. It was a kind of a pet name he had for me.'

It would have been appropriate, too, when they first met, Mary thought, recalling the saucy manner with which Rosie used to talk to him before they were married, and for some time afterwards too, but now the thought that it could ever have been applied to this prematurely aged woman in front of her was so incongruous it caused her a distress she could not hide. Fortunately Rosie did not notice: she was lost in reminiscences.

'He took it in good part all right at first,' she said, 'and I was beginning to feel sorry for what I did when he gave that belittling smile of his: that smile that I hate. "Wait till people hear what a little devil you are!" he said. "Wait till my mother hears! Wait till Violet hears it. They think——" But I didn't wait to hear what they thought or what they didn't think. I just saw red again. You see we were going over to Esmays' that evening and I nearly died when I thought of him telling them everything. "You can tell them what you like," I shouted, "but I won't be there to hear you. I won't be there to-night or any night." I think I must have begun to shout, because I know I shouted out the next thing at him. "I'm not going over to your mother's again as long as I live because I hate her, and I hate your sister, and I hate their house, and I hate everyone I meet in it!" '

'But, Rosie,' cried Mary, interrupting her, 'I always thought you liked them; you were always telling me how well they kept themselves, and how grand their house was. How could you say such things?'

'Because it was true,' said Rosie. 'Like everything else, I tried to put a good face on it when I was talking to you, but I used to hate going over to that house so much that I used to want to scream sometimes when I thought of it.' She looked up at Mary. 'Oh, Mother, you don't understand—you couldn't understand. All the things I am telling you about seem to you to be so small, but small things are harder to bear than big things sometimes. It wouldn't have been so bad if it had been one big thing that was the matter: I could have stood it, like you stood it the time of Patrick; but it was little things, all the time, little things that set me on edge from one end of the day to the other. And going to that house in Raglan Road was one of the worst things I had to stand in my whole life. It was! I tell you it was! I got so that I couldn't stand the thought of it. It wasn't that they weren't nice to me: they did their best, but it was just that they weren't my kind of people. and I wasn't theirs. All they ever did was play cards, night after night; that, and smoking, and drinking. I just didn't fit into the picture at all, and they knew it, and they couldn't help showing it. I used to sit there looking at them playing cards. They wanted to teach me in the beginning, but I didn't want to learn. I told Frank. "I despise card-playing," I said. "Why?" said Frank. But that's the worst of me, Mother, I know what I mean, but I can't explain it. "It's so idle," I said. And of course, he had me there. "Well, I like that!" he said. "You talk of being idle! What do you do all day long but sit down with your hands in your lap looking into the fire?" That was true, I suppose, in a way, but when I used to sit by the fire, I used to be thinking: thinking of the time when we'd have a proper home, perhaps, where I'd have plenty to do all day, not like in the flat, where I had everything done by midday: or thinking we might have a baby perhaps. Because if we had a baby I'd have enough to do: I'd even have an excuse to stay at home at night without having to make up excuses. But Frank didn't understand that. Neither did the Esmays. They never did any thinking. They never gave themselves time to think, with their card parties and their suppers, and their family gatherings. Oh, how I hated them! That's why I flared up at Frank. "I'm not going with you to-night," I said. "I'm not going over there again to-night, or any night!" '

'How long ago was this?' said Mary quietly.

'Oh, it was years ago,' said Rosie.

That was what Mary thought.

'But you went there afterwards, several times, didn't you? You were there last week! You were there last night!'

'I know that,' said Rosie, with a helpless look on her face. 'And I went that night too,' she added. 'But can't you listen to me, Mother? Amn't I telling you about it? That was the first time that Frank began his campaign.'

'Campaign?'

'Will you stop interrupting me, Mother. Amn't I trying to tell you? Oh, you think you've heard all: you haven't heard anything yet. Isn't that why I'm here? Isn't that why I've left him: because of the Campaign. That's what I call it: the Campaign!'

'Call what? I don't understand,' said Mary, but the next instant, seeing the way Rosie's face had begun to twitch nervously, she put out her hand. 'You don't need to tell me anything else if you don't want to tell it, Rosie,' she said. 'If you want to come back home, you can come. That's no reason why you should have to tell me everything. If there is anything you'd rather I didn't know——'

But Rosie raised her eyes.

'Are you afraid to hear it?' she said.

Mary laughed uneasily.

'It's not that bad, I don't suppose,' she said.

'It's bad enough,' said Rosie flatly, in a colourless voice.

Mary made a last protest.

'Perhaps Frank wouldn't want you to be talking like this!'

'——Is it him?' flashed Rosie. 'What does it matter about him?' she cried. Then she threw out her hands. 'I've got to tell you, Mother. Aren't you the only one I have in the world: the only one that I can trust: the only one that will tell me the truth?' She lowered her voice. 'You see, Mother, you don't know anything at all. I kept it all from you. I made up my mind to come and tell you a hundred times, but I never got further than the door. I wonder you didn't see me sometimes walking up and down the street. I even came to the door a few times, but then I'd think of all you'd gone through, and I used to say to myself that I'd bear my own trouble: for another while anyway. But I can't bear anything now,' she cried, beginning to cry again. 'I've gone to pieces.'

That was true. Mary hardly knew what to do: whether to try and stop her from talking, or whether to let her say all she had to say.

'Hadn't you better begin at the beginning?' she said at last.

'It all began that night,' said Rosie. ' "Why aren't you going?" said Frank. As if he didn't know! As if he didn't know I hated going there from the start. But instead of that, he gave that hateful smile, and asked what my reasons were for wanting to stay at home. "Is there anything the matter with you?" he asked. Oh, Mother, if you saw the look on his face; the sly look!'

As if she were stifled, putting up her hand Rosie pushed her hat further back on her head. The gesture was jarring to Mary's nerves, and so too was her dishevelled and disarrayed appearance.

'Take it off altogether,' she said sharply.

But Rosie shook her head.

'Hadn't you better take off your coat,' said Mary, 'and try to take things calmly?'

'Calmly?' As if she had been affronted by the word, Rosie looked up wildly, and then her eyes fell. 'Yes; I must try to be calm,' she said then, quietly. 'That's the trouble, that's the whole trouble, I get so excited.' She looked at Mary. 'I wasn't always like that, Mother, was I?'

'Oh, I suppose we're all excitable by times,' said Mary, cautiously.

'I was telling you about the evening I refused to go to his mother's house with him, wasn't I? Well, that was the first time he began to say things to me.'

'Say things?'

'Yes, to make insinuations, if you like to put it that way; to say mean little things to hurt me. For instance, that evening, the minute I said I wouldn't go to Raglan Road, although at first he got red with anger, and I thought he was going to lash out at me, but instead of that, I saw his face change, and a look came into his eyes that I had never seen in them before: a cruel look. I didn't know for a moment what it could mean, and I got so frightened I began to tremble. But then, all at once, I knew the way he was going to hurt me. I knew! "Why, Rosie," he said, "why, Rosie, my darling, is there anything the matter? You're not feeling out of sorts, are you?" Oh, you don't understand, Mother! But I knew at once what he meant. Oh, the meanness of it! "You're not well, my love?" he went on, and he tried to put his arm around me. "Of course we won't go if you're not feeling up to the mark, although as a matter of fact Mother would be the first to understand. She's always so considerate, particularly for you, my dear. She's always inquiring about you. If she thinks you're looking the least bit pale, she's anxious about you at once. Why, the other night she thought you were looking a bit tired, and she took me to one side and questioned me." But I didn't listen to any more, I can tell you: I saw through him. As if I didn't know what he meant! As if I didn't know what his mother meant; what she was putting into his head!'

'I think you misjudged them,' said Mary wearily, 'both of them, Frank and his mother. It seems to me that they were very kind and considerate! They didn't understand that you were so sensitive.'

'Oh, they understood well enough,' said Rosie. 'They knew what they were doing. That was only the start of it. After that, hardly a day passed without his hinting and making suggestive remarks. And the Esmays were at the back of it. Even Violet, the spiteful thing, had her share in it. Oh, I never knew she'd turn out to be so spiteful. She usedn't to be like that, I'm sure. But since she got married, and had children of her own, there is no standing her at all. Wait till I tell you what she did! Right from the first, she was always calling at the house, with her pram; and always when Frank was at home. You'd think she'd know better than to call when he was there! I know I wouldn't do it if I was in her place, and she was in mine. And the things she used to say. "I know you don't like children, Rosie," she'd say, "but Frank loves to see them, and they love Frank." Then she'd start all sorts of nonsense, making them say his name and wave at him. It was sickening. Horrid, horrid little spoiled brats they were too. And then the pictures of them that were showered on us! I hated the sight of them, but of course I couldn't let anyone see that, and I had to have them framed and put them up all over the house. They're still there! I didn't dare put them away out of sight or she'd go on more about my not liking children. Oh, the meanness of that! The cruelty of it!'

'Perhaps it was just tactlessness,' said Mary, although her heart had begun to ache.

'Oh, how soft you are, Mother,' cried Rosie. 'Was it just tactless, do you think, the way Frank went on about Fido? You remember Fido, the little dog I had years ago, that I had to give away?'

Dimly Mary recalled Fido. For years until that moment she had forgotten that he ever existed. But now she remembered that he was a little Pomeranian, which a friend of Frank's had given to Rosie, and to which she had been very much attached for a time, until quite suddenly she seemed to take an aversion to the little creature and gave him away. She had been puzzled about Rosie's behaviour at the time.

'What kind of things did he say?' she asked. 'Tell me!'

'Oh, I can't think of anything in particular that he said,' Rosie said wearily. 'He was saying things all the time. For instance, whenever we met people with babies, he used to stoop down and pick up Fido in his arms. "This is our baby," he used to say.'

'I see!'

At last Mary had heard enough, and although at the back of her mind she was surprised to think that a person like Frank Esmay would have been disappointed over not having a child, still he had behaved in a way in which no one had a right to behave. It wasn't that she did not feel sorry for him, but Rosie was her concern.

'I wonder what kind of a father he would have made if he had children!' she said.

'That's what I said,' said Rosie, but then as if she remembered something else, she closed her eyes, and an agonized look came over her face, already so racked and haggard.

Desperately Mary tried to recall things she had heard other women say, when she was a young woman: things she had no wish to hear, things that seemed immodest to discuss, but to which now, she passionately wished she had listened.

'Take care!' she said, recalling something of that old talk. 'Maybe it's not altogether your fault that you had no family. Did that ever occur to you? Did it ever occur to him?'

But Rosie put her head down on the table.

'It's not his fault,' she said.

'How do you know?' demanded Mary.

'I know,' said Rosie dully.

Mary was annoyed.

'What do you mean! How do you know? Did you get medical advice?'

Rosie raised her head slowly.

'You're so innocent, Mother,' she said. 'You know nothing of the world. You know nothing of men like Frank, and what they stoop to do when they are drunk.'

For a moment Mary didn't understand. Then she did.

'I don't believe it!' she cried. For all his faults she could not believe that of him. 'Who told you such a thing?' she cried, full of wrath.

Rosie met her eyes with a long stare.

'Who do you think?' she said slowly.

Mary's heart began to beat violently.

She did not any the more believe in her son-in-law's incontinence. That he had lied to Rosie she felt certain, but a more implacable anger than she had yet felt came over her at the thought that he could have invented such a lie in order to torment Rosie.

'That settles it,' she said, getting to her feet. 'When you first came into the house, I thought I'd persuade you to go back to your home, Rosie, but after what you've told me, I don't blame you for not wanting to go back. I would not wonder if you never wished to see him again. And there's no need ever to see him again. Your home is here, as it always was, and your room is upstairs waiting for you, like it always was.' More gentle than she had yet shown herself, she went over and took Rosie's hat from her head.

'Take off your coat, child,' she said. 'Stay here. Don't go back.'

For a few minutes, Rosie made no effort to remove her coat. Then out of the corner of her eye Mary saw that, silently and without rising from her chair, she was trying awkwardly to extricate her arm from the sleeves of the coat, while down her cheeks the tears were coursing.

Wanting to pretend that she had not seen those tears, Mary moved across the kitchen until her back was towards the chair in which Rosie sat.

'I had better take a look in the press and see that I have a pair of sheets for you,' she said. 'They'll need to be aired. And they may need a little attention with a needle. They may be a little bit ripped, or there may be a little tear in them. It's a long time since I used any sheets but the ones for my own bed. And towels? You didn't bring anything with you, I suppose?'

The press of which Mary spoke was by the side of the range. It contained the boiler, that stored the hot water for the house, and above the boiler there were slatted shelves useful for airing linen or underclothing. When Mary opened the door, however, Rosie's first impression was that the shelves had been removed, because the entire space, above, below, on top of, and around about, the boiler, was packed tight with every imaginable kind of article. As far as she could see, soiled clothes and clean clothes were pushed into it indiscriminately. There seemed even to be old rags and bundles of old papers shoved in among the better things. And the manner in which all these things were disposed in the press was only to be described by saying that they were stuffed into it, as if they were so much wadding or packing intended to keep the boiler from falling to one side. Of any kind of order or arrangement there was no vestige. Then too, inside as well as out, the press itself had been so long exposed to the blackening effect of smoke and dust that there was a layer of grime upon the woodwork everywhere, that would have to be scraped with a knife if it were to be removed.

Looking at it, Rosie could not repress a shudder.

That press used to be full of clean sheets and towels, ironed and folded and laid neatly row by row upon its shelves that were always scrubbed and white. Now, so far as she could see, some of its original contents still remained, among the bundles of ragged articles, and they were clean, no doubt, but a bad colour, unironed, and for the most part frayed and worn. Her heart sank.

Just then, Mary managed to pull out a sheet.

'This is torn, I'm afraid,' she said. 'I meant to sew it, but my eyes are very bad lately. Perhaps——'

'Give it to me——' Rosie put out her hand. 'Oh, it's ripped all down the middle?' she said in dismay. 'Haven't you one better than this?'

Mary had no better one.

'Show it to me,' she said, falsely bright. 'Oh, that's the easiest kind of tear to mend,' she cried, as she saw the long gash down the middle of it. 'You won't have to do any patching or darning with that. All you need do is just rip it the whole way down, and sew it up again with the selvedges in the middle.'

'But the outer edges?' exclaimed Rosie. 'They will have to be hemmed?'

'So they will,' said Mary uneasily. 'But not to-night,' she added hurriedly. 'You can do it at your leisure.'

'It will be fraying all the time,' said Rosie.

She felt like crying. How her mother had changed in those few years since she had left home. How she had aged, and how greatly altered she had become in her habits: how careless and slovenly. It was probably because she was tired and without energy. Irrelevantly, it seemed, looking at the sheet in her lap, she spoke out aloud.

'I can't go back, that's one thing certain,' she said.

Mary looked at her.

'I thought that was settled?' she said.

Rosie wavered.

'It doesn't seem fair to you, Mother,' she said, 'to come back like this to you.' Her voice lagged. 'I think I should go back,' she said weakly. 'But the worst of it is I left a note for Frank. I said in it I was going for good.'

'Surely you wouldn't go back to him after what you told me?' asked Mary, but her voice too was flat and unemotional.

'Oh, that happened four years ago,' said Rosie, and there was a dry, hard bitterness in her voice. 'After all, I put up with him since then, so I suppose I could put up with him till the end?'

'What did you say in the note?' asked Mary. 'Maybe he hasn't got it yet.'

'Oh, he has got it by now,' said Rosie.

'Maybe he won't think you are serious,' said Mary.

They looked at each other. Was it hope that shone in Rosie's eyes? Be it what it may, however, after a minute the light in her eyes faded.

'I can't go back,' she said finally. 'He'd only say that was more of it.'

'More of what?'

The pain in Mary's shoulder had begun to throb again, or else it had been throbbing all the time but she had only become conscious of it in the past few minutes. Surely to goodness there was nothing left to hear?

'Didn't I tell you?' said Rosie heavily. 'Didn't I tell you he was always insinuating things? Didn't I tell you that after making my life a misery to me for years, because I hadn't given him a child, didn't I tell you he changed around lately, and began to insinuate that it was a good thing I didn't have any children?'

'What was the meaning of that?' cried Mary.

Rosie looked into her mother's eyes. For one instant she dwelt on the pain she was causing her, and an impulse came over her to spare her this last revelation; but once again, as with Larry long ago, the habits of a lifetime prevailed, and she cast her burden upon her mother's shoulders.

The colour had risen again in her face, a disturbing angry flush. Her whole face had a distraught look.

'I don't know but that there's something in what he says,' she muttered. 'I know one thing, and that is that I'm not the same as I used to be: I know that.'

Mary's heart thundered.

'In the Name of God, what are you trying to say?'

Nervously Rosie laughed.

'Didn't people always say,' she said, 'that there was a great likeness between——' she paused, and looked aside— 'between me and Patrick, I mean,' she said. Then she turned and looked full at Mary: and their eyes were locked in a long terrified stare.

For a moment, Mary's heart seemed to have stopped, and then a rush of blood went to her head. But she was resolved to stay calm.

'I never heard such nonsense,' she said. 'I never saw any resemblance between you. If you were like anyone, you were like Ellie. Who said you were like Patrick? Did Frank say it? If he did, he must have been dreaming. What could he be thinking about to say such a thing?'

As she spoke, she searched Rosie's face to see if she had appeased her. Rosie's face, however, was a poor guide now to her feelings; all blotched and stained with dirty tear marks. But she didn't seem to be appeased.

'You know what he was thinking, Mother?' she said, doggedly.

Yes, Mary knew; but getting to her feet she stood over Rosie's chair.

'The cur!' she said. 'The cur! I hope you had more sense than to listen to him?' she cried anxiously. Then as Rosie said nothing, she leaned down and caught her by the shoulders. 'You didn't pay any attention to him, did you?' she cried. 'You didn't listen to him, I hope. I tell you, if there's anyone queer it's your precious husband. That's it: it's him that's queer. And he's trying to drive you out of your mind too. Do you hear me? What did he say to you? Tell me what he said.'

'Stop shaking me, Mother,' said Rosie, first, and then, having freed herself, she shrugged her shoulders.

'Oh, he's always saying things,' she said. 'I can't remember half what he says.' She put her hand to her head. 'I think he began by asking about Patrick. For years he never mentioned him, and then all at once he began to ask me about him every other day. "How is your brother?" he'd say. At first I didn't know which of them he meant, Patrick or Larry, but when I asked him he gave me such a queer answer that I knew it must be Patrick. "Which of them?" I said. "You know the one I mean," he said. Wasn't that a queer thing to say, Mother?'

If he didn't say anything worse than that, Rosie's nerves were certainly in a bad state, thought Mary.

'I don't think there was anything at all queer about that,' she said. 'You ought to have known he meant Patrick. And I must say I think it was nice of him to ask for your brother like that. I didn't think he had that much good nature in him.'

As if it was good nature that made him ask! Rosie smiled bitterly.

'He just wanted to torment me.'

'But why should it torment you to have him inquire for poor Patrick?' asked Mary.

But Rosie sighed.

'I'm so tired,' she said, 'I explain things so badly. I didn't tell you that he used to choose special times for asking about him. For instance, there was one day he went out, just as the dinner was on the table, after all my trouble in getting it ready, and he didn't come back till late in the evening. Well, I couldn't be expected to behave as if nothing happened when he came back, so I didn't answer him when he spoke to me. I didn't mean to keep it up for long, but I meant to give him a cooling, so I just went on with my work, and didn't say anything to him, no matter what he said to me. That was one of the times he asked for Patrick. And when I didn't answer, he took up a pencil and began to pare it, looking at me out from under his lids. "What was it that first made you notice there was something wrong with him?" he said. There! Do you see now what I mean? Do you see what he was insinuating?'

Mary supposed that she saw what Rosie wished her to see, but she longed to ask her if she might not have misunderstood his remarks, only she saw that Rosie would not listen to her.

'That was a long time ago, wasn't it?' she said instead. 'He hasn't said anything like that lately, has he?'

'Didn't I tell you that he never stops making remarks night and day. Wasn't it something he said this evening that drove me out of the house!'

In all her questioning, Mary had not thought to ask what it was that had brought things to a head on this particular occasion. Interest quickened in her face, which had begun to look so fatigued.

Rosie sighed again.

'I wasn't feeling too good all day, and just about four o'clock I thought maybe I'd take a cup of tea if it was weakly made. So I put on the kettle and made a little pot of tea, and sat down to take it. I was just sitting down when Frank arrived home. He had been out for a walk. We hadn't been getting on too badly for the past few days, so I looked up when he came in and I said he was just in time for a nice cup of tea. I didn't think he'd take it, but I was delighted when he said he'd like it. "I'll get a cup for you," I said, and jumped up to get one. My own tea was poured out, but I put the saucer over the cup and went out to the press in the pantry to get a cup for him. "Here it is now," I said, coming back and pouring out a cup of tea for him, sweetening it and putting milk in if before I handed it to him.

' "Thanks, Rosie," he said, and he said it in a way that made me feel a bit happier than I had been feeling for some time. "What about your own?" he said then, and he nodded at my own cup with the saucer over it. "It will be cold," he said. "Oh, it will be all right," I said, and I was thinking that I wouldn't care whether it was cold or not as long as he was so considerate about me. But all the same, when I lifted the saucer off the cup, and put the cup to my lips, I didn't think it tasted the same as when I took the first sip out of it. I suppose it was a bit cold, or else being covered with the saucer made it draw a bit, made it a bit stronger. Anyway I thought it had a bitter taste. As a matter of fact something the same happened to me once or twice recently with other things! I thought I'd like something or other, and then when it was ready I took a turn against it. But tea was different. You know how I was about tea! I could drink a cup of it at any hour. But whatever came over me this evening, when I came back to it, after one sip I couldn't touch it. But I didn't want Frank to notice that I wasn't taking it, in case it would spoil his enjoyment of his own tea. So I stood up quietly and I went over to the sink intending to pour it away; but the next thing I knew he was standing beside me, and he had me by the arm. Oh, Mother, if you saw his face! If you heard the way he spoke to me!

' "Why didn't you drink that tea?" he said, and I thought the people downstairs would hear him he shouted so loud. Then, without waiting for me to say anything, he shook my arm. "I suppose you think I put something in it?" he said.'

It was absolutely beyond Mary's control to keep back the question that came to her lips.

'Did you think it?' she asked.

But unexpectedly, Rosie gave a gay little laugh—like the laugh she used to have before she was married; very mirthful and musical.

'Not at all,' she cried. 'Why should I think such a thing?' But the next moment her face darkened again. 'I didn't get a chance to tell him that I didn't think it,' she said, 'because he took the cup from me, and held it up to my lips. "If you think there's nothing wrong with it, why don't you drink it?" he demanded, and I thought he was going to pour it down my throat. "Drink it!" he said. "Drink it, I tell you!" and he shouted at me again.

'It was probably the way he shouted that made me nervous, but before I knew what I was doing I flung out my hand and knocked the cup out of his hand. That was what he wanted. "So you did think it!" he said, accusing me with his finger. His eyes bored into me. "You know where you're heading if you keep on this way," he said. Oh, Mother, wasn't that a terrible thing to say to me: wasn't it?'

It was. And yet Mary felt some curious sympathy for Frank Esmay.

'It's a pity you didn't take one sip of it, just to please him—just to show him, I mean,' she said, correcting herself quickly.

'I know that,' said Rosie, and again the answer was unexpectedly calm and normal. 'But I didn't want it, that was all. Honestly, Mother!' Their eyes met: mother and daughter. 'Honestly!' said Rosie again, and then abruptly she lowered her eyes.

'Well,' she said then, defiantly, 'if I did think anything queer it was because he put it into my mind. I would never have dreamed of such a thing! But that was what he wanted, all the time, to put queer things into my mind. He wanted to drive me mad: that's what he wanted. Because then——' She stopped and closed her eyes. It would be intolerable to her, in word or thought, to go further than she had gone.

Suddenly she stood up. And her face had a terrible distorted look. Mary stared at her. It was not the face of a fully normal woman.

'Oh, Mother!' she cried, and leaning across the table she clawed at the edge of it, her fingers unloosening and fastening upon its edges. 'Is it true, do you think? Is it true? What he thinks about me? That's really why I came home to you: to ask you to tell me the truth. I would have asked you long ago only I was always hoping——' she stopped, looking puzzled—'hoping for what?' she said, but rushing on again she left this parenthetical question unanswered. 'Oh, Mother, I'm frightened!'

Suddenly she threw herself into Mary's arms, and all at once she

seemed in need of protection, young again, and helpless. Mary
pressed her close to her. She was a child again: soft, vulnerable.

'Hush, child, hush!' said Mary, and she began to smooth down the
hair that was so dry and dishevelled. There was no doubt that Rosie
was not well, not normal: the dry hair under her hand was only
another symptom of a poor condition of health.

'Is it true? You'll tell me the truth, Mother.'

Mary held her daughter close. For some reason she was not afraid:
it was as if in the long twilight she divined a light about to break upon
them.

'Of course it's not true, my love,' she said calmly, trustingly. 'It's
not true, but you must be calm. You must not give way to foolish
fancies. Hush, hush!'

'Hush! Hush!'

With these words she had stilled convulsive fits of sobbing when
her children were in their cradles. And confident in their power, she
kept saying them, over and over again, until at last Rosie's sobbing
stopped, and she was crying softly. Then, this soft crying ceased too,
and she dried her eyes.

'Everything would have been different if only I had a child,' she
said quietly.

'Perhaps it's all for the best that you haven't,' said Mary.

Startled, Rosie raised her head.

'You don't mean——?'

'I mean nothing,' said Mary, 'but what I said. Isn't it a good thing
you haven't a child now? If you've made up your mind to leave your
husband, isn't it a good thing you haven't a child? You'd have to look
after it, and how could you do that if you wanted to go back to work?
And after a while, I suppose that's what you'll want to do: you'd
hardly be content to do nothing all day. You know you could not
take a job and mind a child at the same time? I'd give you all the
help I could,' she added, looking steadily into Rosie's eyes, but
feeling urged to utter her first and only cautionary words, 'but you
won't have me for ever,' she said.

But Rosie was not listening to this part of what was being said
to her.

'You don't understand,' she cried. 'If I had a child I'd never have
left my husband. And even if I did leave him, I'd have had something.
I wouldn't be all alone, like I am now! Oh, Mother! If you knew the
feeling of loneliness; of emptiness——' she pressed her hand, not to
her heart, but spread wide upon her bosom, as if the feeling she
sought to describe was felt by her whole body, her whole being. 'I

didn't care so much in the beginning,' she whispered, 'but it got worse and worse until now it's more than I can bear!' She looked up. 'That's why I'm frightened,' she said unsteadily, 'not at what Frank said, but because of the way I feel here——' She put her hand again to her bosom. 'When I see other women in the street with their babies in their arms I have to turn away. My own arms ache—oh, but ache! I can hardly bear to see a child now. When I see them playing in the street I turn my face away, and walk past them as fast as I can. One day there were two or three children playing on the pavement and I was walking so fast and trying not to look at them that I didn't see that one of them was sitting on the path playing with stones, and I nearly fell over it. I almost stood on its little hand, trying to save myself from falling. Such a little hand. I wanted to stop and take it in my own, and feel it, but I just rushed on, without stopping, because I was afraid I'd start to cry. And then another day I saw a little kitten in the gutter, and I picked it up and nearly squeezed the life out of it; it was so warm and soft, and living. I closed my eyes and made believe it was a little baby; my baby.' She closed her eyes. 'I could hear its little heart beating.'

As if she could still hear that little heart beating, she said nothing for a few minutes. Then she looked at Mary again.

'I started to cry that day,' she said, 'in the street. Wasn't that terrible, Mother—to start crying in the street. But I couldn't help it. It's always happening to me lately, and I can't help it. But——' and here she took more command of herself than she had done since she came into the house—'but it cannot go on like this,' she said. Resolutely, steadily, she repeated what she had said. 'I cannot go on this way.'

'No, you cannot go on this way,' said Mary, but there was something in her voice that made Rosie look up with surprise, and on her mother's face when she looked at it, she saw that there was a strange expression, unreadable to her, but one which filled her, as a high wind fills a tree, with a trembling of all its members.

'Rosie!'

As if she were afraid to speak, Mary's voice was hesitant, halting. 'I want to tell you something,' she said. 'I know that feeling which you talk about; that loneliness, and that emptiness. I had those same feelings, long ago.' She hesitated for another instant, but taking confidence, she went on more boldly. 'Before each one of you was born, I felt like that,' she said. 'It was worst of all, I think, before Patrick was born. Do you know what I used to say to your father? "I'm aching to hold him in my arms," I used to say. He used to laugh. He didn't understand such feelings, I suppose, being a man, although he was quicker than me to know the cause of such feelings, because of course there is a cause for everything. Rosie. But anyway, as I was saying, I had that empty feeling right up to the day Patrick was born. And then I forgot all about it. "You have your arms filled now," said your father, when he came into the room to see the baby. And afterwards when Patrick was getting fat and heavy and hard to carry, he used to remind me of what I said before he was born, about the way my arms ached to hold him. But I had almost forgotten about the way I felt by that time, until one day I was out for a walk, and I passed by a vacant piece of ground beside the Canal, and there was a woman sitting on the grass—there are houses built on it now, but it used to be a nice place to sit on a summer day. Patrick was getting big enough to take notice of things; the butterflies and the daisies, and the other children that sometimes ran in there to play. This day, however, there was no one there but another woman with a pram, and I didn't take much notice of her until I was going home. But as I was passing, I looked into the pram, half expecting to see a baby about the same size as my baby, but instead of that there was a little thing only a few weeks old, staring up at the sky with two little eyes as blue as if they were bits of mirror giving back the blue sky. I got such a surprise. It was not a year since Patrick was born but somehow I had forgotten that a baby could ever be so small and so soft and helpless. And do you know what I wanted to do! I wanted to stoop down and take it up in my arms and hug it. And suddenly I got that empty feeling again: that aching feeling. And it was so bad I told Tom about it when I went home. Tom only laughed again. He knew better than me what it meant, and the next spring Ellie was born!'

As she spoke, a radiance like the radiance of youth had come over Mary's face.

'Oh, Rosie, it's just like yesterday,' she said, but seeing Rosie's face, she remembered the purpose of her reminiscences.

'But I was telling you about the way I felt,' she said hastily. 'Well, we didn't know then what it meant, but two years later, when Patrick was a big boy, running about, and climbing up on everything, and Ellie was beginning to stumble about on her little fat legs, and getting big too, I was hanging out clothes on the line, and Tom was helping me: he was in his shirt sleeves, I remember, and all of a sudden he looked at the children.

' "Isn't it great they're getting so big," he said. "We'll soon be able to take them out for a day. Before we feel it, they'll be grown up and no bother to you at all." But I stopped him. "Oh, don't talk of them growing up," I cried. "I can't bear to think of a time when they'll be too big to take in my arms: I'd be so lonely for them, my arms ache at the thought of it." I wasn't thinking of what I was saying. But your father looked at me.

' "Don't tell me you have that lonely feeling again?" he said, and he laughed. I was still very young, you know: and so it wasn't till I saw the way your father was looking at me that I knew what he meant, and sure enough he was right! Within a week I knew there was another one of you on the way! And I was obliged to start rummaging in the old clothes chest for the little garments that had got too small for Patrick and Ellie, and to start patching them and darning them to have them ready for the next arrival: Angie. It was Angie that came next, you know——'

But at this point, Rosie, who had been crying quietly, could bear no more.

'Why are you telling me all this?' she cried, piteously.

Why indeed? In the sweetness of recalling those far away days, Mary had forgotten her reason for talking about them. But she had a reason. Now, all at once, however, she realized the enormity of the thought that had occurred to her, and the enormity of the risk she was taking in putting that thought into Rosie's mind. But she had gone too far to draw back.

'Have you no idea, Rosie, of why I am telling all this to you?' she said, her face trembling. 'Have you no idea of what I've been thinking in the past few minutes?'

She hoped to make things easier for both of them by those questions, but Rosie stared back at her without comprehension.

'That feeling you speak about, the loneliness, and the aching in your heart,' said Mary. 'Do you not think it strange that God should have given you such feelings, if—if they were to be without purpose?'

She paused. Desperately she scanned Rosie's face to see if any flicker of her meaning had penetrated to her cheerless mind.

'I don't want to give you false hope,' she said, seeing no light in the other's countenance, 'but I'll tell you one thing more. When I had that feeling long ago myself, I used to think that it was God's way of preparing the heart for the new burden. He was to lay upon it. Do you see what I mean?'

They stared at each other, silent, trembling.

It was just then, while they stared at each other, that, deep in her body, Rosie felt a soft flutter like the flutter of a young bird's wings; a feeling she had never felt before in all her life, but which she understood as truly as the beat of her heart: it was the first stirrings of a life imprisoned within her.

'Oh, Mother!' she cried.

'I may be mistaken,' cried Mary in alarm; 'I may be wrong—I may——'

But Rosie, with her hand on her body, looked up with a light on her face that would never wholly fade from it.

'You're not wrong, Mother,' she said simply. 'I should have known long ago, but I was disappointed, so often, I was deceived so many times, I had stopped thinking that such a thing could ever happen to me.'

Mary O'Grady looked at her daughter. Only a moment before she had despaired of ever seeing a gleam of light on her face again, but now she recoiled from the conflagration of happiness in that face.

'Don't take it too much for granted,' she cried. 'How can you be so sure, all in a minute?'

As if she didn't even hear her, Rosie was looking around her.

'What time is it?' she asked, and seeing the hour on the little tin clock, she began to look around the room for the calendar. 'What date is it?' she asked.

She seemed to have become obsessed with a sudden urgency; with a feeling of there being no time to waste. And more than anything that had passed between them, this air of urgency about her made Mary believe that they were right, both of them, in their suspicions about her condition.

'Will this make any difference in your plans?' she asked, on an impulse, and at the same time she looked around the kitchen. 'This house is no place for you now,' she said, but the next minute her face became violently agitated; so much so that it was hard to say whether it was from pain or from pleasure.

'Just a minute,' she cried, then, and going over to the corner of the room she began to drag out something from under the old sofa, whose springs were now so broken it no longer had any other use but as a repository for old papers and empty boxes. Like everything else in the house except the chair she sat upon, and the bed she slept upon, it was a heaping place for rubbish. But from under it at last she dragged out an old trunk, and opened the lid of it.

What it contained Rosie could not see, but the next minute she saw her mother get up from her knees, and her hands were as black as the tin box which she stretched out towards her.

'But what is this for?' she cried. And to her distress she saw that the tears were streaming down her mother's face.

'Don't you remember it?' cried Mary, glancing down at the box. 'Don't you remember the time I told you that I could pay your way through college, even if Patrick wasn't able to help me? Do you remember that? Do you remember I told you I had the money that Patrick sent back to me from America? He didn't need it, and none of the rest of you needed it either; but I needed it least of all, and it's still here. If I give it to you now will you do as I say with it? Will you take it and go down to Tullamore, and let your child be born there? Will you do that? I've told you about it so often you must nearly feel as if it was home to you. Oh, Rosie, it's the grandest place on earth. I know I've never set foot there since the day that I left it to marry your father, but I'm sure it's just the same as always: things never change in the country, and although your Uncle John is an old man now, he'll not have changed either. He was always a kind brother to me, and he'll be kind to you and your child. You could go to him. I'll write to him to-night. There's no one but himself there all alone in the old home, and he ought to be glad to have you. It's not as if you'd be going to him like a pauper; you'll have enough in this box to pay your way for a long time. Money goes a lot farther in the country than in the city, and there are lots of ways of sparing it, and ways of adding to it also. Here! Take it!' She thrust the box forward. 'Take it,' she cried, and then, as Rosie made no move to put out her hands, a sudden fear dampened the ardour that had burned in her.

'You don't want your child to be born in this miserable place, do you?' she cried.

Rosie shuddered.

'No, I don't want that,' she said slowly, and she put out her hand and took the box from her mother. 'What about you, though? What are you going to do, Mother?' she asked, but although this concern touched her, it seemed to Mary that Rosie only put it forward to give herself time for pondering others.

'Oh, don't mind about me,' said Mary. 'Later on perhaps I'd straighten out things here and go down to see you. You might even find a little cottage near John's house, and then——' All at once, however, she became frightened by the preoccupied look on Rosie's face. 'Will you go, do you think?' she asked abruptly. 'Will I write to your Uncle John?'

Getting no answer, she stood up, and as if to put more force into her words, from a shelf of the dresser she took down a pen and paper and a bottle of ink.

'If I write now, we could post the letter to-night and he'd have it to-morrow,' she said; for she felt that, unseen, some enemy threatened her plans.

But Rosie stood irresolute.

'What about Frank?' she said.

'What about him?' said Mary.

He was the unseen enemy. But although a rancour came over her at the thought of him, she did not fail to see the colour that came into Rosie's face as she said his name.

'Mother! Do you think that if I went away he'd follow me?' she cried, and no one could mistake the note in her voice. 'We could start all over again. Things would be different there; away from his family, and all the temptations of the city.'

'I don't know,' said Mary gravely. 'You know him better than I do. But that is another matter: will I write to your Uncle John or will I not?'

'I suppose you'd better write to him,' said Rosie, but the next moment she leaned over the table. 'Do you think I ought to write to Frank, Mother?' she asked.

But suddenly Mary was very tired.

'I'll leave that to yourself,' she said, but after a minute she put out her hand and laid it on the lid of the box that Rosie had left on the table between them. 'Do as you please,' she said, 'but remember one thing. I'm not giving this money to you, I'm giving it to your child. If you don't want to go to Tullamore, you can tell me now, and I'll put the money away until the child is born.'

Very gently, Rosie laid her hand on the aged and wrinkled hand upon the lid of the box.

'I'll go to Tullamore, Mother,' she said. 'I promise you I'll go. But don't write to Uncle John to-night. Wait until I write to Frank. Wait until I hear from him. He might even——'

Behind her eyes such hope shone it was hard to think it could be ungrounded or false: such love it was hard to think it would not some day be requited.

'Give me that pen,' she said, 'and I'll write to him now; and he'll have it to-morrow.'

She took the pen and paper and the bottle of ink, and clearing a space at the end of the table, she sat down to write. After a few minutes, however, she looked up. She had not written anything.

'When it gets dark,' she said, 'I might walk as far as the house and put it into the letter box. He'd get it to-night then, and maybe—'

'Maybe what?'

'He might come here,' said Rosie humbly, and she took up her pen again.

More than an hour passed, however, and although there had been a continual scratching sound from her pen, and several times there had been the sound of paper being torn into pieces, she still had not written anything to her satisfaction. And Mary, who had moved over to a chair by the fire, had fallen into a kind of doze.

'It's no use,' said Rosie at last, and she stood up. 'I don't know what to say to him,' she said, and a fatigued, despondent look had taken the place of the exhilarated look her countenance had worn when she first sat down. 'What do you think I ought to say?' she asked, looking in Mary's direction, but seeing that her mother was asleep, she felt a catch at her heart, and going closer to her, for the first time since she had come into the house, she looked with anything like concentration at her.

How tired she looked, and how frail! She had been failing for some time. She had seen her declining. But now it almost seemed as if in the short while since they had ceased speaking, she had gone steeper downhill. To think that, however, would be to think that it was her fault, and from such a thought she drew backwards. And yet, if her mother had looked like this when she came into the house this evening, how had she been so engrossed in her own concerns as not to notice that something was wrong?

'Mother?'

Even the very fact that she continued to sleep with someone standing over her was in itself disturbing. And her breathing, although it was regular, should surely be less heavy?

'Mother?' she cried again, her voice sharp with anxiety.

Mary opened her eyes.

'Are you all right, Mother?' asked Rosie, anxiety sharpening her voice still more.

Mary was surprised.

'Why, of course I'm all right,' she said.

'You don't look it then,' said Rosie unsparingly, because for a minute she had been frightened at her mother's appearance. 'You're very white looking,' she said then, trying to be gentler, trying to be kinder, and filled with remorse for the way in which she had laid her own burdens upon her. But she was unskilled in expressing the kind of emotions she now felt. 'You're not giving yourself proper care!' she said, her desire to be warm, to be kind, resulting only in exasperated recrimination.

Now there had been many times of late when Mary had not felt well. There had been times when that pain in her shoulder had been fairly bad. And there had been times when it would have given her ease to have told Rosie how she felt. But she had always resisted her desire to do so, and disguised her discomfort as best she could. To-day, however, she felt better than usual! Even the pain that had been almost incessant of late had ceased to bother her in the past hour or so.

'Why are you looking at me like that?' she asked petulantly. 'I'm all right.'

'Are you sure?' persisted Rosie. 'Are you sleeping well? Are you taking proper meals? Do you get enough exercise?'

For in the answer to one or other of these questions, she hoped to find a cause for the change that had come over her mother. And when the change did not prove attributable to neglect of any kind, gladly even would she attribute it to her own lack of consideration. Because, from the intransigent thought that Time alone had caused that change she shrank back in fear.

'Oh, Mother, I have caused you so much worry,' she said, falling to her knees in front of her. 'I have never spared you, but ran to you with all my troubles. Oh, how selfish I have been! And we were all the same, all of us. I'm so ashamed.' She put her head down on Mary's lap.

Gently Mary put out her hand and began to stroke her hair.

'I never heard such talk,' she said. 'To whom would you turn if you didn't turn to me?' Then, remembering something she had momentarily forgotten, she smiled. 'That's what mothers are for in this world as you'll find out some day,' she said, intending to make a little joke.

But Rosie did not smile.

'I suppose so,' she said dully. And she stood up.

Mary looked after her. She had taken up the unfinished letter she had been writing, and she was staring at it with such a sad expression that Mary half rose from her chair.

'What are you thinking?' she asked, anxiously.

Rosie turned around slowly.

'I was thinking of this child that is coming into the world,' she said, 'and of the way I wanted it so much—at one time. But all of a sudden I began to wonder why I should want it so much. My own life wasn't so wonderful that I should want to bring another life into the world.' Here she turned around to Mary, and forgetting her tender feelings of the previous moment, she spoke accusingly. 'And you, Mother?' she cried. 'What was your life, only misery and sorrow: one sorrow after another? What hope of happiness could you hold out to this child that is on the way?'

'Rosie O'Grady!'

Although with a difficulty she had never experienced before, Mary got fully to her feet.

'Rosie O'Gray! How dare you talk like that! What do you mean? Didn't I have all of you children? Didn't I have your father? And didn't we all have our love and affection for each other? What more could we have had than that?' she asked, wonderingly.

Rosie looked into those eyes, so full of love, into which she had looked only too seldom.

Their love and affection for each other, she thought. That was all they had got from life; but what a joy it had been to them, and for their mother, what a light it had lit in the dark days, through all her earthly sojourn.

But Mary was speaking again.

'If you only knew,' she said, 'how I used to love to watch you, just to look at your faces when you didn't know I was looking at all.' She smiled. 'That's all I'd ask of God for all Eternity, just to see you all again, and look at your faces for ever and ever. And that's what I'm always thinking about lately,' she said, 'thinking about the day when we will all meet again; when we'll all be together for ever more, with no pain, and no partings.' But at this point a shadow came over her face. 'Only there was something that worried me,' she said, and she put up her hand to her head, as if in perplexity. 'What was it, I wonder? It was something about my own mother, and something——' Her face was distressed. Rosie took her hand. It was trembling.

'Don't distress yourself, Mother,' she said.

'But it was important,' said Mary. 'Why can't I remember it? I thought I would go to see some priest and ask him to straighten things out for me. I was so worried about it—whatever it was.'

'Perhaps you were dreaming, Mother?' said Rosie, gently.

Mary looked up at her.

'No, I was awake,' she said.

But it seemed that in thinking so, she might have been mistaken, for even at that very moment, with Rosie's warm fingers clasping her wrist, the room began to fill with a misty vapourousness, and while she was looking at it, Rosie's face became indistinct.

Was it Rosie at all?

For a moment she thought it was Ellie!

But there was always a likeness between Rosie and Ellie. To try to see more clearly, she puckered her face.

'Mother!'

Far, far away, a voice was calling to her, out of the golden mist, but she did not trouble to answer.

It was Ellie! And, ah, how her heart leaped—there was Angie beside her, both of them together, smiling at her in a radiance undimmed by any shadow.

And there were the others: there they all were, together, all smiling at her. And with them was her own mother. They were all smiling at her, and they were stretching out their arms to her, and beckoning to her. But it was not they she was seeking. The heart in the body had known all there was to be known about them. And what she was seeking still was unknown to her. And so although she smiled back at them, her eyes were seeking all the time to penetrate the radiant haze about her. Seeking whom?

Ah there! Away in a distance still more radiant than the place in which she stood, she saw at last what she was seeking; it was a little naked child, that stood with its back towards her.

Oh, for that child to turn its head! Oh, for it to show its face! Such a longing took possession of her that, except for the pulse of that longing, her whole being seemed to melt away.

Yet, how could she feel this longing for a child she had never known, she wondered? Then all at once she knew: it was Rosie's child; Rosie's child, as yet unborn. But why did it not turn its head? Why did she not see its face? And why, though she followed after it, did it seem ever farther and farther from her? She did not understand. But instead of feeling troubled, she felt a tremendous elation, as if she were on the very point of entering into the mystery of all things.

The others will explain everything to me, she thought. And she turned back to find them. For although in the increasing radiance it was hard to make out where they were, she could still hear them calling her name.

'Mother! Mother! Mother!'

Has she fallen asleep again, thought Rosie, as she got no answer?

'Mother!' she said again, very, very gently.

Love such as she had never felt welled up in her, and she looked around her for something to put across her mother's shoulders. There was an old black cardigan lying on the floor. She picked it up and shook it, but as she was about to lay it on her mother's shoulders, she looked with a start again at her face. She was smiling, so serenely, and so untroubled! And she was so still! She was hardly breathing, or else her breathing scarcely stirred the bodice of her old black dress. Did it stir at all?

Instinctively she stretched out her hand to touch the still hands that lay lightly clasped on the old black skirt, but on a second instinct she drew it back, recalling her need to safeguard her own body from shock.

The greatest blow that life could give her had fallen, she knew, upon her, but she had to bear it bravely for the sake of the child in her body.

I must be calm, she thought. I must not give way.—But I must call someone, she thought, and turning she began to run towards the hall door, but here again she recalled her condition, and she began instead to walk as quickly as was possible without agitating herself too much.

And to whom would she look for help? From the neighbours, she supposed, although they had long since become strangers to her. The people passing in the street were hardly less so. Would she call out to the first person she saw?

Her loneliness and friendlessness came home to her as she put her hand to the door to open it. Was she all alone now? she thought, and she opened the door.

And there, coming across the street, making directly toward her with an anxious face, was Frank: her own Frank!

'Oh, Frank!' she cried. 'Thank God you came. Hurry! It's Mother! I think——'

Her face was enough for him: he did not wait to hear what she thought, but hurried past her into the hall and down the passage.

'Oh, Frank!' she cried again, with love and anguish, and as he went past her, she pulled him by the sleeve, and for a moment held him back. 'I have something else to tell you too,' she said— 'afterwards.'

Afterword

IN THE final pages of *Mary O'Grady* the heroine's youngest daughter, Rosie, discovers after several years of marriage, that she is soon to have a baby. Her dying mother looks to the event with unqualified joy. But to the daughter, looking back on both their lives, it appears differently:

> ... forgetting her tender feelings of the previous moment, she spoke accusingly. "And you, Mother?" she cried. "What was your life, only misery and sorrow: one sorrow after another? What hope of happiness could you hold out to this child that is on the way?"

Rosie is taken aback by the alarmed vehemence of her mother's reply:

> "What do you mean? Didn't I have all you children? Didn't I have your father? And didn't we all have our love and affection for each other? What more could we have than that?" she asked wonderingly.

While the daughter is, at least temporarily, baffled by her mother's reply, the reader is not. We have known the heroine long before Rosie was born. The early pages of the novel created a small, intense universe in which the abiding values by which Mary lived were subtly adumbrated: the husband to whom she takes dinner every day along the canal bank; the small house in Ranelagh to which she returns in the afternoon with her children: the vacant ground, a "plot of green grass", where she pauses daily—emblematic of her childhood in the country round Tullamore which she is destined never to revisit, and of the heaven towards which she yearns as life nears its end.

In the last paragraphs of the novel Mary's beatific vision is of consummated motherhood. She sees her dead daughters, Angie and

Ellie, "smiling at her in a radiance undimmed by any shadow" and "with them was her own mother". Finally there is the vision of the "little naked child, that stood with its back to her". This she identifies with Rosie's unborn baby, though the reader may be free to associate it with the madonna and child theme which is central to the Catholic iconography which the author allows to permeate the heroine's consciousness, especially towards the end. Thus in the early chapters of the book, when Mary O'Grady is young, innocent, happily absorbed in her children, the language of her speech, thought and reverie are correspondingly simple, tender and optimistic—the frequency of the word "little" in the author's narrative is a case in point. It took a marvellous feat of both empathy and objectivity to portray that vivid, simple consciousness through the novel. It meant that the author must be consistently *in* the heroine's mind and sensibility, but not of it.

The narrative darkens, the language hardening imperceptibly, as Mary proceeds towards middle age and encounters progressively the sadness of experience. At the end it softens and brightens with her visions of an eternal reward, a development implicit in her character and actions throughout her life. One critic who has accused the author of lapsing into sentimental "subjectivity" in these final pages misses the narrative technique of the book as a whole by confusing the writer with the character, and by missing the subtle blend of sympathy and detachment by which the character is defined and mediated.

Those who identify Mary Lavin with Mary O'Grady would do well to remember that the characters called "Jane" in Jane Austen's fiction are those least like the author herself. This is not to say that there is a schematic sense of distance between the author's view of things and that of the heroine; Mary Lavin is far too instinctual a story-teller for that. But a sensitive reading of the novel will reveal that many of Mary O'Grady's responses and attitudes—her innocence, stubbornness, sentimentality—are almost as much a mystery to the writer as they are to the reader. The most striking and perhaps central example of this creative ambivalence is Mary's apparent excess of piety at the novel's end. I would argue that this development has been delicately anticipated in the narrative by the special quality of her resignation.

Our opening quotation identified Mary as a "mother of sorrows", a phrase out of a familiar Catholic litany. Yet it is clear that she does not see her life as failure. She has lived her role of mother and wife to the full; she has been true to her calling both in human and divine terms. Beside that steadfast conviction the temporal disasters which befall her, and which make up the book's unhappy narrative, are entirely bearable. Hers is an old-fashioned philosophy, sharply challenged by the modern restlessness and self-doubt of her youngest daughter. Mary may be seen as a last representative of an attitude, resilient because unselfconscious, that accepted the trials and calamities of womanhood as part of a severe but not unjust providence. Mary's sufferings are not seen as the workings of a malign fate or an unjust social system. In this sense it is better to resist, at the outset, any easy comparison between her world and that of Hardy's Tess, George Moore's Esther or Zola's Gervaise in *L'Assomoir*—even the world of James Stephens's great story, "Hunger", which opens with such an apposite assertion as "On some people misery comes unrelentingly ... with such a continuous rage that one might say destruction had been sworn against them and that they were doomed beyond appeal, or hope."

There are two reasons why Mary O'Grady's psychology can barely admit, let alone yield to, despair. She is infused with that sense of the life-force which gives such strange vitality to a certain kind of Mary Lavin character recurrent in the novels and short stories; and she is sustained by that Catholic world-view already glanced at. As this world-view has some manifestations not often encountered in Anglo-Saxon literary criticism, it is well to confront its implications before going further.

The book seems to begin and proceed as a purely secular novel. Though the O'Gradys are clearly a Catholic family—we are told in Book V where each attends Mass—we never see them inside a church; the father's burial service is not even glimpsed; we never see them at family prayer, though it would surely have been part of their routine. Even when the second son, Larry, is conscripted into the priesthood by the sinister Father Dowling, we are denied entry to the seminary and its rituals and we are excluded from the young aspirant's inner thoughts, soul-searchings, scruples, examinations of conscience. The contrast with such "Catholic novelists" of the fifties, with Graham Greene, François Mauriac, Evelyn Waugh, Kate O'Brien or Sean O'Faolain, could hardly be more dramatic.

The book's apparent indifference to questions of theology is explained in part by the point of view. Apart from a few exceptional interludes, we view the action through Mary's unquestioning and largely unlettered sensibility. Indeed one of its triumphs is the ease with which that limited consciousness sustains our interest through the moods and events that make up the simple linearity of its plot.

But if Mary is not an intellectual Catholic we are not therefore to assume that her sense of human life *sub specie aeternitatis* is less than coherent. The passiveness with which she accepts the day's vicissitudes and society's dictates is grounded in a network of beliefs and convictions common to her time and background. These beliefs would have been mediated by the liturgy of the Mass, readings from the gospels, and sermons and prayers which stressed—in a manner foreign to most forms of Protestantism—the "family at Nazareth", the obedience, patience and obscurity of the Virgin Mary, her *via dolorosa* to the foot of the cross, and so on. The prayer in which such values are most enshrined is the "Hail, Holy Queen" which every Catholic of her time would have known by heart. Its imagery permeates the language of the novel, especially those phrases which describe humankind as "poor banished children of Eve", this world as a "valley of tears", and which ask that "after this, our exile" we may be shown "the blessed fruit of thy womb, Jesus". Though Mary O'Grady loves her "little home in Ranelagh", she never sees it as permanent. Between Tullamore and paradise it always retains the feeling of an *exilium*. Another Catholic hymn, "Hail Queen of Heaven", salutes the Virgin as "The ocean star/Guide of the wanderer here below"—Kate O'Brien's *Pray for the Wanderer* is a direct quote from it. The O'Grady house, despite its warmth and comfort, survives as an impermanent shelter for exiles, wanderers over sea and land: Patrick crossing the ocean to return, and to leave again; Ellie and Bart restlessly house-hunting; Larry leaving, returning only to leave forever; Rosie in flight from her unhappy marriage, coming back in time to see her mother before she goes on her last journey into death.

When the imagery or doctrine of Catholicism appear in Joyce, for instance, it is nearly always with consciousness and deliberation: one thinks of the opening page where Eileen Vance's hands evoke a phrase from the Litany of Our Lady, "Tower of Ivory"; the explicit doctrine of the hell-fire sermon or the subsequent confession; the symbolic moment in the last chapter where Stephen sees himself as a "priest of eternal imagination, transmuting the daily bread of experience into the radiant body of everliving life". But when in Book V of *Mary O'Grady* the heroine looks round at her deteriorating house she is not consciously echoing Newman's "Lead, kindly light amid the encircling gloom", yet this imagery of light and darkness recurs through the novel, always with a subliminal sense of the religious: ". . . a kind of fog, or smoke or gloom that hung in the very air. It was like a kind of twilight: a perpetual twilight that had stolen into the entire house, that in Tom's time had shone with the gleam of early morning." It is in the return of that gleam that the book ends.

An important function of Mary Lavin's power as a writer of novels and short stories is her empathy with conditions of mind well below the level of her own sophisticated consciousness. Kate O'Brien or Elizabeth Bowen would never choose a heroine like Mary O'Grady. Mary O'Grady is not clever, inventive, subtle or resourceful, but neither is she a stupid, uncomprehending victim of blind natural or oppressive social forces. And though the author is well aware of the inequities of Mary's world it is none of her intention to protest at them, but to follow and understand the destiny of one personality who is hard done by at their hands. If the reader starts from this assumption there is less likelihood of confusing the limitations of the heroine with the self-imposed limitations of the author's intention and perspective.

For the heroine, therefore, life holds out no guarantee of happiness nor, in fairness, any promise of misery. There is joy, love, pain, disappointment, grief, laughter, calamity. These all form part of a pattern mysteriously ordained whose meaning will be revealed after death. It is the lot of the mother to give of herself and to ask little in return. The reward is in the giving, and implicitly in the hereafter. Mary's understanding of life is matched with good health, strong nerves and a disposition simple and unselfish. Against the assault and battery of daily existence this is an invincible combination. The heroine's passivity and resignation, her tendency to act only when acted upon—all the qualities that make the reader impatient—when seen in this light become curiously acceptable. There is no sense of conscious or whining martydom in her cheerful stoicism because she expects little from life except love, which she herself gives in spontaneous abundance. Thus the history of her miseries, delivered often in cruel, unexpected incident and reversal, never reads with the feel or flavour of naturalism, but with a sort of poetic realism that may often wring the heart but rarely depresses the spirit.

Because Mary O'Grady is not an introspective person many of her acts and motivations remain inscrutable: the author allows us to guess, if we wish, at her choices and their causes. Why does a woman to whom motherhood means so much never return to her mother at Tullamore, the land of all her reveries? Perhaps it is because she cannot risk disappointment: one place must remain idyllic in a life so fraught with disaster, real and apprehended. Why does she insist on paying Patrick's fare to America when he has arranged very sensibly to work his passage? Because of a countrywoman's pride? Or because she wants obscurely to punish him with guilt for leaving home? Why in the light of such disregard for her savings did she grudge the doctor's fee that might have saved her husband from death? Parsimony, a peasant reluctance to spend money on health, or a terrified refusal to face the reality of Tom's being fatally ill? Would this last explanation account for her foolish interference in Alice Maguire's illness and the sensible attitude of the girl's parents towards it? Why does she so callously expel the Maguires from her house after her own three days' catalepsy, and why is there no subsequent apology? Shame perhaps, or maybe an unconscious decision to withdraw from the outside world. Why does she acquiesce so easily in the advice of the doctor to leave Patrick locked up for life in a mental institution, even when he has recovered? The curious fact about all such actions in the book is that they seem the sort of things that Mary O'Grady would have done at that time and place. More crucially they illustrate the fact that Mary Lavin is more interested in states of mind than in a Jamesian inquiry as to how these states of mind originated and developed. The great vivid passages in the book are those that transport us into a concrete, sensuously apprehended moment, a present that yields up its sound, taste and odour and remains in the mind long after the narrative has moved on.

The tension of the narrative is supplied by the stasis and permanence of the heroine's consciousness being acted upon by external character and event. She herself is perhaps more type than character, and her occasional moments of instinctual perception bear this out. Looking at her daughter Ellie, in Book II, she senses in her a

> ... core of enmity in her hate against all men, be they brother or husband, the core of enmity that would keep her always, till the last minute of her life, a person with whom to contend. She would never allow herself to rest at ease in the slack chains of familiarity or intimacy. She would be always at heart a stranger to the man she married, and for that reason always, to the last in command of his love. Not like me, thought Mary. I stopped being a woman. I became a mother. But she will always be a woman first, and a wife and mother afterwards.

The dreadful irony is that Mary will never see either of her eldest daughters live to fulfil her characteristic destiny. With their boyfriends, Willie and Bart, Mary's surrogate sons, they die in the plane crash that confirms the heroine in her role of tragedy.

There is a sense in which the characters who surround Mary O'Grady exist to enact her instinctive, prescient apprehension of life as individually fated. Her dread of Patrick's fascination with trains and with the distant mountains foreshadows his emigration to America. His disappointment with the mountains when he visits them—"they're not like mountains any more, they're just ordinary fields"—prefigures the failure of his American ambitions and his return to Ranelagh as a broken man. Mary's fears of the children falling, and of trains and icebergs at sea, are horribly fulfilled in the air disaster. Her distrust of the upper-class Frank Esmay—and her irrational preference for the young librarian whom she has never seen—is justified in the misery of Rosie's marriage. She has almost the solidity of myth, mutely enacting the roles of Rachel and Cassandra in a Dublin suburb.

As Richard Peterson has pointed out, the action of *Mary O'Grady* takes place through thirty troubled years of Irish history yet makes no reference to such major events as the great lock-out of 1913—when the transport union of which Tom must have been a member stayed out of work for six months—The Easter Rising of 1916, the Black and Tan War, the Civil War, the Treaty and the founding of the new state. This may be accounted for by the circumstances in which the book was written: apart from its final section it was produced in one month while the author, a young mother, sat in the sick room with her dying father. The utter privacy of the action and the headlong, almost breathless momentum of the story, are better understood if we know this.

But Mary Lavin's fiction as a whole is outrageously private. The drama of her fictions derives from domestic, quotidian things. A woman opening a cupboard and revealing its contents can come upon the reader, to use Henry James's phrase, "like the surprise of a caravan or the identification of a pirate". Consequently the haunting images of *Mary O'Grady* concern the humblest events and objects. When young Larry is expelled from the seminary he comes home, is unable to find the courage to confront his mother, leaves his suitcase behind the garden hedge and goes on an aimless, miserable walk around the city. Rain falls and the suitcase, forlorn and saturated, lies unseen in the shadow of the hedge, emblem of the failed vocation and of the strained destiny of mother and son.

When, in the last chapter, Mary opens a cupboard to get her daughter bed linen, the effect upon the reader is apocalyptic:

... the entire space, above, below, on top of, and around the boiler, was packed tight with every imaginable kind of article. As far as she could see, soiled clothes and clean clothes were pushed into it indiscriminately ... the press itself had been so long exposed to the blackening effect of smoke and dust that there was a layer of grime upon the woodwork everywhere, that would have to be scraped with a knife to be removed.

The attrition of loss upon the heroine's character could not have been more vividly rendered.

The most harrowing phase of the novel is Patrick's demoralised return from exile. The weird sense of dread that invades the narrative when Mary and Rosie come up the street and see a taxi-cab outside the door and "standing beside the taxi, a man with a big suitcase in his hand", persists through the following chapter as Patrick moves in and out of his mental illness. The alternating sense of relief and terror, the silence of the house as the two women witness his recoveries and relapses, is captured in the most vivid concrete detail. The pathos of his exit to the mental hospital is caught with memorable simplicity:

> But at that very moment a heavy step sounded on the landing overhead, and turning around, all three of them saw Patrick starting to come down the stairs, heavily, bringing both feet together on each step, in the manner of a child. At thc foot of the stairs, he came to a stand. "I'm ready", he said then, simply.

Mary Lavin has remarked that her two novels, *The House in Clewe Street* and *Mary O'Grady*, are really a succession of short stories yoked by a certain violence into continuous plots. I think she underrates her skill with structure—especially the manner in which the stories of Mary, Tom, Patrick, Larry, Rosie, Willie and Angie merge and separate as the action proceeds—but there is a sense in which she is right. The excellence of *Mary O'Grady* resides in its episodes, its single, unique moments plucked out of time, and its tyrannies of cause and effect. Ellie's revulsion at the house which, on an impulse, Bart insists on inspecting in Book III, is so chillingly rendered that it transcends its occasion and could be lifted out as a short story almost without editing:

> The darkness, the foul odours, and the curious damp atmosphere he did not notice at all, so great was the sudden access of excitement which came over him at the thought of entering with her into this sanctuary of silence and privacy. It was as if they stood together at the mouth of some strange cavern where mystery and ecstasy awaited them, and into which they were about to rush headlong, hand and hand together ... But as he glanced at her with a look of rapture, he saw that Ellie was as cold as ice, and the glance she flashed at him was as cold as the little blue lights that, at that moment, gleamed from the diamond on her finger.

He has just recently given her that engagement ring, and she has been overjoyed by its beauty and its implications of devotion and fidelity.

Yet the sentimentality of the warm, proprietary male and the realism of the angry, secret, intransigent woman has seldom been stated with such archetypal force. Which may mean that the parts of *Mary O'Grady* are probably greater than the whole. I insist on remaining partial to its haunting and ineradicable wholeness—which is the personality of its heroine, one of the most memorable characterisations in contemporary fiction.

Augustine Martin, University College, Dublin, 1985

VIRAGO MODERN CLASSICS

The first Virago Modern Classic, *Frost in May* by Antonia White, was published in 1978. It launched a list dedicated to the celebration of women writers and to the rediscovery and reprinting of their works. Its aim was, and is, to demonstrate the existence of a female tradition in fiction which is both enriching and enjoyable. The Leavisite notion of the 'Great Tradition', and the narrow, academic definition of a 'classic', has meant the neglect of a large number of interesting secondary works of fiction. In calling the series 'Modern Classics' we do not necessarily mean 'great' — although this is often the case. Published with new critical and biographical introductions, books are chosen for many reasons: sometimes for their importance in literary history; sometimes because they illuminate particular aspects of womens' lives, both personal and public. They may be classics of comedy or storytelling; their interest can be historical, feminist, political or literary.

Initially the Virago Modern Classics concentrated on English novels and short stories published in the early decades of this century. As the series has grown it has broadened to include works of fiction from different centuries, different countries, cultures and literary traditions. In 1984 the Victorian Classics were launched; there are separate lists of Irish, Scottish, European, American, Australian and other English speaking countries; there are books written by Black women, by Catholic and Jewish women, and a few relevant novels by men. There is, too, a companion series of Non-Fiction Classics constituting biography, autobiography, travel, journalism, essays, poetry, letters and diaries.

By the end of 1986 over 250 titles will have been published in these two series, many of which have been suggested by our readers.